You're a Privileged Woman.

INTRODUCING
PAGES & PRIVILEGES™.

It's our way of thanking you for buying
our books at your favorite retail store.

GET ALL THIS FREE
WITH JUST ONE PROOF OF PURCHASE:

◆ Hotel Discounts up to 60% at home and abroad

◆ Travel Service - Guaranteed lowest published
airfares plus 5% cash back on tickets

◆ $25 Travel Voucher

◆ Sensuous Petite Parfumerie collection ($50 value)

◆ Insider Tips Letter with sneak previews of
upcoming books

◆ Mystery Gift (if you enroll before 6/15/95)

You'll get a FREE personal card, too.
It's your passport to all these benefits— and to
even more great gifts & benefits to come!
There's no club to join. No purchase commitment. No obligation.

As a Privileged Woman,
you'll be entitled to all these Free Benefits. And Free Gifts, too.

To thank you for buying our books, we've designed an exclusive FREE program called *PAGES & PRIVILEGES*™. You can enroll with just one Proof of Purchase, and get the kind of luxuries that, until now, you could only read about.

BIG HOTEL DISCOUNTS

A privileged woman stays in the finest hotels. And so can you—at up to 60% off! Imagine standing in a hotel check-in line and watching as the guest in front of you pays $150 for the same room that's only costing you $60. Your *Pages & Privileges* discounts are good at Sheraton, Marriott, Best Western, Hyatt and thousands of other fine hotels all over the U.S., Canada and Europe.

FREE DISCOUNT TRAVEL SERVICE

A privileged woman is always jetting to romantic places. When <u>you</u> fly, just make one phone call for the lowest published airfare at time of booking—<u>or double the difference back</u>! PLUS—

you'll get a $25 voucher to use the first time you book a flight AND <u>5% cash back on every ticket you buy thereafter through the travel service</u>!

FREE GIFTS!

A privileged woman is always getting wonderful gifts.
Luxuriate in rich fragrances that will stir your senses (and his). This gift-boxed assortment of fine perfumes includes three popular scents, each in a beautiful designer bottle.   <u>Truly Lace</u>...This luxurious fragrance unveils your sensuous side. <u>L'Effleur</u>...discover the romance of the Victorian era with this soft floral. <u>Muguet des bois</u>...a single note floral of singular beauty. This $50 value is yours—FREE when you enroll in *Pages & Privileges*! And it's just the beginning of the gifts and benefits that will be coming your way!

FREE INSIDER TIPS LETTER

A privileged woman is always informed.   And you'll be, too, with our free letter full of fascinating information and sneak previews of upcoming books.

MORE GREAT GIFTS & BENEFITS TO COME

A privileged woman always has a lot to look forward to.
And so will you. You get all these wonderful FREE gifts and benefits now with only one purchase...and there are no additional purchases required. However, each additional retail purchase of Harlequin and Silhouette books brings you a step closer to even more great FREE benefits like half-price movie tickets...and even more FREE gifts like these beautiful fragrance gift baskets:

L'Effleur...This basketful of romance lets you discover L'Effleur from head to toe, heart to home.

Truly Lace...A basket spun with the sensuous luxuries of Truly Lace, including Dusting Powder in a reusable satin and lace covered box.

ENROLL NOW!
Complete the Enrollment Form on the back of this card and become a Privileged Woman today!

Enroll Today in *PAGES & PRIVILEGES*™, **the program that gives you Great Gifts and Benefits with just one purchase!**

Enrollment Form

☐ *Yes!* **I WANT TO BE A** *P*RIVILEGED *W*OMAN.

Enclosed is one *PAGES & PRIVILEGES*™ Proof of Purchase from any Harlequin or Silhouette book currently for sale in stores (Proofs of Purchase are found on the back pages of books) and the store cash register receipt. Please enroll me in *PAGES & PRIVILEGES*™. Send my Welcome Kit and FREE Gifts -- and activate my FREE benefits -- immediately.

NAME (please print)

ADDRESS   **APT. NO**

CITY   **STATE**   **ZIP/POSTAL CODE**

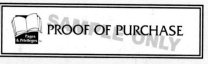 **PROOF OF PURCHASE**

Please allow 6-8 weeks for delivery. Quantities are limited. We reserve the right to substitute items. Enroll before October 31, 1995 and receive one full year of benefits.

NO CLUB! NO COMMITMENT! *Just one purchase brings you great* **Free Gifts** *and* **Benefits!** *(See inside for details.)*

Name of store where this book was purchased_____

Date of purchase_____

Type of store:

    ☐ Bookstore ☐ Supermarket ☐ Drugstore

    ☐ Dept. or discount store (e.g. K-Mart or Walmart)

    ☐ Other (specify)_____

Which Harlequin or Silhouette series do you usually read?

_____

Complete and mail with one Proof of Purchase and store receipt to:
U.S.: *PAGES & PRIVILEGES*™, P.O. Box 1960, Danbury, CT 06813-1960
Canada: *PAGES & PRIVILEGES*™, 49-6A The Donway West, P.O. 813, North York, ON M3C 2E8   PRINTED IN U.S.A

Every woman knows...

THERE'S SOMETHING ABOUT A Cowboy

Stacey Richards—She wants her land...with no strings attached. But according to her grandfather's will, she has to marry sexy Ben Oakes to get it!

Willa Ross—Five years ago, she'd been driven from home for something she didn't do. Now she's back, and rugged Clay Cantrell won't let her forget the past—good or bad.

Brett Sargent—She's gone from being an orphan to part owner of the Carradine ranch. Suddenly Jay Carradine wants to marry her—but is it for love or money?

Hard livin', hard lovin', hard to resist...

Relive the romance....

Three complete novels by your favorite authors!

About the Authors

Candace Schuler—This bestselling author has lived in almost every corner of the U.S., from a schooner anchored in Hawaii's Ala Wai Harbor to a loft in New York's Greenwich Village, as well as the heart of Texas, the frequently frozen plains of Minnesota and, currently, Gaithersburg, Maryland. But in between moves, she's always found time for her first love—writing.

Susan Fox—Susan Fox won two Romance Writers of America Golden Heart awards at the start of her writing career. Having been a lifelong fan of Westerns, she thinks of romantic heroes in terms of Stetsons and boots. This talented author lives in Iowa with her youngest son, Patrick.

Margaret Way—Margaret Way's first romance novel was published twenty-five years ago, and she's been going strong ever since. Known for her wonderfully lyrical descriptions of Australia, she delights in bringing her homeland alive for readers. This prolific author now resides in Queensland with her husband.

THERE'S SOMETHING ABOUT A *Cowboy*

CANDACE SCHULER
SUSAN FOX
MARGARET WAY

Harlequin Books

TORONTO • NEW YORK • LONDON
AMSTERDAM • PARIS • SYDNEY • HAMBURG
STOCKHOLM • ATHENS • TOKYO • MILAN
MADRID • WARSAW • BUDAPEST • AUCKLAND

HARLEQUIN BOOKS

by Request—There's Something About A Cowboy

Copyright © 1995 by Harlequin Enterprises B.V.

ISBN 0-373-20113-3

The publisher acknowledges the copyright holders of the individual works as follows:

WILDCAT
Copyright © 1990 by Candace Schuler

THE BLACK SHEEP
Copyright © 1988 by Susan Fox

DIAMOND VALLEY
Copyright © 1986 by Margaret Way

Printed in U.S.A.

CONTENTS

She'd left home a wildcat...
and come back a woman!

WILDCAT

Candace Schuler

1

STACEY RICHARDS was angry. Furiously angry. The emotion surged through her still body like molten lava heaving unseen beneath the hardened crust of the earth. She closed her eyes, letting herself flow with the feeling for just a moment, almost overwhelmed by the unexpectedness of it. It was the first emotion she'd felt toward her grandfather in the past, endless forty-eight hours.

In the past eleven years.

She didn't count the tears shed yesterday in Marta's motherly arms. They hadn't been for her grandfather but for herself. Tears of weariness, mostly, after the long trip by plane and car, tears of relief and, callous as it might seem, tears of simple happiness at being home again.

I'm home, she'd thought, *and there's no one who can ever send me away again.*

And now this!

Her first impulse was to give in to her anger, to whirl furiously and scream out her rage, but her years at an exclusive school for the daughters of the well-to-do stood her in good stead. She remained facing the window, her proud straight back to the rest of the room, gazing with unseeing eyes at the quiet, sun-scorched courtyard outside. Not by the flicker of an eyelash did she betray how her grandfather's last wishes had hurt and shocked her.

"Do continue, Mr. Barnes," she said to the lawyer, who had fallen silent as if waiting for her reaction. A faint French accent marred what had once been a molasses-thick West Texas drawl. "I'm sure there's more."

She could sense the men in the room looking at each other, wondering silently at her uncharacteristic lack of response. The Stacey of old would have been halfway into a beauty of a tantrum by now. But she wasn't the Stacey of old. Not by a long shot. "Mr. Barnes?" she said coolly, prompting the still-silent man.

Emmett Barnes cleared his throat and resumed reading Henry "Iron" Oakes's last will and testament. But Stacey was no longer listening. Everything it had to say that concerned her and her future had been said. She stood, still facing the window, and watched a large overweight tabby cat wander aimlessly across the courtyard, wondering if it could possibly be the same cat Marta had had eleven years ago.

Eleven years, she thought. *Eleven wasted years*.

They hadn't really been wasted, of course. On the contrary, they'd been worthwhile and productive years. But they slipped away as she stood there, disappearing in the wavering heat outside the window, and she saw herself as she'd been eleven years ago, right here in this very room.

SHE'D BEEN ANGRY then, too. Furiously angry and hurt and rebellious. You're going away to school they told her, leaving no room for argument on that point. But her grandfather, apparently touched by her furious tears, had softened and allowed her to choose where.

"Paris," she'd said defiantly, picking the most foreign, most wicked place her fifteen-year-old mind could imagine. "Paris or nowhere," she'd insisted, hoping he'd say no.

Her grandfather had almost weakened. She could see she'd been getting to him. Paris was so far away from their ranch in West Texas, not only geographically but culturally, as well, and she was so young. She could see her grandfather was wavering, but Ben spoke up then, insisting that she go, and old "Iron" Oakes had finally agreed.

Her grandfather had made her angry, but she was used to his pigheaded stubbornness and could understand it, having inherited so much of it herself. If it had been just him she would probably have cooled down enough to see the logic of his decision. She'd have eventually settled happily into school, coming home each Christmas and summer vacation and then for good when she graduated. It had been Ben's betrayal that hurt so much, hardening her heart against them both.

She'd always loved Ben, it seemed. First with the worshipful adoration of a child for an older brother or favorite uncle, changing imperceptibly over the years into the shy unspoken love of a young girl for a man seven years her senior. Then, the summer that she turned fifteen, she'd blossomed into womanhood so swiftly that the change seemed to have happened overnight. Along with the curves and the luster that came with suddenly finding herself attractive to the opposite sex had come a teasing seductiveness. She'd become a woman—fully grown, she thought—and she'd waited impatiently but confidently for Ben's declaration.

She'd been so sure that he knew how she felt. So sure that he felt the same and had only been waiting for her to grow up a little before declaring his love. And then he'd shattered her confidence, banishing her from his presence and the home she loved in one fell swoop.

"She's growing up wild," he told her grandfather. "Look at her!" He clamped one hand on the back of her neck. "Skintight jeans, a shirt that almost buttons, hair as wild as a range pony's. She looks like a border-town tart!"

"Take your damned hands off me, you damned horse's ass!" Stacey raged, kicking back at him with her booted feet.

His hand closed tighter on her neck and he lifted her so that she was standing on her toes. She reached up and behind her with both hands, grabbing his wrist, swearing at him all the while.

"Let me go, you son of a—"

A button popped on her shirt front, strained past holding by the pressure of her upraised arms. It let go with a ping, momentarily freezing the actions of the three people in the room, and rolled across the polished wood floor, unnaturally loud in the sudden silence. Stacey gasped, her face burning with embarrassment, her hands dropping to pull her shirt together—but not before both men had seen, quite clearly, that she wore no bra beneath the Western-cut shirt,

"You see what I mean?" Ben said fiercely, letting her go.

"You talk like I did that on purpose," Stacey flared defensively. "I didn't. It was your fault, damn you!"

Ben lifted an eyebrow at her grandfather as if to say, See?

"Marta ought to wash your mouth out with soap," Henry Oakes observed mildly. "You talk like one of the hands."

"Marta can't control her anymore," said Ben, tight-lipped. "If she ever could."

"I don't need anyone to control me."

"The hell you don't!" Ben's voice was low and strained. "Unless somebody stops you from throwing yourself at the hands, you're going to end up the bride at a shotgun wedding."

"That's not true!" Stacey raged. "It's not!"

And it wasn't, not really. The only man she'd wanted, then, was him. She'd only flirted with the hands a little, testing herself and her newfound desirability as any young girl would. Why couldn't he see that?

The battle had raged for another week, but when the smoke cleared Stacey found herself packed up like so much unwanted baggage and put on a plane bound for Paris. The boarding school, recommended by the wife of a friend of her grandfather's, was well-known for its ability to make ladies out of the wayward daughters of the well-to-do.

Stacey eventually adjusted to her new environment. She came to enjoy her school and the friends she made there. Under any other circumstances she might have looked upon the whole experience as an exciting adventure. But she could not—*would not*—forgive Ben and, by association, her grandfather for exiling her from the place and the people she loved best.

Stubbornly, she left her grandfather's short and infrequent letters unanswered until he finally ceased to write to her at all. She wrote instead to Marta. Her letters were full of glowing descriptions of Paris and her new friends and exaggerated tales of one exciting adventure after another. She never mentioned how homesick she was and how bored with fashion shows and museums and cooking lessons and how, if she had to spend one more afternoon at one more charming art gallery, she'd scream.

By the time she was ready to leave school the walls had been built so high that she couldn't knock them down by herself. The only acknowledgment of her graduation from home was a large check from her grandfather with instructions to buy herself "something nice," a drugstore card of congratulations signed "with love" from Ben, and a white lace mantilla from Marta.

She wrote Marta a warm note of thanks, draping the mantilla over her headboard where she could see it each day. She deposited the check in her already bulging bank account; her grandfather would know it had been received when he got the quarterly bank statements. The card, after being read over half a dozen times in the unconscious hope of finding some hidden message, she burned.

No one, not even Marta, had mentioned that now that Stacey was supposedly finished she should come home. And Stacey was too proud, or too stubborn, to say that that's exactly what she wanted to do.

Looking back, she could see what a futile gesture it had been and how, when you came right down to it, she was hurting no one but herself. But she was only eighteen at the time, and older, wiser heads should have prevailed, should have ordered her home. She would have gone, gladly. But no one did.

So Stacey took an apartment in the expensive and fashionable seventh district of Paris and lived as any other young Frenchwoman of considerable means would. She partied far into the night and often right into the dawn. She collected art and drove fast, expensive cars and bought more clothes than she needed or could ever wear. She traveled with friends to Cannes for the film festival, to St. Tropez for the sun and to St. Moritz for skiing. And finally, out of sheer boredom, she found herself a job.

It wasn't a very good job, nor did it pay much. But then, Stacey wasn't working for the money, not with the enormous checks that still arrived every quarter. To her surprise, she found that she liked the business world and that she was good at it. Too good, as it turned out, to be challenged for long by the position she held. Very soon, she began looking around her for new fields to conquer. It didn't take long for her to realize that she wasn't qualified for the kind of job she wanted.

Her obvious enthusiasm and cool blond beauty got her in a lot of doors, but knowing how to set a perfect table, how to pick the proper wine, or how to smooth over sticky social situations—all taught at boarding school—were not readily marketable skills.

So Stacey went back to school. Business school. And when she graduated, two years later, she went to work in the secretarial pool of a small but very wealthy international oil company. In only a year and a half, after a brief stop in the accounting department, she found herself in the enviable position of executive assistant to the president.

It was an exciting and challenging job, made more so by the frequent trips to the company's offices in Saudi Arabia, where Stacey's work took her into the oil fields and refineries as well as the executive suite. Her employer, André el-Hamid, a widower of French-Saudi extraction, had homes in both places, as well as offices, and did a great deal of business-related entertaining so that Stacey's excellent social skills, along with her equally excellent business ones, were finally proving useful.

She was happy she told herself stubbornly when the homesickness became too strong. Paris was her home now and that dusty little podunk ranch in West Texas was just a part of someone she used to be. Her friends, her job, her life were in Paris. She'd be bored silly if she ever had to go back.

But it was a lie. And, deep down, she knew it. She'd have gone home like a shot if anyone had even so much as *hinted* that she was wanted back there. But no one had. Not until the telegram that came less than two days ago.

She'd been spending a long weekend, mixing business with pleasure at the country home of her employer when the telegram finally tracked her down.

HENRY HAD FATAL ACCIDENT. BRONC BROKE HIS NECK. YOU ARE NEEDED IMMEDIATELY FOR READING OF WILL. BEN.

There had been no expression of sympathy, nothing to soften the blow. Stunned, she'd left it to André to express the emotions he felt at the callousness of the missive.

"But this is outrageous!" he bellowed, waving the telegram with Gallic intensity. "Who does this Ben think he is to announce such a calamity with so little sensitivity? Annette—" he called a maid to his side "—pack Mademoiselle Richards's bags immediately and have someone bring the car around. Thirty minutes, no more." He waved the maid away, at the same time drawing Stacey with him out of the room, away from the curious stares of his guests. "I am so sorry, *chérie*," he said in a more normal tone of voice, patting her shoulder comfortingly. "This Henry, he was your father?"

"Grandfather," she corrected him in a small emotionless voice. "André, you don't mind too much, do you? My leaving you in the lurch like this?" She made a vague gesture, which encompassed the guests, her job. "I know there's that contract with Monsieur Jordan to be worked out and a thousand other things, but—" she shrugged "—I'll be back as soon as I can."

"Yes, I will mind. Terribly! But that is of no importance now. Your secretary can handle most of it until your return. And Edouard can help out while you are gone. It will do him good." A hard gleam came into his dark eyes. "It is time that playboy son of mine learned from where comes the jam for his bread," he said, but

Stacey didn't laugh as she usually did at André's mangling of American slang. "You go and make ready." He patted her shoulder. "I will call the airport."

"The telegram said immediately, so get me on the first available flight, no matter what the connections are like," she said as she moved toward the stairs. *Home*, a voice sang somewhere in her head, lightening her step as she hurried up to the luxuriously appointed guest room that had been assigned to her. *I'm going home.*

NEARLY EIGHTEEN HOURS and two plane changes later she touched down in Lubbock, Texas. There'd been a stopover of several hours at the Dallas/Fort Worth airport and she'd left the plane, overnight case in hand, to find a ladies room and freshen up. It had helped some but not much, and she still felt rumpled and travel stained and more weary than she could ever remember being before. There was no one familiar to meet her at Lubbock International. Just a lanky young cowboy in faded Levi's and a dusty brown Stetson. He introduced himself, saying, "Hank Watkins, ma'am. Boss sent me to pick you up."

They accomplished the three-hour drive to the ranch in nearly complete silence, the young cowboy having little conversation of his own and Stacey being too tired to draw him out. The air conditioning in the old tan pickup proved inadequate to the Texas sun and they drove with the windows open, both of them preferring the fine, gritty dust to the stifling heat of the closed cab. She sat almost motionless during most of the long drive, her head resting tiredly against the seat back, her eyes barely registering the seemingly endless miles of two-lane highway bordered on both sides by equally endless miles of barbed-wire fence and the flat dusty land that stretched as far as the eye could see.

She seemed to know instinctively, though, when the passing landscape became Iron Oakes land. She straightened, her eyes scanning the horizon eagerly for the first glimpse of the high, arched gate that marked the main entrance to the ranch.

"Stop, please," she instructed the young driver quietly when he turned off the highway, bumping over the metal cattle guard, to pass under the white-painted iron gate.

He pulled to a stop and waited as she got out of the truck. She stood silently, gazing around almost reverently, saying her own private hello to the ranch. She inhaled deeply, breathing in the dust and the heat and the faint, unforgettable perfume of the sparse silvery sage. She could even smell the fainter but no less welcome stench of the oil pumps that dotted the distant horizon. As always, they reminded her of some strange species of insect, though far too many of them were motionless when they should have been pumping the black wealth from beneath the barren-looking ground. It told her, all of it, that she was really, finally home.

She lifted one graceful hand to shade her eyes, straining to see the main house at the end of the long road. She could just make out its outline, surrounded by the huge trees that had been transplanted years ago by her grandfather to shade and protect the house and its inhabitants from the relentless sun. She could see, too, the vague outlines and rooftops of the outbuildings—the barn and bunkhouse and various sheds—that were set out behind and slightly to the south of the main house.

The outbuildings seemed to be bigger than she remembered, and there were more of them. A grain elevator and another barn and several tall, spindly, oddly shaped structures revolving lazily in the almost nonexistent breeze that she finally decided must be some sort of experimental windmills. She sighed, feeling somehow betrayed by these changes to her childhood home, and climbed back into the cab of the truck.

As they got closer to the house she saw even more changes. Small ones in reality, but to Stacey each difference felt like a stab at her heart, and she couldn't see them for the improvements that they were. She closed her eyes wearily, not wanting to see any more, but as the truck bumped over a second set of cattle guards, she opened them again. They had arrived.

The young cowboy busied himself with her suitcases, leaving Stacey to make her own way as he carried them in ahead of her. The tiled front hall was exactly as she remembered it, shadowed and cool after the brutal sun outside. It was full of people, too, or so it seemed to Stacey, who was by then so worn and weary that she could hardly see straight. She saw Ben immediately, though, towering head and shoulders over everyone else in the room.

"Hello, Stacey," he said, his eyes speculative as they ran over her from the sleek coil of her hair to the toes of her snakeskin pumps. "You've changed."

"That was the general idea, wasn't it?" she replied coolly, rising instinctively to the challenge in his voice and his assessing blue eyes.

"It was," he agreed easily. "I'm glad to see that all that money wasn't totally wasted."

Uncle Pete—not a real uncle but, rather, her grandfather's old wildcatting partner—claimed her attention, then, pumping her hand in greeting. He pounded her on the back with his other hand, welcoming her home. And then Ramon, the Iron Oakes gardener and handy man—grown so old now!—made a short welcoming speech, his eyes riveted firmly on the floor as he spoke. Everyone else was new to her. Uncle Pete was just beginning general introductions when Stacey spotted Marta coming toward her like a longhorn cow who had just sighted a lost calf.

"Shame on you," she chided everyone, gathering Stacey to her as if she were no more than ten years old. "Can't you see that she is tired? Worn to the bone! Go, all of you." She leveled a pudgy brown finger at Ben. "You, also, Benito. Go!" She waved them all away and steered Stacey up the wide staircase to the bedrooms on the second floor.

"Come with me, *niña*," Marta said, using the familiar Mexican endearment that Stacey hadn't heard in eleven years. She hustled her charge down the hall. "You are tired, no? Come. You will undress and nap and then, when you have rested, you will eat."

"But lunch," Stacey protested halfheartedly. "I could smell the enchiladas when I came in."

"There will be plenty more when you wake up, *niña*," Marta said, opening a suitcase. She handed Stacey an ivory silk nightgown and pushed her toward the bathroom. "Go wash," she commanded, as if Stacey were a recalcitrant child.

Stacey took the gown and did as she was told, emerging a scant ten minutes later feeling vastly better for the quick wash.

"*Muy bonito,*" complimented Marta, fingering the silky material of her nightgown. "You have grown up very pretty. Benito, he will like that, *si?* Come," she commanded before Stacey could say that she didn't particularly care whether Ben liked the way she'd grown up or not. "Sit here—" she motioned toward the bed "—and brush the tangles from your hair before you sleep. You have had a long trip, no?" she went on, not waiting for, or expecting, an answer as she bustled from the open suitcase to the closet.

Stacey smiled and did as she was told. Marta hadn't changed one iota, bless her; she still treated Stacey like a beloved, if slightly backward, child. "I can do that later, Marta," she said, flicking the brush through her hair.

"Ah, pah!" Marta replied exactly as Stacey had known she would. "It is no trouble. I do it now," she said, citing a familiar refrain, "and it is done. *Si?*"

"*Si,*" Stacey replied, shaking her hair back as she laid the brush on the nightstand.

Marta's busy hands paused in their task. "So fair still," she mused, "just like when you were a little girl." She reached out, touching Stacey's hair lightly. "You have been away too long, I think. It is good to have you home, *niña.*"

"It's good to be home, Marta," Stacey said simply and then, suddenly, without warning, she burst into tears.

"There, there." Marta gathered Stacey comfortingly to her ample bosom. "There my sweet *niña*," she soothed, stroking the shining blond head. "It is all right now. You're home," she chanted, rocking gently until the sobbing quieted and then, finally, ceased. "There! You feel much better now, *sí?*" she said, taking a handkerchief from the bodice of her dress to tenderly wipe the upturned face.

Stacey nodded. "I'm sorry, Marta," she said, taking the handkerchief to finish the job herself. "I don't know what came over me."

"Pah!" Marta made a sound of dismissal, waving aside any explanations or apologies. "You are exhausted," she said. "Come. Into bed."

Smiling, Stacey did as she was told, snuggling gratefully into the cool, crisp white sheets that Marta held open for her. Her eyes drooped heavily. *Heaven*, she thought. *I'm home and it's sheer heaven.*

"Sleep as long as you need to," Marta instructed as she closed the long louvered doors leading to the upper veranda. "When you wake there will be enchiladas and guacamole, *sí?*"

"And Mexican coffee?" came the sleepy question.

"*Sí*, and Mexican coffee," Marta said softly, closing the door behind her as she backed out of the bedroom.

Exhausted, Stacey slept for hours, through lunch and dinner both, waking to full daylight and the furtive sounds of Marta unpacking her suitcase.

"I'm awake, Marta," she said from the bed. "There's no need to be so quiet on my account."

"You have no other black dresses, *niña?*" Marta asked, holding up two delectable Parisian creations obviously meant for evening wear. One was a short, slinky bias-cut satin, the other was a long-sleeved, floor-length sheath with a slit up one side. "Where is your black suit for the funeral?"

Stacey pushed her single cover off and sat up, reaching for the ivory silk robe at the foot of the bed. "There is no black suit. I'll be wearing the dark green dress with the jacket."

"Green! You cannot wear green to your grandfather's funeral. It is not respectful!"

"It's perfectly respectful, Marta," she said firmly, and then added at the housekeeper's reproachful look. "The dress is forest green, after all. You can hardly get any darker than that."

Marta's expression didn't change.

Stacey tightened the belt on her robe and looked away, refusing to feel like a guilty child. "It's not as if I were planning to wear red."

"But you should wear black," insisted Marta, who was herself draped in that color from the lace mantilla that covered her hair to the sturdy, low-heeled shoes on her feet. The worn gold crucifix that Stacey had never seen her without hung on a slender gold chain around her neck. A rosary made of gold filigree and ebony beads was tucked into her belt. "You are his granddaughter."

"His granddaughter that he never saw once in eleven years."

"That was not all his fault, I think."

"No, it wasn't," admitted Stacey, thinking of Ben rather than herself. "But it changes nothing." She paused in gathering together her toilette articles. "I won't be a hypocrite and pretend an emotion I don't feel. Please try to understand, Marta. I can't."

"He missed you terribly," Marta tried one more time.

"Did he?" Stacey shrugged, unmoved. "I find that a bit hard to believe." If he'd missed her, why hadn't he come for her? Why hadn't he, even once, asked her to come home? She paused in the bathroom doorway. "I don't have anything else to wear, anyway, Marta," she said. "Unless you think the beige suit would be better?"

When she finished in the bathroom, Marta was gone. The unpacking had been completed and the bed made. The dark green dress and its matching jacket lay across the ruffled pink bedspread in silent reproach, the white lace mantilla spread out next to it.

Stubbornly refusing to feel guilty, Stacey dressed and did her makeup with a swiftness borne of long practice. She brushed her fine, golden-blond hair away from her face, plaiting it into a sleek French braid, finishing it with a small, flat, grosgrain bow.

The forest green dress was a figure-skimming, linen-look sheath cut with a master hand to subtly hint at the lithesome female form beneath the material. It had a demure boat neck and was sleeveless but the matching jacket made up for that lack, its long sleeves and tailored, boxy styling making her look almost prim.

Defiantly, Stacey added a triple strand of large, milky pearls around her neck, pearl studs in her ears and a discreet spray of expensive perfume before finally draping the lacy mantilla over her head. Then she stepped back and surveyed herself in the large oval mirror over the old-fashioned dresser. *No range pony wildness now,* she thought with satisfaction.

The woman reflected in the mirror looked appropriately subdued, but very chic. She could have been attending the funeral of a business acquaintance. No stranger, seeing Stacey, would suspect that the man being buried today was her grandfather, the man who had raised her from infancy after her parents had been killed.

It struck her suddenly that she hadn't yet seen the body, didn't know what arrangements had been made, didn't know anything at all, really, aside from what had been in Ben's telegram. But it was no use thinking about it now, she told herself. There was nothing she could do about anything at this point, anyway. And Ben had undoubtedly taken care of everything.

BEN DELIVERED THE EULOGY at the graveside, keeping it short and simple, stating the barest statistics of Henry "Iron" Oakes's long and eventful life.

"He died as he would have wanted to, had he been able to choose," Ben said, his deep voice husky with pain. "Quickly, and in the best of cowboy traditions, with his boots on. We must be glad for his sake that it happened that way, no matter how big—" his voice faltered slightly and he paused, visibly gathering himself together "—how big a hole his passing has left in all our lives. We'll miss him." He bent and touched the coffin lightly, almost caressingly. "Goodbye, Henry," he whispered, his blue eyes bright with unshed tears. "God go with you."

Stacey looked away then, feeling as if she were intruding on an intensely private conversation. Seeking something, anything else to focus her attention on, her eyes skimmed over the other mourners gathered around the gravesite.

It was obvious that her grandfather had been well loved and respected, and not only by Ben. The little family cemetery was full to overflowing with ranch hands, friends and neighbors. There were a surprising number of grizzled old men who'd flown in from the nearby oil centers of Houston and Tulsa, as well as from as far away as Anchorage and Mexico City and the oil-rich North Sea off Great Britain's shores. They were old wildcatters like her grandfather and Uncle Pete; some had struck it rich, as "Iron" Oakes had, some had since lost everything in the latest oil bust, and some had never made it at all. But all of them held their hats in their hands in a gesture of respect for a fallen friend.

Marta wept openly, standing there beside Stacey, as did several of the other women. Even Uncle Pete, on her other side, hid suspiciously bright eyes. But Stacey didn't cry. She couldn't. And, standing there, composed and dry-eyed, she could feel the disapproval of those around her. *Unnatural girl*, their eyes said. Stacey stiffened her already straight back and returned the condemning stares with icy dignity. And then the preacher said "Amen" and everyone began filing away from the grave. Ben took her arm, leading her toward a waiting car, and she forgot the disapproving mourners between one breath and the next.

"Emmett Barnes will meet us back at the house," Ben said, settling his big frame behind the wheel of the two-year-old dark blue Lincoln. "He wants to go over Henry's will without any delay."

Stacey reached into her bag for a badly needed cigarette and lit it, completely forgetting that she was trying to quit. "Is all this unseemly haste necessary?"

"Emmett seems to think so. Something in the will's put a burr under his saddle and he wants to get rid of it, pronto." He paused, his glance flickering over her. "It's probably not going to be—"

She stopped him with a toss of her head. The mantilla fell down around her shoulders at the movement. "I'd rather hear it from Mr. Barnes."

Ben shrugged, the fine black cloth of his jacket straining across his wide shoulders. "Suit yourself," he said, and headed the car down the graveled road to the main house.

Stacey sat stiffly, separated from him by two feet of light gray upholstery, and studied him from under her lashes. He'd changed very little in the past eleven years, except to get even bigger and tougher looking, if that were possible, filling out the promise of the broad shoulders that he'd had even as a rangy, wiry teenager.

He'd been fourteen to her six when he first showed up on the ranch, looking for sanctuary with his Aunt Marta after the death of his mother. Over the years, Stacey had learned that his father had been an alcoholic, cold and unfeeling toward his only son when he was sober, abusive when he was drunk. His mother's death had freed him to leave.

Henry had taken an immediate liking to the young Ben, going so far as to invite him to live in the main house like a member of the family. Marta had joyously welcomed him for his own sake, as well as that of her deceased sister, making it part of her life's mission to add weight to his rangy frame. And six-year-old Stacey had unconditionally adored him.

Theirs had been a special relationship then, with Ben filling the role of big brother and protector, Stacey the indulged and adoring kid sister. Two years later, Ben's father died and Henry formally adopted him. Stacey was ecstatic; now Ben was a *real* relative, she'd thought gleefully.

It was then that the rumors started. Ben was the old man's bastard kid, some said behind his back, though no one, not even Ben, knew for sure and none dared ask. Ben had wanted the rumors to be true—even at eight, she'd somehow known that without being told. He'd wanted it fiercely, with all the longing of a boy who'd never known a father's love or basked in the pride that a man was supposed to feel for his only son. Having Henry as his real father would have explained a lot, giving him a reason for the way he'd been treated by the man he'd called father for the first sixteen years of his life.

Stacey had been too young, at first, to understand all the ramifications of the whispered snatches of overhead conversation, despite the fact that she intuitively understood Ben's reaction to them. Years later, when she did understand, she fiercely denied it because if Ben was her grandfather's natural son, it meant he was really her uncle. And she knew you weren't supposed to feel about your uncle the way she was, by then, beginning to feel about Ben.

She studied him now, her eyes not blinded by childish adoration or adolescent infatuation, looking for a resemblance to her grandfather and finding none. Henry Oakes had been fair-haired, as she was, and a smaller man physically than the dark-haired, swarthy-skinned giant who sat beside her now. The only thing you could tell for sure about Ben by looking at him was that he was a Texas rancher.

Even in the somber funeral black his appearance screamed cowboy, she thought. Maybe it was the Western cut of his suit. Or his tan, burned so deep that she doubted he would ever lose it. Or the way his eyes crinkled up at the corners as if he were perpetually squinting into the blazing Texas sun. Or his big, work-callused hands, so strong and capable looking as they rested on the steering wheel. Or—

Her mind veered off suddenly, self-protectively, focusing on the black Stetson on the seat between them, tossed there when he got into the car. *Cowboy,* she thought again, scornfully, trying to imagine a brace of six guns strapped to his long muscular thigh. But he really didn't need them to complete the picture. He had a tough, virile, uncompromising look about him that clearly said he was a man to be reckoned with. A man whom, sooner or later, *she* was going to have to reckon with.

2

"MIZ RICHARDS?" It was the lawyer's voice, calling her back to the present. "Miz Richards?"

Stacey turned from the window to face the three men standing behind her in her grandfather's den, waiting for her reaction to his outrageous will.

The lawyer, Emmett Barnes, stood behind Henry's desk, clearly wishing that he were anywhere but where he was. His hand came up and nervously plucked his shirt collar as if feeling the heat, though the room was cool despite the midsummer sun. His eyes slid away from her steady gaze.

Uncle Pete smiled at her from his place in front of the empty fireplace, a little sheepish, obviously a little worried about what her reaction would be, before returning to his contemplation of the hearth stones.

Only Ben dared to look her squarely in the eyes.

How long his lashes are, she thought irrelevantly, ridiculously long for a man, and as dark as his hair, framing eyes of a startling clear blue. *Almost as blue as mine*, came the unbidden thought, and she wondered again about his parentage. He lounged, apparently completely at his ease, in one of the two big leather chairs facing the desk. His long, hard-muscled legs were stretched out in front of him, the booted feet crossed at the ankles, a well-iced glass of bourbon in one hand. He took a long slow sip, watching her.

"It can be broken, I suppose?" Her words were for the lawyer, but her eyes questioned Ben.

"No, I'm afraid it can't," Emmett Barnes said. "It's ironclad."

"No will is ironclad," Stacey retorted.

"This one is," Ben put in before the lawyer could answer.

"I'm truly sorry, Miz Richards, but I'm afraid Ben's right." Emmett paused, clearing his throat, and then went on uncertainly. "I tried to tell Henry that it was a crazy thing to do, putting it in his will like that. He should have told you his intentions himself. Prepared you."

"Prepared me? As if anything could." Her voice was brittle, and she forced herself to take a deep, calming breath before turning from Ben's measuring gaze to face the lawyer. "I'm sure you did your best, Mr. Barnes— Emmett," she corrected herself. "No one knows better than I what a hard man my grandfather was."

"He was only tryin' to protect you," offered Uncle Pete.

Stacey turned icy blue eyes on him. "From what?"

Pete shrugged and looked down at the toe of his boot.

"He was trying to protect the ranch and his oil companies," she said flatly. "And Ben."

"Now, Stacey, girl," Pete cajoled, trying again. "Be reasonable."

"Was Henry reasonable?" she challenged, her blue eyes glacial as she reached for her sleek leather bag where it lay on a corner of the desk. She rummaged for her cigarette case. "Is this will reasonable?"

"The way he looked at it, he was. It is," Pete said.

"And what about the way I look at it?" She flipped open a gold cigarette case and extracted a long, slender cigarette, lighting it before anyone could move to do it for her. She tossed her head back, inhaling deeply. *Thank heavens for nicotine*, she thought, feeling calm spread through her as the soothing smoke filled her lungs. "Is this will reasonable for me? Or fair?"

She strode angrily to the window and back, her long legs moving gracefully from the hip, pulling the dark green dress tight against the curve of her back with each step. "Did *he once* think about me or how I would feel when this—" her hand arched through the air "—this medieval document was read?"

"Oh, surely not medieval." Ben spoke lazily from the depths of the leather chair.

Stacey whirled, crushing out the just-lit cigarette in an ashtray on the desk as she passed it, and came to stand in front of his chair at the point where his long legs ended.

"Besides," he said, before she could speak, "I can't rightly see what you're squawking about. You'll still be getting your checks regularly." He paused for a moment to emphasize his next words. "If that's what you decide you want."

"You knew," she accused him bitterly. "You knew and you approved, didn't you?"

"No. I didn't know," he said calmly, raising his glass to his lips. He surveyed her over the rim, his eyes traveling slowly from her flushed, angry face to touch lingeringly on her full breasts, rising and falling visibly with her agitation, down to her narrow waist and softly rounded hips, to the long, slender length of her legs, and then back up again.

She'd changed, as he'd said yesterday in the front hall, but not enough to matter. More mature, sleeker, a great deal more polished, maybe, but she was still the most exciting female in the state of Texas. Especially when she was on the verge of a temper tantrum. "But now that I've had a chance to look you over, it doesn't seem like a half-bad idea," he said, just to see if he could push her over the edge. "You grew up real—" a slow, deliberately lascivious smile curved his lips "—nice."

Stacey heard the collective gasp behind her and ignored it, as she tried to ignore her own heightened color. Her reaction wasn't one of outraged modesty, however, or shock that Ben would say such a thing— she told herself she expected no better of him—it was one of overwhelming anger.

She could feel it boiling up in her again, threatening to break the bounds of her hard-won self-control. Her hands clenched by her sides as she imagined hitting him. Or throwing something at his head. With a superb effort of will she forced the feeling down and unclenched her hands as her mouth curved into the semblance of a smile.

"I've had a chance to look you over, too." Her eyes ran disparagingly over the length of him where he lounged in the leather chair. Her smile turned overly sweet and catlike. "Unfortunately, my taste doesn't run to overbearing, ill-mannered, redneck cowpunchers," she said disdainfully. She turned from him, going to sit on a corner of her grandfather's desk.

Her action caused her to miss the admiring gleam that flickered in his eyes for a moment. Stacey had always given as good as she got; he was glad to see that she still did, despite the ice-maiden facade. "You could sell out," he taunted, wondering how far he could push her before the ice would crack clean through.

"And leave you in sole possession of *my* home?" She glared at him through narrowed eyes. "Not a chance. This is my home. My ranch. I've waited nearly eleven years to come back to Iron Oakes, and I'm staying," she said, surprising everyone, including herself. She hadn't intended to stay when she left Paris. She'd told André that she'd be back. "I'm staying," she repeated, realizing that she meant it. "Even if I have to marry a snake like you to do it."

"Now, Miz Richards," Emmett said, claiming her attention as he tried to smooth things over. "There's no need for this unseemly haste."

Her glance flickered unwillingly to Ben for a moment, catching the brief flash of ironic humor. Those had been her exact words to him in the car.

"You have six months to make up your mind, you know," the lawyer went on.

"Six months." She waved her hand in a gesture of dismissal. "And what good does that do me? According to Henry's will, I'd still have to marry Ben at the end of it."

"You might decide to sell your half," Pete began hesitantly and then stopped, wary of the cold light in her eyes as she turned to him.

"No." Stacey's voice was flat and strangely unemotional. "This ranch is half mine and I intend to keep it. And no one—" her icy glance speared Ben for a moment and the glacial lights turned to blue flames "—no one," she repeated, "is ever going to run me off again. No matter what I have to do."

"Yes, of course, but, Miz Richards—"

"You might as well call me Stacey," she said, interrupting the lawyer. "This matter is a little too intimate for us to stand on ceremony, don't you think?" She drew her purse toward her again as she spoke and flipped open the gold cigarette case. This time she held the cigarette to her lips and waited expectantly. It was Emmett who hurriedly drew a lighter from his vest pocket to light it for her.

Stacey nodded her thanks and rose from the edge of the desk, moving with cool, feline grace to sit in the leather chair opposite Ben. The little ritual of the cigarette had given her the time she needed to collect herself. She was in control again.

"I'll have a brandy now, please, Uncle Pete," she said with a slight smile. "Courvoisier, if you have it." She crossed her long, nylon-clad legs and leaned back, deceptively casual. "What about divorce?" she asked Emmett.

"Divorce? Hell's bells, girl, you ain't even married yet," said Pete, handing her the drink in a heavy, straight-sided highball glass.

"I think what the lady means is can she get a quickie Mexico marriage and divorce—"

"Preferably on the same day," Stacey interjected.

"—and still keep half the ranch," Ben finished, ignoring her interruption. "The answer is no."

She looked at Emmett. "Is that right?"

"I'm afraid so, Miz Rich—ah, Stacey. Your grandfather was very specific about that part of the will. If you marry Ben and then later get a divorce, your half of Iron Oakes Ranch reverts to him. Unless there are, ah, children, of course," he said, a red tinge creeping up from under his collar. "In that case, Ben would hold the land in trust until they came of age."

"Even if he beats me?"

"Uh, beg pardon?" Emmett stammered. "Beats you?"

"If I divorce him for cause," she explained, watching Ben for a reaction. She had yet to goad him out of his calm, and he'd pushed her too close to the edge twice already. "You know," she elaborated, "physical brutality, adultery, that sort of thing. Would he still get the ranch?"

"You got no call to go sayin' a thing like that, girl!" Pete exploded, shocked down to his hand-tooled boots. "Ben would never hit no woman." The disapproving look he gave her was darkly significant. "Even if she deserved it."

Stacey barely glanced at him. "Would he?" she persisted, her eyes on Emmett.

"No," he said. "At least, I don't think so," he amended. "Henry made no special provisions as to the cause of divorce."

"I see. So any way you look at it, I lose."

"Not at all," Emmett hastened to reassure her. "This provision of Henry's will applies only to the ranch. Your ownership in other Oakes Enterprises' holdings has nothing to do with whether or not you marry Ben. In fact, you own several oil leases outright—"

"Well, hallelujah," Stacey said dryly, referring to the currently depressed state of Texas oil prices.

"Don't you be scoffing, girl," Pete scolded her. "Things'll turn around soon enough. They always do."

"Yes, that's right," Emmett agreed. "They always do if you can hold on long enough—and there's no question that you can. Henry saw to it that you own some other subsidiary companies of Oakes Enterprises that have nothing to do with oil. It's all right here, if you'd care to read it." He gestured toward the will where it lay on the desk. "If you decide that you can't, ah, comply with this one provision of the will, well, Ben is instructed to pay you a fair market value for half the ranch. Over a reasonable period of time, of course," he added. "But you'd lose nothing financially. In fact, Miz—ah, Stacey, you're a very wealthy young woman. Very wealthy, indeed. With proper management, you'll never want for anything."

"I wouldn't have the ranch."

"No, you wouldn't. But if you'll forgive my saying so, does that matter so much? You haven't lived here since you were fifteen, or so I've been given to understand."

"I was away at school." She blew a cloud of smoke into the air and looked at them through it, silently daring any one of them to refute her words.

"Yes, at first, but more recently by choice," Emmett ventured.

"Not by *my* choice."

"Whose choice, then?" Ben challenged. His voice had a hard, angry edge to it. Who the hell else's choice had it been, if not hers?

"You can ask me that?" Stacey fought the urge to jump up and confront him. "*You?*" she said, her voice like ice. "The low-down snake who convinced my grandfather to send me away in the first place!"

"It was for your own good. And like Emmett said, you weren't at school the whole time, or even most of it. You could have come home anytime you wanted."

Stacey came ramrod straight in her chair. "Anytime I wanted! After the way I was sent away? After no word, not even a lousy postcard?" she said furiously, forgetting the letters that had arrived in the beginning. "Nothing but those damn checks?"

"Whose fault was that?"

"I was fifteen years old!" she defended herself. "A child in a foreign country and away from home for the first time in my life. And you're saying that I should have been the wise one and made the first move?"

"He was a proud man."

"And that excuses him, I suppose?"

"Now, Stacey, girl," Pete soothed uneasily. "Henry was only tryin' to protect you."

"You said that before." She rose with a jerky motion, her cool, calm exterior once again shattered, and moved to stand at the window with her back to the room. "But protect me from what?" she asked after a minute, turning around. "Answer me that, if you can, Uncle Pete. Protect me from what?"

"Well, from—" he shrugged uneasily "—from havin' to come back here, permanentlike, if you didn't want to," he said finally. "You been gone a long time, girl. You might of found yourself a man you didn't want to up and leave."

Stacey's low laugh was bitter. "So he made the provision that I'd have to marry Ben?" she said scornfully. She made a small, disbelieving gesture with her hand that stopped him from thinking up further inane excuses for his old friend. "Henry wrote this will to protect the ranch, to protect Ben, and to punish me," she said, slapping the offending piece of paper with the flat of her hand. Ashes from her cigarette drifted over the desk. "What I can't understand is why he didn't just leave it to Ben outright and save all this argument."

"He knew you'd fight that," Ben said, wondering why the hell Henry hadn't realized that she'd fight this, too. And harder than she would have fought it the other way. He rose from his chair in one fluid motion, graceful for so big a man, and set his empty bourbon glass on the bar.

"But fight this and you stand a good chance of losing it all," he said. "Most Texas juries wouldn't look kindly on a woman who hadn't seen her grandfather—*her only blood relative*," he emphasized, moving toward her as he spoke, "for almost eleven years, fighting like a greedy little bitch to get more. They'd most likely think that you'd got enough already. More than enough, all things considered."

He stopped directly in front of her, deliberately crowding her against the desk. "I think everyone's got a clear idea of how things stand," he said, his eyes touching each of them in turn before coming to rest on Stacey's upturned face.

She stared back at him, her wide blue eyes no longer cool and scornful, but full of the same spit and hellfire as they'd been when she'd gotten angry as a girl. Her finely chiseled jaw was set in the stubborn line he remembered far too well for his own good. Her lush mouth was firmed in anger.

He studied her for a brief moment, the space of a heartbeat only, remembering other times that she had stood just so, staring up at him with daggers in her blue eyes. He'd felt then much as he felt now: frustrated, angry, confused, lustful, not knowing whether he wanted to shake her until her teeth rattled or haul her into his arms and kiss away her bad temper. He hovered for a moment between the two possibilities.

And then Stacey lifted her hand, bringing the half-smoked cigarette to her lips.

Ben frowned and his big hand came up, quick as a cat, swallowing her wrist in his grasp. Before she could twist away he reached up with his other hand and took the cigarette from her. He reached around her to the oversize crystal ashtray on the desk, and crushed it out, ignoring her gasp of protest.

"Nasty habit," he said softly, enjoying the feel of her soft skin beneath his fingers. Had she been this soft eleven years ago? "Not at all ladylike."

Stacey nearly hissed, her anger finally boiling over at his careless assumption of authority. Her fingers curled, the long, beautifully manicured, salmon-pink nails pressing into the back of his hand. He tightened his grip warningly, and then almost painfully, but she persisted, digging her nails into his flesh until they threatened to draw blood.

"You have six months," he said finally, his voice still soft but dangerously so. His eyes were hot as they blazed down into hers. Hot with anger and desire and the wild thrill of standing toe-to-toe with her again.

Stacey returned his glare steadily, giving as good as she got, willing herself to give no outward sign that he'd cowed her. Or aroused her.

Their gazes held for a few seconds more, her nails still pressed into the back of his hand, his fingers still wrapped around her wrist. The two other occupants of the room were silent and still, waiting for the explosion. Seconds ticked by like minutes, neither of them moving, neither of them backing down.

"Hell," Ben swore in disgust and dropped her wrist. He brought his injured hand to his mouth, sucking lightly at the marks that she'd made with her nails. "Marta will have lunch on the table by now and we've wasted enough time already on all this palaverin'," he said, turning toward the door. "I've got work to do yet today."

LUNCH HAD a rather solemn air. Obviously intended by Marta to be both a welcome home to Stacey and a farewell to Henry Oakes, it hovered somewhere in between, neither completely festive nor truly sorrowful.

The table was covered with a fine lace tablecloth and set with delicate crystal glasses and fine English bone china. The silver was Gorham sterling. Stacey stared at it for a moment, surprised. The dining room of her memory had been an uncomfortable and seldom-used room; she remembered eating in the kitchen most of the time, off sturdy crockery.

The table's elegance couldn't be Marta's doing, she knew, because as lovingly as she would care for it, Marta wouldn't know the difference between the finest Waterford crystal and an imitation from the local K mart. Nor would she care. And neither would Henry or Uncle Pete. They'd been roughneck wildcatters in the early years when they'd first formed their partnership, and despite their success, neither of them had ever given a plugged nickle about the so-called finer things in life.

Which, by the process of elimination, left Ben. But Ben was as much a hick cowboy as Henry had been and Pete still was. Wasn't he?

Something of her bafflement must have shown in her face, for she looked up from her brief contemplation of the beautifully set table to find Ben eyeing her sardonically, as if he knew full well what she was thinking.

We're not all quite the rough country hicks that you'd like us to be, his look said clearly.

Stacey turned her head quickly away from him, forcing herself to smile up at Marta instead. "Oh, how wonderful! Enchiladas," she said as the housekeeper proudly placed a steaming plate on the table in front of her.

If the table was set like something out of *House Beautiful*, the food was pure Tex-Mex, a delicious blending of the Texas and Mexican cuisines. Besides the enchiladas made with homemade corn tortillas, there were soft refried beans without which no Mexican meal was complete, spicy Spanish rice with colorful bits of peppers and pimentos, deep-fried turnovers, filled with savory Gulf shrimp, and Marta's special guacamole. Which was hotter than Hades, Stacey remembered belatedly, reaching for her iced tea, but delicious nonetheless.

"Enough," she said at last when Marta offered second helpings of the traditional caramel-topped flan she was serving for dessert. "It's wonderful, all of it, but I've had enough."

"You are too skinny," Marta scolded affectionately.

"No, she's not," Ben said. "I like my women on the slim side."

Stacey rose to the bait immediately. "I'm not your woman."

Ben cocked an eyebrow at her and stood up, his long body seeming to unfold endlessly from behind the table. "Not yet," he agreed easily.

"I could sell out," she reminded him, wishing he wouldn't stand over her like that. Even across the width of the table his great height and breadth of shoulder were intimidating.

He shrugged. "You could," he said. It took all his considerable self-control to appear unconcerned either way. "But you won't."

"You're awfully sure of yourself."

"Sure of you," he corrected. "I saw that greedy little gleam in those big blue eyes of yours. You want this ranch and all the goodies that go with it."

"I don't," she said, and stood to gain whatever advantage her height might give her. She still had to tilt her head a bit to meet his eyes. "I don't care about the money or the oil wells. I—"

"Am I to take that avaricious gleam to mean that you covet me, then?" he mocked softly.

Unaccountably Stacey blushed. She hadn't blushed for years, not since her teens, and even then, it would have taken more than a smart remark like that to make the color come rushing to her cheeks.

"This is my home," she said hotly, looking to Pete for support, but both he and the lawyer had risen when she did and were already backing away from the table.

Did nobody stand up to this bully?

She reached out toward her water glass, itching to fling its contents at his arrogant head. Something in his eyes stopped her, a quiet look, but dangerous nonetheless. She knew, beyond a doubt, that he wouldn't hesitate to retaliate, and with equal certainty, she knew that no one would stop him. Without a word being spoken, she allowed her hand to fall back to her side.

"Smart girl," he said with a wry twist of his mouth. And then he turned, following the other two men out the door, wondering just what he would have done if she hadn't backed down. And why in hell he'd pushed her to the point where she'd had to.

3

STACEY WAS LEFT STANDING openmouthed with impotent fury. "Damn him!" she swore softly.

How many times had he caused her to lose her temper today? Twice? Three times? However many, it was too many. And to think that she, renowned all over Paris for her cool head and icy control, hadn't said a hasty, unconsidered word in years. Probably not since the last time he'd goaded her beyond thinking rationally.

"Damn him." She hit her closed fist on the table in frustration. "Damn him, damn him!"

"Sit, sit." Marta pressed Stacey back into her chair with one hand, pouring her another cup of cinnamon-spiced coffee with the other.

"How can you all let him get away with it?" Stacey fumed. She reached for the narrow leather clutch purse that lay beside her napkin.

"It is his right." Marta didn't pretend to misunderstand. "He has been the *jefe* for a long time now. It is only natural that he should have the respect and obedience of those who live here, no?"

"What about my grandfather? He was the *jefe* of Iron Oakes last time I heard. Didn't he have any say? And Uncle Pete." She fingered the clasp on her gold cigarette case with one hand, opening and closing it. "Does Ben ride roughshod over him, too?"

"But, no, of course not!" Marta sounded shocked that Stacey would even suggest such a thing. "Benito rides rough over no one. And he takes nothing that is not his due." She began stacking plates on a wooden tray. "It is only that your grandfather was not a well man before he died and—"

"Henry was ill before he died? But I thought—" Stacey twisted around in her chair to look at Marta, the temptations of the cigarette case forgotten for the moment. "He was thrown, wasn't he?"

"*Sì*, from that painted devil of a horse. But he was old, *niña*," Marta said, her head bent over her task. "As Señor Pete is old. Old and tired and glad to lay the burden on younger shoulders." She lifted her head, her black eyes twinkling. "And such broad shoulders, no? Benito is much man, *muy hombre, sì?*"

"He's an overgrown, ill-mannered ox," Stacey said grumpily.

"Ah, pah! You are as stubborn as he is." Marta lifted the tray and headed toward the kitchen.

Stacey finished her coffee in solitude, one hand still fiddling with the cigarette case, opening and closing the gold clasp.

Nasty habit.

The words echoed through her mind and she wavered for another moment, torn between smoking just to score a point against Ben and her own good common sense. It was silly, she decided, to continue polluting her lungs just because she was mad at Ben. After all, she'd been mad at Ben for a good portion of the past eleven years and she was probably going to be even madder at him in the future. She left the cigarette case on the table and carried her empty coffee cup into the kitchen.

"That was a truly delicious meal, Marta," she said, hugging the housekeeper from behind. "You remembered all of my favorite dishes. Thank you."

The older woman took refuge in gruffness, pleased and embarrassed by Stacey's warm thanks. "Go to your room and rest. I have work to do." She waved her away with a soapy hand. "Go."

"I've rested enough." She squeezed Marta again, planting a smacking kiss on her cheek before she let her go. "I want to look around."

"Well, look somewhere else, then," Marta scolded her affectionately, "and do not clutter up my kitchen with your foolishness."

Stacey laughed lightly, happily. How many times in the past had Marta chased her from the kitchen for getting in the way? "I'll stay out of your way," she promised, turning to poke into the nooks and crannies of the big cozy room.

Changes had been made inside as well as out, she noted, the beginnings of trepidation tugging at her heartstrings. The old refrigerator had been replaced with a newer model, a dishwasher had been installed, and there was a big double oven in the adobe wall next to the stove. A food processor, as shiny new as if it had just come out of the box, sat on the tiled counter next to the old apple-shaped cookie jar.

"This is quite a machine," Stacey said, touching it lightly. "I'll bet it does everything but plant the crops."

"Ah, pah!" Marta shrugged, up to her elbows in sudsy dishwater, obviously unwilling to trust the fine crystal to the mercies of the new dishwasher.

Stacey smiled to herself, the trepidation beginning to fade. Some things might have changed but not Marta. Marta would always prefer the old, known ways no matter how many new appliances she had.

"Benito bought it," the housekeeper went on. "To save me work, he said. Pah! I only have more to clean."

But Stacey could tell that she was pleased. Not with the new appliances exactly, but with the evidence of Ben's care and concern. Stacey was feeling pretty pleased herself at the moment. Not with Ben's concern, of course, but with the realization that all the modern appliances hadn't taken away from the warm rustic charm of the kitchen she remembered so fondly from her childhood.

The rough-textured, white-washed walls were still the same as she remembered them, touched now with a golden glow by the late-afternoon sunlight streaming through the narrow arched doors that opened onto the courtyard. Marta's carved wooden crucifix still hung above the double doors that gave access to the dining room. The long trestle-style table still ran down the center of the kitchen, surrounded by eight ladderback chairs with woven cane seats.

Stacey ran her fingers over the scarred tabletop, engraved with the name of nearly everyone who had ever eaten in Marta's kitchen. Stacey's was there, several times over. And Ben's. She touched the entwined hearts and initials, hers and Ben's, that had been carved there so long ago. She had been nine or ten at the time, still young enough to cherish a severe case of hero-worship for the teenaged Ben, who had done it to please her.

Nostalgia welled up unexpectedly, filling her with a wistful longing for something that once was and could never be again. Foolish tears filled her eyes. She blinked them back. She was long past hero-worship, and Ben was no hero, anyway. He never had been. She brushed her eyes with the back of her hand. "I guess I'll go rest, after all," she said to Marta, saying the first thing that came to mind as she sidled past the housekeeper.

I'm just tired, Stacey told herself as she hurried through the dining room. *It's the time difference; jet lag; the funeral this morning. I am just tired!* She sniffed determinedly, her steps slowing as she entered the living room.

It, too, had thick, whitewashed adobe walls. The ceilings were low and beamed. The furniture was mostly rich brown leather and oversize, as if it were intended for use by a race of giant men. Stacey smiled through the unshed tears that still shimmered in her eyes.

That was just the image, she thought, that Texas strived to give the rest of the world. Texans were supposed to be bigger, smarter, richer, more generous, more everything than anyone else. Their women were prettier, their horses—and cars—were faster and they drank their whiskey straight. Or so the legend went. Most Texans believed the legend and, from what Stacey had observed in her travels, it seemed that most of the rest of the world believed it, too. Everyone, it seemed, loved a cowboy. A Texas cowboy, in particular.

She wandered around the living room, which, like the kitchen, was chock-full of memories, full of family legends and stories and shared laughter, full of the girl she used to be. The girl she could never be again, she thought wistfully, even if she stayed.

If.

The thought startled her; she'd already made up her mind, hadn't she? Yes, she told herself. Yes, she had. She was home and she was staying. And to hell with the girl she used to be.

She didn't want to be that girl, anyway. That girl had been too highstrung and emotional, too vulnerable, too much in love with a man who'd turned out to be a low-down snake. She was infinitely better off as she was now—especially when it looked as if she might be forced to marry that snake to keep what was hers.

And then, no, she thought in the next instant. She couldn't marry him. The idea was totally ridiculous. But she couldn't lose the ranch, either. Not again. Not ever again. Not even if she had to stand toe-to-toe with Ben Oakes and battle it out for the rest of her natural life.

THE LITTLE jeweled travel alarm buzzed somewhere near her head. Stacey jackknifed to a sitting position, reaching to silence it. She sat still for a moment, the clock cupped in her hands, listening for any sounds of stirring in the silent, sleeping house. There were none.

Satisfied that she had wakened no one else, Stacey put the clock back on the bedside table and swung her long legs out of bed. Aided only by the moonlight that streamed in through the louvered shutters, she slipped into her robe, belting it loosely over the matching silk nightgown that Marta had admired and, barefoot, made her way quietly from her room.

It was dark in the hall. She paused on the top of the stairs, letting her eyes adjust to the darkness before proceeding cautiously, one slow step at a time, down the wide, wooden staircase, automatically avoiding the fifth one from the top that had always creaked.

It was light again at the bottom of the steps, the moonlight shining softly through the glass doors that led out onto the courtyard. It cast its wavering shadows over the solid brown leather furniture, making the oversized chairs and sofa look eerily like large animals hunkered down for sleep.

Stacey shivered slightly, dismissing the thought, and walked toward the doors that led to the courtyard. Opening them, she stood in the night air with her arms wrapped around her middle. The sun had gone down hours ago and one might have expected it to have cooled off by now. But it hadn't. At least, not much. She'd almost forgotten how hot a summer's night in Texas could be. And how beautiful.

Without the clutter of neon signs and city streetlights to compete with, the night sky was an endless expanse of inky blackness lit by thousands upon thousands of tiny, twinkling stars and the bright lantern of a nearly full moon. It shone down, casting its ghostly light over the utter silence of the night and glimmering off the softly splashing water in the fountain in the center of the courtyard. Stacey sighed, hugging herself as she gazed up at the smiling face of the man in the moon. It had been just such a night when she'd taken her last moonlit ride on Iron Oakes's land.

It had been later in the summer, though, not quite so hot, and her companion had been a man. Not Ben who, newly graduated from college, seemed to have no time to spare for her then. And not one of the many boys of her own age who clamored around her that summer like eager bees around a new honeypot. Her companion that night had been an "older" man; in his midtwenties only, but older in comparison to Stacey's fifteen. A new employee not long on the ranch who either didn't know, or, more likely, didn't care, that the *jefe*'s pretty little granddaughter was off limits. Henry hadn't seemed to notice anything amiss, but Ben hadn't liked the attention the new hand paid to her.

"You're just a kid and he's too old for you," he'd said. "Keep away from him."

That was all it took. She'd snuck out one night—after carefully planting a note—to meet her admirer for a midnight ride with some vague idea of making Ben sit up and take notice of her newfound maturity. But her companion had wanted much more than the few innocent kisses Stacey had thought to exchange. When Ben finally caught up with them they were rolling around in the dust near a dying campfire, Stacey all undone and screaming with anger and fear.

Ben had hauled the cowboy off of her with one hand. She'd scrambled away, unaware at first that she'd been rescued, and grabbed up a gnarled piece of mesquite wood to defend herself. But it was unnecessary. Ben had already hit him.

She could still remember the sickening sound of breaking bones as Ben's fist smashed savagely against the other man's nose. The second blow had sent the ranchhand sprawling and in a low, dangerously controlled voice, Ben ordered him off Iron Oakes land. There had been a long, taut silence, she remembered, while the two men measured each other. Her assailant was older and more experienced at brawling, but Ben was bigger, much bigger, and a killing rage boiled in his steely blue eyes.

"Never did like a tease, anyhow," the cowboy said, wiping at the blood that trickled from his nose as he turned away. Only after he was gone, swallowed by the darkness, did Ben turn to Stacey. The look on his face scared her almost more than the attempted rape had done.

"Ben," she said, taking a step back. She lifted the makeshift mesquite wood club she was holding as if to ward him off, her knuckles white with the fierceness of her grip. "It wasn't—I didn't—"

"Don't say a word." He yanked the stick out of her hand and tossed it aside, then reached out and grabbed her by the wrists, shaking her slightly. She stumbled against him and his hands went automatically to her shoulders. He shook her again. "Just don't say a word. I don't want to hear it." He thrust her away from him with a gesture of disgust. "Get on your horse."

"Please, Ben." Her eyes filled. This wasn't how it was supposed to be at all! This wasn't how she'd planned it! He wasn't supposed to push her away in anger and disgust. He was supposed to hold her. Comfort her. Tell her he had never realized how much he loved her until this moment. But something had gone horribly wrong. She reached out to touch him, to placate and plead for understanding. "Please." Her hand touched the middle of his chest.

He went absolutely still.

She could feel his madly, erratically beating heart and the faint wetness of his sweat-dampened chambray shirt. His breathing was harsh and fast. Much faster than it should have been, even considering his mad ride and the thrashing he had just given her attacker.

Hope welled up as she recognized the emotion that gripped him. How many times over the years had Marta smacked her with one hand while holding her close with the other? He was angry because he loved her, that was all, she'd thought, relieved. Angry and afraid for what might have happened to her.

Oh, Ben, dear sweet Ben, her young heart cried out. *You do love me.*

Without conscious volition she moved a step nearer, her other hand reaching out to join the first. "It's all right," she crooned softly, stroking his heaving chest as if soothing a restive horse. "It's all right, Ben. He didn't hurt me. I'm all right."

He moved then, his big rawboned hands coming up to capture hers, pressing the palms flat against the hard, muscled wall of his chest.

"I'm so glad you came after me, Ben," she breathed, swaying toward him, believing that now, at last, the night would turn out as she'd intended it to. "So glad. I didn't mean—"

"No, you didn't mean it." His voice was strained and low. His hands tightened, crushing her fingers in his grasp. "You never mean it, do you? You strut around in those tight jeans with nothing on under your blouse. You wiggle and tease, just like he said, until some poor fool takes you up on it, but you don't mean it."

"Ben!" she said, aghast. What was he saying? Why was he blaming her? She hadn't meant for the man to attack her. "I didn't do anything!" she defended herself. "He tried—"

"He tried what? To take you up on what you offered? Can you blame him?" His eyes, hot, caressing, accusing, traveled over her disheveled form. He let go of one of her hands and reached out to run one callused fingertip over the upper curve of the high, young breast that was partially exposed by her torn shirt.

Stacey stood frozen, paralyzed by his delicate touch and the wondering, wanting, tortured look on his face.

"Could any man blame him?" Ben whispered raggedly, and then shook his head in answer to his own question. "I can't," he said. Both hands moved downward, lightly outlining her budding figure, coming to rest on her denim-sheathed hips. "I'd like to kill the bastard—" his fingers tightened, biting into her "—but I can't really blame him."

Stacey was scarcely aware of what he said, so intent was she on trying to read the expression on his face in the flickering shadows of the dying fire. What she saw there—or thought she saw there—only confused her more.

There was desire in his expression, yes. Even as inexperienced as she was, she could see that. But she could also see that he was fighting that desire. The battle was evident in the tightened line of his full lower lip and his clenched jaw and the pinched, strained look around his eyes. And overlaying it all was a disgust he didn't even try to hide. For her? Was he disgusted by what he'd thought she'd done?

"It wasn't like that, Ben," she said frantically. "Honest, it wasn't! I only rode out with him because you told me not to a-and—" it was so hard to say with him looking at her like that "—and so that you'd come after me," she finished in a small voice.

Ben's eyes flared wide for an instant. "You *wanted* me to come after you?"

"Yes." It was barely a whisper.

"Why?" Just that one word, and his eyes looking at her so strangely.

Didn't he know? she thought. Couldn't he see why?

"Because I . . . because . . ." But she couldn't tell him why, couldn't put into words what she felt now that she was given the chance. Not with him looking at her like that.

"Did you want me to kiss you, Stacey, like he did?" His fingers flexed on the curve of her hips. "Did you?"

She bit her lip and nodded once, hesitantly. This was what she wanted, wasn't it? This is what she had dreamed about for months now? Ben holding her. Ben about to kiss her. And yet . . .

"Say it, Stacey," he demanded roughly. "I want to make sure I understand you." His hands tightened, pulling her unresisting body to his. His breath was hot on her face. "Tell me you want me to kiss you."

"I . . ." But suddenly, standing there with her lower body held to the hardness of his and her hands flat against his heaving chest, she was no longer sure that's what she wanted at all. It hadn't been this way in her daydreams. When she'd thought about it, planned it, it had been all soft and pretty and filled with sweet, warm emotion. But there was nothing soft or pretty or sweet about this. This was all too real. And it was frightening. *He* was frightening.

"Changed your mind again?" he said when she hesitated. His voice was low, as dangerous as a coiled snake. "Decided you don't want me, either, now that it comes right down to it, is that it? All teasing and cute little games and we play by your rules or we don't play at all?" He brought one hand up to the back of her neck and curled his fingers into her long, tangled hair, forcing her head back. "What happens if I don't want to play by your rules? What if I just take what I want?" His eyes burned over her upturned face. Hard, implacable, terrifying eyes. "There's no one here to stop me like I stopped him."

Stacey whimpered and squeezed her eyes closed. She'd never seen this Ben before. Never even guessed that he existed inside the Ben she knew.

"Ben, don't." She arched away from him, pushing against his chest with both hands. It was like pushing against a stone wall. Panic knifed through her. "Please, don't." She lifted wide, tear-filled eyes to his. "Don't."

Their eyes held for a long, taut moment. They were both breathing hard, both tense and stiff, both waiting for what the other would do next. And then Ben shifted his hold and stooped, picking her up before she quite knew what had happened. Without another word he tossed her onto her horse and, with her reins in his hand, mounted his.

They rode back to the house in silence, Stacey being led like an irresponsible child. Two days later, Ben had confronted her grandfather with the accusation that she was "growing up wild" and together the two men had contrived to have her sent away.

Stacey sighed deeply, thinking vaguely of lost innocence and lost love, and brought her wandering mind back to the present. What was past was past, and she had more pressing things to attend to now. Such as her reason for being up in the middle of the night.

She'd set her alarm, taking into account the time difference, so that she could catch André in his Paris office the very first thing in the morning. She needed his advice because, sometime during the evening meal, which Ben never came in for, she'd decided that she was going to need a lawyer. André, with his far-flung oil empire, would know the best. And she was going to need the best if she was going to fight Henry's will and win.

She turned back inside, leaving her memories to float uneasily on the night air, and walked through the dark, sleeping house to her grandfather's den. With fifteen minutes to wait before she could be sure that André would be in his office, she poured herself a small brandy and curled up in the big leather chair she'd occupied just that morning. Sipping her drink in the warm, cocooning darkness, she tried to tell herself that, no, she didn't want a cigarette. Five futile minutes later, she sighed and straightened, reaching for the battered silver box that Henry had always kept full of his own special brand of smokes. *Just one*, she solemnly promised herself, lifting the lid.

The box was full of sour lemon candies.

Making a small sound of annoyance, she sat her drink on the wide arm of the chair and rose to move behind the desk, reaching for the lids of the other small boxes lined up above the leather ink blotter. She found stamps, rubber bands, paper clips and loose change but no cigarettes.

Well, damn, she thought, lifting file folders and loose papers as her search became more frantic. *Henry always had cigarettes. He'd smoked like the proverbial chimney.* Getting desperate as only a quitting smoker can, she reached out and snapped on the small, green-shaded desk lamp to aid her search.

4

RUBBING ABSENTLY at the back of his neck, Ben walked past the row of box stalls, turning off the bright overhead lights as he went. He was hot and tired and sweaty, his neck and upper back aching from the long struggle to help Lone Star deliver her first foal. Because of the mare's extreme nervousness and the added difficulty of a breech birth, he and the vet had nearly lost them both a couple of times. But mother and baby were doing fine now and the Iron Oakes Stable had another potential winner in the awkward, spindly-legged newborn who'd already managed to struggle to her feet for her first meal.

The thought gave Ben a great deal of satisfaction, beyond that of helping a new life safely into the world, because the addition of a racing stable to the Iron Oakes holdings had been his idea. And it was proving to be a good one.

He turned off the last light and pushed open the wide door, stepping out of the barn and into the dark, star-studded night. He headed down the well-worn path to the main house, his sense of satisfaction fading a bit with every step, replaced by a curious mix of feelings made up of wariness and irritation, anger and affection, and something he could only label as nostalgia. Nostalgia brought on by the very natural reminiscing about the past that was part of mourning and—*might as well face it*, he thought—the fact that Stacey had finally come home.

Ah, Stacey.

She'd been the kid sister that he'd never had, an occasional tag-along pest, a preadolescent who'd liked loud music and bright colors. And, finally, a temptation.

It'd been on a night much like this one—still, starry, hot—that he'd finally realized they couldn't go on as they had been that summer so long ago when she'd turned from little girl to woman. Together too much, alone too often.

After that night, he'd deliberately set about convincing Henry that she needed to be sent away for her own good. For his good, too, he admitted, because, naively, he'd thought that the distance would cure him of his unholy craving for her.

It didn't, of course, especially after Marta had finally told him that his desire for Stacey wasn't as unholy as he'd feared. It was time that finally did the trick. Lots of time. For three years, he'd continued to think about her. Despite the anger she'd spewed at him, despite the lack of letters besides those she wrote to Marta, despite everything, he'd thought about how it would be when she finally came home and he could claim her as he wanted to. And he was sure she still wanted him to, under all the hurt feelings and injured pride.

Only she didn't.

Because, when her schooling was complete, she didn't come home. Not even for a visit. His first reaction had been to go to Paris and drag her back by the hair. His next inclination had been to let her rot over there, and good riddance! In the end, he hadn't gone after her and she, perversely, hadn't rotted. And with more time and the wisdom that comes with growing older and realizing that lust won't kill you, the desire had died a natural death. He'd even begun to think of her as a sister he'd once been close to but had grown apart from.

And now she was home. It'd taken threats and tears and shouting to get her to leave Iron Oakes in the first place; it had taken the death of her grandfather to bring her back.

Would she stay now that she was here? This morning in Henry's office, she'd said she would. No, he thought, grinning into the night, she'd gotten good and mad and *threatened* to stay—and marry him if she had to. His grin faded.

"Dammit, Henry," he said to the sky. "Why the hell did you do it? At least you could've told me what you were planning."

He could have prepared himself then, somehow, to deal with it and all the conflicting emotions it had caused. As it was, well . . . He'd prepared himself to be pleasant and overlook his anger at her prolonged absence—the perfectly justified anger he felt on Henry's behalf. He'd been prepared to be magnanimous and forgive her neglect of her home and her aging grandfather.

But she'd walked into the front hall, as cool as you please, and looked around with all the icy disdain of a queen visiting a peasant's hovel. The first words out of her mouth had been a challenge! And she hadn't even sounded Texan! For some reason, that alone made him want to wring her beautiful neck.

He hadn't even known about the will then.

He kicked open the courtyard gate with the toe of his boot, guiltily catching it before it slammed against the adobe brick wall, and shut it behind him, angry with himself for allowing such a stupid, insignificant thing as a French accent to bother him when he had so many other, more important things he could be bothered about instead.

Oh, hell, face it, he thought, unbuttoning his shirt as he headed toward the courtyard fountain, it wasn't the accent that bothered him. He cupped his hands, splashing water over his heated face and chest. It was what that French accent represented. Stacey's long absence from Iron Oakes. Stacey's neglect. Stacey's life in Paris. Stacey's—

His thoughts broke off abruptly as a light came on in Henry's office. He straightened, absently wiping his face with the hem of his shirt, his eyes on the desk lamp glowing between the open curtains of the office.

Speak of the devil, he thought.

Stacey.

She was wearing some sort of movie-queen nightgown, all silk and sleekness in a soft ivory color. Her hair fell to her shoulders, slightly crinkled from the braid she'd worn all day. Her motions as she rummaged through the desk were quick. Almost frantic.

*What in hell is she doing in Henry's office at—*he glanced at his watch—*two-thirty in the morning?*

He took a deep breath and ran his hand through his damp hair, pushing it back, then strode silently, eagerly, across the courtyard and entered the unlatched patio door to Henry's office. "Can I help you find something?"

Stacey jumped as if she'd been scalded. The folder she was holding slid from her fingers, scattering papers across the desk. She reached out with both hands, snatching at them, squinting into the shadows beyond the light cast by the lamp as she stuffed them back into the folder. "Ben?"

He didn't move, didn't say anything else beyond those first accusation-tinged words, but she knew it was Ben. His height and the massiveness of his shoulders, even if he hadn't spoken at all, would have been identification enough.

"Ben," she said again, hating the vaguely guilty catch in her voice. She wasn't doing anything wrong, but it felt as if she was and looked that way, too, she was sure. "I didn't realize anyone else was still up," she offered and knew immediately that it was the wrong thing to say.

"Obviously," came the mocking reply. He walked into the room then, moving with deceptively lazy grace, and sank into the leather chair Stacey had vacated a few minutes earlier. One hand absently rubbed the back of his neck as he continued to watch her. What the hell was she doing, searching through Henry's desk?

Stacey stared back at him just as silently—as calm as a cool mountain lake on the outside, as agitated as a bubbling caldron of hot oil on the inside—waiting for whatever he would say next.

His faded denim workshirt was wet along the edges, hanging loose and open over his muscular torso. His black hair was disheveled, its slight tendency to curl more pronounced with the water that dampened it. And even across the width of the desk he smelled faintly of hay and horses and hardworking man.

The unbidden memory of another time, another night, when he'd looked like that, smelled like that, slipped into her mind, perhaps because she'd so recently been thinking of it. *Is his heart beating like a drum*, she wondered, and then frantically pushed the unwelcome thought away. She didn't want to be reminded or to know. Not now. Not ever.

"I'm sorry if I disturbed you." She knew she hadn't, but good manners—and her screaming nerves—demanded she say something to break the silence that stretched between them.

"I'm sure you are," he agreed. His eyes, those bottomless blue eyes, seemed to mock the inanity of her remark.

"How's the new foal?" she asked, remembering that Uncle Pete had mentioned that Ben was assisting at a difficult delivery.

"Just fine," Ben said, wondering why he didn't just ask her what she was looking for. "Lone Star took her own sweet time tonight, but both she and the new filly are doing fine."

"It was a long labor, wasn't it?" One hand moved aimlessly, fingering each item on the desk's surface.

"It was a breech birth." His eyes followed her wandering hand.

She stilled it, clasping it at her waist with the other. "Oh?"

"We had to turn the foal twice before she finally stayed turned." He sighed and rubbed the back of his neck again, as if trying to ease an ache.

Stacey surprised herself with a vague longing to move behind him and take over for his massaging hand. He looked so tired. So weary and—

"What are you looking for?" he asked abruptly.

The longing to soothe him died just as abruptly. "A cigarette," she said quickly. Too quickly, she thought, and a bit defensively. She could almost hear the apology in her voice. Damn! She had nothing to apologize for. "Couldn't find one, though," she said, shrugging, her voice purposely careless. "Henry give up cigarettes in his old age?" she asked lightly, almost jokingly, in a further effort to erase the apologetic-sounding words.

Ben's head snapped up, his massaging hand stilled at the back of his neck, his blue eyes dark with sudden anger. "He had to quit." His eyes bored into hers. "Doctor's orders."

"Doctor's orders?" she said, momentarily confused by Ben's unexpected anger and the shadow of pain in his eyes.

He stared at her for a long moment before answering, trying to determine if she was really as heartless as she sounded. The Stacey of old had been headstrong and quick to anger but not heartless. Never heartless. He didn't know what this new cool, cosmopolitan, Frenchified Stacey was. It was time, he decided, that he found out.

"He had cancer, Stacey," he said bluntly, his voice gone flat and nearly toneless. He ignored her small shocked gasp and the fluttering of one hand in a vague gesture of denial. "Lung cancer. He was dying slowly, day by agonizing day, of lung cancer. And *that's* why he gave up cigarettes in his old age!"

"I didn't know," Stacey found her voice with difficulty. It was thin and reedy. "I— Your telegram said he was thrown."

"From a horse that should never have been able to toss him. Wouldn't have, if he'd been a well man. But he was sick and in pain. Constant pain, I think, toward the end, though he'd never admit it. Old 'Iron' Oakes! Had to live up to his image." He gave a short bark of harsh, mirthless laughter and picked up Stacey's forgotten glass, tossing down the fiery liquid in one swallow.

"His image killed him," he said reflectively, more to himself than to her. "He wouldn't slow down, wouldn't check into the hospital for any more treatments after the first operation. Said he didn't want any more days than God saw fit to give him."

"Operation?" she echoed faintly. When had Henry had an operation? And why hadn't anyone told her about it?

"Said he wasn't going to die in some damned hospital bed," Ben continued as if he hadn't heard her, "hooked up to some damned machine. He wanted to go fast, with his damned boots on," he added, his voice husky with pain. He sat silently for a few minutes, gazing into the empty glass as if wondering where the drink had gone. "Well, he did that, didn't he?" he said finally, but Stacey hadn't heard him.

Her eyes were closed tightly against the hot tears that threatened to fall, trying to block out the image of her grandfather as sick and frail and dying. He'd always been such a powerful man. Not nearly as big as Ben but barrel chested and ham fisted, full of grandiose schemes and plans that he mostly made come true. He'd been so full of tenacious life, she thought, and their parting had been so angry, their last words so full of accusation and rage.

She remembered suddenly, with sharp, cruel clarity, the faces at the funeral, the condemnation in all those eyes and the way they slid away from hers. It wasn't just that she hadn't shed any tears at Henry's graveside. It was because they all thought she'd known that her grandfather was dying of cancer and hadn't bothered to come home until he was dead. Like a vulture, arriving in time for her share of the spoils.

Damn Henry for not telling her! And damn Ben for telling her now, this way!

"No one told me," she whispered hoarsely. "No one wrote. Marta's letters..." Her voice broke and she paused, struggling to control it. "She never said Henry was sick."

"Would you have cared?" His voice cut into her like a knife.

Stacey's eyes flew open. "Cared! Of course I cared! He was my grandfather! No matter what you think. In spite of everything, I...I loved him." She whirled away, turning her back to him, too proud to allow him to see the tears that finally escaped her control and slid slowly down her cheeks. She stood as straight and stiff as she had at the funeral, as she had that morning at the reading of the will. She wouldn't let them—Henry, Ben, any of them!—see how badly they could still hurt her.

Ben stared at her for a long moment. Her back was ramrod straight, but her shoulders were trembling under the shimmering material of her robe, a sure sign that she was crying.

"Dammit all to hell," he swore softly. He'd never been able to cope with her tears, especially if he'd been the one to cause them. They made him feel helpless and mean. Leather creaked as he rose from the chair. "Stacey..." He came around the desk and put a hand on her shoulder, urging her to turn to him. "I didn't mean to make you cry," he said, sounding weary and resigned, feeling guilty. "Stacey, honey, please don't cry."

She stiffened and pulled away, keeping her back to him, unwilling, as always, for anyone to see her tears. "I'm not crying," she said and sniffed.

"All right," he agreed, forcibly turning her into his arms. "You're not crying."

She stood stiffly for a second or two longer, trying to freeze him out, trying to hate him, but his hand went to her hair, gently stroking, and suddenly she was ten years old and he was the Ben he'd been then. Her friend, her protector, her whole world. She burrowed her face into his bare damp chest and sobbed as if her heart were breaking.

Ben comforted her as best he could, smoothing the fine golden-blond hair, whispering meaningless, consoling words, holding her as he'd once held a hurt child, letting her cry it all out.

And she did.

She cried for the scared fifteen-year-old, alone in Paris and too stubborn to cry for herself. She cried for the homesick career girl, too proud to come home without an invitation. She cried for the woman whose grandfather hadn't allowed her a proper farewell.

"Why didn't you tell me?" she asked when, at last, she could speak again. Her voice was muffled against his chest. "I would have come home, Ben. Nothing could have kept me away, if I'd known. Nothing."

She could feel his cheek against the top of her head and she thought she felt his lips move, but he said nothing in reply, just held her, one hand still gently, absently stroking her hair.

It was imperative, suddenly, that he believe her, that he understand. She could take everyone else thinking she was a cold, selfish bitch, but not Ben. She needed to hear him say that, despite what everyone else thought, he didn't think she was so small and hardhearted that she wouldn't have come home if she had known that her grandfather really needed her.

"I would have come back, Ben," she said again, her hands flat against his chest now, pushing a little away from him to look up anxiously. Her eyes were soft and pleading. Her cheeks were tear streaked.

"Yes," he said softly, the word neither a confirmation nor a denial. He stopped his mindless stroking of her hair, moving his hand so that his palm lay against the side of her neck under the heavy curtain of her tumbled blond waves. Splaying his fingers against the base of her skull, he pressed her head back into his chest. He couldn't take her looking at him that way, all soft and vulnerable and pleading. It made him feel . . . too much. Remember too much.

Stacey resisted the pressure of his hand, refusing to be so easily comforted. "I would have, Ben," she insisted again, her voice barely above a whisper. She searched his face for a sign that he believed her. "I would."

"Yes," he said again. She was so beautiful, staring up at him like that! Her eyes were bluer than he remembered, their color intensified by emotion, shimmering beneath her tears, like bluebonnets after a spring rain. "Stacey," he murmured pleadingly, trying to push her head back down to his chest before she could see the heat that flickered in his own eyes. Heat and hunger and the awareness of a memory. "Stacey, honey, please."

She stilled in his arms, knowing exactly what he was remembering because, suddenly, she was remembering it, too.

It was that long-ago night all over again, she thought, staring up at him, except now they were starting where they'd left off. She could feel the passion growing in him, in his hand at her head and in the tenseness of his big body. And, like the last time, she was afraid. But afraid now of where and, more important, who they were. She wasn't fifteen anymore and crazy in love with a teenager's dream, and this was a Ben she no longer knew or, she told herself fiercely, even wanted to know. She stiffened, looking down, trying to pull away, but she'd hesitated too long.

Even as he warned himself not to, even as he told himself he was making a mistake, Ben tightened his fingers on the back of her neck and drew her closer. His other hand slid from her shoulder to the small of her back.

Stacey pushed his bare chest with the flat of both hands, but that served only to press her lower body

more fully against him. She could feel the rock hardness of his denim-clad thighs against her own softness,
could feel the buckle of his belt pressed against her ab-
domen. It was wonderful and it was frightening and
it—

"Be still," he commanded softly, pushing her chin up
with his thumb. The fingers still splayed along the back
of her neck tightened, holding her head immobile. His
hand on her back pressed her close.

Stacey squeezed her eyes closed. Her hands clenched
into fists against his chest, pushing.

"Look at me," he demanded. The hand at her head
tightened fractionally when she refused. "Stacey, look
at me."

Her eyes flared wide, reflecting fear and defiance and
arousal all at once, the icy disdain she'd so carefully
cultivated forgotten. Their eyes, blue boring into blue,
locked and held, exchanging heat and anger, years of
resentment and hurt and desperate need. Against her
will, she felt her resistance melting away as the flicker
of memory in his eyes became a blue flame, devouring
her.

"No," she managed to say, whether to him or to her
own suddenly raging libido she didn't know, couldn't
tell.

"No," she said as he bent his head toward hers. Her
voice was weaker this time. Her hands against his chest
lost all resistance, unclenching to curl sensuously in the
damp, clinging black hairs. His heart *was* beating like
a drum, she realized.

"Oh, no." It was a last, almost silent plea, but her lips
were parted, a perfect O of instinctive invitation and

Ben's mouth covered hers, taking her past her fears, past the present and into that night more than eleven years ago when all she'd ever wanted was him.

She felt herself give helplessly against him as he staggered back against the desk. Her whole body softened as if any remaining resistance, any lingering defiance, were being drained away at the touch of his lips on hers. She could feel as separate, distinct impressions the short crisp hairs on his chest curling damply around her now passive fingers, the large hand, warm and firm, against the small of her back, the strength of his hard-muscled inner thighs pressing against the outside of hers. She breathed in the musky, thoroughly welcome, male smell of him and pressed closer, burrowing into the notch of his splayed legs.

He groaned, deep in his chest, and the hand on her back shifted, moving lower to caress her bottom and press her more fully against his aching erection. Stacey gave up all coherent thought then, giving way to the glorious, overwhelming onslaught of pure, primal feeling.

Her mouth opened willingly under his. Her hands slid mindlessly up over his chest and shoulders to twine themselves in the damp, curling hair at his nape. Her body collapsed onto his, *into* his, as boneless and pliant as a rag doll.

He moved his hand again, gliding up her slim torso to brush the side of one silk-covered breast. She shifted slightly, bringing her breast more fully under his hand. He shuddered against her, like a man mortally wounded, and kneaded the soft, full flesh that overflowed his palm.

"Stacey." Her name, whispered against her open lips, tasted hot and honey sweet. "Oh, Stacey." His callused fingers probed gently, feverishly, for the opening in her robe.

She turned her body, instinctively allowing him freer access to what he sought. His hand slipped eagerly inside the robe and came up against the frail barrier of her silk nightgown. Stacey could have screamed with frustration. She wanted, desperately, to feel his hand on her bare, yearning flesh. He could have torn her nightgown then and she wouldn't have cared, probably wouldn't have even noticed, if it would have given her what she wanted.

But he didn't tear it. One finger found the V of her gown and followed it upward, over her chest and the inner swell of her breast, to her shoulder. Then his hand slid under the narrow strap, pushing it and the robe downward to bare a smooth rounded shoulder. And still downward, gently forcing one upraised arm from around his neck to hang limply at her side so that it was bared past the elbow and one full white breast was exposed, its rosy tip hardened and straining for his touch. But still Ben moved slowly, agonizingly slowly, not touching her bare flesh until Stacey's nerves were taut with desire and her nipple was swollen with need.

He'd waited so long for this, he thought feverishly, so long, and he wanted it to last forever. His lips left her mouth, planting hot, frantic, moist kisses along her jaw and down her throat and across her smooth bared shoulder.

Stacey's head fell back and she writhed against him, pressing into him, wanting him to please, please,

please, touch her. He murmured something hot and arousing as his mouth found her ear and then his wet tongue probed gently inside, imitating the act they were both dying for.

Stacey moaned and then moaned again as his hand finally closed over her bared breast. He rolled the aching nipple between his thumb and forefinger, making the ache deeper and more intense, driving her desire higher than it had ever gone before.

"I want you, Stacey. Lord, how I want you!" he growled against her ear.

Wordlessly, mindlessly, she pushed her breast into his caressing hand wanting more, wanting everything, because this—as wonderful as it was—just wasn't enough. It had never been enough, she thought. Would never be enough.

He shifted his hand on her back, tightening it around her waist, and drew her up against his body until her toes were just barely touching the floor. She could feel him trembling against her, like a leaf clinging desperately to a limb, buffeted by strong winds. His mouth left off tormenting her ear and he bent, twisting his big body slightly, to take the swollen bud of her breast into his mouth. He sucked gently, seductively, greedily at the hardened pink nipple.

Stacey began to make soft whimpering sounds in her throat. Her arm tightened around his neck. Her back arched to bring him even closer. Her previously limp hand moved, trying to insinuate itself between their locked bodies, reaching for his belt buckle.

"Wait. Stacey, honey," he breathed against her burning flesh. "Not here. Wait." He lifted her as if she weighed no more than a feather and carried her into the shadowed hall and up the dark staircase to her room.

5

SHE HAD A BRIEF MOMENT of panic when he set her
down in her girlhood bedroom. But his lips claimed
hers again and his hand covered her breast and the
panic disappeared as if it had never been.

He backed away after a long sweet moment and
pushed the silk robe and gown off of her other shoulder, down to her waist so that both breasts were bared.
The robe fell to the floor in a shimmering pool at her
feet, but the nightgown clung at her hips. She stood
there, trembling in the moonlight that streamed in
through the half-open louvered doors, her arms and
waist and shoulders looking far too fragile for the lush
ripeness of her white breasts. Her rich, golden hair was
tousled and wild from his hands. Her lips were swollen
from his kisses. Her eyes were narrowed and glazed
with a passion meant for him alone.

"Stacey," he breathed on a ragged sigh. "Oh, Stacey."

Gently, almost reverently, he reached out and placed
a hand over each breast, carefully, so that the pink
crests were pressed against the center of his palms and
his fingers were splayed over the full upper slopes. He
stood there like that for a moment, his eyes closed, not
moving, not speaking, just touching her, his thumbs
brushing softly over the inner swell of her breasts. And

then, his eyes still closed, his face rigid with passion, he began to move his hands over her body—feverishly, frantically—tracing the curves of her shoulders and arms and waist and breasts with his palms. The frenzied caress left trails of fire flickering along her skin and stoked the hot flame of her desire into a raging inferno of need.

"You're so beautiful," he said gruffly, his eyes opening at last. The fire that burned in hers blazed tenfold in his. "I always knew you would be." He drew a deep, unsteady breath. "I dreamed you would be."

She reached out then, wanting to touch him, too, wanting to give him as much pleasure as he was giving her. She ran her long salmon-pink nails lightly over his chest, scraping over his flat male nipples, tugging the dark, crinkly hairs that blurred the definition of his work-honed muscles.

Ben stood very still, his chest pumping like a bellows, watching her face as her hands traveled upward over his massive shoulders. Palms flat, fingers curved against his skin, she slipped them under the opened shirt and down his hard-muscled arms, leaving the damp chambray in a heap on the floor.

She moved toward him then, a small half step to close the little space between them as she reached for his belt buckle. Her foot caught in the tangle of material at their feet and she stumbled. Her breasts flattened against his bare chest. Her outstretched hands pressed against the bulging fly of his jeans.

Something in him snapped, a letting go of whatever slim control he'd been holding on to, and his hands, instead of righting her, toppled her backward onto the bed. With feverish haste he stripped off the rest of his clothes and then dragged Stacey's silk nightgown down off her hips, throwing it carelessly to the floor as his weight pressed her into the bed.

"Stacey." He breathed her name again, over and over, as if to reassure himself that the woman he held was the one he had dreamed about. His hands were everywhere on her body—touching her face and throat and breasts, contouring her belly and thighs, stroking the growing moistness between her legs—until she began to whimper again, softly, deep in her throat. Her body arched in silent supplication, her back lifting from the bed in mindless, aching need.

"Yes, that's it, honey," he panted against her neck. "Yes, right now. I can't wait any longer, either." His words were almost inaudible as he positioned himself over her body. "I've waited so long already," he murmured, opening her thighs even wider with the pressure of his knees. "So long."

But Stacey was past listening to what he said. She heard only the need and desire in his voice, a need and desire that matched her own. Her hands clutched his arms, pulling him to her, and she wrapped her long legs strongly around his hips. Her body arched instinctively, offering herself to him, poised to take whatever he would give.

Ben slipped his hands under her hips, lifting her even higher against him, and took what she offered. Took it feverishly, hungrily, as she gave it. Their bodies moved in a fierce, primitive rhythm for long moments, accompanied by the sounds of his harsh, hurried breathing and Stacey's low moans of pleasure. The muffled thud of flesh striking flesh filled the air around them as their hips came together again and again, faster and then faster still, driving them relentlessly toward the culmination of long-denied desire. And then Stacey stiffened beneath him, hit by an ecstasy so sharp and intense that she cried out his name. Her nails dug into his buttocks as she clung to him with all her strength. He found his release a heartbeat later, a ragged groan of deep satisfaction rumbling up from his chest as his big body tightened like a bow above her.

"Stacey," he sighed. "Stacey." He lowered his chest to hers, wrapping his arms tightly around her, and buried his face in the tangled hair at her neck.

They lay like that for long moments without speaking, their breathing slowly returning to normal, still locked in the closest embrace possible between a man and a woman until Ben finally rolled away from her, onto his side, and propped himself up on one elbow to look down into her flushed face.

Shyly, now that passion was spent, Stacey looked away, unsure of what she might see in his eyes, of what he might see in hers. Now that the reckless, primitive, desperately needy feeling was past and they were two separate people again, she felt curiously defenseless. Curiously alone.

It was as if she'd made too fast a transition in time from the here and now to the past and back again with no time to adjust or evaluate. It had all happened so fast. Everything, all her feelings, had merged for that brief, breathless time; all the love and hate she'd ever felt for Ben, all the anger and hurt, her grief at her grandfather's death and her joy at being home had all tumbled together so that she couldn't tell one from the other. She needed time to sort it all out, time to understand what it all meant, to understand how she felt. She needed, suddenly, to be alone.

Lying there by her side, watching the conflicting emotions chase across her face, Ben could almost feel her slipping away from him. He had to fight the crazy impulse to grab her and hold on tight. "I'm glad that's settled," he said, compelled to bring her back from wherever it was she'd gone.

Stacey turned her head to look up at him. The moonlight filtered through the long shuttered doors, casting dark slanted shadows like some old black and white movie across his face that made it unreadable. She could see his mouth clearly, but that was all.

"Glad what's settled?" she asked.

"Henry's will." Uncertainty warred with the note of sexual satisfaction in his voice. He struggled to overcome it. "We can drive to Lubbock tomorrow and get married."

"Married?" she said very carefully.

"There's no sense wasting any time over it now the decision's been made." He shrugged. "If you really want to, though, I guess it could wait until next week. Marta could arrange some sort of shindig. She'd get a real kick out of it." He stared down at her as he spoke, carefully not touching her, wishing to hell he could read what was going on behind those too-cool blue eyes of hers. They were shuttered now. Guarded. Not begging for his understanding, not shooting sparks of angry defiance, not half-closed with passion and promise. Not anything. She'd been so open, so giving, a moment ago, so much the old Stacey, and now she was . . . Hell, he didn't know *what* she was! Couldn't tell what she wanted.

But if it came right down to it, he didn't know what the hell he wanted, either. Marriage? Did he really want a marriage that'd been dictated by some ornery old wildcatter's will? Or was it just the old guilt raising its ugly head now that he'd gone and done what he'd once been sure would send him straight to hell? Was it really possible that he was thinking of going along with Henry's last wishes because he'd finally bedded Stacey—inviolate, untouchable Stacey—and now he felt he had to marry her? Was that it?

"But if we're going to wait until next week," he said, looking for a way out of the hole he'd dug for himself, "we might as well wait two or three." He shrugged uneasily at the questioning look in her eyes. "I've got two more mares about to foal any day now and—"

Stacey sat up abruptly, turning her back on him, and reached for her robe on the floor. Now that he'd gotten what he'd wanted all along, the lousy, low-down snake was having second thoughts, she thought indignantly, conveniently forgetting that she was having a few second—and third and fourth—thoughts of her own. Just who in the hell did he think he was?

She stood up and shrugged into the robe without a word. The need to be alone, to put some space between them, wasn't just a feeling now, it was an overwhelming urgency. She had to have some space to think, had to decide what this meant to her, what she wanted to do about it. Until then, she wasn't giving anything away. Certainly not any rash promises of marriage, and certainly not to Ben. She tightened the sash on the robe with a savage tug and turned to look down at him. "What makes you think we're getting married?" she said acidly.

He lay very still on the bed, staring up at her. "You made me think we're getting married," he said stubbornly, despite his own doubts about the wisdom of such words. His voice was low, careful, clipped. "Just now."

"Really, Ben." Stacey forced a laugh into her voice. "You're as medieval as Henry's will." She moved toward the dresser as she spoke and picked up a silver-backed hairbrush. "Just because two people go to bed together doesn't mean they're getting married," she said, vigorously brushing her hair as she watched him in the mirror. He still hadn't moved. "Not even in Texas."

"We're not just any two people."

"No." She put the brush down and turned to face him, crossing her arms as she leaned back on the dresser. "We're related. Uncle and niece, remember?"

Ben flinched as if she'd taken a swing at him. That old bugaboo would *not* cause him any more guilt! "Not by blood."

"Maybe." She shrugged, looking very French as she made the gesture. "Maybe not."

Incensed, and not quite sure why, Ben sat up abruptly and reached for his jeans. "You don't believe that any more than I do," he said through clenched teeth, wondering why the hell he didn't just take the out she'd handed him instead of arguing about it. Or tell her the truth, just as Marta had told him eleven years ago.

"Henry wouldn't have put that clause in his will if we were related by blood."

Stacey's eyebrows rose. "Wouldn't he?"

He stood, zipping his jeans, and then faced her, his hands planted firmly on his lean hips. "You know damned well he wouldn't!" he snapped. His eyes bored into hers, turning the full force of his steely gaze on her.

Stacey drew herself up, refusing to be intimidated by him. "No, I *don't* damn well know it!" Her eyes blazed back at him with an equally fierce light. "I haven't got the faintest idea what Henry would or wouldn't do. I hadn't seen him for eleven years, remember? For all I know he could have been senile."

Ben took a menacing half step toward her.

Stacey lifted her chin, refusing to back down, and tossed her head disdainfully, daring him to . . . to something! "Judging by that will of his I'd say he was definitely senile, or damn close to it!"

They were speaking in tense, angry whispers, both of them well aware of the need to keep their argument—and all that had gone before it—quiet.

"Stacey, I'm warning you." He reached out with one hand and grasped her upper arm, giving her a little shake, wondering just what in hell he was warning her about.

Stacey's chin lifted even higher, haughty as an affronted queen. "You don't scare me, cowboy." She didn't even acknowledge the hand on her arm. "There's nothing you can do that would scare me."

Ben shook her again. "What I ought to do is whale the tar out of you," he threatened, frustrated beyond thinking.

"That won't get you what you want."

"Which is?"

"My agreement to Henry's will." All sexual passion between them was forgotten as she glared up at him, her eyes as fiery blue as his. "And full ownership of this ranch without having to pay for it. I know that's what you want, that that's why you—" she faltered slightly "—why you took me to bed just now. You thought I'd just lie back and say yes, didn't you? Well, I won't."

Ben threw both hands up. "Dammit, Stacey, the will didn't have anything to do with—" he waved a hand at the rumpled bed "—that."

"No?" She crossed her arms. "Then what did?"

Good question, he thought. *What did?* "Hell, I don't know. Propinquity? Shared grief? The need to reaffirm life in the face of death? Curiosity about what it would be like after all these years?" He ran a hand through his hair. "How the hell do I know?"

"How about greed?" she suggested.

"Greed?" He knew he'd been...hungry. But greedy? Had she thought he'd been a greedy lover?

"Yes, greed," she said. "As in yours for everything that Henry had. But you're not going to get it, Ben, because no matter what you do, seduce me or beat me, I'm still going to fight you on this. And I'll win, too. You see if I don't," she challenged. "I'm not one of your sweet little West Texas girls anymore, Ben, and I've—"

"Sweet?" he scoffed. "When were you ever sweet?"

"—grown up," she went on, ignoring his sarcasm, "and I won't bow down to the *jefe* of Iron Oakes like some insipid Southern belle simply because he orders it." She poked him in the chest with her finger. "I don't take orders from anyone, Ben. Not anymore."

He stared down at her for a second longer, his jaw clenched, the little pulse in his temple beating furiously as he fought for self-control, wondering how the hell they had got from the passionate embrace on her bed to this equally passionate anger. Wondering, too, why the hell it excited him so. "You turned into a real bitch while you were away," he said at last, needing to say something.

Stacey smiled nastily. "And I've got you to thank for that, don't I?"

Ben raised his hand as if to take her arm again but instead, he made a low sound in his throat, like a growl, and turned away from her. In one quick motion he bent over to scoop up his boots and the rest of his clothes from the floor and headed for the door. "You can't win," he said, pausing in the doorway. "There's no way in hell you can win."

"We'll see," she said, holding her ground until he turned and left the room.

When he was gone, all the emotion in the room seemed to have gone with him. She sagged back against the front of the dresser, wrapping her arms protectively around her middle. Well, she was alone, as she'd wanted to be, but something was wrong. Terribly wrong. She felt betrayed and deserted, somehow, just as she had when they'd sent her to Paris all those years ago. Tears shimmered on her cheeks.

Oh, Ben, she thought, *how can you do this to me? And, how could I have allowed you to—* her mind faltered, not knowing what to call what had passed between them there on the bed. It certainly hadn't been lovemaking—*to do what you did?*

Because there was no getting around it—she *had* allowed it. Had allowed it willingly, had even acted the aggressor when he wasn't moving fast enough to suit her. Ben hadn't used any force. He had, in fact, seemed to be acting under the same sort of mindless compulsion as she'd been. A mindless compulsion that had driven them into each other's arms—and then set them at each other's throats.

Sighing, she crossed the room and dropped on the edge of the bed, running a hand over sheets still warm from their entwined bodies.

Perhaps they'd both just been acting out the memory of a night long ago. Perhaps they'd just finally expressed something that should have been expressed between them years ago and then forgotten.

Resolutely, Stacey straightened her back and dried her tears. She was through crying. She'd shed all the tears she was going to, for her grandfather, for herself and for Ben. She would fight Ben for the ranch, and Pete and Marta, too, if she had to. It was her right. She was, after all, Henry "Iron" Oakes's only blood relative. That should count for something.

With a determined toss of her head, she stood and started back downstairs to her grandfather's office. She still had to call André and get the name of a good lawyer.

6

STACEY AWOKE the next morning heavy eyed and un-rested and lay tiredly for a moment, staring blankly at the ceiling, debating whether it was worth it to get up.

André had been more than helpful last night when she finally called him. He gave her the name of a Dallas lawyer, Lyle Higgins, who, he said, had handled a few things for him over the years when Edouard had gone to school in Texas and he—André—had always been most satisfied with the results.

"We are missing you very much, *chérie*," he said warmly after he'd given her the information she requested. "Edouard does not know which of his ends is up. He has already managed to misplace the Jordan contract and your so lovely files are a disaster."

Stacey laughed obligingly, and told him where he could find an extra copy of the missing contract.

"When are you coming home, *chérie*?" he asked then, and Stacey felt a lump form in her throat at the warm regard in his tone. She fought it down before answering. She was through crying, wasn't she?

"I don't know, André. My grandfather's will is rather complicated. Not for a while and maybe..." She paused. There was really no "maybe" about it. She'd already made up her mind and it wouldn't be fair to André not to give him the news now and let him wait two or three months before she finally told him. She took a deep breath. "André, I'm sorry, I don't know how else to say this. But I won't be coming back. I—"

"Not coming back! But why not? We need you here and you are...you are like family to us. To me, *chérie*." His Saudi accent had gotten thicker, distorting his French as it always did when he was upset or excited. "Why are you not coming home?"

"Oh, André, thank you for those words! You don't know how I needed to hear *someone* say that I was family now. It's been..." Suddenly she found herself telling him all about the details of Henry's will, about the scene in the den after the funeral, about the cancer. About everything, in fact, except what had happened upstairs in the silent, darkened bedroom between her and Ben.

"And you are going to marry this uncle of yours, this Ben?" he asked, very obviously disapproving.

"No, of course I'm not going to marry him, André. But I *am* going to fight him for my half of the ranch."

"And you are never coming back to Paris? Ever?"

Would she go back to Paris? When she had fought Ben and won, when the ranch was half hers, would she want to live here? With Ben? Even if they weren't married?

Yes, she thought, surprising herself. Iron Oakes was her home. "My home is here, André," she said quietly, but forcefully.

And it was, she thought, lying there in her rumpled bed the next morning. Despite everything, the Iron Oakes Ranch was *home* and it was where she was happiest. She couldn't analyze it or explain it, even to herself. It just was. She decided she was going to accept it that way, accept that here in this girlish room with its massive old-fashioned Spanish furniture and its sunshine yellow walls she was far happier than she had ever been in her ultraelegant, ultrafashionable Paris apartment.

She heard the screen door to the kitchen slam as she lay there, heard the click of booted feet over the brick courtyard, then Uncle Pete's Texas twang and the softer, more melodious voice of a man whose mother tongue was Spanish. There was a shout from somewhere beyond the courtyard, muffled by distance, and the booted feet moved away—out toward the barns, she supposed—still talking as they went.

In the silence left behind Stacey heard the unmistakable slap-slap-slap of Marta's hands as they shaped homemade tortillas. The sound evoked a hundred happy childhood memories and served to further strengthen Stacey's resolve and the decision made last night, alone in the aftermath of destructive passion.

Come hell or high water—or Ben—she was here and she was staying!

"But first," she told herself, swinging her long legs out of bed, "first I see that lawyer."

She padded barefoot across the uncarpeted hardwood floor to a small bathroom. It had been a closet at one time; her grandfather had had it converted when she was twelve because, he'd said, a growing girl needed her privacy.

He'd allowed her to pick the colors, and so the tiny room was awash with bright blue tiles running halfway up the walls and a flower-patterned wallpaper in which the predominant color was buttercup yellow. Nothing had been changed, up to and including the flower decals on the mirror and the pink-and-purple paisley bathrobe hanging on a hook behind the door.

"What awful taste I had!" she said aloud as she reached for the gaudy robe.

She shrugged her damp body into it, grimacing at her reflection in the bathroom mirror, and thought longingly of the perfectly plain, perfectly tailored, pearl-colored robe of the finest cashmere hanging on its padded, scented hanger in the walk-in closet of her Paris apartment. Some things, she decided, with a grin at her mirrored self in the too-bright, too-tight robe, would have to be shipped over immediately.

The grin faded as suddenly as it had appeared as she noticed a dark smudge low on her neck. She tugged aside the neckline of the robe to see it better. It was a bruise, a small one, hardly bigger than a dime, just above the curve where her neck and shoulder met. And there was another, fainter one, lower down on the inner curve of her breast. They were, unmistakably, marks made by a man in the throes of passion.

Damn him, she thought furiously, forgetting that she had undoubtedly inflicted the same sort of damage on him. They'd both been overeager and wildly uninhibited last night.

She stared at the faint bruises for a long moment, transfixed by the marks of Ben's possession, and then angrily yanked the robe tight about her. But she could still see the one on her neck where it peeked annoyingly, tauntingly out from the flat collar of the robe, seeming to mock her and remind her of how foolish she'd been.

Quickly she finished her morning ablutions, efficiently plaiting her still-damp hair into a French braid. She applied more makeup than was usual for her, using concealing cream and blusher in an attempt to hide the circles under her eyes and the faint love bite—no, she corrected herself, passion bite—on her neck. A few quick strokes of mascara and a slick of clear gloss and then she returned to the bedroom to stand in uncharacteristic indecision in front of the wide-opened doors of the huge armoire that had become her closet when the bathroom was put in.

The root of her indecision lay in the clothes that hung there. The fashionable, up-to-the-minute wardrobe packed for a long business-related weekend at a French country home was in no way appropriate to life on a working ranch in West Texas. Side by side hung the peach silk lounging pajamas that she had been wearing when the fateful telegram found her, the two black cocktail dresses that Marta had tried and found wanting, the beige suit that she had traveled in and the now infamous dark green Chanel-inspired dress and jacket. Add to that a few pairs of designer slacks and slim skirts in subdued shades of beige, ivory and deep forest green, several tailored silk blouses in coordinating colors and all the appropriate accessories and she still came up zero.

She reached finally for the plainest of the pants, a beige gabardine, front-pleated trouser, and an exactly matching, man-tailored silk blouse. Tossing them across the bed she opened a dresser drawer, looking for the underclothes that Marta had unpacked for her yesterday. What she found brought a gasp of surprise and pleasure to her lips.

Like the robe left hanging on the bathroom door, here too, were her old clothes, neatly folded away with sachets of lavender and rose lovingly tucked between the folds to keep them fresh. Cotton Western-cut shirts and sweaters in the glaringly bright primary colors worn by the old Stacey and soft faded blue jeans, as fashionable now as they had ever been.

"Bless you, Marta," she said aloud as she picked up a pair of the jeans.

Hastily shaking out the folds, she held them up against her. She hadn't grown any taller in the past eleven years and her hips probably weren't much wider, if any. Tossing the garment behind her to the bed, she went back to searching for her underthings. Finally finding what she was looking for, she stepped into a pair of blush pink bikini panties and a matching bra with a flower embroidered in the center of the nearly transparent cups.

She wriggled into the jeans. They were still as tight as ever but, thankfully, she thought, not too tight. She tried on one of her old cotton cowboy shirts but the pearl snaps wouldn't meet over her chest, so she slipped instead into the beige silk blouse, tucking it snugly into her jeans, and automatically fastened a pair of small gold hoops in her pierced ears. A further search didn't turn up any of her old boots, and since her snakeskin pumps would look more than a little ridiculous with the jeans, she stood barefoot in front of the mirror, surveying her finished self.

A snug fit, she decided, twisting around to look over her shoulder at the rear view, but not bad for eleven years. Not bad at all. She turned up the collar of her blouse to further conceal the faint bruise on her neck and then, with a Gallic shrug, nodded to her reflection as if to say, *You'll do*.

Pulling the door closed behind her, she hurried from her room and down the broad staircase, her bare feet making no sound as she crossed the tiled foyer to the den. She made a quick phone call, finding Lyle Higgins most anxious to be of help when she mentioned André's name. They made an appointment for two days hence and she thanked him and hung up. Her next call was to an airline to make reservations on one of the daily flights from Lubbock to Dallas's Love Field. That done, she strolled back through the front hall toward the kitchen and the steady, inviting sound of Marta making homemade tortillas.

"Good morning, Marta," she said, entering through the wide double doors. She didn't bother to look around to assure herself that Ben wasn't there. In the past, he'd always left the house before dawn, and she knew, somehow, that the habit still held.

"Ah, *buenos días, niña*," said Marta, her hands not pausing in their task. "You slept well, *sí*? And now you would like some breakfast?"

"No, no breakfast, thank you, Marta." She headed for the stove where a pot simmered, its rich aroma filling the air. "Just coffee."

But she found herself sitting at one end of the long trestle table, a cup of coffee in front of her, while Marta happily busied herself slicing bread and setting out homemade peach preserves and fresh yellow butter in colorful crockery bowls.

"Benito," she began hesitantly, placing the plate of toast on the table in front of Stacey, "he has told me that you know of Señor Henry's illness."

Stacey didn't look up. "Yes," she said softly, staring into her coffee cup, "he told me about it last night when he came in from the stables. It was something of a shock." Her eyes sought Marta's. "You never wrote me about it, Marta," she said, trying not to sound accusing.

"No, I did not," the housekeeper admitted sadly. "To my shame, I did not. But Señor Henry, he did not want you to know."

"But I had a right," Stacey insisted. "He was my grandfather and I had a right to come back and—oh, I don't know—" she flung a hand out distractedly. "But I could have done something. Anything." She paused. Railing at Marta wouldn't do any good. What was done was done and she knew Marta hadn't kept it from her willingly, anyway.

"*Sí*, you should have been told," Marta agreed. Her hand went to Stacey's hair, smoothing it back as if she were a child. "Such a proud man, he was, your grandfather," she sighed. "He did not want you to see him as he had become, *niña*, but to remember him as he had been. Big and strong." She cupped Stacey's chin, turning her face up to her own. "Can you understand that, my *niña*, and forgive him?"

Stacey flung her arms around Marta's ample form, hugging her tight. "Yes, I understand, Marta," she said and found that she meant it. Henry *had* been a proud man and she understood pride very well. Too well. "I understand. Thank you."

"Ah, pah!" Marta disengaged herself from Stacey's embrace, embarrassed as always by any display of affection for herself. "Eat your toast before it gets cold," she said gruffly, turning back toward her stove.

Stacey grinned and ate a piece of toast, liberally spread with the peach preserves to please Marta. She was toying with a second piece when the screen door opened and Ben walked into the room.

Immediately, it seemed to Stacey as if the large kitchen had suddenly shrunk. No one said a word, not even Marta, as Ben stood just inside the doorway, his eyes adjusting to the dimmer light of the indoors. And then he moved, breaking the spell as his booted feet clicked noisily against the kitchen tiles. He pulled out one of the ladderback chairs. "Any coffee left?" he asked Marta as he turned it backward and straddled it, facing Stacey as he sat down. He tossed his hat on the table and combed his fingers through his disordered hair. His blue eyes raked over Stacey speculatively, assessingly.

She lowered her eyes, unable or unwilling to face him, as one hand stole nervously upward to pull the collar of her shirt more closely around her throat.

"*Sí,*" Marta said in answer to his question, moving to get it for him. She brought the mug to the table but didn't set it down. "You have not taken off your boots," she accused him. "I have just this morning cleaned this floor and now you are tracking it up with dirt!"

He glanced down at the offending boots. "Gee, I'm sorry, Marta." He grinned at her, his strong white teeth looking even whiter against his deep tan. "I forgot."

"Ah, pah! You forgot!" She scolded him fondly, setting the steaming mug down on the table. "You always forget," she continued, lapsing into Spanish.

"I know I do, Marta. I'm sorry." He crossed his forearms on the chair back and leaned forward, gazing up at the housekeeper through his ridiculously long lashes. "Forgive me?" he asked.

Marta threw her plump arms up in a theatrical I-give-up gesture and turned away in pretended annoyance, but she was smiling. When Ben reached out a long arm and tweaked the bow of her apron, untying it, the smile turned to a beam of motherly affection. "Stop that, Benito! You are worse than a baby!" she scolded, slapping his hands and trying to look severe, but failing totally. "Ah, pah!" she said and turned to busy herself at her refuge, the stove.

Stacey watched this foolish play from under her lowered lashes, pretending a great interest in the unwanted toast on her plate. This was a Ben she'd never seen before, she marveled silently. A laughing Ben, showing his affection for Marta with his light-hearted teasing. She wondered when he and Marta had grown so close. Or if they always had been and she'd just never noticed it before because, like most teenagers, she'd always been so wrapped up with how *she* felt.

"Didn't you sleep well?" Ben asked suddenly, breaking into her reverie.

Stacey looked up, startled, realizing belatedly that he was addressing her and not Marta.

"You look a little worn," he elaborated. His eyes touched her face as if seeing under the makeup to the dark circles and then slowly, lingeringly, grazed her throat as if he could see, too, the mark on her neck, even covered as it was by concealer and the collar of her shirt. He smiled.

A slow, knowing smile, thought Stacey. How she'd love to wipe that smirk off his too handsome face! She straightened under his steady gaze, lifting her now-cold coffee to her lips as if she had no idea of what he was referring to, or if she did, that she couldn't care less. "I slept fine, thank you," she said primly, freezing him.

But he wouldn't be so easily frozen. "That's good," he said approvingly, for Marta's benefit she thought, because the housekeeper was listening avidly to their conversation, but his blue eyes still mocked her. Challenged her. "You're ready to go riding, then." The words slipped out before he could stop them; he hadn't meant to invite her to go riding with him. Had he?

"Riding?" She put her cup back on the table but kept her fingers curled around it. She hadn't been for a good, galloping ride in years. She'd love to go riding. But not with Ben. "Not right now, thanks," she said, casting around in her mind for an excuse. If they'd been alone she wouldn't have needed an excuse. She would just say no, but Marta was listening. "I haven't finished my breakfast."

He reached out for the slice of toast on her plate. "I'll help you." He bit into it, making Stacey feel as if it were her he was biting. "You didn't want it, anyway," he added when she started to protest. "Did you?"

"I haven't got any boots," she said then, sticking one bare foot out from under the table. "I found these old jeans in a dresser, but—"

"I thought I recognized the fit," Ben interrupted, his eyes running appreciatively up the length of the slender leg she held out.

Stacey hurriedly pulled it back under the table. Damn! She wouldn't allow him to rattle her again. She would not!

"I have kept your old boots, too, *niña*," Marta was saying. "They are out in the laundry room." She looked pointedly at Ben. "Where yours should be, Benito."

Ben grinned at her. "I'll try to remember that," he said before turning to Stacey. "Any more excuses?" he asked her, wondering why he was pushing. The last thing he wanted was to be alone with her again, except . . .

Stacey looked up into the challenge of his blue eyes and glared at him.

That's why he pushed, he thought. Just to see her flare up that way.

"Why should I go riding with you?" Her tone made a curse of the last word.

Ben shrugged, his shoulders straining against the faded blue of his Western-cut shirt. "I thought you might like to look over the changes in your inheritance," he taunted. "But if you don't want to—" he rose, setting his empty coffee cup on the table "—it's no skin off my nose." He picked up his hat and turned toward the door. "Thanks for the coffee, Marta." He paused. "By the way, there'll be six for dinner tonight. Will that cause you any trouble?"

"Ah, pah! Six is no more trouble than three." She smiled at him and waved him away. "But you must get out of my kitchen so I can work."

Ben grinned and pushed open the screen door, letting it bang after him without another word to Stacey.

She jumped up, nearly toppling her chair. "Wait!" she called and hurried out after him.

The sun-heated bricks of the courtyard were burning hot on her bare feet and she raced past him, hurrying to reach the shaded coolness of the laundry room. Before she could get there, though, she felt herself hoisted into the air from behind, lifted and turned against Ben's broad chest. Automatically, her arms came up to clutch his neck.

He stood still, staring into her face. She stared back, mesmerized by the intense blueness of his eyes. She was so close that she could see the laugh lines crinkling their corners and a small scar, from a run-in with a barbed wire fence if she remembered correctly, just under his left eyebrow. It made him seem vulnerable somehow and strangely sensitive. How odd. Sensitive and vulnerable were two traits that she'd never attributed to Ben before. Seeing them now made her feel uncomfortable and . . . guilty. She squirmed.

His arms tightened of their own volition, stilling her. What was she staring at so intently? What did she see with those cool blue eyes of hers? And why, dammit, did she frown and look away as if she didn't like what she saw?

Her gaze came back to his before he could ask. "Ben," she said hesitantly, questioningly.

"I remember when it took more than a few hot bricks to make you run for your boots," he murmured. His eyes held hers captive as he spoke. His hard male lips were mere inches from her own. She could feel his pulse beating, slowly, steadily, under her hand on his neck. "You've turned into a greenhorn tenderfoot." The words were a caress, as if he'd called her darling.

He's going to kiss me, she thought. And, oh, Lord, how she wanted him too!

"Put me down," she said, panicked at the thought. If he kissed her she'd be lost. She pushed against his chest. "Put me down, Ben," she ordered.

He nodded and set her on her feet. She seemed to hit the ground running toward the laundry room, but it wasn't the heat of the bricks that propelled her—she hardly felt that now. It was the heat in his eyes. She could feel them burning into her back as she ran across the courtyard.

Quickly, she grabbed the first familiar pair of boots she saw, stomping into them barefoot, though she knew she'd pay for that folly later, and hurried out into the sunlight again. She didn't want him to follow her inside. The laundry room was too small and dark and close. She didn't want him that close.

But Ben wasn't coming toward the laundry room. He didn't want to be that close, either. The hell he didn't, he thought savagely, turning in the direction of the high wrought-iron gates that led outside the courtyard. He wanted to be that close and closer. So close that he was inside her again. He pushed open the gate and headed out toward the barn without another word.

Stacey stood for a minute staring after him, watching his long, muscular legs carry him swiftly away from her. And then she broke into a half run after him. Just as she had when she was a little girl, she thought wryly, with a bitter twist to her soft mouth. Ben forging ahead and herself trailing hopefully along behind. Until she'd turned fifteen, and then she'd done the running. But he hadn't chased her.

The barn was only a hundred yards or so beyond the house, about the length of a football field, but it was hot and Ben's stride was long, causing Stacey to take two quick steps to his one. By the time they reached the barn door Stacey's silk shirt was sticking damply to her back between her shoulder blades. She could feel tiny beads of perspiration on her upper lip and at her temples and nape, causing escaping tendrils of hair to curl and cling damply to her moist skin. She surreptitiously daubed her face with the sleeve of her shirt as they entered the shadowed coolness of the barn and almost bumped into Ben as he halted just inside the doorway.

"Riley," he called into the shade-dark barn. "You still here?"

"Yeah, boss, over here," came the muffled reply. A bright, carrot-red head appeared from around the corner of one of the large box stalls, attached to a rakish, freckled face that looked too young for the lean, whipcord body that followed it. He pulled the bottom half of the door closed behind him. "Just checkin' on Lone Star and her new youngun," he said to Ben as his lanky strides ate up the distance between them. "She's got herself the purtiest little filly I ever did—" He broke off, noticing Stacey where she stood just inside the barn door. Her slim figure and pale, golden blond hair was haloed and highlighted by the bright sunlight outside. "Well, maybe not the purtiest," he amended. "You're a mighty purty filly, too," he said to her with a vastly exaggerated twang. "Mighty purty."

"This is Stacey Richards, Henry's granddaughter," Ben said dryly, taking her arm to pull her farther into the barn and out of the revealing sunlight. "*Ms* Richards to you, Romeo. Riley Duggin," he said to Stacey. "Our vet."

The redhead grinned and held out a big, rawboned hand. "Howdy, Miz Richards, ma'am." He winked at her, still exaggerating his drawl. "Real pleased to make your acquaintance, ma'am. 'Deed I am."

Stacey pulled her arm out of Ben's grasp to shake the offered hand and grinned back, charmed by his forthright flirtatiousness. Nobody could flirt like a Texas cowboy—blatantly, playfully, with nothing sly about it. "Please call me Stacey."

Riley stood, his hand still holding hers, gazing with open admiration into her face.

"Uh, could I have my hand please?" she said with a laugh.

"Yes, give the lady her hand back, Riley," Ben said curtly.

Riley dropped her hand like a hot brick and backed away from Ben's frown. "Yes, sir, boss," he said, winking at Stacey. "Yes, sir, don't want to do no rustlin'. No, sir."

Ben snorted with disgust and headed for the stall that Riley had come out of.

Stacey chuckled.

Riley grinned and winked again.

Ben glanced over his shoulder, glaring at them as if they were two kids who were passing notes behind the teacher's back. "You coming?" he demanded peevishly, feeling unaccountably like a fool.

Stacey's chuckle ended in a startled gasp. *If I didn't know better, I'd think he was jealous*, she thought, automatically following them toward the stall.

But she did know better.

What Ben was displaying was pure out-and-out possessiveness, as if she were a...a horse or an oil well that he owned, just like any other of Iron Oakes's vast holdings. He obviously thought he'd staked his claim last night, despite the fight they'd had and what she'd said to the contrary. Well, she thought, stomping along behind him, he had another think coming. He could be as possessive as he wanted and it wouldn't do him one damned bit of good.

"How're they doing this morning?" Ben asked the young vet as he opened the bottom door of the box stall.

"Just fine, boss," Riley said, following the bigger man inside.

Stacey paused in the doorway. "Oh, how lovely!" Inside the stall, nursing greedily, was a downy-coated little filly, not yet a full day old. Her long spindly legs were splayed for balance. Her bottle brush of a tail was twitching like a metronome gone haywire.

"She's a beauty," agreed Ben fondly, reaching out to stroke the fuzzy black coat of the baby. The mare nickered and he lifted his hand to her side. "Good girl," he

crooned to the proud mother. "You did a real fine job."
He circled the mare, smoothing a knowledgeable palm
over her satiny coat as he moved around her, checking
her over for any signs that she wasn't recovering as
quickly as she should from the birth. "The filly's sire is
Black Gold," he said, glancing at Stacey over the animal's back.

She looked up at him blankly. There had never been
any but cow ponies and rodeo stock eleven years ago.
She had no idea what animal Ben was referring to.

"Black Gold," Riley explained before Ben could do
it, "Carl Peabody's champion stud. Over Austin way?"
he added, as if that would clear it up for her. "He won
every race he was in until he injured himself. Includin'
the Preakness." He patted the newborn affectionately.
"This little lady is gonna be a champion racehorse."

Stacey reached out to stroke the nursing baby. "How
can you tell so soon?"

"Bloodlines," Riley said, somehow managing to
cover Stacey's hand with his own. "With Lone Star
for her mamma and Black Gold for a pappy—" he
squeezed her fingers lightly "—why, she wouldn't dare
be anything but a champion, now would she?"

Stacey smiled and drew her hand out from under the
veterinarian's without making an issue of it. But he got
the point, nonetheless. "Maybe she'll turn out to have
four left feet," she joked.

Riley widened his eyes as if scandalized. He tucked
his fingers into the back pockets of his jeans and rocked
back on his heels. "Now she wouldn't da—"

"If you want to take that ride, we'd better get going." Ben bit the words out from between clenched teeth. "Saddle up FlapJack for Miss Richards, would you, Riley?" His voice was perfectly polite, but the words were definitely an order.

Riley looked startled for just a moment. "Sure thing, boss," he said, backing away as Ben came around the mare and exited the stall.

It occurred to Stacey that saddling horses wasn't part of a vet's usual job description, but she said nothing. Ben brushed by her without a glance, and she stood her ground. *What on earth . . . ?* she wondered, lifting puzzled eyes to Riley's.

Riley shrugged. "Ain't nothin' like the green-eyed monster for makin' a rational man plumb unreasonable," he said, grinning at her.

Stacey shook her head. "He's not jeal—"

"You want to take that ride or not?" Ben hollered, his voice cutting across hers.

Riley jerked his head in the direction of the bellow. "Not jealous, huh?" He shrugged. "You sure coulda fooled me."

Stacey stared at the vet, her eyes widening in speculation. Ben jealous? It was an intriguing thought, true, but one she'd already decided was way off base. Jealousy and possessiveness were two entirely different things.

"Stacey, dammit, are you coming?" The voice outside the enclosed box stall held a decidedly testy note.

"You better go before he comes in here an' takes a

horsewhip to me," Riley advised her, his grin even wider.

Stacey felt an answering grin turning up her own lips. Why, she wasn't quite sure.

"Stacey!"

With a last quick smile at Riley, she whirled from the stall and ran to catch up with Ben.

THEY RODE IN UNEASY SILENCE for a good twenty minutes, Stacey mounted on the buckskin gelding called FlapJack, Ben on a big chestnut with the deep chest and narrowed nose of an Arabian and the powerful, stocky legs of a mustang cow pony.

The day was still, with nothing but the creaking of saddle leather and the muffled clip-clop of the horses' shod hoofs on the dry, hard-packed ground to fill the silence between them. The sun was fierce, beating down on Stacey's bare head as they rode. Sweat trickled between her shoulder blades, and her inner thighs were already beginning to feel the effects of being too long out of a saddle. But all that she could handle, even enjoy. It was the sliding, sideways glances of Ben's that finally began to grate on her nerves.

She shifted her weight in the saddle, wondering what he was plotting now. Judging by the scowl on his face it boded ill for someone. *Probably me*, she thought sourly. In which case, she decided, she didn't really care to hear anything he might have to say. Still, it was going to be an awfully long ride if neither of them said a word.

"I won't have you flirting with the hands," he said abruptly, startling her.

Stacey turned her head to look at him. "You what?" It wasn't that she hadn't heard him, it was just that she couldn't believe what she'd heard.

"You heard what I said." He turned in his saddle to face her. "I won't have you flirting with the hands," he repeated. "Not this time."

"Not this time?" she echoed. Her expression went from puzzled to incredulous to indignant in an instant. She drew herself up in the saddle, poised to do battle. "I haven't been flirting with any of your precious hands," she said coolly, tamping down the anger that his words induced. She wasn't going to lose her temper this time, she vowed silently. Not when he was so obviously trying to make her do just that. "In the first place, I haven't met any to flirt with," she said, the very voice of reason. "And in the second, I—" she paused as a thought suddenly occurred to her.

"Ain't nothin' like the green-eyed monster for makin' a rational man plumb unreasonable."

"You don't—" a genuinely amused smile curved her lips "—you don't mean Riley, do you?" she asked.

Ben glared at her, unamused.

Stacey's smile widened. "Well, I'll be be damned! You *do* mean Riley. I don't believe it. The *jefe* of Iron Oakes is jealous of a freckled-faced, wet-behind-the-ears veterinarian."

"Jealousy has nothing to do with it." Ben redirected his eyes forward, glaring at his horse's bobbing head, trying to ignore her gibe and his own growing sense of foolishness. He could feel the tips of his ears turning red. "I just don't want you giving everybody any more cause for talk, that's all."

Stacey's amused smile faded. "Cause for talk?" she said, but she knew what he meant. Their neighbors were already talking about her long absence and her abrupt return and the supposed reason for it. The last thing she wanted to do was add more fuel to the fire, of course, and if Ben thought—

"I want it to stop," he ordered. "Now, before it even gets started. Is that clear?"

Stacey reined in her horse. "*You* want it to stop?" she said, coolness giving way to irritation at his high-handedness. Although she might have agreed with a reasonable request, she objected—strongly—to an order. "And just who asked your opinion?" she demanded, sitting very straight in the saddle. "Who I flirt with, if I flirt with anyone, is none of your business. Which is completely beside the point in this case," she informed him, "because I wasn't flirting with Riley. I said hello. We shook hands. Tell me—" her voice dripped with delicate sarcasm, making her faint French accent more pronounced "—when did this alleged flirtation take place?"

"It started when you got dressed this morning," Ben said levelly, turning to face her again. "When you put on that flimsy blouse that clings so—" he waved a hand in the air "—so graphically to every curve. And when you piled on the makeup like some Las Vegas show-girl."

"Las Vegas showgirl!"

"And those jeans," Ben went on, ignoring her outburst. "You couldn't get them any tighter if you painted them on. They're a blatant invitation to any man who looks at you."

"Invitation to—?" Stacey sputtered. Unconsciously, her hands tightened on the reins, making her horse snort and shake his head.

"Looking like a common streetwalker may be all the rage in Paris," he said, pinning her to the saddle with the fierceness of his gaze. He was being ridiculous, he knew, and insulting, too, but he couldn't seem to stop himself. "You might remember that here in Texas we like our women to dress like ladies."

Stacey's hands clenched into fists on her reins. "Just who the hell do you think you are, Ben Oakes?" she demanded. "An authority on fashion as well as—" The buckskin pranced sideways, made increasingly uneasy by the anger communicated to him through his rider's hold. Stacey reined him in tighter, twisting in the saddle to keep Ben in her line of vision as the horse turned. "How can you say such an insulting thing?" Her eyes narrowed dangerously, shooting sparks. "How *dare* you say such a thing!" she spat out, too angry to care that she was being overly dramatic.

Knowing it would infuriate her even further—wanting to infuriate her—Ben shrugged. "I dare because I'm the *jefe* of Iron Oakes now. I dare because you're living in my house. On my ranch," he added, instinctively knowing the exact thing to say to send her over the edge. "And for as long as you're here, you'll live by my rules. Is that clear?"

"*Your* house!" The horse continued to dance uneasily, but Stacey barely noticed it. "*Your* ranch!"

Ben reached out a gloved hand and caught the bridle of her restive mount. "Yes, *my* ranch. And whether you marry me or not, it'll still be my ranch. Remember that."

Stacey stared at him for a long second, trying desperately to contain the feelings that were boiling up inside her. But they were impossible to control, to contain. Eleven years of hard-won self-control snapped like a tightly strung strand of barbed wire. She uttered a sharp scream of pure, unadulterated rage and launched herself at his head.

Ben was completely unprepared for her attack. A grunt of surprise escaped him as her full, furious weight landed square in his lap. He tried to brace himself in the stirrups and one arm came up, automatically circling her back to keep her from falling. His horse, frightened by the sudden additional weight and the screaming, raging wildcat on his back began to prance wildly, bucking slightly in an effort to rid himself of the unaccustomed burden. Ben tightened his gloved hand on the reins, trying to control the panicked animal. His other hand tightened around Stacey's back, trying to control her.

"*Your* ranch!" she screamed, her clenched fists beating wildly at his head and shoulders in an effort to inflict real and permanent damage. She inadvertently knocked his hat off, sending it flying. "It's not your ranch, do you hear me!" One hand caught in his hair. She curled her fingers and pulled. She saw him wince and yanked again, harder, relishing his yelp of pain. "It will never be your ranch!"

"Stacey, calm down!" He could feel her slipping from his one-armed grasp as the chestnut pranced and shifted under them. "You're going to fall."

His only answer was a two-handed yank on his hair and a knee in his thigh as she scrambled for a better position.

"Dammit, Stacey!" He dropped the reins and reached for her wrists with both hands. The horse reared, toppling them backward. Ben twisted his body, taking Stacey's full weight as they fell. Still holding her tightly, he rolled them away from the dangerous, dancing hoofs of the frightened animal.

Stacey scarcely seemed to notice the fall or the barely averted danger of the horse's hoofs. She half raised to her knees, still consumed by the burning need to hurt Ben in any way she could.

He lay passively for a moment, stunned by the fall, his arms crossed protectively over his face, his chest heaving, sucking in great gulps of air to replace the wind that had been knocked out of him. One of Stacey's fists connected with his jaw. With a grunt of pain, he levered himself up and rolled over, trapping her beneath him. Grasping a flailing hand in each of his, he pinned her wrists to the ground on either side of her head, holding her immobile with his weight as he fought to catch his breath.

But Stacey didn't quit. She squirmed wildly, screaming abuse in his ear. Her slim body heaved as she tried to throw him off. Her booted feet kicked uselessly, hitting nothing except her heels on the ground. Enraged anew by his easy ability to hold her down, she retaliated in the only way left to her. She bit him, sinking her teeth into his shoulder with murderous intent.

He reared back pulling his torso out of harm's way. "Dammit, Stacey. That's enough!"

She snarled like a cornered cat and lifted her head again, her teeth bared to take another bite.

He yanked her arms up over her head, manacling her wrists to the ground with one hand, and grabbed her chin in his gloved fingers. "Stop it," he ordered, holding her head immobile. He'd started it, he knew, and he probably deserved to have a strip taken off him, but enough was enough. She was going to hurt herself—or cause him to hurt her—if she kept on this way. "Stop it! Now!" he bellowed into her face.

She stilled, glaring at him defiantly. Her blue eyes were glistening with rage. Her cheeks were flushed with temper and heat and exertion. She was breathing hard, almost panting, and her lips were parted slightly, showing her small, even teeth.

"Same old Stacey," he said with a curious sense of satisfaction. Was this why he'd goaded her so unmercifully? To see how much of the old Stacey was left under the polished veneer of the new?

"Same old Ben," she hissed, trying to twist her chin out of his iron grasp.

He let her, his gaze shifting lower, taking in the madly beating pulse in her slender white throat and, still lower, to her heaving breasts, their every curve revealed by the damply clinging silk shirt. A couple of buttons were missing on the shirt, torn off in her wild struggles, revealing the edges of her pale pink bra and the soft swell of her creamy flesh.

"At least you wear a bra now," he said, his eyes drinking in her exposed cleavage as if mesmerized. He'd tasted her there last night, touched his tongue to that very spot. Without thinking, he bent his head as if to taste her again.

Stacey dug one booted heel into the ground beneath her and arched violently, trying to throw him off. But it was useless; all she succeeded in doing was to further expose her body to his avid gaze.

"Temper, temper," he chided softly, lifting his head to look up into her face. A sudden frown creased his forehead and his gaze traveled back down, his hard fingers sliding down the slim column of her throat to settle on the small, faint bruise on her neck. Worn leather separated his skin from hers. Without taking his eyes off of the bruise, he lifted his hand to his mouth, pulled the glove off with his teeth, and tossed it aside. Then, very gently, he placed his thumb on the mark as if testing for size or shape.

Stacey lay stiffly under him, panting with exertion and temper, sternly forbidding her traitorous body to melt at the sudden, unexpected gentleness of his callused touch and the concern in his eyes. "Don't," she said through clenched teeth. Her eyes shot sparks of helpless fury at the top of his bent head. "Don't touch me."

Ben ignored her protest. He moved his hand to her breast with slow deliberation, nudging aside the silk shirt to fully expose the other faint purple mark. Then he looked up at her, his eyes filled with guilt—and a curiously possessive, almost triumphant light.

"Did I do this?" he asked softly. His index finger brushed lightly, back and forth, over the tangible remnant of their shared passion.

"Yes," she spat at him.

"I'm sorry," he said, very low. And he was, in a way. Sorry that he'd hurt her, but not at all sorry that she wore the marks of his possession. "I didn't mean to hurt you."

"But you did, anyway!" she accused, even though he hadn't really hurt her, not last night, anyway. She'd been so far gone in passion herself that she couldn't have said when the marks were made. But she wasn't going to admit that to him. At the moment, she could barely admit it to herself.

Her eyes held his for an endless second as she tried to silently telegraph messages of repugnance and hate, but communicated instead only pain and bewilderment and some other, sweeter emotion that she couldn't name. Ben reacted to it unconsciously, his expression softening as hers did, his touch becoming even more feather-light and caressing. Against her will, Stacey felt her anger draining away from her, as if it were seeping slowly out into the hot, dry earth beneath her back. She struggled not to let it go; it was all she had to protect herself, she thought desperately.

"I'm sorry, honey," Ben said. He bent his head, lightly pressing his lips over the mark on her neck. "I swear, I didn't mean to hurt you." His head moved lower and his hand cupped her breast, lifting it to his lips as he kissed the faint purplish mark that marred her white flesh. "I never meant to hurt you," he murmured against her skin, nuzzling his face against her breasts. "Never."

Something in her loosened. Some emotion that had been sitting painfully, tightly coiled in her chest slowly unfurled, releasing her furious anger and resettled itself in her stomach. The hands that had been curled into claws in his relentless hold uncurled and opened. Her body, stiff and unyielding beneath his, relaxed and became pliant. Her stubborn, rebellious mind pushed all his hateful words and actions and intentions into the background to be thought about some other time when the demands of her too weak body weren't clamoring to be heard.

She couldn't fight him and herself, she thought despairingly. She didn't even want to fight him—not now, not anymore. But she wouldn't make it easy for him, either. If he wanted her, now, like this, then he would have to take her. Literally.

Ben sensed the change in her almost immediately. He lifted his head from the scented valley of her breasts to look questioningly into her face. Her eyes, half closed against the glare of the sun overhead, seemed to signal her surrender. He released her wrists cautiously, as if fearing she might turn on him again. But her hands lay passively where he had held them, thrown above her head, the palms opened and facing upward like delicate, defenseless flowers. Very slowly, he shifted his weight and lifted himself to one elbow, gazing down at her motionless form.

Her once pristine silk blouse was dusty and torn, the missing buttons leaving it open halfway down the front to expose her breasts in their transparent wisp of pink silk. Her fine blond hair had escaped its neat braid and wavy tendrils curled damply along her forehead and temples and snaked across her white neck. Her eyes were fully closed, the long, mascaraed lashes lying against her cheeks like wounded butterflies.

It was unnatural and unnerving for her to be so still, so meek and passive. He didn't like her this way, with all the fight and fire and personality gone out of her. It wasn't what he wanted at all. It wasn't Stacey, not his Stacey, and it frightened him. Angered him. Made him want to do something so she'd sit up and spit at him again. He lifted his hand from her breast and reached up, brushing the damp tendrils of hair away from her face.

She didn't move, either to acknowledge him, or to squirm away from his touch.

Experimentally, he let his fingers trail down her jaw and across her closed lips, and then lower, down the satin length of her throat to her fragile upper chest.

She lay perfectly still.

He brushed his fingertips lightly over the upper slopes of her breasts.

She didn't respond.

Deliberately then, trying to incite a reaction—any reaction—he traced the contours of the dainty silk flower embroidered on her bra.

The rosy nipple surged into prominence even before he touched it, betraying her need of him, but Stacey wouldn't—*couldn't*—allow herself to move or in any way acknowledge his touch.

Desperate now, he unclasped the front closure of her bra, smoothing it back to reveal the gleaming satin of one white breast. He bent his black head, once again touching his lips to the love bite on the inner curve.

Not an eyelash flickered.

He brushed his lips over the slope of her breast to her nipple. Slowly, he circled the distended bud with the tip of his tongue, around and around the sensitive areola, the way his fingertip had traced the flower, pausing now and then to blow softly against her wet, gleaming flesh.

Except for the goose bumps that rose up along her chest and arms, Stacey didn't move a muscle. She just lay there, limp.

Ben moved his hand downward, skimming over the curves of her waist and hips to trail his fingers seductively up her inner thigh.

Though it was killing her, she didn't acknowledge him by so much as a whimper.

Cursing softly to himself, Ben opened his lips over her breast, taking as much of it as he could inside the wet cavern of his mouth. He cupped his palm between her legs at the same time, caressing her through her jeans.

Stacey tensed beneath him. Her lax hands clenched. *I won't respond,* she thought furiously. *I won't give him the satisfaction!* But the feeling that, moments ago, had settled in her stomach coiled tighter, and then tighter still, burning low in her belly. His mouth, sucking so sweetly, so greedily at her breast, urged her to arch into him. His hand, moving in slow circles between her thighs, urged her to surrender completely to the most erotic caress she'd ever experienced. She longed, with all her passionate being to respond to him. But she wouldn't give in to him now. She couldn't! He'd provoked her anger and her rage. She wouldn't allow him to provoke her passion, too.

She willed herself to lie there, tense and still, her eyes squeezed shut, her nails biting into her own palms, calling upon every last slender shred of self-control she possessed to resist him—and herself. It wasn't easy. It was, in fact, the hardest thing she'd ever done. Her whole body was screaming at her to give in.

Yes, it urged, *Yes, let him love you!*

And then, just when she might have snapped, just when she couldn't have stood even another second of his delicious, wickedly seductive torment, he rolled away from her with a low, muffled curse and sprang to his feet.

"All right, Stacey, you win," he said.

She opened her eyes to see him standing over her, one hand outstretched to pull her to her feet.

"Get up."

She sat up a little shakily and took his offered hand, allowing him to haul her to her feet. Without a word, without so much as another glance in his direction, she bent her head and began fastening her bra and blouse. Her hands were shaking.

Ben turned away, ostensibly to look for his hat and the glove he'd thrown aside, unable to stand there and watch her fumble for her buttons without reaching out to help her—or take her in his arms again. He felt like a damn fool. Worse, like a rapist, as if he'd beaten her into submission and had his evil way. No matter that he hadn't had his way, he still felt guilty. He had plenty to feel guilty about, he thought, snatching up the black Stetson that lay on the ground. He beat it against his leg to rid it of some of the dust and jammed it on his head.

He'd accused her of flirting when she hadn't been; he'd taunted her by calling Iron Oakes *his* ranch; he'd handled her crudely and cruelly. And not just today.

Last night his handling had left bruises on her soft flesh. Bruises that he'd been macho enough to feel smug about, he thought with disgust, like some teenage Lothario with more hormones than brains!

"Dammit to hell!" he muttered, bending over to pick up his discarded glove. Straightening, he pursed his lips and issued a piercing, two-note whistle.

The chestnut horse, grazing contentedly a short distance away, raised his head at his master's command and obediently trotted over to Ben with the buckskin following closely behind. He reached out and gathered both sets of dangling reins in one hand.

"You ready to go back?" he asked, staring at his horse's head to avoid looking at her. He was afraid of what he'd see in her eyes if he did—accusation, loathing, fear. Whatever it was, it wouldn't be anything he didn't deserve.

"Yes," she said quietly, not looking at him, either, afraid he'd see the desire she couldn't quite hide.

"Mount up, then." He braced his shoulder against the buckskin and cupped his hand for her booted foot, ready to toss her into the saddle as he'd always done. But she was already mounting herself, her left hand grasping the saddle horn, her foot in the stirrup.

She held out her hand. "My reins," she said, still not looking at him.

"Oh, yeah. Sure." He flexed his knees, circling one arm under FlapJack's neck, and brought the two lengths of leather together over the animal's withers. "Here."

She reached to take them, then gasped and drew back.

"Hell, Stacey, I'm not—" he began, thinking she'd drawn back in fear.

"Your face," she said.

He frowned. "My what?"

"Your face. It's—" she lifted her hand toward him then let it drop "—bruised."

He fingered his jaw, moving it experimentally back and forth. A spot about midway between his ear and chin was slightly tender to the touch. A tiny, self-mocking smile curved his lips. His eyes met hers. "I guess that makes us even."

"I guess," she mumbled, looking away again.

He sighed and extended the reins toward her. "Here, Stacey, take them."

She took them with a mumbled thanks.

Ben continued to stand there, his shoulder against the horse, staring up at her. He wanted to say...something. To explain. But explain what? How could he explain anything when he didn't know himself what had made him act the way he had? There was no rational explanation for the way he'd taunted her. Bullied her. Frightened her. But he could apologize, he thought. He owed her that much, at least.

She looked at him then, leaning forward in the saddle to touch his jaw with gentle fingers. "I'm sorry about your face," she murmured, truly appalled at the damage she'd inflicted, and more than a little embarrassed that she'd lost control to the point of actually hitting someone. Even Ben. It didn't fit in with the image she wanted to have of herself. "Really sorry."

Her apology, so sweetly offered, so obviously sincere, made him feel even worse. "Don't be." He covered the back of her hand with his, crushing it to his cheek so briefly that she wasn't completely sure, afterward, that he had actually done it. "I deserved it." He turned away abruptly and mounted his horse. "I have some work to do out at the cattle pens," he said. "Inoculations and branding. Can you find your way back to the house?"

"Yes, of course, I—" she began, but he'd already whirled the big chestnut and headed off across the flat land, away from her. Stacey sighed—a deep, heartfelt, confused, shaky sigh—and lifted a hand to shade her eyes as she watched the cloud of dust that boiled up behind his retreating figure.

"I deserved it," he'd said. But did he mean for what he'd said and done today? Or for last night?

She hoped not. It gave her a sad, strangely empty feeling to think he might be regretting what had happened between them last night in the shadowed darkness of her room because, to her, last night had been . . . it had been . . .

Last night was a mistake, she told herself sternly, clamping a lid on the idiotic sentiments that threatened to overcome her. It had been a thoroughly stupid mistake. A foolish and unfortunate incident that had changed nothing, settled nothing. They were still what they'd been before last night happened. Distant relatives. Strangers. Enemies, even. But not lovers. Never lovers, not in the truest, best sense of the word. The knowledge hurt somewhere deep inside of her.

With a hard yank on the reins, she turned FlapJack in the opposite direction from the one Ben had taken and set her heels to the horse's sides, leaning low over his neck as he surged forward. They ran a mile or more, woman and horse, pounding furiously over the hot, dry ground as if the devil himself were after them. Stacey urged her mount faster and faster still, running from herself, from Ben, from all the painful decisions made or still to be made. Running...

The horse stumbled, his hoof grazing some unseen rodent hole, throwing Stacey forward in the saddle so that she had to clutch his mane to keep from falling. Cursing under her breath, she regained her balance and pulled gently on the reins, slowing the horse to a halt. She could feel his sides heaving between her legs. Hot puffs of air billowed from his flared nostrils.

Immediately contrite at her callous use of the willing animal, she dismounted and ran her hands expertly down his legs, checking for any damage that might have been done by his near fall, cooing soothingly to the horse all the while. His neck and chest were damp with sweat, but thankfully, he was whole.

She remounted and gazed around her to get her bearing, unsure how far or in what direction they'd run. Sighting a familiar landmark, she gathered up the reins and spoke softly to the horse, urging him to a cooling walk. They moved slowly in the direction of the little family cemetery where Henry Oakes had been buried yesterday morning. Swinging out of the saddle, she tied FlapJack to the white wrought-iron fence surrounding the tidy plot—not at all sure that he would respond to her whistle—and pushed open the gate.

It was green in the cemetery, just as it was around the house, thanks to its windmill-generated irrigation system that watered daily, and a few transplanted oaks and red maples. The trees weren't as large as the ones surrounding the house because they'd been planted later, but they still offered shade and the welcome illusion of coolness.

Her parents were buried here. The two simple marble markers that stood side by side were engraved with names and dates that meant little to her. She'd been less than six months old when a fatal auto accident claimed their lives. They were snapshots in a photo album, less real to her than the woman buried beneath the impressive headstone next to her grandfather's grave.

She trailed her hand over the gleaming white marble angel that marked the resting place of Constance O'Flannery Oakes, the beloved and eternally mourned wife of Henry Oakes. She'd died before Stacey was born, before her own daughter was old enough to start school, but there was a painting of her hanging opposite the big brass bed in Henry's bedroom, and Stacey had come to know her through that. Connie Oakes had been a gentle soul, fair and delicate with a sweet smile and understanding eyes.

"She was the only person could ever calm ol' Henry down when he was a ragin' or turn him aside from some fool scheme," Uncle Pete told her once. "Jes one of her sweet smiles was all it took. An' she would'a done anythin' fer him. Anythin' a'tall. Couldn't find no finer woman."

Stacey sank to her knees beside her grandfather's grave, reaching out to sift the new-mounded earth through her fingers, wondering if Grandmother Connie would have been able to "turn him aside" from his latest—last—fool scheme. Whatever it was.

"Oh, Henry," she whispered. "Why did you do this to me? Why? Your Connie wouldn't have liked it." She cocked her head sideways, looking at the headstone as if Henry Oakes were sitting there in front of her. "I know you had a reason," she rationalized. "You always do—did," she amended, patting the earth as if to soothe. "I just wish you could tell me what it was."

She fell silent, as if she actually expected some kind of answer, but the air was still and quiet except for the occasional gentle snorting of FlapJack, tied at the fence, and the rhythmic creaking of the windmill. A hawk soared through the sky above her, a rattler slithered through the prairie grasses just beyond the fence, a lone cow lowed somewhere off in the far distance and still she sat—thinking, remembering, drinking in the peacefulness around her and, finally, making her own peace with the memory of her grandfather.

Theirs had been a stormy relationship those last few years they'd had together. They'd both hurled some hurtful words at each other, leaving unsaid other words that should have been spoken. They were both too stubborn and too proud and too much alike to have done anything else, she realized. But it didn't really matter. Not now. Not anymore. What mattered was the relationship they'd shared for the first fifteen years of her life.

"Goodbye, Henry," she said softly, getting to her feet. She looked down at the simple headstone, adorned with the Iron Oakes brand, and smiled. "I love you. I've always loved you."

STACEY STOOD in front of her bedroom mirror trying to adjust an oblong scarf of peach-and-ivory silk around her neck to fall in graceful folds. She'd had a shower when she came in from her ride, and a brief, uneasy nap to rid herself of a nagging sun-and-emotion-induced headache. Her hair was coiled into a smooth French twist at the back of her head. Her makeup was fresh and expertly applied. Her slim body was clothed in peach silk evening pajamas with a loose, dolman-sleeved top and slim, tapered pants that made her legs look elegantly long.

She was herself again, she thought with relief. Cool. Collected. Completely in control.

As long as no one noticed the touch of sunburn on her nose and forehead, she amended, or looked too closely at the palms of her hands, blistered by the leather reins, or the heels of her feet, blistered, too, from wearing her old cowboy boots without socks. They were painful where the straps of her delicate high-heeled sandals rubbed against them. The insides of her thighs ached, too, and her backside from the unaccustomed hours in the saddle today.

Impatiently she untied the scarf and retied it into a big pussycat bow, standing back to study the effect. No, she thought—tied that way it spoiled the sleek lines of her outfit, besides being much too obvious. She looked like a teenager trying to hide a hickey from her parents. She pulled the scarf off altogether, but that was worse. The wide neckline of the top, meant to slide easily off either shoulder, exposed the faint purplish mark on her neck completely.

It looked huge to Stacey, obvious and noticeable, like a brand. It could be nothing other than what it was; a mark inflicted by a man in the throes of passion. She couldn't pass it off, like her torn, dusty blouse as being caused by a fall from her horse.

That had been her excuse when she'd brought FlapJack back to the barn—that she'd taken a fall. Riley had looked at her a little strangely but seemed to believe her story.

She draped the scarf around her throat again, letting the ends trail down the back instead of the front. Worn like that, it looked more like an intended part of the outfit instead of an afterthought. Rummaging through her jewelry case, she fastened on big square earrings of hammered gold and slipped a matching cuff bracelet on her left wrist. Satisfied that she'd done her best, she shrugged at her reflected image and left the room.

Her high heels clicked noisily on the stairs, masking the low murmur of voices coming from the living room, announcing her descent to anyone who might have been listening for it. As she reached the bottom of the staircase Ben appeared in the arched doorway. Her first cowardly impulse was to turn and run back to the safety of her room, but she resisted it. She stood, outwardly poised, on the bottom step. She looked, he thought, as fragile and elegant and as cool as a crystal glass of peach sherbet.

He stood without moving, staring back at her, his black head nearly brushing the curving arch. Instead of his usual denim jeans and workshirt, he wore well-tailored black slacks that fitted snugly over his flat belly and narrow hips and fell to just the right length over a pair of cowboy boots made of exotic blue-sheened eel skin. His white shirt with its pearl snaps and Western-cut yoke emphasized his wide, powerful shoulders and chest. A silver concha buckle decorated his belt. He wore no tie, not even a Western string one, and the collar of his shirt was left open, exposing a small wedge of the dark curling hair on his chest. A small bruise stood out sharply on his clean-shaven jaw.

"You're looking well after your fall," he said. The way he emphasized the last word told her he'd heard her story from Marta or Riley, and was amused. His eyes went significantly to the flowing scarf at her neck and he grinned conspiratorily.

Almost against her will, Stacey found herself grinning back, feeling like a co-conspirator who shared a secret with him, a secret that must be hidden from everyone else. She wondered what story he had told to explain away the small bruise on his jaw. Her grin faded. Suppose he'd said he'd fallen, too?

He moved toward her reaching out to cover her hand where it rested on the newel post.

Stacey snatched her hand back automatically, fearful of what his slightest touch did to her.

Ben's eyes flickered up in surprise and a sort of pain crossed his face, but the expression was gone before Stacey could be sure she'd read it right.

"I won't bite you," he said, and the word "again" hung in the air between them. Unconsciously, he curled his hand around the newel post, pressing his fingers into the wood.

"Is that a promise?" she shot back. But the words, even to her own ears, sounded more like a plea than the sarcastic rejoinder she'd intended them to be.

At her words his eyes went again, deliberately, to the scarf draped across her throat. Her hand stole upward, nervously fingering the length of silk, as if reassuring herself that the mark of his mouth was still hidden.

I've faced down an Arab sheik who once tried to buy me from André, she reminded herself. *I've easily turned off countless playboys of all nationalities with just a polite smile. So why can't I do it with Ben?* She dropped her hand to her side, her back stiffening proudly. *I will not allow him to intimidate me,* she told herself bravely, ignoring the agitated fluttering of her pulse as their eyes met again.

Let him see how icy she could be, she thought. How really cold and unmelting. Maybe that would protect her from the heat in his eyes. But surprisingly, she saw no heat there now, just two eyes as blue and unreadable as the summer sky over Texas gazing back at her. Waiting.

In that instant she felt, somehow, as if he'd defeated her. Bested her in some way she couldn't understand. He could so easily affect her, stirring her to hot rage or hotter passion, but she could stir him only if he chose to let her. And if he didn't choose then . . . nothing.

Damn him! she thought vehemently. And damn her own weak will where he was concerned.

With a toss of her head, she tore her eyes away from his and swept past him, through the archway and into the living room. Ignoring the pain of her shoe straps where they rubbed against her blistered heels, she crossed the room to join the little group by the open patio doors. Three of the group were men—Uncle Pete, the redheaded vet, Riley, and a Mexican *vacquero* of about fifty with a lean, wiry body and weather-beaten skin. The fourth person was a lovely young woman with a cascade of dark curls tumbling to her shoulders and dark liquid eyes. She looked up, smiling as Stacey approached them, and poked Riley in the side with her elbow. He broke off whatever he was saying and held out his hand.

"Good to see you all in one piece after your fall," he said, hardly a trace of twang coloring his voice now as he moved aside to make room for her in their circle. "How're you feeling?"

Stacey glanced up at him, looking for the barb in his words. His eyes still twinkled as irrepressibly as she remembered from this afternoon, but she could see no hidden meaning in them. "Much better, thank you," she said, taking a second, closer look at him. His hair still blazed carroty red, faint freckles still dusted his nose, but he seemed older than what she'd first thought. It was his voice, of course. "What happened to the accent?" she asked, smiling up at him.

He grinned, unabashed at being caught in his little deception, and turned to introduce her. "Stacey Richards, meet Francisco Montoya. Cisco's the Iron Oakes foreman," he told her. "Been here for the past—" he looked at the foreman "—for what? The past five years or so?"

"Six," he said in his musically accented English. He shifted his drink and held out a hand to Stacey. "Good evening, Señorita Richards."

"Call me Stacey, please."

"Stacey," he said obediently, releasing her hand.

"And this is Linda Montoya, Cisco's daughter," Riley said. "She's on summer vacation from college."

The two women shook hands. "What college?" Stacey asked pleasantly.

"SMU. I'm a junior." She smiled at her beaming father and corrected herself. "Going to be a junior next fall."

"SMU's a wonderful school, I've heard," Stacey said. It was where she would have liked to have gone.

"Yes, it is," Linda agreed.

"Heard you got throw'd," Pete said then, adding his two bits to the conversation with characteristic disregard for what was being discussed. "Marta was all wound up about it, but you don't look much hurt to me."

"Just my pride, Uncle Pete," she said and then tried to change the subject. The less said about her "fall," the better. "How's a girl get a drink around here?"

"What would you like?" asked Riley.

"White wine, please." She smiled up at him. "Or red, or rosé." She shrugged delicately, recalling that Iron

Oakes had never had much of a wine cellar. "Whatever's open."

He moved away to get it for her and Pete went on as if there hadn't been an interruption. "Never heard of ol' FlapJack throwin' nobody afore," he said. "He's a pure gentle animal."

"He didn't exactly throw me, Uncle Pete," Stacey told him. "It was my fault entirely." She paused to flash a smile of thanks at Riley for her wine and took a small sip before continuing. The white wine was crisp and refreshing. "He stepped in a hole. And I went off over his head."

"Ridin' hellbent for leather, I'll be bound," Pete said gruffly, giving her an approving slap on the back that caused her to choke a little on her wine. "This li'l girl always did know jes one way to ride a horse," he said to no one in particular. "And that was at a dead run. Caused poor ol' Marta no end a grief, she did. One way or t'other." He grinned, pleased. "Never knowed if you was gonna find her with her arm broke or behavin' real unladylike and beatin' up on some poor cowboy who daren't defend himself. Had a real mean temper, she did." He chuckled to himself as if something funny had just occurred to him. "Ol' Ben came in today lookin' like you'd been beatin' up on him," he informed her.

Stacey gasped and choked on her wine again, tipping the glass in the process so that Riley reached out to rescue it from her suddenly clumsy fingers. Pete started pounding her on the back. "Hell's bells, girl, if you cain't keep it down, don't drink it."

"Sorry," she mumbled, trying to avoid his helping hand. "I usually handle my liquor better," she laughed shakily, "but it went down the wrong way. I'm fine, really."

Riley handed her back her glass. "Okay, now?"

"Fine, thanks," she said, avoiding looking at him as she took the glass. Riley was no dummy, despite his aw-shucks-ma'am looks, and she'd gotten the distinct impression this afternoon that he only half believed her story, no matter how politely he'd pretended to believe it. "Did Ben say how he hurt himself?" she asked Pete as casually as she could manage.

"A little heifer kicked me when I tried to brand her," said a mocking voice behind her.

"Objected to your handling, did she?" The words were out before she could stop them. She knew better than to needle Ben, especially in front of an audience, but she just couldn't seem to help it.

"At first," he said, "but then she just bowed to the inevitable and let it happen. Like they all do," he added softly. He knew she couldn't respond to that without giving herself away.

If she hadn't already, she realized belatedly. Uncle Pete looked faintly puzzled at the biting undercurrents in their apparently harmless comments and Francisco Montoya wore an uneasy expression as if he, too, sensed something not said. Linda's dark eyes were bright with speculation. Riley's darted back and forth between her face and Ben's.

She didn't know what he saw, if anything, in Ben's face because he still stood behind her and she refused to turn around. If she had, she would have seen that his expression was as carefully bland as her own, giving nothing away and so making Riley even more suspicious.

"Come, everyone. Supper is ready," Marta announced from the arched doorway, diffusing the tension. Everyone turned with visible relief toward the dining room.

The table was again beautifully set, with the addition of candles and cut flowers tonight. Ben steered everyone to their seats as unobtrusively and graciously as André would have done, gallantly seating Marta before taking his own chair at one end of the table. Stacey found herself seated at the opposite end, so that every time she looked up across the expanse of old lace and sparkling crystal she encountered Ben.

He no longer looked at all like the hick cowboy she'd tried to convince herself he was. If the truth were known, he'd stopped being a hick in her mind sometime during the heated encounter of the previous night. But the truth wasn't known, even to her, and she was amazed at how he seemed to be filling her eyes with a hundred different aspects of himself.

He looked as if he belonged sitting there at the head of the gracious table, as at home among these elegant surroundings as he was on the back of his chestnut cow pony. He had an aura of competence and command and power that was somehow right in both places. Not power just by virtue of his size and obvious strength, but on the basis of sheer personality. He dominated the table in a very subtle way. It was to him that everyone turned for agreement or confirmation of a point in dispute. It was for him they told their jokes and their stories. It was his approval and laughter they sought as their reward.

He threw his head back now in rich enjoyment of something Pete said, and Stacey found herself unwillingly fascinated by the play of muscles in his strong, brown throat and the flash of his teeth, sparkling white against the tan of his face and by his hard, masculine lips, parted in laughter. He reached for his wineglass, his big hand looking stronger and more tanned in contrast to the fragile crystal, and brought it to his lips. Stacey felt suddenly as if she were that glass, so fragile and helpless under the onslaught of his hand and lips.

She looked away, replying quite coherently and with apparent interest to a question from Riley. She managed, in fact, to appear interested and interesting to everyone at the table, speaking when she was spoken to, laughing in the right places and contributing much of her own to the general conversation. Her years at finishing school and as André's official hostess had taught her the trick of appearing to be fascinated by conversation she was only half listening to while her mind was busy elsewhere. And tonight, try as she might, her mind was very definitely elsewhere. Not far elsewhere, just to the other end of the table, but she couldn't seem to help herself.

She watched silently with an unacknowledged ache somewhere deep inside her when Ben's black head bent companionably toward Linda, who sat on his left, as he listened earnestly to whatever she was saying. He smiled and reached out to teasingly tweak a dangling tendril of her dark hair. The back of his hand brushed her cheek caressingly. His smile softened his lips as even laughter hadn't done and his face was full of genuine warmth and tenderness as he looked down at the young woman.

The way he used to look at me, remembered Stacey with a pang, *before I grew up and we started hating each other.*

Does he love her? she wondered, looking away when she couldn't bear to watch any longer. He didn't look like a man in love, she thought, but then, who could tell from appearances? Ben had never been one to display his emotions openly. Still, she had to admit that Linda would be perfect for him. She was sweet and charming; she was a Texan to her bones; and she obviously had a giant-size crush on the *jefe* of Iron Oakes. It would be a miracle, really, if the feeling weren't mutual.

Stacey glanced back down the length of the table, unable to keep her eyes away for long. Ben and Linda were still deep in conversation. He seemed to be trying to reassure her of something, shaking his head and then turning to Marta, who sat on his other side, to back up whatever he'd said.

Marta agreed with an emphatic nod and Ben laughed again, reaching out to pat Linda's hand where it lay on the table. Linda smiled up at him then, apparently reassured.

Stacey's fingers tightened on her fork as if she intended to break it in half with just her bare hands. She lowered her eyes to her plate, afraid that someone might see the emotion that burned in them.

Jealousy. Oh, the jealousy! It twisted in her stomach as strongly and as painfully as it ever had in her love-sick teens. She realized, miserably and unwillingly, that she hadn't yet grown out of loving Ben. She would probably never grow out of loving him, hating him, wanting him.

She took a deep breath, consciously drawing back from the edge of the overwhelming emotion on which she hovered for only a very few seconds, endless though they'd seemed. She became aware that her nails were pressed painfully into her palm and she looked at her hand, realizing with a shock that she held the fork as if it were a weapon. Carefully she uncurled her fingers and put the utensil down next to her plate, looking around the table to see if anyone had noticed her lapse.

No one had. They were all busy with the business of finishing dinner and selecting their desserts from the mouth watering pantry tray that Marta's helper, Consuela had brought into the dining room.

"Uncle Pete," Stacey said as casually as she could to the man on her right, shaking her head at Consuela to decline the offered desserts. "I need to get to the Lubbock airport tomorrow. Do you think that nice kid—Hank, wasn't it?—would be free to drive me into town?"

"You ain't leavin' already, girl?" Pete said, his gravelly voice carrying down the length of the table. "You jes got here! Ain't nothin' been settled yet an' you ain't made no weddin' plans or . . ." He caught the look in Stacey's eyes and for once in his life was aware of having said something he shouldn't. "Or nuthin'," he finished lamely.

"I have no intention of making any wedding plans," she said. "I'd merely like to go into Dallas for a few days." She shrugged. "Do a little shopping and—" she paused, deliberately seeking Ben's eyes to issue her challenge directly "—see my lawyer about contesting Henry's will."

There, it was said out loud. The gauntlet thrown down. Her intentions made clear. *Now let's see what he does with it,* she thought, feeling unaccountably victorious until she caught sigh of Marta's astonished face. The older woman shook her head slightly, shocked and disapproving. One did not challenge the *jefe* publicly, her look said clearly. Not unless one wanted a public reprisal in return.

But Ben's words, when he answered her challenge, were mild. "I'm going to Dallas myself tomorrow," he said, not even bothering to pick up the gauntlet she'd thrown. Not even seeming to realize, she thought, that one had been cast at his feet. "You can hitch a ride with me."

She shook her head. A drive from the ranch to Dallas was much too long a time to be trapped in a car with only Ben for company. They'd tear each other apart. "I'd rather fly, thanks."

"You will be."

Stacey looked at him blankly.

"We had an airstrip put in a few years ago," he explained. "Just a small one, but it serves the purpose."

"And a helicopter pad," Pete added, his tone of voice indicating disapproval.

"Really?" Stacey was interested in spite of herself. "What for?"

"Herdin' cattle," Pete told her, shooting a look of good-natured disgust at Ben. "College boy here calls it modern ranchin'."

Ben laughed obligingly at what was obviously an often heard refrain and then turned his attention back to Stacey. "Do you think you can manage to be up before ten tomorrow?" he asked her. "I'd like to get an early start."

"I think I can manage that, yes," she said, and turned away as Consuela offered her an after-dinner drink. "Courvoisier, please," she said to the maid. She rose from her chair with the heavy crystal brandy snifter in her hand. "Let's have our coffee and afters on the patio, shall we?" she said to the table at large, moving toward the courtyard with all the grace and assurance of a young queen.

Ben had placed her at one end of the table, she told herself. It was traditionally the place of the hostess. Probably he'd only intended to seat her as far away from him as possible, with no intention of conferring any sort of status on her. But, dammit, she *was* the hostess in this house. It was time she started acting like it.

"Bring the coffee trolley outside, Consuela," she said, avoiding Marta's eye as she moved down the length of the table toward the patio doors. "It's much too lovely a night to waste indoors."

9

STACEY SAT QUIETLY, her long nylon-clad legs crossed at the knee, her hands resting easily on the padded arms of the chair as she waited, with seeming patience, for the lawyer to finish reading her grandfather's will.

She was aware that she created a very cool picture, but the image she presented was misleading because she was anything but calm. She hadn't been calm or cool or really sure of anything since she left Paris. *Couldn't he read any faster?* she asked herself, staring at the lawyer's bent, balding head, willing him to finish. He seemed to sense her eyes on him and looked up quickly, catching her impatience before she could hide it.

"Just a couple more paragraphs," he reassured her with a smile.

Stacey returned his smile and shook her head slightly as if denying her impatience, wanting him, for some reason, not to know how important this was to her. But he had already returned to his perusal of the will.

Silly, she chided herself silently. One is supposed to hide nothing from one's lawyer. André had taught her that. You found a lawyer you could trust, he said, and then you trusted him. Always, of course, paying him very well to ensure that he stayed trustworthy. She smiled, thinking of André.

"May I ask you a question?" the lawyer asked, interrupting her thoughts, and Stacey nodded. "What do you want?"

"What do I want?" she echoed, slightly puzzled. Wasn't it obvious what she wanted?

"You don't like the will as it's written, obviously, or you wouldn't be here. So the next question is what do you want? Am I supposed to look for a way to disinherit Ben Oakes and this—" he looked down briefly "—this Peter Crawley totally, or—"

"Oh, no," Stacey interrupted. "That's not what I want at all! Uncle Pete is . . . was Henry's partner," she explained, "from their earliest wildcatting days. He's not actually my uncle, not by blood, but he's always been at Iron Oakes. Uncle Pete is family. Just like Marta and like Ben," she added honestly because Ben had been, still was, part of her family no matter how she felt about him now.

"I take it, then, that you don't want to disinherit Mr. Oakes, either," he prodded patiently, when her voice trailed off.

"No," she said slowly. "I want Ben to have everything Henry felt was due him. Even half the ranch. That's only fair. He's worked it all these years. But I also want what's due me and I don't want to have to marry Ben to get it."

"That clause applies only to the ranch," Lyle Higgins pointed out, thinking that perhaps she didn't clearly understand the terms of the will. "There are no strings attached to the other bequests."

"I understand that," she assured him.

"And Mr. Oakes has to pay you for what would have been your share of the ranch, so you would lose nothing."

"Yes, I understand that, too," she said, becoming impatient. Did André really think that Lyle Higgins was the best lawyer in Texas? He seemed just a tad slow to her. "What you don't understand, Mr. Higgins, is that what I *want* is my half of the ranch. Not the money, the ranch."

"Ah," he said. "First question answered. Now for the second. Why?"

"Because it's my home. I grew up there." Her hands fluttered for a moment in front of her as she tried to explain, and as if she had suddenly become aware of them, she clasped them together in her lap. "I want it, that's all," she said finally, quietly. "And I don't want to have to marry Ben to get it." She looked the lawyer straight in the eyes. "Can you help me?"

"That depends, Miss Richards, on several things." He paused, looking vaguely uncomfortable and Stacey wondered what was coming. "If you'll forgive me for asking, how are you and Ben Oakes related? Aside from legally, that is. I mean, is he, ah . . ."

"You mean is Ben Henry's bastard?" she said crudely when he hesitated. "No, he isn't. Not literally, anyway." She reached for her handbag. "Forgive me. Bad joke," she said, rummaging through the purse for her cigarette case. "Damn," she swore under her breath when she couldn't find it.

"Problem, Miss Richards?"

Yes, there was a problem. But not one he could do anything about. It was just that every time the supposed relationship between Ben and herself was mentioned lately she started falling to pieces. He was *not* related to her by blood! Why did everyone need to ask that question?

"I seemed to have misplaced my cigarettes," she said finally, because Lyle Higgins was waiting for an answer to his question.

"Allow me." Mr. Higgins came around his desk and offered her one of his from an enameled box, lighting it for her before he sat down again.

Stacey inhaled deeply, even though she didn't really like American cigarettes, feeling the rush of soothing smoke invade her lungs before she spoke. "When Ben was first adopted," she began reluctantly, "there were rumors. Lots of rumors. Some are still probably floating around but—" she shook her head, causing the gold hoops in her ears to swing gently "—none of them were or are true."

"How can you be sure of that? Was it ever investigated?"

She shrugged. "I don't really know, but its not relevant, anyway." She paused and took a long, slow drag on her cigarette, gathering together her thoughts to tell this man how she knew.

He sat quietly, hands clasped on his desk, waiting for her answer.

"I'm sure because Henry loved Ben," she said after a minute. "Very much. And the feeling is . . . was mutual. They were as devoted as any real father and son. More so, maybe," she continued, reflectively, "for having chosen that relationship. If Henry had even *suspected* that Ben was his biological son, he'd have

said so. Hell," she reached over and crushed out the
half-smoked cigarette, "he'd have taken out a front-
page ad in every newspaper in Texas to announce the
fact. And besides that," she went on, unconsciously
using almost the same words that Ben had said to her,
"if Ben and I were related *that* way, by blood, if there
had been any doubt at all in Henry's mind that Ben
might really be my uncle, then he'd never have put in
the marriage clause. My grandfather was a hard man,
Mr. Higgins, and he made up a lot of his own rules as
he went along, but he had a strong moral streak. Relig-
ious, even. He was raised a Baptist, you know, even
though he didn't actively practice, and he would have
considered even the possibility of such a thing highly
immoral."

"Can it be proved one way or another?"

Stacey shrugged, indicating that she didn't know. "Is
it important?"

"It could be our whole case."

He had her full, undivided attention then. "How?"

"Under Texas law, Miss Richards, a marriage between an uncle and niece who are related by whole or
half blood is illegal. It carries a two- to ten-year peni-
tentiary sentence, plus, of course, automatic dissolu-
tion of the marriage. However, marriage between an
uncle and niece related by adoption alone carries no
such restrictions."

"Which is my situation exactly, so I don't see how
that—" she began but he held up his hand and, when
she was silent, continued.

"You don't know, *for sure*—" he emphasized the
words "—if that's your situation or not, do you, Miss

Richards?" he said slowly. "Your blood relationship to Ben Oakes, or lack of it, has never been proved one way or the other."

"You mean—" Stacey leaned forward in her chair "—I could just say that I *believe* that Ben is my blood uncle and—" light was beginning to dawn "—and the burden of proof would be on him to prove I was wrong. Is that what you're saying."

"Exactly."

"Could I have another cigarette, please?" she said, needing time for what she'd just heard to sink in. She inhaled deeply as he lit it for her. "Thank you," she said absently, leaning back in her chair.

She didn't have to prove anything then, she thought, she had only to insinuate it. No, it couldn't be that easy. Nothing involving Ben was easy.

"What if Ben can prove it?" she asked. "That he's not Henry's biological son, I mean. There must be records of some sort, mustn't there? From a hospital or something. Or Marta," she said, remembering. "Marta Suarez is our housekeeper," she explained. "She's mentioned in the will, too. Ben is Marta's sister's child." She frowned. "I think. At least, that's what I remember being told."

The lawyer shrugged. "If he can prove he's not your grandfather's biological son, then your case would be more difficult, of course, but not impossible. We would merely contend that *you* have always looked upon Mr. Oakes as your uncle, or your older brother, and that any other relationship would be morally abhorrent to you. Not sound legal grounds, I admit, but highly emotional ones. And juries are often swayed by emotion."

The word hit her with the force of a punch to the gut. Juries. She hadn't thought of juries before. She'd been imagining this while thing on paper, like one of André's oil deals. Rather impersonal. But juries?

Her face flamed suddenly, remembering the passion shared in her darkened bedroom, his big calloused hands, hot and eager on her body and his mouth—his avid, greedy mouth—as it hungrily caressed hers. Her own as she caressed him. Definitely not actions a woman permits to a man that she thinks of as an uncle.

If she took Ben to court, challenged him with the emotional case that Mr. Higgins suggested, he could tear her apart. But would he? She didn't know. But she did know that she hadn't thought of him as an uncle since she was fourteen. And she knew that he knew it, too. Marta knew it. Even Uncle Pete probably knew it. If they were brought into court, where would their loyalties lie? Would they side with her or with the *jefe* of Iron Oakes?

"No, I don't think so," she said, not realizing that she'd spoken aloud until the lawyer looked at her questioningly. "I don't think I can take it into court, not on those grounds. It sounds so—" her hand fluttered "—so sordid. If there was something else, some other way, maybe. But not on that basis—" she shook her head "—I don't know."

"In most cases I'd agree, Miss Richards. It certainly isn't the most savory way to go about it. But in this instance it might be the best way. Not the only way, mind you, just the best."

"Why?" Stacey asked, her stare intent as she waited for his answer.

"Well, in the first place, any court hearing would be here in Texas. Mr. Oakes's home ground. Yes, I know you were born here," he said quickly, anticipating her, "but you don't live here now. You're a foreigner. You look foreign. You have a foreign accent. Very faint, true, but there.

"Secondly, you yourself have told me that you haven't lived on the ranch for eleven years, not even been back for a visit. You have a job in Paris, an apartment. Also, you've been receiving a very hefty monthly income from your grandfather these past eleven years. He hasn't stinted in his care of you, even though you've shown an apparent lack of proper family feeling.

"I said 'apparent,' Miss Richards," he added when she opened her mouth to speak, "and it is appearances that we must concern ourselves with. Moreover, and most detrimentally, you lose nothing, financially speaking, as the will now stands. Your monthly income will continue." He glanced down at the will. "You will own several Oakes Enterprises oil leases and other subsidiaries outright *and* you will be financially compensated for half of the Iron Oakes Ranch if you decide to sell. In short, Miss Richards, you've been remembered most generously in your grandfather's will and I'm afraid that any attempt to overthrow this one clause, except on the grounds I have already mentioned, is doomed to failure."

"That's what Ben said," Stacey said after a minute. "He said most Texas juries wouldn't take kindly to a woman who hadn't seen her grandfather in eleven years fighting like a greedy bitch to get more," she repeated hollowly, looking down at the cigarette in her hand. "He said they'd most likely think I'd gotten enough already, considering the circumstances."

"I'm afraid he's right, Miss Richards. I'm sorry."

"I'm sorry, too." She looked up at him. "Just one more question and then I won't take up any more of your time." She smiled a little wanly. "Could Ben refuse to marry me?" she said, asking the question she hadn't dared to consider before now. She'd been so sure the will could be broken that she hadn't thought the question would be necessary.

"Refuse to marry you? I'm afraid I don't understand."

"The will says that I have six months to marry Ben or the ranch becomes completely his. But it says nothing about his having to marry me. I was wondering if he could stall for those six months and cheat me out of it altogether, even if I had made it clear that I was willing to marry him?"

Lyle Higgins looked down at the will, reading the clause in question and then reading it again.

"I'm afraid you're right, Miss Richards. Your grandfather's will doesn't specifically state that Mr. Oakes must marry you, but—" he glanced at it again "—it certainly implies it. I would say that your grandfather felt it unnecessary to bind his son by putting it in writing. He has merely assumed that his wishes would be carried out. That you would be allowed to choose." He looked at her closely. "Do you have reason to believe that Mr. Oakes won't honor his father's wishes?"

Stacey stood up, crushing out her cigarette as she did so. "I don't know," she said, picking up her copy of the will from the lawyer's desk. "I don't even know if I want to find out." She offered her hand. "Thank you for your time, Mr. Higgins," she said formally. "I appreciate your seeing me on such short notice. I'll be in touch if I decide to pursue the matter."

"I'm sorry that I couldn't be more encouraging, Miss Richards," he said as he ushered her to the door. "Please give André my best when you see him again."

"Yes, I'll do that." She smiled, but the smile faded as the door closed soundlessly behind her.

The long black limousine she'd hired was parked at the curb, waiting for her. The driver, John, moved hurriedly from his place behind the wheel at the sight of her and pulled open the rear passenger door. "Where to, Miss Richards?" he asked as she slid into the air-conditioned coolness of the back seat.

She considered the question as she rummaged almost frantically through her purse for her cigarette case, again without finding it. Where was the damn thing? Her fingers brushed a business card—Ben's. She turned it over slowly and read the address that he had scribbled on the back.

It was a North Dallas address in one of the new town house developments. He was here often enough, he'd said this morning when he gave it to her, to warrant having a permanent address. But she didn't want to go to Ben's town house. He might be there. And the less time she had to spend with him the better.

The plane ride this morning with just the two of them in the cockpit of the tiny Piper Cherokee had been bad enough. She should have known that Ben would pilot it himself and that there would be no third person to lessen the tension between them. It'd been just as uncomfortable as Stacey had feared it would be. Their conversation was abrupt and infrequent, focusing mainly on comments about the view. Ben didn't touch her except to hand her into and out of the plane, but Stacey could feel him watching her occasionally out of the corner of his eye. She'd refused to acknowledge even this brief contact and hunched her shoulders, turning to gaze out the side window as if transfixed by the flat landscape passing below them. But she could still feel his eyes touching her.

"Miss Richards?" the chauffeur asked again and Stacey looked up to find him watching her in the mirror.

She flushed, feeling as if she had been caught in some forbidden act. "Ah, have you got a cigarette?" she said. "I seem to have lost mine and I'm about to have a fit."

He extended a pack toward her, one long arm reaching over the back seat.

She pulled one from the offered pack. "Thank you." She lit it hurriedly and took a deep, calming drag. The strong tobacco burned as it went down but, magically, it seemed to steady her shaking fingers. *Great way to quit smoking*, she thought, *three cigarettes before lunch.*

"Decided where you'd like to go now, Miss Richards?" John asked then.

"Oh, yes. I'm sorry." Stacey fingered the card in her hand, rubbing her thumb across the embossed lettering on the front. She still didn't want to go to Ben's town house. "I want to go shopping," she decided suddenly.

She'd mentioned that she wanted to do some shopping, hadn't she? Okay, she'd go shopping. "Let's try Neiman Marcus first," she said, stuffing Ben's business card back into her purse.

"Wait here, please," she instructed when the limo had pulled to a stop in front of the department store. "I'll meet you at this entrance in, oh, an hour and a half, two hours at the most," she said, sliding out of the car as John opened the door to assist her.

She walked quickly past the designer departments, headed determinedly toward sportswear. What was needed, she had already decided, were some casual clothes more appropriate to life on the ranch than the ones she'd brought with her. Quickly, she picked out three pairs of size eight Calvin Klein denim jeans, several Liz Claibourne and Gloria Vanderbilt tops in various styles and colors to go with both the jeans and the pants she'd brought with her, and an armload of cotton T-shirts in assorted colors.

Before she'd finished in the sportswear department she'd added three shorts-and-camisole-top playsuits, two bright cotton gauze sundresses by California designer Patti Cappalli and a big straw sun hat that she knew she'd never wear because she never wore hats. But she bought it, anyway.

Finished there, she headed toward the shoe department and bought six pairs of knee socks in bright solids, two pairs of canvas sneakers, white and navy, and two pairs of casual flat sandals by Beene Bag, both of which were absurdly expensive. "Done," she congratulated herself as she headed toward the exit.

But her eye was caught by an extravagant display in the lingerie department. She stopped short, causing at least two other shoppers to detour sharply to avoid careening into her. She had to spend at least one night, maybe two, alone with Ben in what she assumed was a small town house and all she had was that damned white silk gown and robe. Resolutely she searched out the most covered-up nightwear she could find.

Nothing the least suggestive about this, she thought with satisfaction as she paid for pale blue man-tailored pajamas and a full length navy blue robe of the finest wool. She politely declined the salesgirl's offer to have them monogrammed for her.

"Now where?" asked John as she deposited herself and her purchases in the back seat of the limo.

"Well, I need some boots," she said, still unwilling to chance running into Ben at the town house. If she stayed out long enough he was bound to be out by the time she got there. "What's the best Western-wear store in town these days?"

John considered a moment, looking at her in his rearview mirror, taking note of the expensive jewelry, the chic upswept hairdo, the large number of shopping bags with their exclusive Neiman Marcus label. "That would be The Wild Buffalo," he said. "Pretty steep, price-wise, though."

"But it's the best?"

"Yep."

"The Wild Buffalo it is, then," she said gaily, suddenly feeling as light-hearted as if she didn't have a care in the world beyond spending as much money as fast as humanly possible.

Thirty minutes later and several thousand dollars poorer, Stacey again tossed an armload of shopping bags into the back seat of the limo. She'd succumbed without a fight to the salesman's persuasion and purchased two pairs of boots, new riding gloves, a gray cowboy hat—cowboy hats being the one kind of hat she did wear—several pearl-snap Western-cut shirts and an extravagant and practically useless fur vest made of luxurious red fox with dozens of fox tails adorning the hem. She'd bought presents, too: a bronze paperweight in the shape of an oil derrick for André, engraved silver belt buckles, feathered hatbands and colorful Western bandanas to send to friends in Paris.

"Looks like more than boots," John commented with an indulgent grin.

Stacey nodded slowly and looked at the piles of packages heaped on the back seat and overflowing into the front with a rather dazed expression. She hardly remembered buying all that. She blinked as if waking up, suddenly realizing she'd been doing what she'd done those first years in Paris. Buying, always buying, as if trying to fill a void or solve her problems by throwing money around. The light-hearted feeling was gone in an instant, leaving her feeling drained and exhausted.

"Where to now?" asked John when her eyes met his in the rearview mirror.

"Home, I think, would be best," she said, giving him the address.

He helped her inside with her packages, thanked her for her generous tip and was gone. Stacey was left standing alone in the middle of Ben's cream-and-rust living room.

It was a nice room. The glass tables, high beamed ceiling and one wall of stereo and video equipment made it modern, and the pit sofa covered in rust-colored corduroy velvet, the brick fireplace, the plants and the paintings made it comfortable. But Stacey barely registered her surroundings.

She was aghast at the vast numbers of shopping bags and boxes spilling over the sofa cushions and onto the thick pile cream carpet. She'd spent literally thousands of dollars on things she had no earthly need for! What was happening to her, she asked herself. Where was all that self-control and cool common sense that André was always praising her for?

"A little shopping!" she said aloud, the sound of her own voice making her start nervously.

Almost guiltily she gathered up as many shopping bags as she could carry and hurried across the living room to an open doorway that looked as if it might lead to the bedrooms. She found herself in a short tiled hall-way with three more doors opening off it. She peeked into the first room, catching a glimpse of thick sand-colored carpet.

"Ben?" she called softly, just to be sure. Getting no answer, she shouldered open the door and went in.

The room wasn't large but the sand-colored carpet was an extremely low pile, fine wool weave and cov-ered the walls and the ceiling as well as the floor, giv-ing the impression of an endless expanse of desert. Even the woodwork and the louvered doors of the closet all along one wall were painted the same color so that they blended in, defying the casual eye to guess at the real dimensions of the room.

There were only a few pieces of furniture and Stacey's gaze was drawn immediately to the king-size bed centered on the longest wall. It was covered with a heavy Indian blanket in jewel colors of turquoise, beige and coral. A huge hammered-brass Aztec sunburst hung on the wall above it in place of the more usual headboard. There were traditional Mexican leather-and-lattice tables on either side of the big bed. A rounded barrel chair of the same material sat in front of a parson's desk with burnished brass fittings.

She didn't need to see the slacks and shirt thrown carelessly across the foot of the bed or the size twelve-and-a-half cowboy boots on the floor beside it to tell her that this was Ben's bedroom. It was very much like him, she thought, extremely masculine, almost primitive, Western to the core. She backed hastily out of the room, as if Ben himself and not just his clothes were lying on the bed.

The next room she poked her nose into was a bathroom and the one after that another bedroom. A neutral room, neither overly masculine nor feminine, with a turquoise carpet and smooth cream walls. The tailored bedspread and drapes were made of matching fabric in a small geometric print in rust, cream and turquoise, as was the upholstered armchair in front of the window. Bleached wood bedside tables, a long, low dresser and an unusual wall mirror with a latticed frame made up the rest of the furnishings.

Stacey's suitcases sat unopened at the foot of the shiny brass bed. With a sigh of relief she kicked off her high-heeled pumps and dropped her packages on the floor. Then she hurried back into the living room for the rest of her purchases. She came to an abrupt halt just inside the doorway, her hand lifting automatically to stifle her gasp of surprise as Ben straightened and turned toward her, a piece of paper in his hand.

Stacey stood where she was, rooted to the spot, the fingers of one hand still touching her lips, her eyes wide. Never, she thought in that one shocked second, never had she seen such a beautiful man! He stood there on the cream carpet, his feet bare, like a statue cast in polished bronze, wearing only black swim trunks and a turquoise towel slung casually around his neck.

"I saw the limo pull up," he said, speaking first.

"Where were you?" was all she could manage. She felt like a gawky schoolgirl catching her first glimpse of a near-naked man. She hoped fervently that she wasn't blushing.

"Doing laps." He gestured over his shoulder toward the wall of windows behind him with their view of the swimming pool sparkling from across the width of the manicured lawn.

Stacey hadn't noticed the view when she came in and she barely glanced at it now. She was too busy watching the fascinating ripple of muscle under the thick pelt of chest hair as he gestured behind him. She remembered how it had curled around her fingers when she touched him and how it felt, rather coarse and crinkly, beneath her exploring hands. She yearned, with fierce intensity, to touch him again, and her eyes caressed the mat of black hair, following it to where it narrowed on his flat belly, curling around his exposed navel and then disappeared temptingly into the black swim trunks.

She saw the muscles of his stomach contract suddenly, tightening as if he'd abruptly sucked in his breath, and her eyes flew guiltily to his face, her own flaming hotly. She caught a brief look of fierce, unbridled desire in Ben's eyes before she tore her gaze away to focus blindly on the jumble of packages still on the sofa.

You came in here to get those, she told herself sternly. *So get them and get out. Get away. Quickly.*

She moved forward determinedly, her eyes fixed on the brightly colored packages, afraid if she looked up at Ben again, looked at that strong, gleaming body, into those fierce blue eyes, she would be lost forever. Carefully, she stepped around him and began picking up the rest of her packages.

He watched her walk around him, careful not to touch him in any way, and felt his guts twist. Was she that afraid of him? Or that disgusted by him? "Looks like you had a busy afternoon," he said, because he had to say something. His hand came into her field of vision, the receipt from The Wild Buffalo held out to her.

The feeling of guilt at her overindulgence came rushing back and, with it, irrational anger at Ben for making her feel that way. She welcomed both feelings gladly. They were better, far better, than the dangerous, delicious feelings that the sight of his lean, unclothed body had aroused in her.

"It's my money," she snapped, snatching the receipt from his fingers without looking up. "You had no right to pry!"

She felt his hand on her upper arm, detaining her when she would have turned away, back to the relative safety of the guestroom. "That was just a comment, honey," he said softly, reassuringly, as if she were a young animal that needed soothing. "Not a criticism. The receipt was lying on the floor and I picked it up. I'm sorry if you thought I was prying." His bare brown shoulders lifted in a shrug. "I was just curious, I guess, to see what kind of things you'd buy for yourself."

"They're not all for me," she said almost defensively, confused by this sudden change in mood that she sensed in him.

"No," he agreed absently, wondering at her defensive tone, and then, "Let's call a truce, shall we, Stacey? At least for tonight."

"A truce?" she echoed hesitantly.

"All this fencing and feinting around each other." He paused and ran a hand through his damp, curling hair. "I'll make reservations somewhere for dinner. We'll eat out, in public, like two old friends. We'll forget about the other night, the ranch, Henry's damn will. We'll talk instead of jumping down each other's throat." He looked down at her and smiled hopefully. "How does that sound to you? Truce?"

"That sounds fine," she agreed slowly, except that, strangely enough, she didn't want to be his friend, not anymore. Not when her pulses were racing madly out of control at just the sight of him. She couldn't forget the other night, even if he could. But he was right. They had to talk. Really talk. "Truce," she said.

"Good." He dropped her arm then, already heading for the telephone. "You can have the bathroom first," he said as he dialed. "I'll give you an hour's head start."

10

THE RESTAURANT he took her to was an elegant private club housed in what had once been someone's home— if something so huge could be called a home—in the exclusive Turtle Creek area of Dallas. It was the area where the city's very oldest money still lived.

The Cipango Club, Ben told her as they turned into the curved, porticoed driveway, had at one time been an exclusive and illicit gambling establishment with bootleg liquor and rooms available upstairs. It was also said that during the same time a gentleman never brought his own wife to dine and play at the club except on New Year's Eve. Or so the legend went. Whether it was true was anybody's guess.

In any case, it was an entirely respectable club now, and wives were allowed anytime, he smilingly informed her.

Happily, the club had managed to retain a great deal of the glamour and ambience of that earlier, more reckless era. A pretty receptionist in a long evening dress sat at a desk just inside the door to check memberships and reservations. She didn't even glance at her book when Ben stopped at her desk. "Good evening, Mr. Oakes," she said, her smile warmer than was strictly necessary. "Would you like to be seated in the dining room immediately, or would you prefer to go into the bar first?"

"The dining room, please, Cassie," he said, and she smiled again, extending her arm gracefully to motion them into the main lobby and from there into the dining room.

The appointments were quietly lush and faintly art deco with a fireplace and a cushioned sofa and armchairs in the mirrored lobby and extravagant arrangements of fresh flowers throughout. As they stepped up into the main lobby Stacey caught sight of their reflection in the mirrored walls. For just a brief instant, she thought she was looking at another couple.

What a stunning pair, she thought in that moment before she realized that the blue eyes looking back at her were her own. *Well, we do make a stunning couple,* she insisted to herself. Her own image was slender and pale in a black silk sheath of a dress that left her shoulders and arms totally bare. Her skin seemed to have the sheen of a pearl, gleaming in the low lights that reflected off the mirrors and sparkled on the diamond-studded hoops in her ears.

Ben, so tall and dark beside her, stood head and shoulders over her own not insignificant height even in her highest black heels. He looked magnificent in a pale gray, summer-weight suit and immaculate gray cowboy boots. His crisp white shirt only served to emphasize the swarthiness of his skin and the midnight black of his hair where it just touched the collar in back. His tie was silk, an elegant gray-and-scarlet stripe. He looked totally correct and appropriate for the occasion, but it seemed to Stacey as if his rampant masculinity was only intensified by the sophisticated clothes he wore and the refined atmosphere in which he found himself. It was a masculinity that served to enhance and emphasize her own femininity.

Never, she thought, had she looked so fragile and so female as she did now, standing next to Ben while he exchanged pleasantries with the tuxedoed maître d'.

"Stacey?" Ben said softly. His hand at the small of her back urged her forward, and she came out of her daze to follow the maître d' to their table.

After they ordered drinks from a waiter who identified himself as Mark, they sat silently.

Stacey gazed around her, wondering what to say. Talk, he'd said. Like old friends, he'd said. Well, what did old friends talk about? Old times? Common interests? No, old times for them were a touchy subject, and as for common interests, well, what did they have in common except the ranch and Henry? She stole a look at him through her lowered lashes. The ranch and Henry she amended, and that hot, almost painfully sweet feeling that flamed so easily, too easily, between them.

"This is a lovely place," she said finally. "So elegant. I didn't expect—"

"You didn't expect it in a hick place like Texas?" he interrupted, "or you didn't expect a hick like me to know about it?"

Her eyes flew up to his, genuinely contrite. "Oh, no, that's not what I meant at all!" she began, but he was smiling at her, a teasing glint in his blue eyes. "All right, yes," she said, smiling back at him. "That's what I meant. But I take it back. Texas isn't a hick place, or at least Dallas isn't and—" her lashes fluttered down and then up again "—neither are you," she said softly.

"Well, thank you for that," he said lightly, but the look in his eyes was anything but light. Their eyes held for a heartbeat or two, each seeking something from the other, asking questions that as yet had no answers.

"May I offer the lady a rose?" asked another waiter at Ben's elbow.

Ben nodded his assent, his eyes never leaving Stacey's, and for a confused moment she thought his nod was meant to agree with whatever she'd just silently asked him. She felt herself begin to color delicately and then the waiter came between them, presenting her with a single, perfect red rose theatrically offered on a small satin pillow. She reached for it, breaking eye contact with Ben, and brought it to her nose, inhaling the sweet, heady fragrance.

"For the rose," the waiter said, setting a crystal bud vase on the table and then Mark appeared at her other side with her aperitif, offering the menus and his own recommendations for their meal.

Ben turned to the waiter, after asking Stacey's preferences, and ordered for both of them. The wine steward appeared as Mark retreated and another few minutes were spent in earnest discussion over the wine list.

"Does that meet with your approval?" Ben asked as he handed the leather-covered wine list back to the sommelier.

"Yes, that's fine," Stacey said, though she had no idea what he had ordered.

"Good." He leaned forward, both elbows on the table, one big hand idly twisting his bourbon glass on the snowy cloth. "Tell me about your life in Paris," he said conversationally. He'd wanted to know for a long, long time.

"There's nothing much to tell. I work." Stacey shrugged delicately. "I live."

"There's eleven years' worth," Ben said.

She laughed softly, though there was nothing funny in what he had said. "Yes," she said and began to tell him about boarding school and business school. She described her apartment and her job, telling him how much she enjoyed working for André's oil company and about their trips to Saudi Arabia and, laughingly, about the sheik who'd once tried to purchase her favors. Consciously or unconsciously she painted a rosy picture, leaving out the loneliness and the homesickness and the years of hurt.

"Your turn," she said when she'd run out of things she could, or would, tell him.

He answered her queries about his life in the same way, telling her about the improvements he had brought to the ranch; about his race horses and the Santa Gertrudis cattle he was breeding; about the small, experimental herd of buffalo being raised, he hoped, for market. He talked about the modern windmills she'd seen on her drive to the main house, about the "helicopter herding" and Pete's disgust with it, and about the land he'd loaned to some Texas Tech college students who were convinced that a common desert weed was the answer to the nation's alternative energy problems.

"Who knows?" he laughed. "Maybe they're right. And if they are I want to be one of the first to know about it."

"I'm sure you will be," Stacey agreed.

They kept up their informative, if light-hearted, conversation all through the escargot appetizers and the tossed salad with its delicious blue cheese dressing. They paused for a few minutes for the small ritual of the wine tasting and then laughed together like children at the obvious disapproval of the sommelier over Ben's choice; a compromise rosé to compliment both Ben's Steak Diane and Stacey's sauteed red snapper in lemon sauce.

Neither of them mentioned Henry or the will or what they were going to do about it. She didn't mention any men, except quite casually in passing, though there'd been two who'd been important to her at different times in her life. He didn't mention women, either, though she knew that in eleven years there must have been two or three. She studied him appreciatively, toying with her wineglass as she listened to him expound authoritatively on the subject of oil and energy. Probably, she thought, suppressing a stab of jealousy, the women in his life numbered more like five or six. If not more.

The meal was over more quickly than she could believe and they sat there with their coffee, watching silently as their waiter made a small, pleasant production of warming their brandy in the big crystal snifters. He set them on the table with a flourish and then offered Ben a cigar to properly cap the meal.

"Do you mind?" Ben asked Stacey, his hand poised over the open humidor.

"Nasty habit," she teased, smiling her assent, and he grinned at her.

"Smoke if you want to," he said magnanimously.

"Gee, thanks," Stacey drawled, letting him know with her eyes and her tone of voice that she hadn't forgotten his reaction the last time she'd smoked in his presence, and that she was amused by his condescending offer to let her do so now. "But I've either lost or misplaced my cigarette case and I had a couple of American cigarettes already today. They tasted rather awful." She shrugged expressively. "I can forgo it."

"If you'll excuse me," interrupted the waiter, "we carry Gauloises cigarettes."

"Really? That would be lovely," she said, and Mark hurried off to get them for her.

"He knew you were French," Ben said, eyeing her speculatively over the snifter of brandy. Smoke from the cigar held in the same hand drifted between them.

"But I'm not French. I'm a Texan," she objected.

"You look French. Especially when you give that little shrug. No American woman—no. No Texas woman," he amended, "moves quite that way. I don't mean it as a criticism. I like it," he said when she looked about to speak, belatedly realizing he did like it—very much. "It makes you different." His voice dropped intimately. "Mysterious."

He looked away from her as the waiter appeared at his elbow. "Thank you, Mark," he said, taking the pack of cigarettes. "I'll take care of it." He placed a cigarette between his lips, lighting it with the burning end of his cigar. He took it from his mouth with two fingers, turning his wrist, and held it against her closed lips.

"Take it," he ordered softly and it was as if he had said *Kiss me* instead.

Stacey took it between her lips and inhaled, feeling as if she could taste his mouth on the burning cigarette, knowing it was impossible. Her hand came up to take it from his fingers. "Thank you," she murmured shakily. She glanced down nervously at the pack of Gauloises lying on the table, at the black matchbook with the gold lettering, the coffee cups and brandy snifters and Ben's hands, brown and strong against the white tablecloth and the even whiter cuffs of his shirt. He held the cigar lightly between his first two fingers in the American way.

"Ben," she said, "we have to talk." It couldn't be put off any longer, could it? They *had* to talk. She had to tell him what the lawyer had said about breaking the will. And she had to tell him what she was going to do now.

He made a dismissive little movement with the hand holding the cigar. "We are talking."

"Ben, please don't make this any more difficult than it has to be." She glanced up at him quickly and then down again just as quickly, unable t read his eyes. "I saw a lawyer today," she began, hesitant but determined, "and he said that I . . . that you . . ." She floundered.

"He said that there was no way out, didn't he?" Ben said in a low voice. "For either of us." His voice was hard, grating against her ears, and her eyes flew to his face.

He didn't really want to marry her, she realized, despite what he'd said the other night. He didn't want to be forced into it any more than she did. He was trapped, too, by Henry's will. Trapped by the love he'd felt for his adoptive father and his adopted home.

"So you see why we have to talk?" she whispered.

"Yes," he agreed, dreading it, "but later. Not now. We have a truce for tonight, remember?" He laid his cigar in an ashtray. "No discussion of Henry and his damned will allowed." He stood up and held out his hand. "Dance with me," he ordered and then added when she hesitated, "Please?"

Silently, unable to resist him, not even wanting to resist him, Stacey crushed out her cigarette and put her hand in his, allowing him to draw her with him onto the dance floor. She tried to hold herself stiffly at first, keeping a sane few inches between them. Ben seemed to acquiesce, clasping his big hands loosely at the small of her back, but she soon realized that his casual hold on her was just as intimate, if not more so, than if he'd held her tightly to him. She could feel his eyes on her face, touching her bare neck and shoulders and the deep, shadowy cleft between her breasts.

Her own hands rested rather uneasily on his chest and she kept her eyes fixed determinedly on his striped tie and his snowy white shirtfront, refusing to look up. The shirt was so fine that, this close, she could see the faint shadow of the dark chest hair under it and feel the heat of his skin beneath her fingers. *Trust Ben*, she thought, with a faint, secret smile, *not to be wearing something so mundane as an undershirt*.

"Let me in on the joke?" he whispered, wondering what had caused that small, catlike smile to curve her lips.

She could feel his warm, brandy-scented breath stir the fine, wispy hairs at her temple. "You're not wearing an undershirt," she said without thinking about it first. If she had she might have realized how aware of him it revealed her to be.

He grinned. Somehow, without looking up into his face, she knew that. "Neither are you," he teased, and she felt his eyes run over her again, touching her face and hair and her smooth bare shoulders.

Her hand went to her neck as if to cover the bruise there, though it was now so faint that a dab of concealing cream had hidden it completely. He didn't seem to notice her instinctive, protective reaction to his wandering gaze.

"In fact," he continued, "you don't look as if you're wearing much of anything. Not that I'm complaining." His arms loosened a fraction and his eyes ran the length of her slender figure. He sighed theatrically. "The men of the world owe a great debt of gratitude to French designers," he said and then, as if it had just occurred to him. "That is French, isn't it?"

"Yes," she nodded, wondering vaguely where all this was leading to. "St. Laurent."

"Uh-huh. Thought so," he said, and she finally looked up at him through her lashes and was startled by the look in his eyes. They were hot—burning hot—and hungry, completely at odds with the light, almost playful, conversation they were having.

"Dance," he said softly and she realized she'd stopped moving to stare up at him, her own eyes mirroring, had she but known it, the expression burning in his. "Stop looking at me like that and dance," he whispered, his voice ragged. His words were no longer playful.

Her eyes fell swiftly, protectively, afraid of what she might have revealed to him in that brief glance. His arms tightened around her, pulling her close. She didn't resist.

Yes, she thought, turning her face into his shoulder, hiding from him and from herself. *Yes*, it was better this way, dancing sightless and silently. She couldn't give herself away if he couldn't see her face, she thought, if he couldn't see the unwilling, unwanted love burning in her eyes. *Oh, Ben*, she almost cried aloud, *I don't want to love you. I don't!*

"I've tried to fight it," he whispered raggedly against her ear.

For a crazy moment she thought she'd spoken aloud and that he was answering her. But, no, it wasn't love he had to fight.

"I thought I could control it," he continued, his voice low and harsh, "but I can't, I never could! I just look at you . . . see you standing there so cool and remote and so incredibly beautiful and I want you again. More than I've ever wanted anything." His hands shifted, cupping her shoulders to hold her a little away from him so that he could look down into her face. His own was harsh and tortured as she stared up at him. "Do you realize what it's cost me to admit that? Can you imagine what it does to my self-respect to know I can't keep my hands off you?" His fingers dug into her shoulders almost painfully.

She shook her head in denial, hardly aware that she did so. No, it wasn't love he fought, it was lust. He wanted her and he hated himself for wanting her.

"And then the other night, when we made love, it was so incredibly good. So ..." He shook his head as if to clear it and his hands slid slowly down her arms to clasp her fingers in his, crushing them in his anguished grasp. "It only made me want you more," he said. "Now that I know how you are, how you look...." One hand came up to touch her face and his eyes held hers for what seemed like endless seconds, searching. "How you respond when you're naked in my arms."

Stacey caught her breath at that, gasping audibly for air, her eyes wide with unwilling arousal. As much as he might despise himself for wanting her, she despised herself even more for responding so hungrily to the heat in his eyes. A heat she knew, because he'd just told her, that was backed by nothing but lust. And yet, even knowing that, her single most driving impulse at the moment was to turn her lips into the hand touching her cheek and tickle his palm with her tongue. Fighting him, fighting herself, she turned her face away.

His hand dropped and she heard a sound from him like a ragged sigh, but she wasn't sure. "Let's get out of here," he said, his voice low and fierce, "before I make an even bigger fool of myself than I already have." Placing his hand at the small of her back, he steered her to their table.

So, wanting her made him a fool, did it? Then what, she wondered, did loving him make her?

"Will there be anything else, Mr. Oakes?" asked Mark, the perfect waiter, appearing at the table as if by magic.

"Just the check," Ben said shortly.

As he signed it, adding a generous tip, Stacey shakily gathered up her tiny satin evening bag, stuffing the cigarettes into it, and turned toward the lobby, leaving Ben to follow behind her. If she could have left without making a scene, called a cab or walked back to the town house, she would have. But the pretty receptionist was watching her, rather enviously she realized, and Ben was just behind her. She pushed open the outer door, needing to keep as much space between them as possible, needing to keep away from the heat of his big body—and keep him from feeling the heat in her own.

"Miss . . . ma'am," she heard the waiter's voice behind her. "Your rose."

She turned and reached for the flower automatically, a stiff smile of thanks curving her lips and then nodded another thank-you as the valet held open the car door for her. She didn't say a word on the short drive back to the town house and neither did Ben. She sat stiffly, clutching the rose tightly in one hand as if it were a lifeline. She wanted a cigarette, but she was trembling so badly that she was afraid she wouldn't be able to light it.

It's okay, she told herself, *you'll be there soon and you can lock yourself in the bedroom and smoke the whole damned pack.*

"Stacey? We're here."

She heard Ben's voice as if from a long way away, and like an automaton, she reached for the door handle and pushed it open. Ben came swiftly around the car and she felt his hand on her elbow, guiding her up the walkway and onto the well-lit porch of the town house. She heard the click of his key in the lock, then the door was open, the soft diffused track lights were snapped on, her purse was taken from her. She knew she was behaving strangely, like a sleepwalker, but she couldn't seem to help it. Only by blocking out all emotion, all awareness, could she keep from throwing herself into Ben's arms and begging him to take what was already his, what had always been his.

"Let go," she heard him say.

She looked down as both his hands covered one of hers. She still clutched the rose and it was that that Ben wanted her to release. She opened her fingers, letting him take it from her. She'd been clutching it so tightly that a lone thorn had imbedded itself in the soft pad of flesh at the base of her thumb.

She blinked like someone waking from a dream as Ben raised her wounded hand to his mouth and pulled out the tiny thorn with his teeth. "They're supposed to be thornless hybrids," he said. The words were light, but the tone wasn't. "I'll have to speak to Mark." Then, having disposed of the thorn, he gently kissed the spot where it had been.

His lips were warm against her palm for several seconds and she could feel the firm, hard line of his jaw under her passive fingers. "Don't," she said then, trying to pull her hand away.

Ben held on to it for a brief second longer, filled with indecision, and then he dropped it and turned abruptly away from her. "I'm going to have a brandy," he said, his voice weary. He opened a bar that was cleverly concealed in the wall of electronic equipment. "How about you?" He half turned, the brandy decanter in his hand.

"No, I'm going to bed," she said hesitantly. "I—"

"You were right, Stacey," he interrupted, loath to let her go just yet. "We need to talk."

"Yes," she sighed wearily. They did need to talk. They couldn't go on like this, constantly sparring with each other, advancing and retreating. Although what good talking would do them, she didn't know.

She went to sit in the farthest corner of the pit sofa, kicked off her high-heeled shoes and curled her legs up under her protectively, her hands clasped over her bent knees. She didn't reach for the drink that Ben held out to her, but made a little motion with her head, indicating to him that he should set it down on the glass coffee table.

She was scared to touch him, she admitted to herself, even so casually and impersonally. Scared that she wouldn't be able to talk, not reasonably, if she touched him.

He took a large swallow of his drink and set it down on the table next to hers. Then he stripped off his suit coat, tossing it carelessly over an arm of the sofa and one big hand came up, tugging loose his tie and unbuttoning the top two buttons of his shirt as he sank onto the sofa near her.

"So?" he said, reaching for his glass again with one hand, handing hers across to her with the other. She took it carefully, avoiding contact with his fingers. "You saw your lawyer today," he stated. "Now what happens?"

She took a sip of her drink, buying time. "I don't know." And it was true, she didn't. She'd been so sure before she'd seen the lawyer, positive that Henry's will could be easily broken. And now, finding out that it was probably going to take an unsavory court battle, she was uncertain and afraid. "I just don't know."

Ben sighed, leaning his head back against the sofa cushions, eyes closed. He was so damned tired. Of everything; the ranch, Henry's will, fighting himself, fighting her, wanting and not having. "Well, what advice did your lawyer give you?" He opened his eyes and looked at her.

She looked into her glass. "You know what he said. The same thing you did. That it would take a court case. And that no Texas jury could be counted on to see my side of it, not unless I..." She shrugged and then stilled the movement guiltily, remembering how he said it made her look—different and mysterious and foreign. "I'm not Texan enough anymore, I guess," she said, unwilling to tell him all the unpleasant details of what the lawyer had said.

"Not unless what?" he prompted.

She shrugged again, staring down into her brandy glass as if it held all the secrets of the universe.

"Come on, Stacey, you might as well tell me and get it over with."

She took a deep sip of her drink and then brought it to her lap, cradling it between her palms. "He said that I'd either have to prove that we were really related by blood or—"

"Which we're not."

"—or, I'd have to convince the jury that I've always thought of you as my real uncle and that I . . . that I'd feel incestuous at any thought of an . . . intimate relationship with you."

"And do you?"

She took another sip of her drink. "No," she admitted softly.

Ben let out a breath he didn't know he'd been holding. "So where does that leave us?"

"I don't know." She hesitated, waiting for him to say something.

He just continued looking at her, waiting for her to go on.

"I guess it means we end up in court," she said slowly, feeling compelled to answer him. "Where all I have to do is convince a jury that I've always believed Henry was your real father."

"Henry *was* my real father," Ben said forcefully. "He just wasn't my biological father. Some no-account rodeo cowboy was my real father."

"How do you know that?"

His hesitation was so brief as to be nonexistent. Telling her would be breaking a confidence that even Henry hadn't been a party to but she had to know. He wanted her to know. "I know because Marta told me," he said. "And Marta would know because she's my mother."

Stacey's eyes widened. "Marta's your mother?" she whispered. "*Our* Marta?"

"Yes, our Marta."

"But how? Why? I don't understand."

"What's to understand? She was sixteen and pregnant by a cowboy who told her he loved her, then took off as soon as he found out there was going to be a baby. Abortion was out because of her religion and—"

Stacey gasped. "Not abortion," she protested, aghast at the thought of there never being a Ben.

"No," he agreed, "not abortion. Adoption. Of a sort," he added wearily.

"Of a sort?" Stacey prompted when he didn't immediately continue.

"Her older sister, Elena, was married to an Anglo rancher in New Mexico," he said quietly, staring into his glass. "Six years married, but there weren't any children, and Elena was desperate for a child." He swirled the liquid in his glass, watching it as if the sight fascinated him. "It seemed like the ideal solution at the time," he said, repeating what Marta had told him all those years ago. "One that was supposed to solve everybody's problem. My mother wouldn't be forced to give up her child to strangers, I'd never have to know I was illegitimate, and Elena would save her marriage. But it didn't work out that way." He lifted the glass to his lips and took a deep swallow, relishing the burning as it went down. "My *father*—" his lip curled at the word "—couldn't reconcile himself to the fact that someone else's bastard was the only son he was ever going to have, but he couldn't quite bring bring himself to refute me, either."

"Oh, Ben." Compassion gripped her heart and stung her eyes at the thought of all the pain his few words encompassed. For him. For Marta. For Elena. And even for Elena's husband. "Ben." Her hand came up to touch his face. "I'm so sorry. It must have been awful for you."

He shrugged away from her touch, uncomfortable with her pity. He didn't want pity from Stacey. He never had. "It wasn't fun," he admitted. "But it was over a long time ago."

"I'm still sorry," she said.

"Yeah, well..." He upended his drink, draining it, then reached out and set it on the glass-topped coffee table. "So where do we go from here, Stacey?"

He knew as well as she did that she wouldn't be taking it to court now. Marta was the only mother she'd ever known. The woman who'd bandaged her scraped knees and seen that she'd done her homework and explained the mysteries of her changing body. She'd never do anything to hurt Marta.

And having it known that she'd borne a child out of wedlock would hurt her deeply because, though an illegitimate baby might not be a big thing to most people these days, it would be to Marta, who still went to Mass twice a week.

Marta had made her decision years ago, Stacey thought. She'd given up her baby to be raised by another woman, she'd left her home to avoid bringing shame on her family, she'd denied herself the pleasure and pride of declaring Ben her son to all the world, even when that world would no longer condemn her. On top of all that, she'd lived with all the guilt and doubts and pain her decisions had certainly brought her. For Stacey to challenge it now, to bring it out in the open for everyone to comment over, would be the worst sort of betrayal.

So, no matter how much she wanted the ranch, no matter how desperately she craved to own a part of her childhood home, she couldn't go after it at Marta's expense. Which meant, unless Ben was willing to just give it to her with no strings attached, she'd have to walk away from it. Again.

"Stacey?"

"I guess—" her voice trembled "—I guess it's up to you," she said. She twisted the brandy glass in her hand, swirling the amber liquid against the sides of the snifter as he'd done just a moment ago.

"The decision is yours," he said firmly. He wasn't going to force her into anything. Not again. Not ever again.

"I can't," she said, realizing it was true. She couldn't make the decision. It was asking too much of her. She wanted him to make the decision for both of them. She wanted him to take the responsibility out of her hands. She wanted, she realized, for him to say that he loved her. Needed her. Wanted to marry her.

But she knew he wasn't going to.

"The decision is yours," he repeated. "Henry wanted it that way."

Stacey nodded, her eyes closed. *Yes, Henry,* she thought. But what, really, had Henry wanted? Had he intended that she should say yes to Ben? Or had he wanted her to say no?

"Stacey?" He extended a tentative hand toward her.

She shot up suddenly, slamming her glass down on the tabletop. "Don't push me, Ben," she said, half pleading, half commanding. "I don't know. I just don't know!"

"Are you going to drag this out for the whole six months, then?"

"No! I couldn't stand that!"

"Then make a decision!" He reached for her hand again, pulling her back down on the sofa. "What do you want, Stacey?"

You, she wanted to say, as the touch of his hand ignited her, *just you*. She should have pulled away then but she didn't. Couldn't.

"The ranch?" he persisted relentlessly. "Or Paris?"

Were those her only choices? The ranch or Paris and nothing in between?

"I . . ." She hesitated uncertainly. Her whole future depended on her next words. Could she tell him what she wanted? Could she bare her pride that far and trust that he wouldn't trample on it? "I want the ranch," she said. Her voice was low, a mere thread of sound, but surprisingly firm.

"Even if I go with it? And I *do* go with it, Stacey, make no mistake about that," he said, wanting her to say that what she really wanted was him and to hell with the ranch. "Is that what you want?"

"I want the ranch," she said again, too full of pride and left-over hurt feelings to admit the real truth.

"All right." He yanked her into his arms. "All right, Stacey, let's see what we have to look forward to for the rest of our lives."

She went into his arms without a struggle, without a whimper of protest and lifted her open mouth to his descending one. *So what if it's only lust on his part*, she asked herself as their mouths fused and their tongues engaged in a passionate ballet, she had love enough for two. Plenty of marriages, good solid marriages, had been founded on far less. She could teach him to love her. He wanted her desperately, she could tell. Surely it was only a tiny step from that wanting to love. She *could* make him love her.

She felt his hand in her hair, loosening the pins so that it fell in heavy waves to her shoulders. His lips left off their exploration of her eager mouth to press moist, hungry kisses along her cheeks and jaw to her ear.

"I love to take your hair down," he whispered raggedly. "It's like messing up a prim little lady and turning her into a tigress." His tongue circled her ear and she quivered, her nails pressing into his shoulder. He thrilled to that small sign of her desire. "Or a wildcat," he said then. "My wildcat."

He pulled back a little to look into her face. Her hair was spread in wild disarray over his arm and shoulder, her eyes were smoldering, half closed with passion, her lips were red and slightly parted. He ran the tip of one finger slowly from her nose, down across her parted lips, to her chin and along the long slender line of her throat and chest to close possessively over one full breast. "Are you my wildcat, Stacey?" he asked huskily, his eyes roving over the seductive splendor of her flushed face.

"Yes." The word was almost inaudible. Her hand came up, pressing his to the warm, wanting curve of her breast. "Yes, Ben, I—" But she got no further.

She heard him take a deep, ragged breath, felt his fingers curve around her breast, kneading, and then somehow, in one smooth motion he managed to turn her pliant body so that she lay on the sofa. His long, hard length pressed her into the cushions. She welcomed his weight holding her down, welcomed his tongue as it once again sought entrance to the sweet, moist recesses of her mouth, welcomed the feel of his big, warm hand as he nudged aside the top of her dress to caress the swollen breast beneath.

"At least I can make you want me," he said into the warmth of her skin.

Stacey arched her body and her arms cradled him close, urging his moist, eager mouth to her breast. She wanted to tell him, over and over, that he didn't *make* her want him because she couldn't help wanting him. Just as she couldn't help loving him. But something held her back. Pride, stubbornness, the need to hear him say it first, to commit himself before she did. . . . Something.

"Stacey," he moaned. "Stacey, honey, I want you." His voice was muffled against her throat. His movements against her were almost frantic, his hands avid and greedy. "Say you want me, too, Stacey." He pressed his hips against her, letting her feel his raging desire and need. "Say it."

But she couldn't.

It would be the same as the last time, she thought. They'd make love frantically, like passionate, starving animals and then, afterward, when there should be closeness and sharing and whispered endearments, there'd be . . . She didn't know what there would be. Nothing, probably. Shame. Uneasiness. Anger. Wary distrust. She couldn't take that again. Not ever again. Not from Ben.

Her body went lax beneath his. "Let me up." She pushed his chest when he didn't immediately release her. "Ben, let me up."

He stilled, his body tensing, his arms hard around her, unable to believe what he'd heard. He raised his head slightly. "Stacey?"

"Let me up," she repeated. "Please."

Her eyes were closed. Her body passive beneath his except for the slender hands pressing against his chest. *Like yesterday.* He'd gone after her like an animal again, he thought, disgusted with himself. He'd mauled her. Manhandled her. Hurt her. She must think he was some kind of crazed beast. He pushed himself up and off her, filled with self-loathing. "I'm sorry, Stacey."

She sat up slowly, pulling her dress up over her breasts. "Don't be," she said, her head down. "You can't help how you feel any more than I can."

"Stacey," he said, anguished. "I—"

"Please, don't apologize." She had to get away from him now, before she gave in again, before she threw herself into his arms and begged him to finish what they'd started. She stood. "If you'll excuse me," she said with admirable calm, for which she was ever after proud of herself. "It's been a long day and I'd like to go to bed." Her eyes met his briefly. "Alone."

He stepped back and let her pass him. There was nothing else to say. Nothing else to do.

She left the room with her head held high, picking up her purse and the now-wilting rose as she went. She managed to keep up her calm facade until the bedroom door closed quietly behind her. Then she turned the lock, dropping her shoes and purse and the faded flower on the carpet. Her whole body slumped and shrank inward as if she'd been hit in the stomach. Her arms came up to hug her upper body protectively.

This is what it would be like if I stayed, she thought. She was a fool to think she could make him love her. A fool! Oh, it might work for a while. He would probably be faithful as long as he still hungered for her body. But inevitably, there would come a day when someone else—someone like Linda Montoya, perhaps—would come along and he'd fall in love.

And when that happened she would surely die.

So she couldn't stay. No matter how much she wanted to, she just couldn't. The ranch didn't matter now, if it ever really had. All that mattered was Ben. She loved him too much to marry him and then have to watch him drift away from her. And he would. Eventually. She was sure of it.

If he loved her just a little she might have stood a chance of keeping him. But he didn't love her. He only wanted her, and that wasn't good enough.

She bent over and picked up her evening bag, finding and lighting a cigarette, and sat down on the edge of the brass bed, waiting for the soothing rush of smoke to work its magic and stop the shaking of her fingers enough so that she could use the telephone.

"André," she said calmly when she had made the connection. There was no trace of tears in her voice. "There's been a change of plans here and I'm returning to Paris after all. Do you think there's a chance I could have my old job back?"

ALONE IN THE LIVING ROOM Ben sat in the dark, drinking himself into insensibility in an effort to drown out the pain of losing her all over again. He'd thought it had hurt the first time, when he'd been little more than a boy in a man's body. But he'd been wrong. The second time around was far worse. Because now he knew just exactly what he was losing.

ANDRE WAS OVERJOYED to be getting back his beautiful and efficient assistant. Stacey had known he would be. He hadn't had time, in the few days she'd been gone, to even begin looking for someone to replace her.

"Not that it would be possible, *chérie,*" he said gallantly, "because you are irreplaceable. But I am puzzled. You were so adamant about staying on your ranch. I despaired of ever seeing you again."

"I just changed my mind, André," she answered him. "Texas and the ranch just aren't my cup of tea anymore. And I missed Paris—and you too, of course—terribly."

That, in essence, was what she planned to tell Ben the next morning when she finally emerged from her bedroom with her suitcases already packed and a taxi summoned by phone.

He was standing in front of the stove with his back to her, his calves and feet bare beneath the hem of a white terry robe. His hair was damp, as if he'd just showered. There was a glass of tomato juice on the counter beside him and the smell of coffee permeated the air like strong perfume. He'd apparently weathered the night with no ill effects—unlike her. Stacey took a deep breath, fixed a cool smile on her face and walked into the room.

"Would you like some eggs?" he asked without turning around.

"Just coffee, thanks," she said, trying to sound breezily insouciant as she reached for the glass coffeepot on the counter. "I haven't got time for anything else."

"Haven't got time?" He turned around to look at her, a spatula in one hand, a pan of scrambled eggs in the other. His bare chest peeked out from between the loosely crossed lapels on his robe. His jaw was unshaven. His bloodshot eyes narrowed as he took in her polished appearance. "Are you going someplace?"

She busied herself with pouring out a cup of coffee. "Home," she said, as if it were the most natural thing in the world to say.

Ben put the spatula in the frying pan and set them both on the counter with no thought for the tiled surface. "Home? To the ranch?" he asked.

"Home." Her eyes flickered to his for a brief instant and then went back to the sugar she was stirring into her coffee. "To Paris."

Something twisted in his gut. "Paris?"

"Yes." She lifted the cup to her lips and took a quick sip. She'd put too much sugar in it. "I've decided that I just couldn't stand to live on the ranch," she said coolly, so intent on her hiding her true emotions that she couldn't see his for what they were. "You helped me make up my mind actually. Dinner last night and...everything. That lovely little club reminded me of just what I'd be giving up. And for what?" She shrugged and took another sip of the too sweet coffee. "A piece of dry desert land and half a herd of dirty cattle?" She shook her head as if at her own brief folly. "I decided it just wasn't worth it," she lied. "I mean really, Ben, can you honestly see me living at Iron Oakes, in that old-fashioned barn of a house, with Uncle Pete and all those hick hands?" She could see the anger building in his eyes, the anger and something else, but she refused to be deterred. "Married to *you*? Way out in the boonies with so few of the luxuries of life and no culture to speak of, after the way I've lived?"

She shrugged again deliberately, dismissively, subtly drawing his attention to the beautifully cut raw silk slacks, the soft silk blouse and the high-heeled snake-skin shoes, all in the same shade of deep forest green. A gold buckled snakeskin belt encircled her slim waist, gold hoops were in her ears and two fine gold chains, one with a diamond studded nugget, adorned her white throat. Her hair was swept up into a sleek coil, not a strand out of place, and she wore her new fox fur vest over all.

Its luxurious reddish color, the profusion of dangling tails at the hem, the basic impracticality of it made her look, she knew, sophisticated, spoiled and frivolous. Very much, in fact, as if she'd never in her entire life been near, or wanted to be near, anything so mundane as a cattle ranch.

No, he thought, *I really can't see Stacey on the ranch. Not this Stacey.*

"I'd get restless for the bright lights, the art galleries, the fabulous shopping..." She shrugged again and tried a careless little laugh, managing it quite well, she thought, despite the fact that it sounded a bit shrill. "Do you know, I haven't even had a decent croissant since I left home?"

She paused as if waiting for an answer, but he just stood there, staring at her with that bland, blank look on his face. As if, she thought, he was waiting for her to finish saying whatever it was she felt she had to say so he could go back to his breakfast.

"And besides, there's André," she said, pride alone driving her now. Her words were intended to show him that what had happened between them meant as little to her as it obviously had to him. "Uncle Pete was right, you know. About what he said in the den that day. I do have a man in Paris, a lover. I thought I could leave him but—" again that maddening little shrug that made him want to strangle her "—I find that I can't."

He could feel the veins throbbing in his temples, pounding out the measured beat of his blood as if it were flowing out of him. He could feel his heart begin to crack. But he pressed his lips together and said nothing. Because, he thought, if he said anything at all he'd end up begging her to stay. And he wasn't quite reduced to that. Yet.

Stacey's fingers curled around the coffee cup in her hand, waiting. Hoping. Giving him one last chance. A single word would've sent her rushing into his arms. Just a single word.

Stay. That's all you have to say, Ben, she pleaded silently. *Stay.*

Pride alone kept him from reaching for her. *Go,* he thought. *Just get it the hell over with and go before I make an even bigger fool of myself!*

The doorbell rang as they stood there, a shrill sound that made Stacey jump even though she'd been expecting it. "That will be my taxi," she said. "No, don't bother to see me out," she added, though Ben had made no attempt to do so. She put her coffee cup down and picked up her two suitcases, turning to go, and then paused in the door for one last look.

Ben stood with his hands in the pockets of his robe, his bare ankles crossed as he leaned back against the counter. "Have a good trip," he said pleasantly, though it was killing him.

Stacey felt her heart begin to break. She stiffened her back. "You can have Marta send along what I've left behind," she said. "She has my address."

Ben straightened as the front door closed behind her. He drew his hands out of his pockets and deliberately, slowly, as if it pained him to do so, uncurled his clenched fists. He raised them to his face, pressing his thumbs into the throbbing, soul-deep ache behind his glittering eyes.

HER APARTMENT was exactly as she'd left it, though why she expected it to be any different she wasn't sure. She'd been gone less than a week, after all, and no one but the daily maid would have been in it during that time. Bernadine always left things exactly as she found them. But still, she'd expected it to be different, perhaps because she herself felt so different.

She unpacked her suitcases methodically, hanging what needed to be hung on padded, scented hangers in her huge walk-in closet, folding other things away in sachet-lined drawers, setting aside whatever needed to be cleaned or laundered for Bernadine to attend to. She was putting away her toiletries, fitting her perfumes and makeup neatly into their places on the bathroom shelves when she met her own eyes in the mirror. She paused in her task and flipped on the circle of makeup lights that surrounded it, leaning forward to study her reflection in the bright glare.

She'd changed, yes, but how? Her hand lifted, her fingers smoothing gently, curiously over her jawline and brow bones seeking...something. Her face was the same one that had stared back at her last week. The same clean jawline, the same fair creamy skin, the same pale pink lips and cheeks that always needed cosmetic help to keep her from looking like a porcelain doll, the same blue eyes.

Stacey stared into her eyes.

There was the change.

For all her adult life, she'd always been cool and rather remote looking. The image was partly the natural result of her pale hair and skin, partly a cultivated manner of reserve that had gradually become second nature. But her eyes she knew, because more than one person had told her, had always managed to hint at the real, warm woman beneath the image. Always before there'd been the hope, she realized, that one day she would go home to Iron Oakes—and to Ben. That hope was what had kept her warm and real for the past eleven years. It was what had saved her from becoming, in reality, the icy career woman she pretended to be. Now that hope was gone—forever—and her face showed it.

She felt as if all the warmth in her had gone up in flames, ignited by the blazing heat in Ben, and now that she'd moved away from his heat her own was gone, too, burned out with just the ashes left. Fine, cold ashes.

I should hate him for that, she thought, *but I can't. Somehow, I can't. He didn't ask Henry to make that will. If this whole, sorry mess is anybody's fault,* she thought, *it's Henry's.* But she couldn't find it in her heart to hate Henry, either. She couldn't find anything in her heart at all.

Shivering slightly, she switched off the glaring circle of makeup lights and quickly finished her unpacking, studiously avoiding looking into her own face.

She ran a bath then and, once dry, wrapped herself in another ivory silk nightgown and snuggled into the cashmere robe she'd thought of so longingly that morning at Iron Oakes. She wandered rather listlessly out into her tiny kitchen, intending to make herself some scrambled eggs and toast and a pot of good, strong coffee. She wasn't really hungry but it'd been hours since her last meal—at the Cipango with Ben—and she knew she should eat something. In the end, though, she ate only three or four bites of her make-shift meal and scraped the rest into the garbage. Leaving the dishes for Bernadine to do when she came in to clean in the morning, Stacey carried her coffee from the tiny kitchen, through the almost equally tiny but exquisitely chic dining room into the living room.

She set the cup and saucer down on a delicate end table and moved across the pale gray carpet to turn on the radio, selecting a soothing classical station as she did almost every night when she came home from work. Before sitting down she switched on the electric fire in the small fireplace with its white marble mantelpiece.

She picked up her cup then, and tucked her bare feet up under her as she sipped her coffee and stared broodingly into the flames flickering over the fake logs, shivering slightly.

In less than a week she'd forgotten how cold it could get in Paris, even in the middle of July. Not that the fire offered any real warmth. One relied on the central heating for that and, because it was summer, the heat was, of course, turned off. She snuggled deeper into her cashmere robe, pulling the shawl collar up around her neck and tucked her feet farther under her. The coffee, her usual dark French roast, tasted weak and unappetizing, and the classical music playing softly on the radio failed to relax her. She put the cup aside and stood up, moving restlessly to the radio to change the station and then abruptly shut it off. She went to stand in front of the fire, her hands extended to the warmth.

She was cold, so cold, both inside and out, and the fire gave off only a feeble warmth. It wasn't enough to heat the coldness that seemed to surround her. She turned from it, her arms wrapped around her upper body in what was quickly becoming an habitual gesture and gazed around her living room. But even the sight of the beautifully decorated room failed to warm her. It was cold, too, she told herself, though it wasn't really true. Cold and formal and almost overpoweringly feminine.

Plush, pale gray carpet covered the living-room floor, giving way to the beautiful black-and-white marble squares of the dining room and the small foyer. The walls throughout were pale ice blue. The furniture was delicate and expensive, upholstered in pale shades

of blue and gray silk brocade. Pale, pearl gray velvet
drapes, pulled back over sheer white undercurtains,
framed a lovely view of Paris's lights. There was an exquisite enameled clock centered on the white marble
mantel with heavy silver candlesticks flanking it on either end.

It was apparent, Stacey realized for the first time, that
no man shared the apartment with her and—she told
herself inaccurately—apparent, too, that no man was
welcome in this frigid bower of femininity. It seemed
to her now to be cloyingly feminine. Perhaps that was
why, she mused, she'd been so conscious of the overwhelming masculinity of Iron Oakes.

So be it, she thought, telling herself that she didn't
care. The apartment was hers, a clear reflection and
extension of her personality. She was now, in reality,
cold and formal and icily feminine as opposed to what
she had once been; hot-tempered and impetuous and
warmly female. *Well, good*, she thought. It was safer
that way.

She switched off the electric fire and went into her
bedroom. The walls were pale blue in here, too, like the
rest of the apartment. The carpet was a floral Aubus-
son in shades of blue and cream and pink. The bed was
a huge gilt four poster dressed with pristine, frilly white
linens and draped with white lace bed curtains lined
with the palest pink silk she could find. It was a fantasy room fit for a princess. Each component, from the
main pieces of furniture to the pink crystal perfume at-
omizers had been lovingly put together to make a
pleasing whole.

Usually it brought a smile of satisfaction and contentment to her lips. Tonight she didn't even turn on a light to appreciate its beauty but instead just crawled into the bed, still wearing her robe, and pulled the comforter up over her head, seeking warmth.

SHE AWOKE EARLY, just as dawn was beginning to color the sky. Her arms were wrapped tightly around one of the pillows, and she was still burrowed like a small hurt animal under the lace-trimmed comforter.

And still cold. So cold.

She rose swiftly, scarcely glancing at the pink-tinged view of a slowly awakening Paris framed in her bedroom window, and quickly made herself ready for work. Showered, her pale face made up with warming colors of ivory foundation and peach-hued blusher, she dressed warmly in a long-sleeved, deep violet silk shirtwaist dress, matching pumps and a cream colored blazer. Automatically, practically without conscious thought, she accessorized her rather severe outfit with small gold hoops in her ears and a long gold chain looped twice around her neck to lie, softly gleaming, against the deep violet of her dress. A tiny lavender lace handkerchief peeked jauntily from the breast pocket of her blazer.

She had nearly three uninterrupted hours at the office before anyone else arrived, and she put it to good use, reorganizing the files that André's son, Edouard, had managed to reduce to inefficient chaos in the short time she'd been gone. She was just finishing up, on her knees before the lowest file drawer, when she heard the door open behind her.

"Stacey," exclaimed André in surprised delight. "You are back so soon! When you called, *mon Dieu*, it was only yesterday, was it not? I did not expect you back so soon. But I am pleased you are home, *chérie*. Very pleased." He came forward as he spoke, helping her to her feet, and then kissed her warmly on both cheeks. He held her away from him a little, still clasping her hands in both of his. "We have missed you very much. It is good to have you with us." He peered into her face with almost parental concern. "But perhaps you have come back too soon? You look a bit worn," he said worriedly. "You have had a long trip and a trying time, *oui*? Perhaps you should go home and rest for a few days. You look tired," he said, though tired wasn't exactly what he meant. He couldn't have put into words exactly what he meant. "As beautiful as ever, *chérie*, but tired."

Stacey laughed lightly, touched by his warm greeting. "I'm fine, André, really," she assured him, "and very eager to get back to work." She gently pulled her hands from his, "Let me get you your coffee, and perhaps a croissant to celebrate this prodigal's return? Do you know I haven't had a croissant since I left here? I'm dying for one," she said, moving toward the door. "Then you can fill me in on what progress has been made on the Jordan contract."

André nodded and let her go. When she returned with two coffees and the promised croissants they settled down to work, busy with all the things that hadn't been properly seen to by Edouard. In a very few minutes it was as if she'd never left. People popped in to say hello and welcome her back and express their belated condolences on the loss of her grandfather. Just before lunch, Edouard el-Hamid made a brief appearance. Seeing Stacey working busily at what had yesterday looked as if it was destined to be his desk, he hurried forward, kissing her hands in a lavish and theatrical display of gratitude for her return, and just as quickly hurried out again.

Things continued to be that way—busy—all the rest of the day. And the week. And the month. Stacey welcomed the frantic pace, seeing it as the perfect way to forget.

HER TWENTY-SEVENTH BIRTHDAY came and went. André bought her flowers to mark the occasion and took her to an extravagant lunch at her favorite little bistro. She received a loving, worried letter from Marta along with a trunk containing all of the clothes she'd left behind. But there was nothing from Ben.

Stacey shrugged and told herself that she didn't care and that it was better that way. Nothing was to be gained, she reasoned, from further contact with him. They had nothing to say to each other. Nothing at all.

She threw herself even more energetically into her work, telling herself daily that she was free of him now, finally, but she knew it was a lie. The cold she felt began to work itself deeper. Even when she accompanied André to Saudi Arabia to finalize the Jordan deal she felt the cold. It was becoming a part of her now, an accepted fact. In a way it was a good thing, she rationalized. It insulated her from feeling any pain and it made her a better employee to André because, she told herself, she had no emotional involvements to sidetrack her from the business at hand.

But André was becoming worried. "*Chérie*," he said to her one day near the Christmas holidays as he was preparing to leave for the afternoon, "why don't you take the rest of the afternoon off, too?" He waved a hand expressively. "Go shopping. Get your hair done. I give you leave."

Stacey looked up from her desk and smiled at him. "You just feel guilty for leaving early," she teased.

"*Non*, I do not. Well, perhaps, just a little but—" he smiled "—that is no reason for you not to take advantage of my guilt. Besides, when I am gone there is no work for you to do, *oui*?"

"When you are gone, André, is when I can get the most work done!" she informed him.

André shrugged dismissively. "Perhaps, but I am worried about you, *chérie*. You are working too hard, too much." He smiled at her faintly amused expression. "Yes, I know. I should be glad that you do since I benefit from your dedication. But you are a young, beautiful woman and I am a Frenchman before I am a businessman. I hate to see such a woman waste herself as you are doing. You should have a man. Someone special to spoil you." His Saudi accent was becoming more evident and Stacey was touched by his very real concern for her.

"What makes you think I don't?"

"*Mon Dieu!* Do not think you can pull so easily the sheep over my eyes! If you had a man he would not allow you to spend so many of your hours here when you could be spending them more pleasantly with him.

Non, you cannot fool me! You have no special man, *chérie*."

"Oh, all right, André, I don't have a special man," she admitted laughingly. "But I'm a career girl, not a homemaker. I like my job and I like working for you," she assured him. "And besides, I see lots of men," she lied.

"Lots of men?" he echoed, unconvinced. "Who? When?"

"Tonight." She fabricated the when, adroitly skipping over the who part of his question. "I'm going to a Christmas party, and as soon as I finish proofing this report I'm going home to get ready."

"You are not pulling on my arm?" he said doubtfully.

"Leg," she corrected. "Pulling your leg. And no, I'm not, André." He still failed to look convinced. "Have I ever lied to you?" she asked.

André smiled then and chucked her under the chin. "Women always lie, *chérie*. They cannot help it." He laughed uproariously at her expression of mock outrage. "But come. Leave this report and I will drive you home."

"Remember," he said when he had dropped her in front of her apartment. "I will expect a detailed report on this party you are going to. And on this nonexistent man!"

Stacey actually did have a party she could go to—she hadn't lied to André about that. She had invitations to dozens of holiday parties, but she hadn't, until now, thought of going to any of them because she just wasn't in a party mood.

She kept thinking of Christmas in Texas, remembering the Mexican chocolate that Marta made for everyone to drink as they sat around the Christmas tree. They'd always had an old-fashioned tree decorated with red and green balls, strings of popcorn, tiny woven straw donkeys and angels and hammered metal stars and crosses that gave it a distinctly Southwestern flavor. She could see Marta's precious nativity scene set up on the mantel, its tiny figures carved of wood and painted by hand. The three kings all wore sombreros and serapes, as did the figure of Joseph. The gentle Mary's skirts were brightly hued, her braids long and black, partially covered by a white mantilla. Even the baby Jesus wore a gaily striped serape as his swaddling clothes.

There'd always been a *piñata*, too, hung from the ceiling in the front hall and filled with small toys and hard candies for all the ranch children, including Stacey, to try to knock down, spilling its riches for everyone.

And the food! There would be rich fruitcake from Corsicana, Texas—the only kind Marta would buy—and homemade pralines, rich with caramel and pecans, and Marta's special Mexican cinnamon cookies. For Christmas dinner there would be Turkey *Mole*, a traditional festival dish reputed to have been invented by the Mexican nuns at the convent of Santa Rosa in the sixteenth century.

Marta used to tell the legend each year as Stacey stirred the simmering *Mole*, redolent with tomatoes and onions and garlic, plus almonds and raisins and sesame seeds and always a bit of ground chocolate. A curious hodgepodge of ingredients, to be sure, but her mouth watered at the thought of the dish.

The thought of what she was missing at Iron Oakes, seeing in her mind's eye all of her family sitting down to Christmas dinner—without her—had made Stacey apathetic and unenthusiastic toward any celebration of the season. But, she thought now, perhaps André was right.

Maybe she *was* wasting herself. There were dozens of men, hundreds probably, who were capable of arousing in her the same sort of response as Ben had done. Of course there were, she told herself firmly. Ben wasn't the only man in the world, not by a long shot. And just because she couldn't have an Iron Oakes' Christmas didn't mean she should deny herself any celebration at all.

Stacey went to the party that night, and several others during the holiday season, up to and including the huge New Year's Eve bash that André always hosted. He was happy to see her there, apparently enjoying herself, and happier still when she allowed an attractive, unattached male to see her home. He wouldn't have been so happy to know that, after a chaste goodnight kiss, the attractive man was sent on his way. Just as had several other men who had been allowed to escort her to and from some of the parties had been sent away. She just couldn't seem to take that final step and say the words that would invite them in.

Damn you, Ben, damn you to hell! she would think when the door closed on a mildly puzzled or sometimes downright angry escort of the evening. *That was a nice man,* she would tell herself after one of them had gone, *an attractive man, totally charming. And he leaves me cold.* And then she would undress and wrap herself in a nightgown and robe, crawling into bed with the covers pulled up over her head to dream, unwillingly, of Ben.

ALL TOO SOON January sped to a close and, with it, the will's six-month deadline approached and passed. The ranch was Ben's now, all Ben's. It was lost to her forever. She stayed home from work that day, locked in her apartment, and cried until her eyes were almost swollen shut and her pale complexion was blotched and red. This was the end of it then. It was no longer possible for her to change her mind.

Solemnly, she gathered up her mementos of Iron Oakes—her copy of Henry's will, some old photographs, the white lace mantilla Marta had given her—and switched on the electric fire in the fireplace. Ritualistically she began to burn them. First Henry's will, then the snapshots. But when it came time to consign Marta's gift to the flames she found that she couldn't do it. So she folded it away instead and hid it, out of sight, in a bottom drawer of her dresser.

EARLY IN FEBRUARY André made a request of her. "I must ask you to do something personal for me, *chérie*."

Stacey put aside the papers she was working on. "Yes, of course, André. What is it?"

"You will not be so eager when you hear what it is," he warned, then went on to explain. "My house, as you know, is still undergoing renovations."

Stacey smiled. Everyone in the building knew about André's house. A relatively small project to begin with, it had grown until nearly every room of what amounted to a small mansion was affected. André shouted daily at someone about his house, or had Stacey shout for him.

"I must entertain a client."

"Monsieur Verdant?" Stacey guessed correctly.

"*Oui*. Verdant," André nodded. "I cannot entertain him properly in my home and . . ." His voice trailed off suggestively.

"Would my apartment be big enough?" she offered, knowing very well what he was leading up to.

"It would be perfect!" André smiled with relief. "You are a treasure, *chérie*, a pearl without price!"

Stacey only smiled. "When is this little soirée to take place?" she asked, her pen held poised over the desk calendar to make a note of the date.

"Tonight."

"Tonight?" Stacey suppressed a sigh and looked up at him, the pen still in her hand. "That's not much notice, André," she reproved him gently, and he grinned rather sheepishly. "How many will there be?" she asked then, and they launched into a brief discussion of the particulars involved.

"Just cocktails," said André, "and some sort of hors d'oeuvres. I will leave that to you, *chérie*," he said, waving a hand in the air expressively. "We have tickets for the opera, you know."

Yes, she knew because she had made the reservations.

"So everything must run like a watch."

"Like clockwork," she corrected automatically. André looked at her quizzically. "Run like clockwork," she repeated.

"Watch, clockwork—" he shrugged "—it is all the same. Go, *chérie*, and see that it does."

"Is there anything special you'd like in the way of food?"

"I leave it entirely to you," he told her.

Stacey nodded, smiling indulgently, and went through to her own office. In less than ten minutes she had tidied up her desk and was ready to do André's bidding.

"I'll be gone for the rest of the day, Nicole," she said to her secretary as she paused to belt a street-length fur coat around her slender waist. She glanced at her watch, mentally juggling errands. "If Monsieur Verdant calls put him directly through to André, please. Anybody else, just take a message." She settled a fur beret jauntily on her head and pulled on dark leather gloves as she gave her instructions. "Let's see, did I leave anything out?"

"No, *mademoiselle*," said the secretary and then briefly repeated Stacey's instructions back to her.

"Good." Stacey smiled, her hand poised to push open the door. "Thank you, Nicole," she said and then stepped out into the cold winter air. She paused for a moment, turning up the collar of her coat against the chill and hailed a cab.

TWO HOURS LATER she made her precarious way to her building, laden with shopping bags and paper-wrapped flowers, the cabbie trailing along behind her with his arms full, too. She shouldered open the lobby door, pushed the elevator button with her elbow and then stood in front of her apartment door juggling packages and searching for her keys. She could feel the huge bouquet slipping from under her arm and she shifted it hurriedly, transferring the strap of her purse to her teeth as she did so.

"Here, let me take that for you," said a man's voice, speaking in English. A big, tanned hand reached out to take the purse and rescue the precariously held flowers.

Stacey's eyes flew up in stunned surprise, the automatic, "*Merci, monsieur,*" dying on her lips. "Ben," she mouthed soundlessly. "How . . . when . . ." But words failed her. She'd never expected to see him again, especially not here in Paris, at her apartment. She didn't know what to say, how to react.

"Hello, Stacey," he said in that deceptively lazy way of his.

"Hello, Ben," she managed then, her wits beginning to return. They stood gazing at each other for a breathless minute, both of them wondering what to say now that they'd said hello.

12

"MADEMOISELLE," said the cabbie on a plaintive note, breaking the spell that held them.

"Oh, *pardon, monsieur.* Ben, would you get those please?" she said, finally managing to dig out her keys and open the door. "You can put them right over there, on the sideboard." She turned to the cabbie, handing him his fare, *"Merci, monsieur,"* she dismissed him. The cabbie bowed slightly and left.

Stacey closed the door behind him and then took a deep, calming breath before turning around. "Well," she said and then hesitated. *What now?* she wondered. She couldn't ask him any of the things she really wanted to. Do you lie awake nights, thinking and remembering, the way I do? Do you ache inside? Has your heart turned to ice? No, she couldn't ask him those questions. "How are you, Ben?" she asked instead.

"I'm fine." He put his hands in his pockets to keep from reaching for her. "And you?"

"I'm fine, too." She gave a nervous laugh. "I'm fine, you're fine. We're both fine. Isn't that nice?" She realized suddenly that she was babbling. Her hands were clasped tightly in front of her. She dropped them to her sides. "I'm going to go take off my coat," she said. "The kitchen's that way, through the dining room. Make yourself a drink. I won't be a minute."

But she was considerably more than a minute.

She hurried to the relative sanctuary of her room and, once there, leaned for a moment against the closed door, her eyes shut tight against the vision of Ben standing on the black-and-white marble floor of her foyer.

Ben! Why was he here? What did he want? Why couldn't he just leave her alone? She'd almost—almost!—gotten over him, she lied to herself. She'd almost reached the point that she wasn't thinking about him every minute of every day. Oh, damn him, why was he here? And then, unbidden, unwelcome, came the thought, *I'm glad! Whatever the reason, I'm glad.*

The secret recesses of her heart conjured up the picture of him that her eyes had so recently seen. He looked so handsome, so big, standing there in her tiny foyer. He was so overwhelmingly the best of the quintessential American male in his jeans and cowboy boots and the heavy sheepskin-lined suede jacket with its furry collar turned up around his tanned face. The lights of the crystal chandelier glinted off his black hair and played up the tiny squint lines at the corners of his blue eyes. Just remembering how he'd looked made her knees weak.

She pushed herself away from the door and methodically removed her coat and hat, putting them away. She debated for a brief moment about changing her clothes and then decided against it. Her jade-green silk shirtwaist, accented by a heavy triple strand of pearls, was quite presentable—feminine and businesslike both. Besides, she'd only have to change again for André's cocktail party.

André's party! For a few minutes she'd completely forgotten about it. She made a quick telephone call to Bernadine, engaging her services for the evening, and then hurried to the bathroom to smooth her hair and check her makeup. It was perfect, as usual, and not a hair was out of place. She turned on the taps, running cold water over the throbbing pulses in her wrists in an unconscious effort to cool her suddenly too-warm self. She realized then, with a small shock of surprise, that for the first time in months she wasn't cold.

Her eyes went to the mirror. Her cheeks were faintly flushed, her eyes were bright with . . . what? Anticipation? Excitement? Fear? Or a little of all three, perhaps? She didn't know, and she told herself very firmly, she didn't want to know. She turned off the taps, dried her hands and went determinedly out into the kitchen.

Ben had made himself a drink as she'd suggested, apparently having had no trouble finding the bourbon and the bar glasses. He'd taken off his sheepskin jacket, which was draped casually over the back of a kitchen chair, and was busy unpacking her groceries. He looked huge—he *was* huge—moving around in her small kitchen.

She stood watching him for a few seconds, admiring the fit of the soft white turtleneck sweater he wore and the way it stretched across the muscles of his back as he put away the pâtés and cheeses and fitted the bottles of wine into her small refrigerator.

"You always seem to be shopping," he said, startling her. She hadn't realized he was aware of her presence behind him. "First it was clothes, now food." He glanced over his shoulder, his grin intended to take the sting out of his words. "Good thing you're a rich bitch, the way you like to spend money," he teased. He thought maybe he should have kept his feeble jokes to himself when she frowned.

"Not my money," she said, coming into the room to help him. "André's money. It's his party."

Ben's face changed suddenly and the grin faded. He turned away from her. "How is André?" he asked tightly.

Now what brought that on? she wondered. And then she remembered. Ben thought André was her lover, because she'd wanted him to think that. Well, she still wanted him to think that. It was better that way, infinitely better. "André is exceedingly fine," she said.

Ben nodded shortly and turned back to the grocery sack.

She stared at him for a few seconds, wondering where to begin, what questions to ask. Because there *were* questions to be asked. He hadn't come to Paris on a whim. "Why are you here, Ben?"

He turned to her, resting his lean hips back against the kitchen counter, and folded his arms across his broad chest. "It's about Henry's will," he said, watching her for a reaction. He didn't know what he expected, nor even quite what he wanted. But whatever it was, it *wasn't* the quick frown that creased her brows.

"Henry's will? I thought we'd settled that." She stared up at him, puzzled and strangely excited. "Iron Oakes is yours." Her eyes fell and then fluttered upward again. "Isn't it?"

He shook his head. "Not entirely."

"Not entirely?" Stacey echoed faintly. Her voice shook. What did he mean, *Not entirely?*

"There are some final papers for you to sign."

"Papers?" she said. What papers? And why couldn't he have just mailed them? Why come all the way to Paris? There had to be more to it than that.

"Mademoiselle" came a voice from the direction of the foyer, "it is I, Bernadine."

"In here, Bernadine," Stacey called, her eyes still holding Ben's. "We're in the kitchen."

An older woman, gray haired and comfortably plump in a plain black dress, joined them in the kitchen. *"Bonjour, mademoiselle,"* she said, and then her eyes flickered to Ben. They widened with a true French-woman's appreciation for a superb male specimen.

"Bernadine, this is—" Stacey paused only half a second "—my uncle from America, Ben Oakes. Ben this is Madame Bernadine Bonnard. She's going to help with the party tonight."

"Your uncle, *mademoiselle?*" Bernadine asked in French, not sure she'd heard right.

"Yes, my uncle," Stacey said firmly.

Bernadine shrugged expressively as if to say that she didn't really believe Stacey, but if that's what she wanted to pretend then she, Bernadine, would go along with it. *"Bonjour,* Monsieur Oakes," she said, inclining her head.

"Pleased to meet you, ma'am," Ben replied easily.

"Come on, Uncle Ben," said Stacey. "Let's get out of the kitchen and let Bernadine get to it."

Ben smiled a farewell at the maid and picked up his sheepskin jacket, following Stacey out of the kitchen.

"Where are you going?" she demanded as he continued on toward the front door.

"To my hotel."

"You can't drop a bombshell like that and then just leave—"

"Look, Stacey," he interrupted, "obviously you're having a party tonight and this is something we need to talk about without interruptions. It's not exactly party chatter. I'll come back tomorrow." He shrugged into his jacket, moving toward the door.

"Wait!" she commanded as his hand reached for the door knob. "Come back tonight."

He looked at her questioningly from under lowered lids.

"It's a cocktail party and everyone will be leaving for the opera at eight-thirty," she explained.

"Not you?"

She shook her head. "*Flying Dutchman* tonight. I don't appreciate Wagner." She reached for his coat sleeve. "Come back at, oh, quarter to nine. Everyone will be gone then. We can talk about—" a tiny pause "—about Henry's will."

He nodded, but for some reason she wasn't appeased.

Her fingers tightened on his sleeve. "Promise you'll come back," she demanded, needing to hear him say he would.

"I promise," he said softly, staring down into her upraised face. It was the face that had haunted his dreams for months now. Fine-boned, fragile yet strong, beautiful. Quickly, before he could tell himself not to, he raised his hands, cupping her face, and touched his lips to hers. It was just a brief kiss, one that even Bernadine would have thought entirely appropriate between an uncle and niece had she happened to see it. But its briefness wasn't the whole story.

In that scant second that his lips claimed hers, Stacey felt herself suffused with warmth as a most unniecely heat flooded her body. Ben felt like a starving man who'd been granted a small taste of ambrosia. He sighed softly—a sigh that was echoed by Stacey—and his hands fell from her face.

"See you later, honey," he said, his voice sounding unnaturally rough to his own ears.

Stacey stood for a few short moments, trembling a little, one hand raised wonderingly to her lips as she stared at the closed door.

Why had he kissed her, she wondered vaguely and then, why, oh why, had she made him promise to come back later, when everyone would be gone and she would be alone? Stupid, she berated herself. And yet, at the same time, she couldn't completely ignore that rebellious part of her that was eagerly anticipating his return.

Call his hotel and cancel, her mind urged her, *tell him you've changed your mind. That you're going to the opera, after all.* But which hotel? She didn't know, did she? So she couldn't call, could she? Of course not! She turned back toward the kitchen, conveniently forgetting that a few telephone calls to some of the best hotels in Paris would easily reveal his whereabouts.

"There will be seven for cocktails, Bernadine, including myself," she said, giving the maid a few last minute instructions. "All of the guests will be leaving promptly at eight-thirty so it won't be a late evening for you. Monsieur el-Hamid has seats for the opera," she explained. "You can set everything up buffet style in the dining room, okay? Oh, and use the big blue glass bowl for the flowers."

"*Oui, mademoiselle, très bien,*" Bernadine answered placidly, already pulling platters and serving trays from their places.

Stacey went to her room then, confident that everything was well under control in Bernadine's capable hands, and began to ready herself for the evening ahead.

She lingered in her bath, reveling in the warmth and fragrance, and then dried herself lingeringly, smoothing on Opium lotion, dusting scented powder over her satiny legs and arms and flat belly.

She wandered back and forth between her bathroom and bedroom; fixing her hair, applying a heavier, more glamorous evening makeup with deep, smokey shadow emphasizing her blue eyes and clear red lipstick that made her skin seem even more porcelain pale by contrast. She began to dress then, when she was satisfied that her face and hair were as perfect as she could make them.

She slipped into her undergarments—a frilly little garter belt made mostly of black lace, a pair of high-cut tap pants and a strapless bra the color of coffee with lots of cream, also liberally frosted with black lace. Sitting on the velvet covered stool in front of her dressing table, she smoothed fine black stockings up her legs, fastening them to the garters. Then she stood up, ready for the dress.

She'd known since the door closed behind Ben that she was going to wear it. She'd bought it on a whim because she'd fallen in love with it at first sight. Now she knew that she had purchased it for just such an occasion as this, when she would need all the self-confidence that such a dress could give her. She lifted it off its padded hanger and slipped into it. It settled around her like a sigh, soft and shimmery.

The season's latest "little black dress," done this year in tissue-thin, gleaming panne velvet, irresistibly ornamented with a thin braid of gold silk cord along the wide bandeau neck and at the seams of the dropped shoulders. The narrow, chemise style just skimmed over her full breasts and slender hips, hinting at the body beneath it. It stopped two inches above her knees.

She stepped into plain black satin pumps with three-inch heels and tiny gold bows on the toes, fastened sparkling gold-and-diamond drops in her ears and then added one more perfect jewel, a gold butterfly with diamond-tipped feelers in the coil of her upswept hair. She stood back and smiled at the coolly elegant, leggy creature in the mirror. She was ready now. Ready for anything—or anyone.

She left the bedroom, hoping it was true.

"Ah, *mademoiselle!*" exclaimed Bernadine as Stacey appeared in the kitchen to check on the progress of the party preparation. "You look *superbe!*" she said effusively.

"Thank you, Bernadine. How are things going in here?"

"All is in readiness," Bernadine replied, motioning toward the dining room table. "All that is needed now are your guests, *n'est-ce pas?*"

"The table is beautiful, Bernadine. Simply beautiful."

And indeed it was. The pâtés rested atop white paper-lace doilies on silver trays, the cheeses were displayed on a bed of tender green ferns, the bite-size crepes were kept warm in a silver chafing pan, the luscious golden pears and red apples were mounded in a big crystal bowl to show them off to best advantage, the breads and assorted crackers were piled into silver gilt baskets lined with blue linens. All of it was artistically and efficiently arranged on the oval cherrywood table with a stack of pure white china plates, two rows of sparkling crystal wine glasses, a spray of gleaming cutlery and, in the center, a truly magnificent arrangement of white roses and baby's breath in a blue glass bowl.

Satisfied that everything was perfect in the dining room, Stacey wandered into the living room and prowled nervously around, twitching a table skirt here, adjusting a pillow there, turning off one lamp and switching on another, opening the drapes to their fullest to take advantage of her really rather spectacular view of the City of Light. The doorbell chimed, its three-toned bell echoing throughout the apartment. Stacey heard Bernadine's unhurried footsteps on the marble tiles as she moved to open the door and then, a second later, the distinctively accented rumble of André's voice.

She let out her breath, unaware until this minute that she'd been holding it, realizing that she'd been unconsciously poised, tensed, to hear Ben's deep, lazy drawl. Somehow, for some unexplainable reason, she thought he'd come back early and crash the party... or something.

Some part of her, also for some unexplainable—or unacknowledgeable—reason had halfway wanted him to. Because somewhere, deep in the most feminine recesses of her being, she'd wanted the chance to show him off to her Paris friends, just once, even if it was only as her uncle.

She went forward to greet her guests, a warm smile of welcome on her lips. "Come in," she said warmly, holding out both her hands to André.

"Ah, Stacey, *chérie*, how beautiful you look!" He kissed her on both cheeks, then leaned back to look at her again. *"Exquise!"* he said and kissed her cheeks a second time.

"Thank you, André," she returned his salute in like manner and then turned to hold out a graceful hand to Monsieur Verdant. *"Bienvenue!"* she said, welcoming him. Bernadine came forward to take their coats as introductions were made all around.

Stacey shook hands with Madame Verdant, an elegant woman dressed in a brown velvet Chanel evening suit with a big-collared gold tissue blouse, and Mademoiselle Verdant, a bright-eyed girl of about eighteen in the latest bit of bright nonsense of Zandra Rhodes and impossibly red hair that was only just saved from being punk by the way it curled on her neck and forehead.

"Call me Rivi," she said, ignoring the quelling glance of her mother. "Mademoiselle Verdant sounds so stuffy." She shrugged expressively, her shining copper-colored lips pursing distastefully and then she smiled again. "Hey, I like your dress!"

Stacey smiled, thanking her, and turned to her last two guests, Monsieur and Madame Carpentier, other business associates of André's. She extended her hand graciously and her smile froze.

Ben had come early after all. He stood just behind the Carpentiers, smiling lazily at her over their heads, looking very pleased with himself and very handsome and elegant in a black tuxedo.

"Magnifique!" Rivi whispered sotto voce, her bright eyes round with admiration. "That man, he is something serious, *oui?*" she said to no one in particular and grinned in open and very youthful provocation at the object of her admiration.

Stacey recovered herself quickly, thankful that although Ben might have understood—no, definitely understood from the look in his eyes—the first word of Rivi's praise he couldn't have understood it all.

"Do come in, Ben," she managed to say with commendable calm, despite the excited fluttering of her pulse. "I'd like you to meet the rest of my guests. This is Ben Oakes, everyone, my un—a relative from America," she said and introduced everyone in turn.

"And this," she said, tucking a hand in André's elbow and drawing him forward, "is André, my boss and very good friend." She smiled at André, putting a subtle emphasis on the word "friend." "Isn't that so, André?"

"*Oui*," agreed André, smiling back at her. He looked at Ben. "So you are Ben Oakes," he said consideringly in English, a little hardness creeping into his voice. "The man who has caused our Stacey so much—" he paused "—annoyance."

Stacey's eyes flew to Ben's face to see how he would take that. He smiled a hard-edged, dangerous smile.

"The very one," he agreed quite pleasantly except for the gleam in his eyes, "and likely to cause her even more—" he paused infinitesimally as André had done "—annoyance in the future."

Their eyes held for the briefest of moments, like two challenging male animals, intent on sizing each other up.

So this is Stacey's lover, Ben thought. He was a little old for her and not very loverlike in his attitude toward her. In fact, Ben decided, if she hadn't already told him about it, he'd have never guessed at the relationship between them. *If*, he thought suddenly, *there was a relationship—that kind of relationship—between them.*

André smiled then, a small smile of satisfaction, and he nodded once. "*Bien*," he said and extended his hand.

The hardness went out of Ben's eyes as he reached out to meet it. "Glad to make your acquaintance at last," he said. They shook, very much as if a silent deal had just been most agreeably concluded.

Stacey's eyes flickered back and forth between them, wondering what had just happened. It seemed as if they liked and even understood each other. And yet nothing had been said and only that very brief, almost hostile, look had passed between them before they shook hands.

She shrugged, a tiny, uneasy movement of her shoulders. "Let's all go into the living room, shall we?" she invited. She made a slight movement with her hand, unseen by anyone but Bernadine, who followed them into the softly lit gray-and-blue room with a tray of glasses and wine bottles in a silver cooler.

Comfortably settled, drinks in hand they began to converse about the usual things that people who don't really know each other well talk about: movies, books, the opera to be seen that night. Stacey noticed, without seeming to, that Ben and young Rivi Verdant weren't participating in the general conversation. Sitting side by side in a corner of the sofa, they were carrying on a semiprivate conversation of their own.

"I just love Americans!" Rivi was saying in delightfully accented English. "They are so different," she went on, her lashes fluttering up and down flirtatiously, blatantly inviting Ben to flirt back. "Are all Americans as big as you?" she asked.

"Only the ones from Texas," Ben drawled.

"Tex-sas," Rivi cooed. "Tell me about Tex-sas, *s'il vous plaît*. I have seen it on the television, oh, many times. Tell me about J.R. Is he really so mean?"

Stacey turned away, a delicate sneer on her lips as she tuned out his explanation about how the fictional J. R. Ewing and the rest of the Ewing clan as seen on the television series "Dallas" had no bearing on reality.

Jealousy stabbed at her vitals and she clenched her fingers around the champagne flute in her hand, appalled that she responded so . . . so viscerally to something that was really so basically innocent. After all, she told herself, Rivi might be flirting for all she was worth, but the only reaction she was getting from Ben was one of amused indulgence. And yet, it was all she could do not to leap across the room and scratch the eyes out of Mademoiselle Rivi's harmless, empty little head.

André made a comment then, about the time, and everyone rose, en masse, and wandered toward the dining room to sample the delicacies that had been prepared for them.

"I just love champagne!" Rivi sparkled up at Ben. "It so tickles my nose."

"Tell me," said André a few minutes later as he drew Ben into conversation. "What is it that you do in Texas?"

Stacey watched with growing apprehension as they talked, too far away for her to be able to hear what was said, too friendly for her to fool herself into thinking that they were acting like rivals for her favors.

And then, suddenly, it was time to leave for the opera. There was a flurry of fur coats and cheek kissing and André whispered in her ear. "I like your Ben," he said. "Mademoiselle Rivi was quite right. He is something very serious."

"He's not my Ben," Stacey started to protest, but André only smiled and put a finger to her lips, silencing her. And then he turned and shepherded his guests out the door.

Stacey stood for a moment, her hand on the doorknob, gathering the courage to go back into the living room and face Ben. The time had come to find out why he'd traveled all the way to Paris. She couldn't really

believe it was just to get her to sign some papers, whatever they were. There had to be more to it than that. But
she had no idea what it could possibly be. Well, she decided, whatever it was, she wanted it over as quickly
as possible.

13

BEN WAS WAITING for her when she returned to the living room. He'd removed his tuxedo jacket. Stacey could see it crumpled on the floor behind him, obviously fallen from the back of the chair where he'd carelessly flung it. His bow tie was undone, hanging loose around his neck, and the top few buttons of his pleated white dress shirt were unbuttoned. The pleats—narrow, discreet, stylish—seemed to emphasize the rampant masculinity of their wearer.

And how well he knows it, thought Stacey, forgetting or ignoring the fact that her own dress emphasized what was most female about her.

He extended a brimming tulip-shaped champagne glass toward her. "Come and sit down," he said easily when she took it. "Bernadine's fixed us a big plate of everything." He motioned toward the plate on the coffee table, laden with slices of cheese and pâté, wedges of ripe fruit and rounds of bread spread thickly with fresh, yellow butter.

Sitting, Stacey set her champagne flute on the coffee table and reached for the plate, layering a slice of rich pâté on a piece of buttered bread. She bit into it hungrily. "How did you ask her to do this?" she asked. "She speaks very little English and I know you don't speak French. Do you?" she tacked on suspiciously.

He shook his head. "I didn't have to ask," he said, spreading Camembert on a wedge of sweet, juicy pear. He grinned. "I guess I just looked hungry. Your Bernadine is a lot like Marta, always trying to feed somebody."

"How is Marta?" Stacey asked softly.

"She's fine." Ben bit into his pear and paused, swallowing. "Misses you a lot. She was hurt that you didn't say goodbye," he said carefully, watching Stacey. She'd been good and angry, too, accusing Ben of driving her precious *niña* away.

Stacey reached for her champagne glass just to have something to do. "I wrote to her and explained."

"Um-hmm," he said, his mouth full of food. "Explained what?"

Stacey's head came up at his tone. "Why I left, of course. What else would I explain? I said I loved her and would miss her, but that I just couldn't see myself living at Iron Oakes anymore." Her voice began to shake a little. Why was Ben questioning her like this? It was a sure bet that he'd seen her letter to Marta, so why this cross-examination? "I said that my life was here now and—"

"Did you tell her about André? That you were coming back to be with your lover?" He knew, now, that André wasn't her lover and never had been. She'd lied to him about that. It made him wonder what else she'd lied to him about.

"Well, not in those exact words," Stacey said. "But, yes, I told her about André." She paused and then looked up at him, defiance in her eyes as she stared into his. "Why are we going over this?" she asked, almost pleadingly. "I'm sure Marta showed you the letter. She always does. You already know what I told her."

Ben nodded. "But you lied," he said, pinning her into the corner of the sofa with the look in his eyes, laser hot as they bored into her. "And I'm just beginning to realize it."

"Lied?" she said indignantly, trying to quell him with an imperious lift of her head.

"Lied," he said flatly, inordinately pleased by the fact. He didn't usually like being lied to, but in this instance, it thrilled him. "André is no more your lover than Uncle Pete is," he stated matter-of-factly. "He's your boss and your good friend, like you said, but that's all."

"That's all *now*," she lied again, looking down into the champagne glass in her hand. She twisted it by the stem. She didn't know why all this seemed to be so important to him, why he even cared what her relationship with André was or was not. It didn't matter now. Iron Oakes was his.

"Not entirely." The words echoed in her mind, warning her of some unknown danger. Why not entirely? Why not...but the thought slipped away as she looked up and encountered the burning heat in his eyes.

He still wanted her, she realized, a shock of something like high-voltage electricity tingling along her nerve endings. Had he really come all this way just because he still wanted her, she wondered incredulously. And did he really think she'd fall into his arms because he had?

"The affair was over a few months ago," she said with a careless shrug, trying desperately to keep herself from doing just that. Because, heaven help her, she still wanted him, too. Wanted him with an intensity and a fire that had not, after all, turned to cold ashes. It had merely been banked somewhere deep within her and was now, ignited by his presence, threatening to explode and burn out of control. If he touched her, if she allowed him to reach her in any way, the flames would consume her completely. "And you know me. Off with the old, on with the new."

"Who?" he asked.

"What does it matter who?" She shifted away from him, reaching out to set her untouched champagne on the coffee table. "Besides, it's none of your business."

He reached and captured her hand. "I think you're lying again," he said softly.

She jerked her hand away, frightened by what his slightest touch did to her already churning insides, and stood up, moving out of his reach. "I don't care what you think," she said tersely, her back to him.

She heard him move, felt his hand on her shoulder and she whirled out of his reach again, facing him. "Don't touch me," she warned softly and then, "Oh, why don't you go back to the ranch where you belong and leave me alone! Just go home."

He reached out and grasped her shoulders, forcing her to stand still and face him. "Home?" he queried, encouraged by her unthinking reference to Iron Oakes as home. "Isn't this your home?"

No, she wanted to say, to scream. *No this isn't my home.* But she didn't. "You're hurting me," she said calmly.

His face paled at her softly spoken words, and a taut, strained line twisted his mouth in a self-directed grimace of disgust. "I'm sorry," he said, loosening his hold on her. "I always seem to be hurting you, one way or another."

"*Pardon, mademoiselle,*" said Bernadine hesitantly from the doorway. "I am ready to leave now. Is there anything further you or the *monsieur* wish before I go?"

"No nothing, thank you, Bernadine," she said, speaking in French as the maid had done. "You did a lovely job with the table. The flowers were beautiful."

"*Merci, mademoiselle.* If that is all then, *bonne nuit.*" She turned to go and then stopped short, catching sight of Ben's dinner jacket where it lay in a crumpled heap on the floor. Tsking softly, she moved forward to pick it up. As she did so something shiny fell out of one of the pockets. She stooped to pick it up. "*Mademoiselle,* it is the cigarette case you thought you had lost!" She crossed the room to hand it to Stacey. "How considerate of the handsome *monsieur* to bring it for you from America, *n'est-ce pas?*"

"Yes, very considerate," acknowledged Stacey softly.

There was a small, tense silence after Bernadine had gone. Stacey stood staring down at the cigarette case, turning it over and over in her slim fingers. "Where did you find it?" she said at last, her eyes still fixed on the gold case in her hands.

"On the table where you left it that first day."

Her eyes flew up to his, wide and questioning. "You had it all this time?"

He nodded slowly, holding her eyes with his, careful not to touch her in any other way. "It was in my breast pocket at the Cipango," he admitted. "I could have given it to you then, when you wanted a cigarette, but—" He lifted his big shoulders in a shrug, looking not the least bit French as he did it but totally, thoroughly American and male and very, very dear to her.

"Why?" she said softly, almost on a whisper as something fluttered in the region of her heart.

"It reminded me of you," he said and his hand reached out to her, softly touching her cheek in a brief, careful caress. "Slim and elegant and cool." His hand dropped. "I wanted something of you."

"I don't understand, Ben," she said, but she thought she was beginning to, a little. Maybe. Tentative hope surged through her. "Why would you want something of mine?"

He looked at her for a long, silent minute, debating his answer. A lie would be a sop to his pride, already bruised by chasing her to Paris and not having her fall into his arms on sight. The truth would get everything out in the open at last. It might also make him more miserable. But, hell, he thought, pride had already made him as miserable as he ever wanted to be. "Because I love you," he said, abruptly deciding to tell the truth. He had to say it to her, at least once.

"You love me?" she echoed, scarcely daring to believe that she'd heard him right. The wild fluttering of her heart became a hammer in her chest, threatening to choke off her breath. She stood silently, staring at him with wide, startled eyes.

He took her silence for disbelief or perhaps disgust. Turning away from her, he ran a hand through his black hair. "I've loved you since you were just a kid," he admitted raggedly, determined to lay it all out on the table now that he'd started. "Like a sister at first. The sweet, adoring little sister that I never had, offering the unconditional love that no one had ever given me before. And then, that summer I graduated from Tech and came back to Iron Oakes for good, you'd changed. My little sister was gone ... changed into a woman, and I couldn't make myself see you as a sister anymore. How I wanted you then! And how I hated myself for wanting you!" he grated through clenched teeth. "A little girl of fifteen and I could barely keep my hands off you!"

"I wanted you, too," Stacey said to his back.

"You only thought you did, which made it all the worse, all the harder for me to resist." He turned to look down into her face and his gaze was fiercely tender. "You weren't old enough to know what you wanted," he explained as his eyes roamed hungrily over her upraised face. "You were just a half-grown kid, eager to know what life was all about. Any man would have done." His hands clenched, the knuckles showing white. "And I couldn't stand that, either! That's why I got you sent away, you know, I couldn't—wouldn't—let myself be the one and I couldn't bear to stand by and watch it be somebody else."

"No," she breathed, her eyes reading and returning the hunger in his. "There was never anyone else, Ben. It was only you, then."

"And now?" he asked very, very softly. He felt as if his whole life depended on her answer.

Stacey scarcely paused to think about what she was saying. She, too, had had enough of false pride. It was a cold companion, and a poor substitute for the love she wanted and needed. "It's always been you," she answered him, her heart in her eyes. "All my life it's been

you. Even those eleven years when I...when I thought
you didn't want me and I tried to hate you for it, it was
still you, Ben." Her hands fluttered up between them.
"I can't seem to help it."

He reached for her hands, pulling her to him gently,
carefully, and she heard him sigh, a deep, ragged sound,
as his arms folded her to him. They stood like that for
a few, endless minutes, holding each other close, her
head against the muscled wall of his chest, his cheek
against her hair. They were content, for the moment,
just to hold each other.

In a little while, though, contentment alone wasn't
enough. She felt his lips against the top of her head and
his hands on her back began to move in small, caressing circles. She pulled a little away from his gentle embrace to look up into his face.

"Make love to me, Ben," she said softly. "Please. Before I die from wanting you."

She saw the flare of hungry passion in his face and,
more importantly, the love that was shining in his eyes,
as he silently bent and lifted her in his arms. Her own
curled around his neck.

"Which way?" he asked hoarsely. Silently, she
pointed the way to her bedroom.

He set her on her feet by the big four-poster bed, letting her body slide slowly down the hard length of his
as he did so. His hands came up and slowly, carefully,
his eyes never leaving her face, he took the gold butterfly from her hair and laid it on her bedside table. Then,
one by one, he removed the pins that held the heavy
blond coil in place. When all the pins were out, scattered carelessly on the carpet, he combed his hands

sensuously through the golden curtain of her hair, loosening and fluffing it around her face.

"Wildcat," he growled, low, his hands on either side of her face. "My wildcat."

"Yes," Stacey breathed, turning her lips into his hand as instinct had so often urged her to do. Her tongue came out to seductively tickle his palm. Ben groaned and his hands fell to her shoulders.

"How does this thing come off?" he demanded, a ragged note of impatient passion in his voice. He struggled to control it.

"Over my head," she instructed, raising her arms. "Just pull."

She stood docilely as he carefully pulled the velvet dress off over her head, watching in fascination as his eyes widened appreciatively and then narrowed in helpless desire as he devoured her scantily clad form. She was barely covered by the silk and lace of her wickedly sexy, seductively female undergarments. He looked around for somewhere to lay the fragile dress, but Stacey reached out, taking it from him, and dropped it carelessly to the floor.

And then she became the aggressor. Her slender fingers slowly unbuttoned his cuffs and then removed the studs from the front of his shirt, pressing tiny, teasing kisses along his furred chest as each new bit of skin was revealed. She pulled the shirttail from the waistband of his slacks and, boldly holding his eyes, lowered her hand to the buckle of his belt.

"Stacey," he breathed raggedly, pushed to his limit by her frank desire. "Stacey, honey, slow down." He reached for her hands, pulling them away from his starving body. He meant to go slowly this time. To love her slowly and tenderly, with the exquisite care she deserved.

But Stacey wouldn't let him. She pressed up against him, going up on tiptoe, and fused their mouths together. They clung—hot, wet and so very hungry for each other. Their tongues came seeking each other's sweetness, their teeth nibbled at each other's lips, their heads turned and twisted, searching out new angles, new pressures, new pleasures. Ben let go of her hands to wrap his arms around her pliant, willing body. Her hands went immediately to his belt buckle.

"Please," she whispered into his mouth. "Please, Ben." She lowered her hand a bit, touching him through the fabric of his slacks, and curled her fingers around the length and hardness of him. "I need you so much."

Ben moaned and pulled her down onto the bed. They feasted on each other—touching and stroking all the sweet, hidden places, their mouths still feeding passionately on the other as if neither could ever get enough. Ben broke away, finally, one hand coming up to curve against her cheek.

"This is just us," he said intently, staring into her eyes. "No memories of some other night. No crazy will, pushing us at each other. Just you and me. Here and now."

"Just us," she murmured. "Just us." Just the two of them, following the dictates of their yearning hearts.

He unhooked her bra, tossing it to the floor, and tenderly covered her bared breast with his right hand. "Tell me if I hurt you, honey," he said against her neck. "I don't want to hurt you, ever again."

"You can't hurt me, Ben. Not now," she said, meaning emotional, not physical, hurt. As far as she was concerned, he'd never hurt her physically. He didn't have it in him to hurt her physically. She touched his cheek, arching her back as she guided his mouth to her breast. "Not when I know you love me."

But he was determined to handle her gently just the same. Obeying her silent directions, he slid down her body and took her nipple into his mouth. Slowly, tenderly, he sucked on her, teasing the hardened peak until she was writhing beneath him. He ran his hand down her torso to where the white satin skin of her thigh was exposed between the hem of the lace-covered tap pants and the top of her stockings. Unerringly, his fingers slid up under the wide-legged panties, honing in on the shadowed delta between her legs.

She stiffened and arched higher, pushing her breast into his mouth. One hand clutched at his hair. "Oh, yes, Ben. Yes. Please," she murmured frantically. Her legs opened wider, the moist feminine core of her needing his touch, all of her eager for the completion of his love. Her hands urged him to cover her body with the weight and strength of his.

"Slow down, honey," he whispered, trying to hold himself back. His hand retreated to her thigh in an effort to cool both of them down. "Take it easy."

"No," she pouted. "I don't want to take it easy. I want you to take me." She ran her hands down the front of his body and opened the fly of his pants. "Now," she demanded, slipping her hand inside to caress him.

Ben groaned and fell back against the bed, helpless as a child under her caressing hands. "Stacey, honey, please…" He didn't know if he was begging her to stop or to go on.

But Stacey knew. She lifted her hips off the bed, sliding off her underpants so that she was clad in only her lacy black garter belt and stockings. Then she rose up on her knees and began to undress him.

She was beautiful, he thought, gazing up at her through passion-drugged eyes. She was female incarnate—feral, deliciously wanton, hungry, wanting, giving. Her face was flushed and eager, her eyes glowing, her lips parted and gleaming in the dim light streaming in through the open bedroom door. Her hair was in wild disarray. Her breasts were full and creamy, thrusting toward him, the pink nipples hard and pointed with desire. Her slim waist flowed into the alluring, palm-pleasing curve of her hips. The soft downy triangle of blond hair between her thighs was enticingly, excitingly, lasciviously framed by the black lace of her garter belt. Her long slim legs were encased in fantasy-inspiring sheer black stockings.

"Stacey, honey," he moaned again. He lay flat on his back in her frilly, feminine bed, his once pristine dress shirt off one arm and wrinkled under him, his pants down around his thighs. "You're killing me."

She lifted her head, her hands stilling against his engorged body. "Do you want me to stop?"

"No! No," he breathed. "I may be dying of pleasure, but I'm not crazy." He groaned as her hands continued their fevered caresses. "Not yet."

"You will be," she promised, stroking him. "We both will."

He reached for her then, his big hands closing over the curve of her hips. "Let's go crazy together," he whispered raggedly, lifting her over him.

Stacey complied eagerly. Swinging one leg across his supine body, she balanced one hand on his damp chest and reached between them to position him. She gasped when he entered her that first tiny bit, her body tensing in anticipation of the pleasure to come. She stilled, savoring the feeling for just a moment. Impatiently, Ben's hands tightened on her hips, and he pulled her down, hard, burying himself to the hilt in her moist receptive warmth. She cried out, nearly screaming his name with the intensity of the feelings that filled her.

He went stiff beneath her. "Stacey?" Had he hurt her again? Had he—?

But she was moving on him, rocking above him in mounting ecstasy. "Ben-Ben-Ben-Ben," she chanted. "Love me. Love me."

He hadn't hurt her, but still, he hesitated. Their first coupling had been so frenzied, so rushed and primitive, that he'd wanted this time to be different. He'd wanted to go slowly with her, to show her how much he loved her. He wanted to take the time to cherish her body and to show her he could be gentle. But she obviously didn't want that. And, truthfully, neither did he. There would be plenty of time for gentleness later. They had a whole lifetime of "laters" now.

He tightened his hands on her gyrating hips, his biceps bunching and coiling as he helped her lift and lower herself above him. Their bodies pulled tighter, straining toward each other, striving to give the ultimate pleasure to each other while taking it for themselves.

Stacey peaked first. Her body tensed into one long line, her spine arching, her head falling back as completion took her. Ben uttered a triumphant shout and let go of her hips to push himself upright. His arms went around her back, holding her quivering body tight. He took her mouth in a searing kiss and exploded into an ecstasy of his own.

They floated back down to the bed in a cloud of sensual, loving feelings, arms locked around each other, pressing kisses against cheeks and chins and foreheads. Two pairs of eyes gazed at each other, glazed with emotional tears and the satisfaction of a long-denied passion, finally fulfilled. Two pairs of lips smiled and whispered loving endearments. Two souls joined, exalting in contentment and joy and love. Two exhausted bodies snuggled underneath the rose-strewn comforter and fell asleep.

STACEY AWOKE, minutes or maybe hours later, and knew instinctively that she was alone. She shot to a sitting position in the big bed, her hand reaching out for the place where Ben should have been.

He's gone, she thought in sudden panic. *He's left me again!*

But no, his clothes were in a crumpled heap on the velvet-covered chair by the bed. He wouldn't have gone any farther than the front door of her apartment without his clothes, she told herself as sweet reason mercifully returned. She lay back on the pillows, sighing contentedly, to wait for him to return to her from

wherever he'd gone. Barely a moment later, she heard
a low, muffled curse and sat up again to see Ben's shape
silhouetted by the faint light shining in the foyer behind him.

"Ben," she called softly, reaching out to turn on the
silk-shaded lamp by the bed. It cast a warm, pink glow
over his naked body. "Are you okay?"

"Stubbed my toe," he mumbled and then held up an
opened bottle of champagne. "I got thirsty," he said
with a grin. "Here." He handed her two champagne
flutes, leaning over the bed to release the folded sheaf
of papers tucked under his arm. "Hold these while I get
in." He pulled back the covers, the champagne bottle
still held in one hand, and climbed into bed beside her.
Fluffing up the pillows behind him, he leaned back and
grinned at her happily. "Aren't you going to read
them?" he asked, indicating the folded papers in her lap.

"What is it?" she asked hesitantly, almost afraid to
touch them. He'd mentioned some papers he had for her
to sign. These, then, were them.

"Open it," he urged, grinning, as he took the champagne glasses from her.

Stacey shrugged and picked up the legal-size document. Very slowly, she unfolded it and began to read.
In a few minutes she looked up at him, her eyes wide.
"But, Ben," she said as if he didn't already know what
it contained, "this is a deed to Iron Oakes. To half of
Iron Oakes," she corrected herself. "In my name! I don't
understand. It's yours now. Henry's will—"

Ben plucked the papers from her fingers, replacing
them with a brimming glass of champagne. "After a
great deal of thought, I came to the considered opinion

that Henry wrote that clause with the sole intention of forcing you to stay on at Iron Oakes once you finally came back," he told her. "He never said anything, but I think he knew how I feel about you," he said gently. "I think he always knew. Or maybe Marta told him. And I think maybe he thought that if he got you to come back and stay for a while, then I would do the rest and keep you there for good."

"This is why you came all this way? To give me this?"

He nodded. "I thought if I came in person instead of mailing it that you might give me another chance."

"But—" Emotion clogged her voice.

He placed a gentle finger over her lips. "It's yours," he said firmly. "No matter what." He lifted his glass and clicked it against hers. "To us," he said, leaning over to kiss her softly before he drank.

"To us," Stacey agreed, staring at him over the rim of her glass. She couldn't believe it—the ranch and Ben, too, sitting here in her bed!

Propped up among the frilly white linens, with the champagne glass in his hand, he looked like some virile Arabian sheikh at leisure with his favorite concubine. The lacy comforter pulled up around his lean middle made his furred chest look harder and broader in contrast. The pink glow all around him from the bedside lamp and the silk bed hangings made his tanned face and hard-muscled arms look darker, and his hair blacker. Everything, in fact, that was masculine about him seemed more so set against the ultrafeminine surroundings of her bedroom.

"Oh, I do love you, Ben!" she burst out impulsively, suddenly giddy with happiness and love.

"Enough to marry me?" he asked. "No, wait," he held up his hand as she started to answer him. "Think about it, Stacey. Think hard. Do you love me enough to give up all this?" he said, making a motion with his glass that took in the room and her apartment with all its chic elegance and all the sophisticated people who went with that kind of environment. "Enough to come back to Texas with me? Back to that dusty little ranch and its dirty cattle and hick cowboys?" He tossed her words back at her. "This cowboy in particular?"

"Oh, Ben. I didn't mean that!" she cried. "You know I didn't mean any of it! I just said it because I was hurt and angry and so—" she hesitated and then plunged ahead "—so full of wounded pride that I couldn't see straight. I said the worst things I could think of to hurt you, too."

"Well, you did," he said seriously. "You nearly broke my heart clean in two."

"Oh, Ben. I'm sorry. I—"

He put a finger to her lips. "No, don't say it. We've both said and done a passel of things we're sorry for. Let's just forget them and start over from here, okay?"

"But, I—" There was so much she wanted to say. So much to apologize for and explain.

"Okay?" he said again.

Stacey nodded. "Okay." She pursed her lips against his finger in a fleeting kiss. "I love you so much," she whispered, turning her face up to his.

"I love you, too." He kissed her tenderly. "More than I can ever tell you."

She smiled dreamily and tilted her head to nuzzle his throat. Her mouth opened against his skin, tasting the salty-sweetness of him. She felt him shiver under the touch of her lips. "Try to tell me," she said as the fierce flame of love and desire flickered hotly through her veins, making her want him again. She kissed his neck and shoulders and whatever else she could reach while they were both holding champagne glasses. "Show me how much you love me."

Without a word, Ben turned, reaching sideways and slightly behind him to set his champagne glass on the nightstand.

On impulse Stacey tilted her own glass, spilling what was left of the icy contents over her bare breasts. It trickled coldly down her stomach, making her shiver, but Ben didn't seem to notice what she'd done. She giggled under her breath and handed him her glass to put on the nightstand next to his.

"Now," he said, turning back to take her into his arms again. "This time we're going to do it my way. Nice and slow and—Geez!" he yelped as his torso came into contact with her wet breasts and belly. "What's this?"

"My champagne. I spilled it," she explained, laughing softly, "all over me. It's sticky," she complained, glancing up at him from under her lashes, "and cold." She shivered delicately to emphasize her point.

Ben grinned wickedly and pushed her down into the pillows. "Poor baby is cold," he drawled, an expression of mock concern in his blue eyes as he bent his head and began to lick at the sticky wetness on her breasts. "I'll fix it," he said. "I'll make you nice and warm again." He lifted his head for a moment to look into her lambent eyes. His own were burning with love and passion and single-minded determination. "But it's going to take a long, slow time," he warned her. "And you're going to be on fire before I'm finished."

Stacey laughed in pure glee and pulled him down to her again. "Take as long as you want," she whispered. "I like the heat."

The black sheep had finally
returned to the fold!

THE BLACK SHEEP

Susan Fox

CHAPTER ONE

WILLA ROSS walked up the grassy incline, silently taking a spot just off to the side of the large group of mourners who had gathered for the graveside service. She didn't join her Aunt Tess and her cousin, Paige, the only ones seated beneath the emerald canopy that shaded the flower-draped casket; her estrangement from them and her late uncle, Calvin Harding, had been too traumatic and had lasted too long for her to believe she would have been welcome there.

So she remained where she was, the small ridge of sod she was standing on affording her a clear view of the minister and what remained of her family, her position there also making it easier for her to slip away later unnoticed.

From where he stood with the other pallbearers, Clayton Cantrell's dark gaze veered toward the movement at the edge of the crowd, catching sight of Willa the moment she stopped a few feet short of the other mourners. A shock wave of rage and grief rolled over him and settled like a rock in his middle as recognition pounded through him.

Slim, clad in a simple fawn-colored dress he suspected was a subtle indication that she didn't mourn too deeply for her Uncle Cal, Willa Ross looked little different from the mischievous minx she'd been as a teenager. Though her sandy-brown hair had been twisted into a prim knot that suggested maturity, her features were much the same delicate, pretty ones they'd been at seventeen. Five years had only enhanced the beauty she'd had back then.

The weight inside him began to twist. It was because of Willa Ross that his kid sister, Angela, had been denied the same chance to mature or grow to womanhood. Because of Willa Ross, little Angie lay just over the hill in a grave next to their parents'.

The bitterness he thought had eased over the years suddenly filled his heart and deepened the harsh grooves that bracketed his mouth.

"Shall we recite the Lord's Prayer?" the minister suggested, then bowed his head as he began, "'Our Father, Who art in Heaven...'"

Willa didn't bow her head as everyone else did, taking the opportunity as she repeated the words of the prayer softly to study her aunt. The past five years hadn't been kind to her Aunt Tess. Willa's green eyes welled with tears as she noted how frail and sickly the woman looked, her complexion lined and chalky, her hair shot through with gray. Aunt Tess's small hands were slightly gnarled now and lay trembling in a desolate clasp in her lap.

Willa would have given anything to be the one at her aunt's side, the one who consoled and offered strength, the one to share her sorrow. But Willa was the family outcast, unsure even now just how welcome her presence would be. She had been unable to stay away from this service, prepared to be satisfied with only a distant glimpse of the woman who'd raised her after her parents' deaths, yet miserable with the secret, gut-wrenching hope that the horrible rift between them could somehow miraculously be healed now that her Uncle Cal was dead.

"'And forgive us our sins as we forgive those who sin against us...'"

Clay Cantrell repeated the words by rote, without thought to their meaning, his hard black eyes fixed on Willa's face, callous to the heartsick curve of her soft mouth and the aura of melancholia about her.

As if Willa sensed his hostility, her gaze suddenly swung, then impacted with his.

Black eyes cold with dislike caused the words of the prayer to lodge in her throat. Abruptly silenced, Willa couldn't look away from that tanned, ruggedly handsome face with its strong, well-constructed contours and bold male cut of mouth, couldn't resist letting her eyes make a quick assessment of the tall, wide-shouldered, lean-hipped body that was nearly a foot taller than her own. Dark-haired, dressed entirely in black, from the Stetson he held in his hand to his suit and dress boots, Clay Cantrell was a towering, intimidating man—almost frightening—and nothing like the tolerant, indulgent older brother of her best friend she'd known him to be so long ago.

"Amen." The minister concluded the recitation, then led the mourners in a verse from what she recognized was one of Aunt Tess's favorite hymns. As Willa forced herself to focus on her aunt and avoid looking Clay's way again, she mouthed the words of the hymn, her chest suddenly too tight with pain for any sound to come out.

Coming here had been a mistake. One glimpse of Clay Cantrell's grim expression had convinced her of that.

It was at just the moment the minister began to make a few last remarks about Calvin Harding's passing that Aunt Tess turned her head and let her pained gaze sweep over the crowd. Taken by surprise, Willa didn't move those first few seconds. And then it was too late.

Tess Harding's glance connected with Willa's, and for a stunned moment, neither could react. Then, as if suddenly oblivious to the concluding service, Tess got unsteadily to her feet. A ripple of surprise rustled through the crowd as Tess laid her handbag on her chair. The minister hesitated, then hastily finished his last sentence, a frown of concern on his face as Tess started to walk away. Paige rose from her chair, clearly startled by her mother's behavior.

Willa felt as if she'd turned to stone, sick with apprehension as her aunt headed grimly toward her. By then, everyone else was turning to see who or what it was Tess was staring at so intently. All sound and movement halted as Willa was recognized.

It took every bit of strength Willa had just to stand there, teetering on the razor's edge of taut nerves as she waited for her aunt's rejection or acceptance. She had the horrifying sensation that the woman coming toward her so determinedly was someone she didn't know at all, and she tried valiantly to steel herself against certain rejection.

And then Tess's grim expression eased. Hope surged in Willa's heart as Tess's mouth curved into a watery smile. Just as Willa started forward to grasp her aunt's outstretched hands, Tess suddenly faltered, stopped, then collapsed onto the grass.

For the first few seconds no one but Willa moved; it was as if no one could believe his eyes. Distantly Willa heard her cousin shriek as she fell to her knees and searched at her aunt's wrist for a pulse. Terror beat a sickening cadence in her chest as she detected nothing. And then the chaos began.

"Someone get my medical bag!" Dr. Elliot came rushing over, then crouched to gently move Tess onto her back. The minister bustled to Willa's side and helped her to her feet. She watched helplessly as the doctor felt for a pulse, relieved when he appeared to find it. Already his station wagon was being driven off the cemetery lane toward them while one of the mourners came running ahead with his medical bag. In seconds he was alternately listening with his stethoscope and issuing orders.

Willa was startled by a strident feminine indictment.

"This is your fault."

Willa turned dazed eyes toward her cousin, Paige.

"Why did you have to show up?" the brunette demanded. "My God, if she dies..."

Clay Cantrell was at Paige's side instantly, his arm going around her consolingly.

"If she dies—" Paige repeated tremulously, unable to voice the threat as she turned her face and pressed it against Clay's chest, her heartrending sobs racking her slim frame and causing Clay to wrap her more tightly in his arms.

Over Paige's perfectly coiffed head, Clay's dark eyes were livid with accusation as they bore down on Willa. He quickly surveyed the large crowd of mourners comprised of ranching neighbors and townspeople. Their expressions echoed both the sympathy felt toward Paige and the harsh reproach directed toward Willa.

"I think you'd better clear out." Clay's deep voice rumbled threateningly and a muscle worked at his jaw.

Willa cast a worried glance at her aunt first, then was forced to step a little out of the way as a couple of men lifted a portable stretcher from the back of the doctor's station wagon.

"Please, Clay, make her go." Paige's plea was partly muffled against the lapel of Clay's suit jacket.

"Willa?" Clay's voice was a chilling menace.

Daring to hesitate, Willa tore her eyes from the warning in Clay's. "Will she be all right?" she asked the doctor as her aunt was lifted onto the stretcher.

"Don't know," he answered gruffly as he waited for the stretcher to be loaded into the back of his car. Willa was dismissed with a curt turn of his head. "Would you like to ride along, Paige?" the doctor asked her cousin solicitously.

Willa stepped back as Dr. Elliot brushed past her to escort Paige to the front passenger seat of the car. In moments, the doctor was in the back with his patient, while a volunteer drove the big vehicle over the unbroken sod to the lane, then on toward the highway and town.

Wanting to follow, Willa hurried across the grass toward where she had double-parked her car earlier. She had almost reached it, when she heard the long stride of booted feet behind her. Sensing instantly who it was, she tried to increase her pace, but steellike fingers caught her arm and swung her roughly around.

Wary green eyes flew upward to meet the black intensity of Clay's, not surprised by the flat, unfriendly depths.

"What the hell are you doing here?"

Willa tried to pull out of his grip but couldn't. "Paying my last respects," she answered, her voice bearing the faintest hint of insolence.

And that insolence riled him. Clay released her arm, aware that the dark feelings she aroused made him capable of bruising her.

"The funeral's over, so you can move on," he advised.

"I'm going to the hospital," she said, her slim body rigid with defiance.

"No one wants you there."

Clay felt something inside him soften at the anguish that flickered over her face before she could mask it. That Willa had suffered these past years was apparent to him, now that he could see the haunting evidence of it in her eyes.

But suffering and sadness were things he didn't want to see, changes he didn't want to acknowledge. This girl's actions had taken his sister's life and he'd be damned if he'd let himself feel sorry for her.

"Go back to wherever it is you came from. There's nothing for you here," he said, the harshness in his voice a denial of the compassion that had tugged at him those few moments.

"I want to make certain Aunt Tess is all right."

"I think you've done enough."

Clay's words robbed her of breath as his implication hit her squarely in the chest. *He blamed her for this, too.* The realization was staggering, but somehow she managed to withstand the pain and return his condemning stare. It was hard to believe that this man's affection for his sister had once extended to her.

Willa turned and walked the last steps to the car. She was just about to reach for the door handle, when Clay reached around her and opened it for her.

"Don't go to the hospital, Willa. You'll just upset everyone again and stir up the past."

"Maybe it needs to be stirred up," she challenged quietly, turning her head to look up at his iron expression.

"She's a sick woman, Willa. If you want another death on your conscience, then go on over to that hospital," he prodded, and Willa's face went ashen.

Without another word, she got into her car, not even looking Clay's way when he closed the door beside her. Fumbling in her purse for the key, she jammed it into the ignition and gave it a twist. As she drove away, she cast a last glance in the rearview mirror at the tall dark-haired man dressed in black who watched her go.

WILLA STEPPED OUT of the service station rest room, changed from her dress, stockings and heels into a plaid shirt, jeans and her well-worn western boots. Her dark blond hair had been released from confinement and tumbled freely just past her shoulders.

She went directly to her car, passing up a last opportunity for a quick meal at the truck-stop diner next door. She wasn't fit to be seen after the storm of heartbroken tears that had left her eyes puffy and red with bruiselike shadows beneath them. The few cosmetics she carried in her purse had covered over some of the evidence, but not enough for her to feel comfortable in public.

She quickly tossed her things into the small suitcase in the trunk. Next to it, the larger case she'd filled with enough clothes to last a week mocked her. She'd had such hope when she'd packed it. Now she knew those hopes were gone. There was truly no going back. Even if she could, there would be no way to expose the horrible lies of the past without further jeopardizing her aunt's health. Judging from the hostility shown her by everyone at the funeral, no one would believe her now any more than they had then. The realization depressed her.

She'd not gone to the hospital, after all, too frightened that Clay was right. She couldn't bear to have another life on her conscience. Feeling responsible for her best friend's death when they were both seventeen was bad enough.

Willa slammed the trunk closed the instant the old memory stirred, determined to keep it suppressed. She'd learned never to let it totally surface, though it often haunted her dreams and made her nights long, restless ordeals.

The late-model car started easily, as it always did, and Willa slipped it into gear, heading out of the gas station for the interstate to continue her long drive home. She was still only about fifty miles from Cascade. Fifty miles from her real home, came the thought before Willa pushed it away.

These days, home was the D & R, a little ranch over two hundred miles from Cascade, Wyoming, just northeast of Colorado Springs, Colorado, and had been for the past three years. She was part-owner of a modest ranch where she and her partner, Ivy Dayton, raised quarter horses. Willa ran the ranch and helped train the horses, while Ivy saw to their breeding and took them to horse shows. Willa had sunk a major portion of the money she'd inherited from her parents into her half of the ranch. It had been a prosperous investment for her, and one that had demanded long, tiring hours—just what Willa had needed—until Ivy sent word from a horse show in Wyoming that she'd read Calvin Harding's obituary. Willa knew she had to attend at least some part of his funeral.

It was Uncle Cal who had banished Willa from their home the day she turned eighteen, warning her never to come back. Although Aunt Tess had tearfully begged him to reconsider, in the end she had submitted to his edict. Willa had been on her own from then on.

Remembering Tess's reluctance to throw her out had inspired the crazy idea that perhaps she and her aunt could be reconciled now that her uncle was no longer alive to prevent it. She knew now that it just wasn't to be.

At the next interchange, a state patrol car came down the ramp, merging into the lane a few car lengths behind her. Willa automatically glanced at her speedometer and continued on, confident she was obeying the speed limit.

Startled by the patrol car's siren a few moments later, she checked her rearview mirror to see the cruiser bearing down on her, red lights flashing. Willa pulled onto the shoulder as quickly and safely as possible, fully expecting the patrolman to drive on past since she hadn't been violating any traffic law. To her surprise, he pulled up behind her, then got out of his car to approach hers.

Tension knotted painfully in her stomach as she recalled the other time she'd had to deal with a lawman. She'd never got over it. To this day she felt intimidated by police officers, frightened to attract their attention in any way, frightened that her word wouldn't be believed and she'd again be subjected to another traumatic questioning.

Seeing the patrolman beside the car, Willa hastily rolled down her window.

"Evening, miss. Would your name happen to be Willa Ross?"

Though the patrolman was a model of courtesy and respect, Willa felt a sharp tingle of apprehension. She nodded.

"Well, Miss Ross, I'm sorry to relate to you that it seems you have a family emergency back in Cascade. They've requested that we try to locate you and provide you with an escort back as soon as possible."

Willa's chest went tight. Suddenly she feared the worst. "Do you know any of the details?" she got out around a tongue thick with emotion. Her aunt had died; she just knew it.

The patrolman shook his head. "No, miss, I'm afraid I don't, but I was under the impression they were in a big hurry for you to get back there. Thought you might have been across the state line by now. Lucky you aren't, since it'll take that much less time for you to get back."

Willa was having a difficult time keeping back her tears. If the patrolman felt there was reason to hurry, it might mean her aunt was still alive. The request for Willa's presence would have had to be her aunt's idea—and one Paige would never have stood for unless it had been a deathbed request.

"Are you all right, miss?"

"I'll be all right," she assured the officer.

"You sure?" The patrolman's concern for her was genuine, and she felt herself relax. She could see compassion in his warm brown gaze and wondered why the sheriff who'd confronted her five years earlier hadn't possessed even an ounce of this officer's humanity.

"I'll be fine. You mentioned an escort?"

"That I did," he said with a smile, which she found herself returning. "If you'll follow me, Miss Ross, we'll get started."

They were back on the interstate in moments and, after making use of a turnaround for emergency vehicles, they were headed north toward Cascade.

"Thank you so much, Officer," Willa said once they'd reached the hospital and she got out of her car. The patrolman had left his cruiser idling just a few feet away to come over and speak to her.

"My pleasure, Miss Ross," he returned with a smile. "Good luck." Willa nodded her acceptance, then hurried on in to the emergency entrance. Discovering that her aunt had been taken to the cardiac care unit, she went directly to the elevators.

She'd pressed the button for the third floor before she allowed herself to again consider why her "family" had asked the highway patrol to summon her back to Cascade. Her aunt was evidently not expected to live. A crush of guilt came down on her. If she'd not attended the funeral and given her aunt a shock, Tess wouldn't be lying in the CCU about to die. Willa looked down at her clenched hands. She didn't know how she could bear the responsibility for a death a second time.

The elevator doors slid open and Willa stepped out, going directly to the nurses' station, where she was directed to the wing that housed the CCU. Willa did her best to harden herself to the reception she knew was waiting, realizing the moment she stepped into the crowded waiting room that she wouldn't have the strength to develop that kind of hard veneer. The most she could manage was to mask her feelings and project the illusion of toughness.

It was one of her aunt's closest friends, Mabel Asner, who first saw her and announced, "Well, now, here's Willa Ross." The small, plump woman fixed a critical eye on Willa's blue plaid shirt and jeans. The quiet conversations in the small room ceased. There wasn't a face in the room that offered any kind of welcome, and more than one gaze went directly to Clay Cantrell, as if to gauge his reaction to her arrival.

Clay's flinty expression revealed nothing as he stood leaning against the far wall, his suit coat, tie and vest discarded, his crisp white shirt partially unbuttoned. Diamond-hard eyes went over Willa from head to toe, their cold scrutiny sending a chill through her.

Next to him Paige sat staring at her accusingly, and Willa felt the old anger rise and swell. The enmity between the two cousins was too strong to go undetected. There wasn't a person in the small room who didn't feel it—or misjudge its reason. As it always had been, Paige was everyone's darling, her long jet hair, violet eyes and satiny perfect skin enchanting them all. Unfortunately the high regard everyone had for Tess caused them to believe Paige possessed the same fine qualities of gentleness and good character her mother did. Few other than Willa and Paige herself knew the truth of that.

Willa took a quick breath and started across the room to her cousin. "How is she?" Willa asked, already knowing what kind of response her question would get.

"Dr. Elliot says she's stabilized. No thanks to you," Paige added.

"I'm surprised you went to all the trouble of having the state patrol track me down."

Paige's eyes were half-lidded with contempt. "Mother was asking for you. The doctor thought it wise to cater to her, or you wouldn't be here. I wouldn't have let you get within a hundred miles of her a second time," Paige vowed, and by the whispering that went on in the room behind Willa she knew most felt the same way. Tess was a well-liked woman, and in view of the recent death of her husband, her friends would naturally feel very protective of her. Willa felt hurt that anyone would think her aunt had to be protected from her.

"When can I see her?"

"If she doesn't mention you when she wakes up again, then never."

Willa felt her face go bloodless. It was no less than she should have expected. Perhaps the delicate lines of strain on her cousin's lovely face were there more out of fear for herself than grief for her late father or worry for her mother's life. Only Willa knew what secrets Paige concealed beneath the cruelty and scorn she showed her. She could easily imagine Paige's eagerness to have her out of their lives again and away from Cascade forever.

"Paige." Dr. Elliot stood in the doorway, beckoning her into the privacy of the hall. Paige rose gracefully and glanced back beseechingly at Clay, who then escorted her out. Willa was left standing awkwardly in the waiting room, staring after them. Anxiously she watched for any sign that the doctor was delivering bad news, relieved when Paige's face darkened in anger rather than agony.

"You'd better step out here, too," the doctor called to Willa from the hall, the stern way he looked and spoke to her making his disapproval evident.

Willa hurried to comply, her heart racing. Just as she reached the small group, Paige made a little sound of despair, then pulled her arm from Clay's to rush down the hall to the nearest rest room. Mabel Asner rose immediately to go after Paige and offer consolation. And probably, Willa thought unkindly, to be the first to glean whatever grist for gossip she could.

"You can step in for five minutes, Willa, not a moment more," Doc Elliot cautioned, then warned, "She can't take any kind of upset right now, so don't you give her any."

"I wouldn't," Willa said, stung at his tone.

"Your presence alone might do it," he pronounced. "If it even looks like this is too much for her, I want you out of there. I won't care how much Tess says she wants to see you, I'll forbid it. Understand?"

Willa's cheeks reddened. She was outraged at being spoken to in such a manner. Her green eyes were flashing. "I understand completely." She clenched her teeth on a more scathing retort, mindful of the fact that she had another chance with her aunt because it was this man's professional opinion that Tess ought to have her wish.

"All right," he said reluctantly, watching her closely. "Tell one of the nurses outside the unit who you are before you go in."

Willa turned and walked toward the end of the corridor to the short hall that led to the CCU. She tried to ignore the booted steps that shadowed hers as Clay fell in beside her. He didn't say a word to her until she stopped to speak to the nurse.

"I'll be watching, Willa."

Willa's eyes flew to his, his quiet warning telling her plainly just how great the chasm of hostility and mistrust between them was.

"You do that, Clay," she murmured as he took a position in front of the observation window, his masculine stance bearing the cold, unrelenting arrogance of an enemy.

CHAPTER TWO

WILLA ENTERED the cardiac unit, hesitating just inside the door as the enormity of it all struck her. Aunt Tess was lying in one of four beds, and Willa's heart ached at the number of wires and tubes connected to her frail body. The constant click, whir and blip of the life-monitoring equipment in the room emphasized how gravely ill each patient was. As she approached Tess's bed, she was suddenly terrified that her visit would be too much for her aunt.

Willa glanced back anxiously at the nurse who had accompanied her and who was now standing at the foot of Tess's bed. The nurse nodded her encouragement and Willa reached out hesitantly to touch her aunt's thin hand.

"I'm here, Aunt Tess."

Tess's eyes fluttered a moment before opening fully and finding Willa.

"Willa." Tess mouthed her name more than spoke it, clearly weak. Her dove-gray eyes were soft, and her pale lips twitched with the extra effort it took to smile. Willa's heart was wrung mercilessly and she gently pressed her aunt's hand between both of hers. "Missed you so," she whispered, and Willa felt the sharp sting of tears.

"I've missed you, too, Auntie." Willa's voice wobbled as she rubbed the back of her aunt's hand.

"Please...stay," Tess said. "I want you with me."

"I will," Willa vowed, distressed when her aunt's eyes fell shut. She was willing to promise her anything if it would keep her alive and make her well.

Tess opened her eyes again. "Kept your room...just the way it was." She blinked as if her eyelids were heavy weights, then appeared to rest a moment. "I want you to come home."

Willa's eyes clogged with more tears. Going back to the Circle H ranch was impossible now, but there was no reason for her aunt to know that just yet. Since she and Tess had had no contact with each other the past five years, Tess didn't know about the life she'd made for herself in Colorado.

The nurse stepped forward and touched Willa's shoulder, signaling her it was time to leave. It was obvious Tess was already too spent to talk longer.

"I have to leave now, Aunt Tess," Willa said, leaning down to kiss her aunt's cheek. "Get a good night's rest. I'll be back in the morning."

Tess's eyes closed a last time and she drifted off into exhausted slumber. Willa tenderly released her hand and backed away from the bed. She was shaking and her eyes were blurred as she followed the nurse from the unit.

"A lot of it's the medication she's on," the nurse explained reassuringly when she saw Willa's flushed face.

"Will she live?" Willa had to ask the question.

"She's stable. The next forty-eight hours will tell." The nurse glanced back at Tess. "She was sure determined to see you."

Willa was too emotional to respond to the nurse's comment or linger. She hurriedly stepped into the hall as the tears began. Unfortunately Clay was still waiting, and she made a swift effort to control herself. What she felt was too deep and too personal to be witnessed by a man who held such ill will toward her.

"What did she say?"

"I'm surprised you don't read lips," Willa hedged as she started to walk away from him. Blindly she fumbled through her purse for Kleenex, hoping to stem the fountain of threatening tears by blowing her nose. She stopped just before she reached the doorway into the main hall, unable to suppress a sob of frustration when she discovered that all she had left was a single shredded tissue.

"Here." Clay's gruff voice drew her attention to the spotless white handkerchief he pressed into her fingers.

"Thanks." Willa turned away from him, her back rigid. She used the hankie to muffle her sudden attack of sniffles.

Clay watched, detecting the tremors that went through her small body, irritated that he couldn't be indifferent to her feelings. But, then, something about Willa had always affected him, even when she'd been a child. Clay's mouth formed a bitter line as his dark gaze wandered down her slim back to her shapely backside and her jeans-clad legs. Something else about

Willa was affecting him now, and he was damn sure he wanted no part of it.

Willa quickly blotted her eyes, acutely aware of Clay's impatience. "I'll see that you get your hankie back," she said as she stuffed it in her bag, then stepped into the main hall to leave. Clay's voice stopped her.

"You got a place to stay?"

Willa looked up at Clay, surprised. "The motel I stayed at last night may still have a vacancy."

"Good." He nodded, clearly satisfied with her answer. Willa suddenly understood.

"Don't worry, Clay. I wouldn't think of imposing on my cousin."

"Just so you don't get it in your head to take advantage of either her or Tess," he said, his hard gaze pinning hers. "They're both too vulnerable right now."

Willa felt a spurt of anger. "So you're their self-appointed protector," she concluded mockingly, her lips twisting. "If I were you, I'd mind my own business."

Clay's eyes glittered. "You are my business," he growled. "And until you leave town permanently, I plan to keep an eye on you."

"I'm sure Paige will have something to say about that," Willa retorted, having already guessed Paige and Clay were either involved or about to be. The thought galled her.

"You're the last woman Paige needs to be jealous of."

Willa gave him a wry smile. "Paige won't be jealous, Clay. She'll be worried."

Willa's implication lay heavily in the sudden silence between them. Clay's dark gaze was livid with rage and a muscle worked wildly in his jaw as he glared down at her.

"You aren't a seventeen-year-old kid this time, Willa," he said in a low, burning voice. "This time you'll pay for anything you do. I'll see to it."

Willa's eyes were overbright as the bitterness and sense of betrayal that had festered inside her for five years surged to the surface. "Just make sure you've got all the facts," she said, then added pointedly, "this time."

Willa turned and walked briskly down the hall to the elevators, her heart little more than a throbbing wound in her chest.

The pain hadn't subsided by the time she'd ordered a take-out sandwich at the café down the street from the hospital, then made her way back to the small road-side motel at the edge of town.

Bleakly she stared at the cold, deli-style sandwich, unable to eat more than a couple of bites. The hot coffee tasted good, its warmth taking the edge off her raw feelings, but nothing could quite deaden the twisting sense of betrayal that churned within her.

It was a good thing, she realized now, that she'd repressed much of the devastation she'd experienced after Angie's death when Clay had turned against her. She wouldn't have been able to bear up half so well these past years if she hadn't. It had been bad enough that Uncle Cal had automatically sided with Paige, unable to believe that his precious daughter was anything less than perfect; when most of the friends Willa thought she and her cousin shared had taken Paige's side, she'd been crushed.

But when Clay joined the rest, choosing to believe Paige instead of her, that had been the final blow. Surely he'd known her better than that, she thought despairingly.

Clay's defection had been a betrayal of her trust and deep affection for him. In the more than seven years she and Angie had been best friends—and almost inseparable—she'd never once lied to Clay. Oh, she and Angie had both been a handful, their good-humored pranks often directed toward him, but he'd treated her like a second little sister. Willa had idolized him.

When Angie was killed and Willa was blamed for her death, she'd lost everyone she loved, including Clay. The compounded grief had been almost more than she could bear.

Willa rose suddenly from her chair, wadding the sandwich into its wrapper before flinging it into the trash.

"What does it matter, anyway?" she demanded of herself aloud as she savagely raked her trembling fingers through her hair. Though she hadn't caused Angie's death, she hadn't been able to save her life, either. The horror of that truth would haunt her for the rest of her life.

"YOU'RE LOOKING MUCH BETTER today, Aunt Tess," Willa offered quietly, all too aware of Paige's sullen presence at the other side of the bed.

A week had gone by since the funeral, a week since her aunt had first been admitted to the hospital. Today was her second day out of the Cardiac Care Unit and in her own private room. The doctor had assured them all that in spite of the fact that Tess's recovery would be slower than normal due to her grief over her husband's death, she was doing well, and Willa's relief knew no bounds.

On the other hand, now that Tess was recovering, Willa would have to think about leaving soon. And judging by the killing looks Paige flashed her every now and then, soon was not nearly quick enough.

"I'm feeling much, much better, Willa," Tess said, her eyes twinkling fondly as she gazed at her niece. "Having you back has been like a tonic."

Willa shoved her hands into her jeans pockets, suddenly nervous. Every time she had been allowed into the CCU to visit her aunt, Tess had talked as if Willa were back in Cascade for good. Willa's gentle hints to the contrary were always met by such confusion and distress that she feared she might be adversely affecting her aunt's health. Was now a good time to reintroduce the idea that she would soon have to head back to Colorado?

"I've got a woman coming in today to do your hair for you, Mother," Paige interjected before either of them could speak again. "Think how good it will feel to have it washed and done up."

"You already mentioned it, Paige," Tess said, her eyes never leaving Willa's. "Right now, I want to talk to Willa about the ranch before I run out of steam."

Paige's face paled. "Please, Mother, don't."

Tess glanced over at her daughter and Willa witnessed a stubbornness she'd not known her aunt to be capable of. Willa was intrigued.

"We went over this last night, Paige, and I don't want to rehash any of it. In another week, you'll be going on a new assignment for that modeling agency and I'll be stuck here without anyone to keep an eye on things. From what Willa's told me about the place she's working, she'd be perfect for the job." Tess turned her head and looked at Willa, catching the surprise on Willa's face as the true meaning of the words dawned on her.

While Tess had asked a number of questions about Willa's life and what she was doing now, her questions had been more specifically about Willa's abilities. The way people in Cascade seemed to feel about her, Willa hadn't been comfortable confiding all the details of her life to anyone, not even her aunt. And now, with Paige hovering in the room, Willa was not about to mention that she was half-owner of the D & R Ranch.

"I need your help, Willa," Tess began earnestly, her eyes searching hers. "Ever since Cal took sick four years back, the ranch hasn't been doing very well. We had to let go of all but two of the hands. One quit a few weeks ago. The other—" Tess shook her head "—has a problem with liquor. He says he only does his drinking in the bunkhouse or in town, but he's come in for a meal plenty of times smelling of whiskey. Of course, even if he was sober I don't think he could handle things," Tess added.

Willa somehow had to forestall the question she sensed Tess was leading up to. She opened her mouth to decline, but the pained entreaty in her aunt's eyes stopped her.

"I need someone to take over for me or I'll lose everything. Cal worked so hard for that ranch. I can't lose it now." Her soft gray eyes grew misty. "I know you've got hard feelings against Cal, but it would mean an awful lot to me if you'd stay on and help out."

"Mother," Paige murmured crossly, "we don't need her."

"I need her," Tess said firmly, the mistiness fading as she overruled her daughter.

Willa couldn't believe what she was hearing. Never mind the fact that her aunt had grown a bit more assertive over the years; she was not only asking Willa to stay, but to take on a job even an experienced rancher would find a challenge. It was hard enough these days to turn a profit in ranching, but to be asked to stabilize a ranch that was in trouble was an undertaking that Willa wasn't sure she was any match for.

The D & R was about the same size operation as the Harding ranch and she'd managed that, but if the Circle H was too far gone, she wasn't certain good management was enough to bring it back. She and Ivy had started out breaking even and had been careful to avoid most of the pitfalls that might have put them under a crippling debt load. Staying profitable was much, much easier than forcing a losing operation to pay. Besides, she and Ivy had always worked as a team. This time she'd be on her own. Her first instinct was to decline her aunt's request.

"I don't think I'm the person for the job, Auntie," Willa said, wanting to let her aunt down gently.

"I can't think of anyone better," Tess countered. "And you'd be home, Willa. That's something I've wanted since the day Cal sent you away."

"I'm not sure I could handle it," Willa admitted. "If the Circle H is in too much trouble, I might not be able to help you hang on to it, anyway. You need someone with a lot more experience than I have." Even if she took the job there was no guarantee that she would be able to save the failing ranch. If it failed, anyway, after she took over, she knew she'd automatically be blamed. Willa didn't want to be assigned that kind of responsibility.

"Paige has offered to put some of her money into it, at least to take care of wages and repairs. That should help a lot. But she—"

"I offered to put a sizable amount of money into the ranch if you could find a competent foreman," Paige corrected. "I'm not at all convinced that Willa's competent. What does a female hired hand know about managing a ranch? Besides, you said she works with horses. Ours is a cattle operation. It's a job for a man."

"You know better than that, Paige," Tess chided, shaking her head. "You know I'm not much on this women's lib stuff, but I don't see any sense in a woman holding back from a man's job if it's what she wants and she can do it. Besides, Willa was working alongside your father and his hired men when you were still playing with dolls. If there's something she doesn't know about ranching, it's not much.''

Tess's outspoken confidence brought a lump to Willa's throat.

''All right then, Mother,'' Paige said, tossing her dark mane of hair defiantly, ''I'll make it clearer. I don't want Willa here.''

The fatigue that had gradually crept over Aunt Tess's face was suddenly dispelled, and her soft eyes went stern. ''Your father was wrong to send Willa away, Paige. There wasn't a day went by that I didn't regret letting him have his way. Now that she's back—'' Tess turned to Willa, her gaze growing warm as she put out her hand and grasped Willa's ''—I'm determined to find some way to keep her here.''

Willa's lips moved into a tremulous smile as she squeezed her aunt's hand.

''Please, Willa,'' Tess coaxed. ''At least go out to the ranch and look things over.''

Willa's eyes shied from the hopeful look on her aunt's face. ''Even if I said yes, what about Clay Cantrell?''

''Yes, Mother,'' Paige stepped in eagerly. ''What about Clay? How do you think he'd feel with Willa around—as a reminder?''

Willa stiffened and flashed a look across the bed, unable to keep from glaring at her cousin. Her cheeks took on a dull flush as she saw the smug look on Paige's expertly made-up face. Suddenly, more than anything, Willa wanted to make that smug look disappear.

"All right, Auntie," she heard herself say. Her eyes came back to catch the excited look in her aunt's. "I'll go out and take a look at the Circle H. But before I decide, I want to talk to Clay."

The lines of age and stress on her aunt's face relaxed. "I'll give him a call."

"No, Aunt Tess," Willa said firmly. "If I decide to stay, Clay and I will have to get along without a go-between. I'll talk to him."

"All right, Willa. Handle it your way. I trust you."

Willa suddenly felt uncomfortable with her aunt's overstated confidence in her, wary of what she expected. "I want you to understand that this arrangement won't be permanent." Willa's heart sank as she saw that her caution had no dampening effect on her aunt's enthusiasm. It was as if Tess were ignoring any words she didn't want to hear. Willa had to make it clearer.

"I'll only fill in until things get straightened out and I can find a good foreman for you."

Aunt Tess's brow wrinkled only slightly at Willa's words. "We'll work something out," she said as she leaned back against her pillows, her strength waning.

Neither saw the look of fear that crossed Paige's lovely features.

CLAY CANTRELL'S Orion Ranch lay just to the south of the much smaller Circle H. Willa could have taken a horse and ridden to the house in a bit more than half the time it would take her to drive her car from the Circle H ranch house to the highway, then over to the

Orion Ranch, but the days when little formality was observed had died with Angie.

Willa knew she wouldn't be welcome at Orion, though just how unwelcome remained to be seen. At the moment, she was too furious to care.

She was worn out and discouraged, angry over the condition of the Circle H. She'd driven out to the ranch as her aunt had asked, and was truly shocked by the run-down appearance of the house and buildings. Everything could stand a fresh coat of paint and easily half the corrals near the barn were becoming overgrown with weeds. Old wind damage done to the barn roof had not been repaired and the resulting leak had produced several moldy bales of hay in the loft.

Signs of waste and laziness were everywhere, from the sloppy storage of hay and feed to the poorly kept stalls in the barn that hadn't been mucked out properly for weeks. The stench had been overpowering.

Then she'd met Art Boles, the Circle H's hired hand, and had been outraged at both his drunken state and his bad manners. He'd refused to cooperate with her, the insolence in his gaze challenging her right to any information. The few answers he'd supplied to her many questions had been evasive at best. Willa had finally selected and saddled a horse, then ridden out alone to look over as much of the ranch as possible that afternoon.

There wasn't a fence on the place that didn't need some kind of repair. Cattle that should have been accustomed to being worked were as wild as deer and almost as elusive. Willa's outrage mounted when she caught sight of at least three unbranded calves that, judging from their sizes, had been born well before spring roundup and therefore, should already have been carrying the Circle H brand.

When she'd at last returned to the barn and asked Art Boles to see to her horse, he'd grudgingly done so, while she headed for the machine shed to look over the equipment. At least everything there had seemed in good shape. Until she'd got to the tractor and discovered parts of its engine had been disassembled—ostensibly to make a repair—then been left lying on a bench nearby.

In a matter of days, the hay pasture would need to be cut and baled, but the tractor was out of commission and apparently had been for quite some time. If this was more of Art Boles's handiwork, there was no telling whether the tractor would ever be serviceable again.

Willa had stomped over to the bunkhouse in a fine fury. This time Boles was defensive, his manner bordering on belligerence.

"Too much work for one man," he'd grumbled. "And what the hell gives you the right to come snoopin' around here, anyway? Who did you say you was?"

Willa hadn't been taken in by his sudden bout of amnesia. "We discussed who I was and why I was here hours ago, Mr. Boles. What we haven't discussed is what you've been doing to earn your wages."

Art Boles had drawn himself up and blustered, "I don't have to answer to you."

Willa had nodded in agreement, her mouth set in a sour slash. "That may change, Mr. Boles. If it does, I

can assure you that you won't have to answer to me
long, since you'll be out of a job." Not trusting herself to keep from ordering him off the Circle H at that
very moment, Willa had turned and gone to her car.
It sickened her to think that Art Boles had been col-
lecting the wages Tess had been hard put to pay, while
he'd given very little work in exchange.

Willa was reminded of Clay's eagerness to make
sure she didn't take advantage of her aunt. He'd
threatened to keep a close eye on her, when all the time
he'd overlooked what Art Boles had been doing. Willa
made up her mind to point that out to him if he objected too strongly to her staying on at the Circle H.

Because she was going to stay, she'd decided. Tess
did need her help, if for nothing more than to fire Art
Boles and hire her a competent foreman and one or
two conscientious ranch hands. Surely Clay could bear
to put up with her presence in his part of the country
for a few weeks. She had little doubt that Ivy could
manage the D & R without her for a while, since their
foreman, Deke Bailey, could easily fill in for Willa.

Too soon she reached the turnoff and in less time
than she remembered, she was braking to a stop in
front of the Cantrell ranch house.

Designed to harmonize with the natural terrain, the
house was built from trees grown on the ranch itself,
the long, thick logs giving the sprawling single-story
structure a formidable ruggedness and a feeling of
permanence.

Willa had spent a lot of time in that house and on
this ranch. She and Angie had been fast friends, the
fact that they were the same age and had both been

orphaned linking them together in a very special way. Bright, enthusiastic, irrepressible, they'd both been a challenge for Clay, who seemed to be the only one who could tolerate their antics for long. Willa had envied Angie her elder brother until she'd matured enough to develop a mild crush on him.

From then on, Clay had become a romantic curiosity, fueling her adolescent daydreams and presenting Willa with what she considered a safe challenge for her rapidly developing feminine charms. The day she decided to unleash those charms on him was the day she learned that it wasn't safe to play kissing games with Clay Cantrell.

Willa's lips curved slightly. She was unable even in the face of a bitter encounter with Clay to suppress the recollection. He'd had too great an influence on her growing up, had claimed too much of her affection for Willa to totally banish his memory. No matter what the outcome of this visit, Clay, like Angie, would always claim a lion's share of her love.

Willa's anger faded. She didn't want her presence to hurt Clay. Perhaps there was a way to convince him to tolerate her long enough for her to help her aunt get the ranch back on the rails. Clay had always been a reasonable man and it was certain he had a sizable soft spot for her aunt and cousin, even if he could no longer summon any fondness for her. Maybe that would be enough.

Leaving the keys in the ignition, Willa opened her car door and stepped out, hoping the warm, early evening breeze had carried the sound of her arrival into the house. She'd known better than to phone Clay to ask his permission to come here, but she didn't want to take him too much by surprise.

She went up the front walk to the door, hesitating only a moment more before she knocked. She waited a bit, chafed a nervous palm against her jeans, then knocked again. The door opened just as she lowered her hand.

"Hello, Clay."

Clay Cantrell's six-foot-four height filled the doorway, the breadth of his shoulders taking up a good share of its width. He didn't seem surprised to see her, but his eyes held a cold challenge.

"I'd like to talk to you, if I may," she said, resolving to cling to her good memories of him rather than dwell on the animosity he held toward her now. Clay had been a good friend once, and though he'd betrayed her friendship by believing the worst about her, even she had to admit that the grim circumstances back then would have pushed any friendship to the breaking point. "Please, Clay," she added softly.

The moments ticked by, until Willa was certain he wasn't going to allow her into his house. At last he stood aside and gestured for her to enter.

The moment Willa crossed the threshold it was like stepping backward in time. Nothing had changed inside the large, ruggedly furnished room, from the heavy leather and wood furniture to the American Indian artifacts that decorated the walls and the heavy woven rugs scattered here and there on the polished wood floor. Willa's eyes went instantly to the mantel above the stone fireplace.

Angie's high school graduation picture was still there. Though Angie had been killed only a few weeks before graduation, she and Willa had had their portraits done months earlier.

The ache of grief and regret that had never totally left Willa came pulsing back as she was reminded that the other portrait that had once shared pride of place on that mantel—her own—had been removed.

"You said you wanted to talk."

Clay's deep voice startled her and she turned quickly toward the somber-faced man. There was no hint of softness in his flinty expression, just an impenetrable hardness that reminded her of the last time she'd stood before him in this room—the time she'd tried to tell him about the accident. He'd been drinking heavily that night. "Get out of this house!" he'd roared, too grief stricken at the sight of her to allow her even a moment to explain before he grabbed her arm and ushered her roughly to the door. She had been inconsolable.

Suddenly the longing to again try telling Clay what had really happened when Angie was killed—and to at last be believed—was overwhelming. Was the lie he'd accepted five years earlier still stronger than the truth? Did she have the courage to find out?

The memory of her aunt collapsing in the cemetery brought Willa back to reality. What would it do to Tess if she were to again insist that Paige's reckless driving had caused the accident? Tess's love for her daughter and pride in her were enormous. The mere suggestion of the truth could be enough to seriously threaten her aunt's life.

Willa felt the old helplessness stir. She could say nothing. In the eyes of everyone in and around Cascade, and particularly in Clay's, she would have to remain the spineless little liar who'd repaid her aunt and uncle for taking her in by telling horrible lies about their darling Paige. Besides, Clay had already made his choice. Five years earlier, Willa had been prepared to beg him to believe her. But she wouldn't beg him now—or ever. Pride stiffened her spine. She would never again plead for anyone's trust.

"I suppose Paige called to tell you why I'm here," she began, already sensing Paige had.

"She called earlier today. Said Tess had asked you to stay on and take over the Circle H." Clay's voice was bitterly cynical.

"Then you also know that Tess asked me to go out and look things over, and that I might be stopping by," she said.

"She told me that, too."

"I've decided to stay," Willa said simply, shoving her nervous fingers into her jeans pockets.

"No."

Willa felt her heart recoil at that one word, spoken so softly, yet so harshly.

"The Circle H is in bad shape," Willa persisted. "I plan to stay just long enough to help straighten things out for Aunt Tess and find someone reliable to take over. I doubt if I'd be around for more than a month at the outside."

Clay gave a sarcastic chuckle. "What could you do?"

Willa's chin lifted at his skepticism as she declared softly, "A lot more than my aunt's many friends and neighbors have done."

Clay's hard expression didn't alter; he must have expected her to say something like that. "Tess's too damned proud to allow much help."

"She's always been that way," Willa agreed. "But she's asked for my help. I want to do it, Clay. I'd like to try."

Clay couldn't help but read the shadowy longing in Willa's green eyes. Her face was stiff and her lips were pressed together with the effort she made to hide her feelings from him. He knew that look as well as he'd known her once upon a time. Those big green eyes had always managed to betray enough of what was going on in her pretty head that he'd teased her frequently about being able to read her like a book. Their relationship had evolved into a game of sorts, one that they'd both played at, a shallow flirtation that had permitted him to harmlessly assuage his attraction to her.

Clay felt himself grow cold. He didn't want to remember that or anything else about Willa Ross. He wanted to harden himself to everything about her but the more he tried the more difficult it became. The seventeen-year-old imp he'd been half in love with was gone; in her place was this serious, melancholy young woman who looked as if she never smiled or had a carefree thought. It was because he could tell that she was trying to conceal it all from him and not play on his sympathy that he felt something penetrate his bitterness and sink deeply into his heart.

"Then I reckon we'd both better stay out of each other's way," he growled irritably as he turned away and pushed a calloused hand through his dark hair.

The painful tension in her body eased with relief, but Willa suddenly felt unbearably sad.

I don't want to hurt you, Clay, she wanted to say. *If there were any way I could go back to that day and do just one tiny thing different...*

Willa was glad he couldn't see her face just then. "Tess will be relieved. Thanks." Willa stared a moment more at that proud set of shoulders before she turned and left quietly.

CHAPTER THREE

WILLA WAS UP EARLY the next morning. She'd been unable to reach her partner, Ivy Dayton, by phone the night before, so she made the call as soon as she got up, hoping to catch Ivy before she left the house.

"Take whatever time you need," Ivy said without hesitation after Willa had related the details of her aunt's situation. "Deke and I can hire some summer help if we need to."

"Thanks a lot, Ivy. I really appreciate it."

"Shucks, it's no more'n you'd do for me," Ivy said dismissively, and Willa smiled at the image she had of her red-haired, freckle-faced friend, who was almost eight years her senior. Ivy was a big-hearted country girl, generous to a fault, just a bit flamboyant, but savvy and as tough as nails when it came to doing business. "You just take care of yourself up there."

"Don't worry. I've grown up some in the past five years," Willa replied, not needing to say more since Ivy knew everything.

Ivy gave an inelegant snort. "So has that cousin of yours. Now that you're back she's bound to be nervous as a weasel and twice as sneaky. You already know what she's capable of when it comes to saving her own hide."

Willa grimaced at the reminder but was grateful for Ivy's unswerving loyalty. She and Ivy had worked together for a year on a big ranch in Kansas before Ivy had suggested a partnership that would pool their talents and their money. Though widowed at twenty-five, Ivy had managed to save most of the money from her husband's estate, and with what she'd put away of her earnings, had been ready to buy something of her own. By then, Willa had already confided her past to Ivy, and it was Ivy's steadfast friendship and belief in her that had eased the pain of estrangement from family and friends that Willa had felt so acutely.

"I'll be careful, Ivy. Thanks."

"Let me know if you need anything."

"I will. Call you in another week or so," Willa said, then returned the phone to its cradle.

It didn't take long to pack and check out of the motel. Though it was still too early to visit her aunt, Willa managed to slip into her room just as Dr. Elliot finished Tess's morning exam and was about to leave.

"Visiting hours don't start for another couple of hours, young lady," he scolded, though the smile on his face negated his gruff tone. Dr. Elliot's attitude toward her had softened considerably in the past few days, and Willa smiled back easily.

"Five minutes?"

"Let's just don't make it a habit," he said, then exited briskly from the room.

"You've decided to say," Tess concluded, a sunny smile on her face. Tess looked even better this morning and Willa marveled at her growing improvement.

"I have. But only for a few weeks—a month, maybe," Willa cautioned gently. "I can only take so much time from my job."

Tess's brow furrowed slightly. "You enjoy working with horses then. Well, there's no reason the Circle H can't begin to make a changeover to horse breeding," she reasoned and Willa went tense.

Panicked by her aunt's seeming determination for her to stay permanently, yet realizing that Tess might not be ready to face the shock of learning that her niece's prior obligations went much farther than those of a hired hand, Willa spoke quickly. "Let's just wait and see, Aunt Tess. Any decisions like that should be made later when you're better and we see how things go."

Willa didn't add that there were no guarantees the Circle H could survive. And since she hadn't yet gone over the books or delved too deeply into just how dire the ranch's finances were, she didn't want to paint too discouraging a picture, either. If she could, she intended to shelter her aunt from as much worry and unpleasantness as possible.

"Did you talk to Clay?"

"I went over to Orion last night. There won't be any problem with him." Willa was confident of that. Clay might object to her staying on, and there would naturally be some unpleasant moments between the two of them, but he wouldn't deliberately cause trouble.

"Good." Tess leaned back against her pillows. "I want you to stop by the lawyer's office today and see what needs to be done for you to get into the ranch accounts and handle my business. He should have everything ready for you to sign. When are you going to move into the house?''

"Later today. I've got a few errands to do in town after I talk to your lawyer.''

Tess nodded her approval. "Paige has been staying with some of her friends, so you might need to buy groceries. And Willa—'' Tess looked troubled "—whatever you decide to do about Art Boles is fine with me.''

"Don't worry, Aunt Tess. I can handle him." Willa forced her lips into a curve to allay her aunt's concern. Actually, firing Art Boles was a task she didn't look forward to, but neither did she want to have a man like him working on the Circle H.

"If you get too busy, don't worry about driving all the way back to town tonight for visiting hours. You'll likely be tired," Tess predicted.

"I'll give you a call if I can't make it," Willa said, and after a few last words, she left the hospital.

"I JUST HOPE YOU KNOW what you're doing firing Art Boles," Paige said snidely from the doorway, cigarette in hand. Willa glanced up from the books she'd been poring over all evening, frowning at the reminder of the scene Art Boles had made that afternoon after she'd fired him and handed him a check for the balance of his wages. "He was probably the only cowhand in the county who'd work for you.''

"He wasn't working, period," Willa reminded her cousin. "What do you want, Paige?" she demanded ungraciously, not feeling particularly obliged to be polite. She was tired and planned to be up at first light the next morning.

"I'd like to talk," Paige answered, sauntering into the room and picking up the small crystal ashtray that sat on the corner of the desk at which Willa was working.

"I'm not too interested in anything you have to say," Willa said coldly as she closed the ledgers and stacked them. She wasn't thrilled that Paige had decided to return to the ranch earlier that day.

"You might be, Cousin," Paige went on haughtily, having perched her long, elegant body on the arm of the nearest wing chair. Chicly clad in a blue silk dress that Willa was certain was a designer original, Paige looked every bit the fashion model. The stunning combination of long, wavy raven tresses, clear luminescent skin and exotic violet eyes made her a natural. Willa had no idea how well Paige had done for herself, since she hadn't been in contact with her aunt these past years, but there was a sophisticated, well-cared-for look about Paige that fairly shouted success. "If you and I can't come to some kind of understanding, Mother's going to be the one who suffers the most."

"Scared?" Willa challenged, though the realization brought her little satisfaction. In spite of what Paige had done, Willa hated the antagonism between them. She knew instinctively that she suffered the ill will they bore each other much more acutely than Paige.

Paige's face flushed with guilt and resentment, but she didn't respond to Willa's taunt. "I'm sure you realize how precarious mother's health is."

Willa came to her feet and grabbed up the ledgers. "How convenient for you," she murmured as she turned away and shoved them into the low cabinet beneath the double windows.

"It could literally kill Mother if you were to start trouble," Paige persisted.

Willa struggled to suppress her anger as she turned to face her cousin. "I get the message."

"That's good," Paige said, her brow arched. Then, to Willa's surprise, Paige's haughty look altered. "For what it's worth, Willa, I'm sorry."

Willa couldn't have been more shocked, but managed to keep it to herself.

"I was terrified of what would happen to me if I told the truth," Paige began, then shrugged uncomfortably. "You were always so strong and so brave, I thought you'd survive it all better than I could. And since Clay was your friend, I was certain he'd forgive you a lot more easily than he'd forgive me." Paige was watching Willa closely. "I had no idea Daddy would throw you out or that people would react as strongly as they all did." Paige hesitated before her chin went up defensively. "If it makes any difference, I would have come forward if Clay had decided to press charges."

Willa stared, unable to fully believe what she was hearing. She knew instinctively that she was the only one who had ever heard this confession and strongly suspected Paige would not only never repeat it, but would hereafter insist even more vigorously that Willa had been at fault.

"I don't think you would have admitted the truth even then, Paige," Willa scoffed. "If you couldn't tell your own mother and father the truth, I doubt you would have had the courage to face going to court and risk being placed in some kind of juvenile detention until you were eighteen."

"My life would have been ruined," Paige snapped, dropping all pretense of contrition. "You didn't have any big ambitions. All you ever wanted to do was live on a ranch someplace like a common cowhand."

"So my future didn't count," Willa concluded grimly, then shook her head. "Cal and Tess worshipped you, Paige. They loved you as much as any parents could love their child. I don't think there was anything they would have denied you. How is it you turned out so wrong?"

Paige's face reddened as she bent her head and crushed her cigarette out violently in the ashtray.

"Just remember what I said about Mother," she warned as her head came up and she pinned Willa with an icy stare. "And don't plan to stay around too long."

Paige rose from the chair arm, tossed down the ashtray, then swept regally from the room.

WILLA SPENT the next two days mucking out the barn and readying the loft for hay before she patched the barn roof. She'd hired a mechanic to come to the ranch and repair the tractor, then had him take a look at her uncle's old red pickup while he was there. Getting the pickup in good driving order had cost more than Willa had anticipated, but the truck was a necessity, and the price of a new one was well beyond what her aunt could afford this year. Willa cringed as she calculated that it wouldn't be too many more months before the truck would need new tires.

So far, there had been little response to the ads she'd placed locally for a foreman and ranch hands. She'd had a couple of calls from Casper and Cheyenne, but it would be next week before any of the respondents from outside Cascade could get to the Circle H for an interview. In the meantime, she had estimated the cost of repairs around the ranch and had decided to get started buying supplies.

Willa became so absorbed in her solitary ranch work that she managed to set aside any uneasy thoughts she'd had about doing business in the small community. Though she visited her aunt daily, she'd had little contact with anyone beyond Paige and the hospital staff. Consequently, her first trip to the lumberyard to buy barbed wire and fence posts was an abrupt awakening.

"I believe I was next," she said firmly as she stepped up to the counter and the short man in blue coveralls, who was in charge of writing up the orders. In spite of the fact that she'd been one of the first to arrive that morning, the man had ignored her to wait on other customers. Taken aback by the clerk's deliberate rudeness, she'd not been quite able to believe she was actually being snubbed, until his repeated oversights became too blatant to be ignored.

"You'll have to wait your turn, miss," he said, then looked past her to the next person in line.

"I have waited my turn," Willa insisted, raising her voice just enough to be heard by everyone in the vicinity as she stepped aside to block the man behind her from moving forward. The quiet conversations around them ceased, and when the clerk flushed self-consciously, Willa sensed everyone's attention was on them.

"I need fifteen rolls of wire and about one hundred wood posts," she said briskly, staring challengingly at the clerk until his gaze veered from hers to glance over her left shoulder.

Intuition sent a sharp tingle through her and she turned her head, her lips tightening as she caught sight of Clay Cantrell standing a few feet away. Concluding that he'd been among those who had entered the store after her and that he had probably seen everything that had gone on, she returned her attention to the clerk.

"Obviously your company can afford to lose business from the Circle H," she said, then turned away, incensed that taking her business to the lumberyard in the next town meant driving her uncle's pickup and trailer almost ninety extra miles.

She'd walked halfway to the door, when the clerk called out to her. "Miss Ross? Did you say fifteen rolls of wire and one hundred wood fence posts?" Willa halted, turned, then noted that Clay was now nowhere in sight. To her surprise, the clerk was bustling toward her, hastily scrawling her order on his clipboard. "If you'll just pay for this up front, you can pick up your order in the yard.'' The man hurriedly initialed the papers and held them toward her expectantly, his low "Sorry for the delay, miss" apologetic enough to induce her to take them.

Without so much as a glance at anyone, Willa collected the rest of the hardware items on her list, paid for them, then went out to drive the truck and small trailer into the yard behind the store to be loaded. Fortunately her trip to the feed store went better, as did her trip to pick up a few groceries, which she placed in the cab next to the small cooler she'd brought along to stow perishables in. By the time she'd gone to the bank and opened a personal checking account it was well past lunchtime, and Willa stopped at a small restaurant on the outskirts of Cascade.

A favorite of hers when she was growing up, Cristy's had been the best place in town for hamburgers and tenderloins, and Willa looked forward to reacquainting herself with one of the hot sandwiches Cristy's was known for.

The moment she walked into the restaurant she saw Clay sitting with three other men at a table toward the front, the remnants of his lunch before him as he lingered over a cup of coffee. He hadn't seen her yet, so she glanced around, looking for a place to sit. Though the lunch counter was filled and the dining area crowded, Willa managed to find a small empty booth midway back. The waitress, whom Willa recognized from years before as Laureen, bustled up, set down a glass of water and started to hand Willa a menu, when she suddenly stopped.

Willa had reached up for the menu and taken hold of it before Laureen's tight expression registered. A testing tug of the menu told Willa the woman was having second thoughts about giving it to her. Only after an awkward moment did the waitress release the menu and murmur a perfunctory greeting before turning and rushing away.

Willa scarcely looked at the menu once she saw that her favorite dishes were still listed. She laid the menu down to indicate her readiness to order, but sat there for more than ten minutes before Laureen started in her direction. Then, coffeepot in hand, the waitress worked the tables and booths in her area, adroitly managing to ignore Willa in much the same way she'd been ignored at the lumberyard.

Embarrassment and anger brought a high flush to Willa's cheeks as she glanced around and noticed the number of curious eyes fixed on her that suddenly looked down or away. The only pair of eyes that didn't shy from hers were the expressionless black ones that watched her from the table near the front of the restaurant.

Willa realized that Clay had seen her shortly after she'd come in and that he'd been watching her for quite some time when his gaze traveled from her to Laureen as the woman continued to avoid taking her order.

Just then Laureen glanced in Clay's direction as if seeking approval. That brief meeting of gazes was all Willa needed to see. With stiff dignity, she slid to the edge of the booth, then rose to walk calmly to the door. Inwardly she was seething with a chaotic mixture of hurt and barely controlled anger, but she was careful not to let it show on her face.

She'd not thought Clay capable of using his influence to cause her problems and public embarrassment, but he clearly had that day, at least twice. Or had he? Perhaps she would have been treated the same whether he'd been present or not. Perhaps this was the way of some to indicate their allegiance to Clay and their sympathy for the pain her presence might be causing him.

Cascade was a small rural town, and as such was subject to the same kind of attitudes and prejudices common to most small towns. Willa guessed that many people in the area believed she'd got off too easily when Angie was killed, and now felt quite justified in dealing out a bit of vengeance on Angie's behalf. It saddened Willa to recall that she'd known most of these people once. Cascade was a good, close-knit community, made up of good, law-abiding people. Knowing that made the injustice of their actions doubly hard to take. Willa had to admit now that Paige's fear of being socially ostracized was well-founded, though it in no way excused the actions she'd taken to avoid it.

Willa walked to the truck and made a quick check that the load was secure inside the trailer before she got behind the wheel and started for the ranch.

Either way, there wasn't much she could do about what people thought of her except get on with her job. The sooner the ranch was doing better and she found someone capable to run it, the sooner she could leave and go back to Colorado, where she was welcome and her word was worth something.

She was almost a mile from the turnoff to the Orion Ranch, when she glanced into her side mirror and saw a big silver-and-black pickup gaining steadily on her much slower truck and trailer.

Just at the moment she was distracted her truck seemed to hit a hard bump. Startled, Willa jerked her attention back to the road as the truck lapsed into the staccato jarring that indicated a flat tire. Moaning in disgust, Willa slowed the vehicle, then pulled carefully onto the graveled shoulder. The silver-and-black pickup whizzed on past as she brought her truck to a stop but left the engine running.

Willa grabbed her work gloves from the seat, resigned to unhitching the trailer and unloading the heavy spools of wire from the truck bed before she could begin to change the tire. When she got out, she noted unhappily that the left rear tire rim was already resting on the deflated remains of the rubber.

She reached into the back of the truck bed for a cement block to place beneath the wagon tongue of the trailer to keep it elevated while she unhitched it and disconnected the trailer lights. As a precaution, she slid a fence post behind the trailer tires to keep the trailer from rolling away on the slight incline. Once she got back into the truck and moved it forward a few feet, she switched off the engine, set the brake, then got out to place a block just ahead of one of the front tires of the pickup to keep it steady while she changed the tire. She had just let down the tailgate of the truck to unload the wire, when she heard a vehicle approach.

The silver-and-black pickup that had passed her moments earlier was coming back down the highway toward her. Since she didn't expect it to stop, she climbed onto the tailgate and reached for the first spool of wire. To her surprise, the vehicle slowed, then turned onto the graveled shoulder, where it stopped headlight to headlight with her truck. Willa was startled when she saw who was driving.

Clay Cantrell opened the door, then stepped down, and Willa guessed from the fixed line of his mouth that he had felt obligated to come back and lend his assistance, no matter how distasteful he found the idea. The dark sunglasses he wore probably hid a wealth of loathing for her. She could well imagine the cold unfriendly depths of those midnight-black eyes, and decided that very instant to refuse any offer of help.

Just as she bent down to maneuver the spool of wire to the edge of the tailgate so she could lower it to the ground, Clay reached into the truck and took hold of it.

"I can get it," she said quickly, her green eyes flashing in his direction as she held the spool immovable. Clay ignored her and gave the spool a yank that dared her to get into a tug-of-war with him. "I don't need your help."

The stern line of Clay's mouth slanted humorlessly, but he made no response. Instead he moved the spool to the tailgate then lowered it to the ground.

"I mean it, Clay," she said as he leaned back into the truck to reach for the next spool. "I don't need your help."

"You get it, anyway," he snarled as he reached in and got a grip on one of the spools. "Are you going to get busy, or do I have to do this alone?" Before she could respond, he was pulling the roll past her forcing Willa to step aside to assist him. In no time, they had unloaded all the rolls.

"Thanks," she said grudgingly. "I can take care of the rest myself."

Giving every impression that he hadn't heard a word, Clay slammed the tailgate shut, then got down on one knee to get the spare tire from the rack beneath the truck bed. "You gotta jack?" he growled as he worked.

"Yes, but I can take care of things now," Willa repeated as she started to kneel down to reach for the spare herself.

Clay's icy voice stopped her. "I haven't got the time or the patience to argue with you, Willa."

Willa hesitated, then straightened and stalked off to get the jack and lug wrench from behind the seat in the cab, intending to refuse any further help. When she returned with the tools, Clay dropped the spare on the ground, letting it wobble and fall onto its side.

"This one's damn near as flat as the other one," he said, depressing the wall of the tire with the toe of his boot. Willa watched, a sinking sensation in her stomach as the new problem registered.

Willa tossed the tools down, then raised her arm to blot the perspiration from her forehead with her sleeve. What a predicament she was in. She wasn't so foolish as to refuse Clay's help now, not when her only other choice was to walk the five or six miles back to town in the heat and take the chance that someone would make off with the fencing while she was getting the spare fixed. It stung to realize she wasn't quite as self-sufficient as she'd thought, but what really stung was the fact that she was in a position that made it more sensible to ask Clay for his help than to spurn it. Assuming, that is, he was still of a mind to give it. Choking back a good bit of her pride, she dropped her arm and looked up at him, seeing twin images of herself reflected in his dark glasses.

"You don't happen to have a portable air tank in the back of your truck, do you?" she asked, forced to set aside any lingering resistance to his help.

"Probably wouldn't do any good," he said, reaching down to grip the spindle hole and lift the useless spare before he carried it to the trailer and laid it on top of the fence posts. That done, he turned and walked to his truck without another word.

Shocked that he was apparently leaving her to her own devices along the deserted stretch of highway, Willa could only stare for a moment. Then, determined not to let him just drive away, she hurried after him.

"I can pay you to haul the wire and the trailer to the Circle H, Clay," she said as she caught up with him.

"I don't want your money," he grumbled as he walked around to the back of his pickup.

"I can't just leave that fencing here," she persisted as he whipped off his sunglasses and shoved them into his shirt pocket. "I know this section of the road is pretty quiet. But I can't afford to take the chance. You know how much money it represents."

Clay shot her a black look. "I didn't hear anyone say you had to." With that he crouched to take the spare from the rack beneath his truck.

Willa understood then that he intended to loan her his spare tire and she felt her face flush with chagrin. "I really appreciate this," she said when he straightened and began rolling the tire to her pickup.

"I'm not doing it for you," he replied coldly, and Willa stiffened, scrambling to harden herself to his obvious dislike.

When they reached the back of her truck, she briskly took over, laboring to conceal her emotions as she loosened the lug nuts of the damaged tire before she positioned the jack and began to raise the truck. While she pumped the jack handle, Clay crouched once more and finished removing the tire. In no more than a few moments, the spare was in place and Clay was tightening the lugs.

"That wasn't the truth, Willa," he said suddenly, his voice going a little rough. He turned his head and looked at her, his dark eyes catching the shadows of hurt that lingered in her green gaze. "What I said just now about not doing this for you. It wasn't the truth."

Willa was suddenly overcome with sentiment, painfully aware that this small bit of tenderness from Clay was somehow much harder to take than his earlier show of disdain. She bent her head abruptly so he couldn't see the watery fullness that sprang to her eyes, as she made a project of lowering the jack, then pulling it from beneath the truck. Clay gave the lugs an extra turn before he straightened.

"Thanks, Clay," she managed, fighting to keep the huskiness from her voice as she avoided his gaze and reached for the lug wrench. By the time she'd returned it and the jack to their place behind the seat in the cab, Clay had opened the tailgate of the pickup and was about to load the first spool of wire.

They worked in silence until the wire was loaded and they'd got the trailer hitched to the truck. Willa retrieved the fence post she'd braced the trailer tires with while Clay hooked up the trailer lights and tossed the cement block back into the pickup. Willa was just about to climb into the cab, when Clay's fingers closed gently around her arm.

"About what happened in town today," he began, "I had nothing to do with it."

"I'd guessed that already. Thanks again for your help," she said, so deeply unnerved by his touch and by his unexpected change that all she wanted to do was flee. She forced a grateful curve to her lips and tried to look up at him, but her gaze went no higher than his shirt front. "I'll have your spare back to you as soon as possible."

As if he'd just become aware that he was touching her, he pulled his hand away. "Don't forget that hankie," he reminded her gruffly.

"I won't," she promised, then turned away from him to get into the truck.

"It's awfully damned hard to have you around here again, Willa," he said quietly, yet his candid admission communicated a gentleness that took her by surprise.

For just an instant, the years of estrangement fell away and Willa turned her head to look up fully into Clay's solemn countenance. Beneath his unconsciously intimidating look was an ache, a longing she recognized and understood. For a mere fraction of a second a familiar feeling of closeness surged between them. It was almost as if Angie had never died and Willa had never gone away.

Suddenly frightened that her own longings were blinding her to the hostility she should have been seeing, Willa sighed, then echoed grimly, "It's awfully damned hard to be here, Clay."

Willa stepped up into the truck and pulled the door closed, tugging off her gloves as she waited for Clay to stop staring at her and walk away. Just when she thought she couldn't bear another moment, Clay turned and started toward his truck. Willa hurriedly twisted the key in the ignition, then waited for Clay to back his vehicle out of the way.

She checked her mirror for traffic, then pulled slowly back onto the highway, the old pickup laboring under its load. She wasn't surprised when Clay turned his truck around and followed her past the turnoff to Orion. When she slowed, then got off the highway on the short road to the Circle H, the silver-and-black pickup stopped and managed an efficient three-point turn on the pavement to head back the other way.

CHAPTER FOUR

HER HAT BRIM SHADING HER FACE from the high midday sun, Willa drove the tractor and hay wagon beneath the wide second story door of the barn to begin the wearing process of levering the large bales of fragrant hay she'd collected from the hay field into the loft. The efficiency of the loft fork and pulley system made the job easier, but some assistance would have helped even more.

Willa thought instantly of Paige, who was up at the ranch house either reading a magazine or in the midst of her daily aerobic workout. Just having someone drive the tractor while Willa tossed the bales on the wagon would have been better than nothing, but Paige had resisted the idea all week, making excuses that ranged from not being good at driving a tractor to the negative effects of too much sun and wind on her complexion.

In addition to an aversion to outdoor work, Paige couldn't seem to manage to prepare a decent meal for the two of them. Paige could subsist on lettuce leaves and cottage cheese, but Willa needed something much more substantial to carry her through a dawn-to-dusk workday. It was no wonder Willa had grown frustrated and irritable this past week. TV dinners and cold sandwiches were not exactly the staples of good nutrition, but Willa rarely had the time or energy to fix herself something better.

That Paige didn't try to help her in even the smallest way only increased the animosity between the two cousins. Paige's too obvious scheme to discourage Willa into leaving was coming along so well that only with the utmost self-control was Willa able to conceal her discontent from Paige. She couldn't wait until she left for her next modeling assignment. With any luck it would be tomorrow, since the photo shoot had already been delayed a few days. Still, Willa cautioned herself not to count on anything until Paige was actually on the plane.

It had been a week since Willa had carted the wire and fencing home, yet she'd accomplished little but the most necessary fence repairs along with her daily checks on the cattle. The small hay pasture had needed to be mown and baled, and since Willa was forced to work the physically exhausting job alone, the other work around the ranch had fallen even further behind.

To top it all off, the two ranch hands she'd interviewed the day before had turned out to be unsatisfactory. One had a criminal record she was certain her aunt would be uncomfortable with. The other had seemed too much of a know-it-all, too often criticizing his past bosses for Willa to believe he'd make the type of loyal, dependable employee Aunt Tess needed.

There had been other calls that week in response to the ad, but only three would agree to come to an interview. It seemed that too many people knew about the problems on the Circle H and either were looking for something with a less shaky future or were hoping for better wages than Willa could promise. And, as much as she wished it weren't so, there were probably more than a few men who simply didn't want to work for Willa Ross, much less for a woman.

Willa finished putting up the hay, then started toward the house to grab a sandwich and exchange her coffee thermos for a larger one filled with ice water before she headed back to the hay pasture. She had just washed up and had set the water thermos in the kitchen sink to fill while she made a quick lunch, when she heard the sound of a vehicle coming up the driveway.

Clay Cantrell's pickup rolled past the house, stopping midway to the barn. Willa groaned as she recalled that although she'd had the tire fixed and replaced on her uncle's old truck, she hadn't got around to dropping Clay's spare off at Orion. She hurriedly slapped her sandwich together and left it on the kitchen counter to dash to the basement to get Clay's handkerchief from the ironing board.

She was just coming up the stairs, when she heard Paige's throaty voice.

"She's not much more competent than Art Boles," Paige was saying. "And I don't know what she does with her time, either. She doesn't have much to show for it except the bills she's been running up. I wish I could convince Mother to open her eyes, but you know how sentimental she is. I just hope Willa has an attack of conscience and doesn't hurt Mom too much this time. She just couldn't take it, Clay."

Willa's cheeks were burning with fury as she stepped into the kitchen and closed the door to the basement with quiet force. Paige was dressed in a lilac form-fitting exercise outfit that clung to her slim body like a second skin, and she was using it to advantage, having struck a pose calculated to look unconsciously seductive. Willa felt a sharp stab of something distressing like jealousy as she swiftly noted what a perfect physical match Paige's brunette looks were for Clay's imposing masculinity.

"You might know a bit more about how I spend my time if you could manage to get out of bed by noon," Willa remarked coolly as she crossed to where Paige and Clay stood just inside the back porch door. "Here's your hankie," she said to Clay, braving his disapproving expression as she held out the laundered, neatly pressed handkerchief for him to take. "If you'll give me a minute, I'll go get your spare." Willa turned away and got out some waxed paper to wrap her sandwich in as Paige led Clay toward the living room.

Doing her best to ignore the flirtatious note that came into her cousin's lowered voice as her words became indistinct, Willa selected fruit from the refrigerator and Twinkies from the bread box, then, along with her sandwich, placed them in a brown paper bag. Willa delayed a bit longer for a quick glass of cold milk before she added a handful of ice cubes to the thermos. She'd collected her lunch and the thermos and had carried it all back out to the hay wagon when Clay caught up with her.

"You've got a section of fence down and about fifty head of cattle out," he told her as she set the lunch sack and thermos on the tractor.

Willa was instantly alarmed. "Where?"

"On Orion."

Willa was unaware of the slight droop of her narrow shoulders as she glanced uneasily toward the cloud-mantled mountains miles to the west. "I've still got a lot of hay in the field, Clay, and it's supposed to storm tonight."

Clay's voice was hard when he spoke. "Your aunt hired you to run this ranch, Willa. If you can't handle it, maybe you ought to step aside."

Willa's gaze swung back to his, her green eyes blazing as the effects of the heat, hard work and frustration of the past few days sent her temper skyward. "If you think you can do as good with almost no money and no help, plus an overabundance of critics who are standing over you waiting for you to fail, you're welcome to try, Mr. Millionaire Rancher." She jabbed a slim finger at his chest angrily. "Until then, either run those cattle back onto the Circle H and patch the fence yourself until I can get to it, or let them graze and send me the bill. I've got hay to get in."

With that Willa turned her back on him and climbed onto the tractor. "Your spare is in the pickup," she called over her shoulder as she started the engine and pulled away from the barn to head down the long twin tracks that led to the hay field.

WILLA WAS TOO EXHAUSTED and miserable to feel angry any longer at either Clay or her cousin as she trudged from the barn to the house that evening. Sweat-mingled hay chaff and dust had worked their way beneath her clothing all day and were now plastered to her skin by the downpour that had begun just as she'd driven the last wagon of hay from the field. The only dry comfortable place was inside her boots, but her feet were too sore for her to enjoy it.

At least the last wagon of hay had stayed dry, thanks to the tarpaulin she'd thrown over it just moments before the rain started. She'd pulled the hay wagon into the barn, resigned to unloading it in the morning so she could feed the horses and get up to the house for the brisk shower she hoped would pound away the scratchy hay chaff and revive her for the book work she needed to do before she made an early night of it.

The thought of spending a good share of the day tomorrow fixing fence and rounding up cattle was too tiring for her to contemplate, and she regretted now that she hadn't hired at least one of the men she'd decided was unsuitable. Willa made a mental note never to interview anyone after the kind of day she'd just put in. There was no telling what kind of person she'd get for her aunt if she gave in to desperation.

Thinking of Aunt Tess suddenly brought a pang of sadness. Willa hadn't had time to visit her much this week and it looked as if she wouldn't tonight, either. But that would have to change once Paige went on her assignment, since Tess would naturally miss her daughter's frequent visits. And since Tess was still struggling with her recovery and her grief over losing Cal, she'd need just that much more love and emotional support.

Willa didn't know what she'd do when her aunt was released from the hospital and sent home. She supposed she or Paige would have to see to hiring a nurse to look after Tess during the day while Willa was out working.

"And it would help a lot if that nurse could double as a housekeeper and cook," Willa said aloud to herself, then felt guilty for the selfish thought. Even though she was about to stare another TV dinner in the face—and wasn't certain whether she might rather prefer to go hungry—she had no right to consider anyone's comfort but her aunt's, since it was Tess's money that would be spent. Willa had the sudden idea as she reached the back porch and pried off her muddy boots that perhaps she should consider drawing on her personal bank account to hire a cook, but dismissed the idea. She was having enough trouble finding a foreman and a couple of ranch hands. In view of the way everyone in their small community felt about her, Willa doubted she'd find any woman in the area who would want to come in to cook and clean house for her.

Willa had stepped from the back porch into the kitchen and set the thermos on the counter, when she noticed the folded sheet of pink stationery propped up on the kitchen table. She walked over and picked it up, then heard the familiar sound of Clay's truck coming up the drive. She didn't have the energy to face a confrontation with him. Hurriedly, she skimmed the note her cousin had left informing her she'd gone to New York.

Relieved that Paige was finally gone, Willa tossed down the paper and quickly closed the back door. With any luck, she could get into the shower and pretend she didn't know Clay was there. Surely he'd leave if he got no response to his knock and couldn't find her down at the barn.

Moments later, Willa stepped beneath the sharp needles of hot water in the shower, lathering her hair twice before going after her skin with a shower brush and soap. She lingered under the hot spray, twisting the shower nozzle until the water pulsed down soothingly on her aching arms and shoulders. Too soon the water began to cool, and Willa reluctantly turned off the faucets and opened the shower door to reach for a towel.

After putting on the short terry robe she'd laid out, she quickly combed the wet tangles from her hair, then blow-dried it to a silky cloud of honey-brown that waved past her shoulders. Revived, but resigned to one of the frozen dinners waiting for her in the freezer and the load of book work she'd been putting off, Willa went downstairs, her bare feet soothed by the gentle abrasion of the rug on their tired soles.

Except for the kitchen, the house was darkened, the only other light coming through the windows from the yard and an occasional flash of lightning as the storm began to reintensify. Willa had just reached the doorway to the kitchen, when it registered that she hadn't turned on any lights downstairs when she'd come in.

"Hope you don't mind that I let myself in."

Clay's low drawl startled her as she stepped into the kitchen and saw him sprawled comfortably on one of the chairs at the table, a booted foot resting on his thigh, his Stetson upended on the cupboard near the back door.

"What are you doing here?" she demanded, her hand going automatically to the loose V of her robe as Clay's dark eyes made a slow journey downward. Willa caught her breath as Clay's gaze lingered first on the swell of her breasts, then on the slim length of thigh, knee and ankle that the short robe left uncovered. There was a pronounced glimmer of male appreciation in those midnight-black eyes before they shuttered themselves and returned to her face.

"I had one or two things I wanted to talk over with you tonight."

As she forced herself to recover from the heat that still lingered in the wake of that look, her lips thinned skeptically. "I'll just bet," she murmured, thinking of his criticism and Paige's when she'd come back to the house at midday. Willa crossed the room to the pantry and stepped around the corner to the large chest-style freezer. "I'm in no mood to hear any more about how incompetent I am or how many bills I'm running up," she called out to him as she started to rummage through the stack of boxed dinners.

"How old are you now, Willa, twenty-two?"

When she realized Clay was beside her, Willa straightened abruptly, hastily yanking down the short robe that had hiked up when she'd bent to look into the freezer. She flung an irritated glance at him and caught the unnerving blackness in his eyes as he forced his attention from her fully exposed leg to meet her gaze.

Several charged heartbeats of time thudded between them as green eyes melded with black. Clay was too close. The large pantry was suddenly dwarfed by his nearness, a nearness that pulsed with his rawly masculine presence and seemed to smother her with an odd lethargy.

As if the storm outside were somehow a barometer of the rising sensual voltage that arced between them, a long, slow-building rumble of thunder began, vibrating the kitchen windows and making itself felt as the floor beneath their feet began to tremble.

Neither of them moved or spoke as the thunder rolled steadily toward its crescendo, neither of them quite able to look away from the other as frail tendrils of feeling wove their way between them.

Willa suddenly remembered that time at Angie's birthday party when she'd managed to maneuver Clay away from their guests and lead him to the small stand of trees well past the stone patio at the Orion ranch house. She'd been sixteen, almost seventeen.

Over Aunt Tess's objection, Willa had bought a daring little ivory halter dress with a deep V neckline and no back for Angie's party with the secret intent of bringing home to Clay just how grown-up she was and how ladylike she could be.

She'd had a crush on him then, and since one or two of the schoolboys who'd been smitten with her had seemed to like kissing her, she'd decided the time had come to see if her kisses would have a similar effect on Clay.

Unfortunately the much older Clay Cantrell had made all the boys her age seem so green and shallow that she'd found kissing them not much of a thrill. Kissing Clay was to be a kind of experiment, an adventure. It had been deliciously dangerous to anticipate what it would be like to kiss a man like him, one who was so tall and strong, one who was so exciting to be around that she'd started to feel odd little flutters in the pit of her stomach whenever he was near.

Just like now, she realized hazily as the thunder grew deafening. But for those few small measures of time she was caught up more in her memory. . . .

"I think this is far enough," Clay had said as he caught her hand and tugged her to a halt just past the first cluster of trees. There had been something quite intense about the way he'd looked at her then, something she'd seen only an inkling of before, and she'd felt both frightened and excited. When he didn't release her hand, but continued to hold it in the calloused warmth of his own, Willa had felt encouraged, almost confident, though she'd also felt alarmingly weak-kneed standing so close to him.

"You never asked me to dance tonight," she said breathlessly as she took that daring step nearer, practically forcing him to take her into his arms. When Clay obliged it seemed like the most natural thing in the world for her to reach up and place her hands on the back of his neck to draw him down those few inches.

Amazingly, magically, Clay's firm male mouth alighted gently on hers and Willa tried to kiss him as best she knew how, thoroughly shocked when Clay showed not even a hint of the enthusiasm her boyfriends had shown. When she drew back, Clay chuckled at her disappointed expression, and she felt insulted. Unable to bear the thought that Clay was laughing at her, she started to pull away, so furious that she almost struck him.

"Come back here, minx," he said in a low, rough voice as he pulled her back into his arms and held her slim resisting body against the male hardness of his. "You're too damned young to be seducing older men," he growled. "If you learn your lesson tonight, maybe you'll want to wait a couple more years before you try this again."

With that, he lowered his head and took her lips with a force that had almost made her faint. Indeed, she fairly melted beneath the sensual assault of his mouth. But when he pressed past her lips and invaded her mouth she became like a rag doll in his arms. When his mouth finally released hers she was too dazed to move, so overwhelmed that all she could do was cling weakly to him.

"Damned if I know which of us learned the lesson," she thought she heard him mutter, but she was too confused by the anger she sensed in him to be certain. He thrust her away from him and turned his back on her with a rough "You'd better get back to the party."

She did what he asked—for once—but had waited in abject misery for him to follow, so afraid that her foolishness had separated them forever that she'd almost gone home. But when he appeared a few minutes later, he acted as if nothing had happened, and she was so relieved that she'd never pulled another stunt like that—or wanted to—with anyone else again....

Willa recovered from the recollection and from somewhere found her voice. "W-what did you say?"

Clay didn't answer for a moment, and Willa felt the warm feeling of lethargy spread over her anew as he took another step toward her.

Suddenly she sensed that Clay was going to kiss her, and the realization was staggering.

But this time, he wouldn't be a man kissing a precocious teenager, she reminded herself dizzily. This time, he was a man about to kiss a woman he despised on every level, a woman whom he believed had caused his sister's death. Remembering that sobered her, and when she saw the tight anger that crossed Clay's features she knew he had remembered it, too.

The long, slow roll of thunder peaked with a crash, then ebbed into the loud drum of rain on the roof.

"How old are you, damn it?" he repeated, wrenching them both from those emotion-charged moments.

"What's that got to do with anything?" she hedged, sensing instantly what he was up to.

"Twenty-two?" he persisted.

"Twenty-two, going on eighty tonight," she said on an out-rush of weary breath as she turned and pulled the freezer door closed, banishing the last of the bittersweet memory as she concentrated on something more immediate. Perhaps the next few nights she'd eat at a restaurant in town on her way to the hospital to visit her aunt. But tonight she'd settle for a glass of

milk and a peanut butter sandwich, suddenly put off
by the thought of another frozen dinner.

"You've taken on a lot for someone your age,"
Clay pointed out a bit less sternly, but she could tell he
was straining to be diplomatic.

Willa turned fully toward him, a wry twist to one
corner of her mouth as she attempted to step around
him. "Well, that's life, Clay," she said in a flippant
tone meant to provoke. "It rarely waits until you're
old enough or smart enough. Ready or not, here it
comes." Willa moved past him, perversely letting her
hip and thigh brush against his as she did so, though
his swift intake of breath gave her much less satisfaction than she'd hoped.

"I assume you're trying to make a point," she said
as she heard him follow her back into the kitchen. She
pulled open the cupboard door where the peanut butter was kept, then set the jar on the counter next to the
bread box before she got out a plate and butter knife.

"Paige said you turned down a couple of men who
came out to apply for work. Was there something
wrong with them, or were you just being too choosy?"

Clay's question revealed a world of suspicion. Net-
tled, Willa stepped aside and yanked open the refrigerator to get out milk and a jar of her aunt's homemade jelly.

"I explained to Paige why I didn't hire those men,"
she said as she set the milk and jelly on the counter
next to the peanut butter and closed the refrigerator
door. "No one would scream louder than she would
if I'd hired either one of them. But," she added,
flashing a sarcastic smile at him as she reached for a

loaf of bread, "I'm sure she figured if she gave the truth just the right little twist she could have you over here making a nuisance of yourself."

Willa turned back to making her sandwich when Clay's expression darkened. "Both men's resumés are in on the desk in the den. Since you've obviously decided you're going to butt in on Circle H business, you might as well charge on in and see for yourself. It's pretty clear my word still means less than nothing to you."

Thick silence filled the room. Even the storm quieted for those next few seconds. Willa worked at her sandwich with jerky movements, her eyes blinded by the angry tears that had suddenly sluiced up from the old hurt inside.

She'd thought her friendship with Angie had included Clay, that the closeness and trust there'd been between the three of them had been unshakable. But Clay had never given her a chance to speak for herself after the accident; he'd already made up his mind. He'd believed Paige, a girl he hadn't known half as well as he'd known her, a girl who had no compunction about telling little white lies, one who'd often put just enough of a slant on the truth to get herself out of hot water, one who'd taken every possible advantage of a tragic situation, because Willa had been so close to death herself that Paige had initially believed she'd die, too, and that no one would ever find out who'd really been driving that day.

"Well, how about it, Clay?" she prodded, unable to calm her roiling emotions as an idea came to her. "While you're at it, you might as well look over the books and see how much money I've been bleeding out of the accounts. Come on.'' Willa tossed down the butter knife, wiped her hands on a dish towel, then stalked out of the kitchen and down the darkened hall to the den. She'd flung open the door and turned on every light in the room before she heard him walking down the hall after her.

Still stinging from the old betrayal, she got out the ranch ledgers, scooped up the bills and receipts she'd planned to tend to that night, then thumped them down in the middle of the desk as Clay stepped into the room. She spied the resumés on the corner of the desk and snatched them to add to the stack. When she looked up, she was trembling, but pride kept her from allowing anything to show but the anger she felt.

"Come on, let's get this over with," she invited irritably.

Clay's face was a stony mask. "That's not necessary."

"Oh, but it is," Willa said, straightening, her green eyes glittering. "I insist. It's time you learned to look at all the facts...and time someone called Paige's bluff." Willa reached out and gave the stack of ledgers and papers before her a little shove in his direction. "It's all here. Since yours is a surprise visit I haven't had time to alter any of the evidence."

When Clay still made no move to inspect the things she'd set out, Willa picked up the resumés and began reading them out loud, adding the impressions she'd formed during the interviews and her reasons for not hiring either man. Next she opened the ledgers and gave him a brief rundown of how much money there was in the accounts, before she began listing the expenses she'd incurred, as well as the ones she'd decided could wait.

"Added to that, I have no idea how much loss we'll show on the cattle, since the tallies at spring roundup were incomplete. Whoever was in charge missed branding—and I assume counting and vaccinating—several of the calves. Oh, I forgot," she went on acidly, "we've got only two good horses and we'll undoubtedly take another loss when the others go to auction and I have to buy replacements."

"That's enough," Clay said roughly just as she was about to add something else.

"Yes, that is enough. I agree," she said, pulling her robe a bit more snugly around herself and cinching the sash tighter around her small waist. "So you'll excuse me if I'm just a little slow getting things done or if it looks as if I'm spending my aunt into bankruptcy. As I told you before, I'll leave when I hire a couple of ranch hands and find someone competent to run the Circle H."

Clay was staring across the desk at her. He had finally stepped nearer to look at everything she'd laid out for him and Willa was certain at that moment that she hated him for needing a closer look at the evidence despite her invitation and his earlier protest.

"That's why I wanted to talk to you. I think I have a way to accomplish everything right away."

Willa watched him warily. "How?"

"Let me take over the search for a foreman and ranch hands. Until then, I can spare three or four of my men to come over and get things in order." Clay stopped, giving her a moment to consider.

Willa made the first objection that came to mind. "You can see from the books that I can't afford to pay wages for that many men."

"I'll be good for the wages. Paige already agreed to take care of supplies and operating expenses provided you leave the ranch."

Willa's lips twisted cynically. She should have known Paige was in on this.

"What about Aunt Tess?"

Clay misunderstood her question. "She won't know about the wages. Paige said Tess has made arrangements to stay with her friend Mabel Asner in town until she's strong enough to take care of herself. Everything should be finished by then."

Willa swallowed hard, her mouth dry as dust as she sensed Clay's eagerness to have her accept the proposal he and Paige had cooked up. That he was this close to Paige and was clearly involved with her made Willa feel slightly ill. But, then, she thought meanly, maybe he deserved to be hoodwinked by Paige.

"And if I go along with your idea, I could be gone by—let's say—tomorrow?" she offered, her light brows raised in question.

Clay's granite expression relaxed and he nodded, clearly relieved by her response.

"You know, don't you, that Aunt Tess has plans for me to stay on," she said, already guessing that neither he nor Paige had considered how Tess would feel about her leaving so soon. "Not that I intend to," she added when Clay's eyes hardened, "but tomorrow would be a bit too abrupt, don't you think?"

"How soon do you think it could be?" he shot back, and Willa was cut to her soul by his persistence—his obsession to banish her not only from his life, but from that of the only blood relative who would claim her.

The sadness she had managed to keep at bay most of the time began to overwhelm her and she shook her head, unable for a moment to speak. "You're pretty anxious to have me gone, aren't you?" she asked, forcing her voice to remain steady.

Clay stared at her a moment. "What do you think?"

"I think you must hate me an awful lot," she answered with soft candor.

Clay swore, his dark eyes suddenly glinting with pain-mingled anger. "Damn it all to hell, Willa, what do you expect?" he demanded, then exhaled irritably, running strong tanned fingers through his dark hair as he regained control of himself. In a more civilized voice he asked, "What about my proposal?"

Willa didn't answer right away as she struggled not to show how much his outright admission of hatred had hurt. Somehow she rallied, marshaling her pride, her manner as cold, aloof—as resolute—as she could manage.

"I'll think it over, but it's only fair to tell you that I want to stay—for Aunt Tess."

Clay's mouth slanted, and he looked away a moment as he shook his head. "I can't understand why you're doing this, Willa," he said, his voice laced with exasperation. "You and Paige are at each other's throats, half the town doesn't want to do business with you, and I'll bet you don't have one friend left around here, do you?"

Clay's gaze came back to hers challengingly, and when Willa didn't respond, he continued on, suddenly relentless. "You should have realized by now that when Tess asked you to stay on and help her, she was making more of an emotional request than a sound business decision. You're risking the loss of this ranch because you have some crazy idea that saving it is going to make up for other things. Other things," he said as his stern voice went somber, "that you can't atone for. I just hope you see sense before it goes too far."

"Is that all you have to say?" Willa asked brittlely.

"That's about it."

"Then I'd appreciate it if you'd leave," she said, managing to hold Clay's gaze without flinching until he turned from her and strode from the room. She listened to the muffled sound of his booted feet in the carpeted hall, listened when they reached the kitchen and thudded toward the porch door. The booted steps halted there and it was several moments before she heard the back door open, then close.

When it did, Willa sat down at the desk, the paperwork forgotten as a feeling of deep depression dragged her heart downward.

CHAPTER FIVE

THE WYOMING SKY was a bright blue, the storm clouds of three days before had long evaporated. The afternoon sun was hot, but the steady breeze that hummed through the stand of pines near Angela Cantrell's grave was cooling.

Willa had put off this visit to Angie's grave site for days—years, in fact. She'd been too severely injured in the accident to attend the funeral. When she'd recovered, she hadn't been able to come, either, as forbidden to do so by her own heart as by her uncle's order.

But now she was here, and the deep grief and sense of loss she still felt was amplified by the fact that today would have been Angie's twenty-third birthday. As Willa stopped at the foot of Angie's grave and stared at the brief lifespan indicated on the marble headstone, the heaviness in her chest grew unbearable as she whispered a soft "Hi, Ang."

Willa squeezed her eyes closed and the memory of Angie that she carried in her mind became unnaturally sharp. What she saw was a seventeen-year-old girl with dark, curly hair, merry brown eyes and coltishly long legs. Willa could still see the mischievous gleam in Angie's eyes and the ornery curve of her mouth as the two of them cooked up some piece of devilry—usually directed at Clay because his good-natured retaliation could be counted on.

"I had to come here today," she whispered at last, easily picturing her best friend's quick smile of welcome. "It's been more than five years, and since it's your birthday..." Willa's voice trailed away as she looked down with tear-blurred eyes at the bouquet of miniature pink roses she held in a cone of florist's tissue. "I brought you these."

Willa stepped to the headstone and crouched down, removing the flowers from the tissue. Suddenly the sense of Angie's presence was so real that Willa half expected to see Angie leaning an elbow on the headstone, grinning down at her. The feeling was so remarkably strong that it was almost a shock not to see her friend standing there. A little unnerved, but comforted in an unexpected way, Willa felt her tension recede.

She lowered herself to the ground, sitting cross-legged at the side of the grave, any sense that she was trespassing gone. One by one, Willa separated the roses and leaned over to place them in the slim receptacle in front of the stone. When she was finished, she rested her elbows on her thighs and sat with her head bowed and her fingers combed deeply into her hair.

CLAY CANTRELL drove his truck beneath the scrolled iron arch that marked the entrance to the cemetery. As much as he'd wanted to ignore this anniversary, the melancholia he'd been feeling all day prevented it. Angie had loved parties and a good time and there was no way he could let her birthday go by without doing what little he could to remember it. It seemed that everything bright and fun had gone out of his life when Angie had died, and for the longest time, he'd thought the grieving would never stop. Eventually it had and he'd got over her death, but there were still times when those tender wounds were pricked. More so now that Willa was back. Just having her around had resurrected the pain, and suddenly this sentimental anniversary had once again become almost unbearable.

The moment Clay turned left at the fork of the one lane road that led to the far end of the cemetery, he saw Willa's car. His mouth tightened grimly as he glanced beyond it toward the hill and the cluster of pines that stood between the road and the Cantrell family plot. That Willa would visit Angie's grave angered him and as he drew his truck to a halt behind her car, he vowed to do something about it.

"I'M SO SORRY, Ang," Willa whispered, her forehead in her hands as the tears finally broke. "I wasn't strong enough. Maybe you were already...gone... before I could get to you." Willa paused, fighting to keep the worst of the memory repressed. "I guess I'll never know for sure." For several minutes, tears of that remembered agony slid in a torrent down her cheeks. At last she raised her head and looked again at the name on the headstone, Angela Elaine Cantrell, and the birth and death dates just seventeen years apart.

The tears continued, but as the sense of uncomforted grief finally eased, Willa slowly began to feel better. Coming here had been a release, a chance to talk things over with an old friend, a time to ask for forgiveness and find it. As crazy as it seemed, Willa somehow knew now that Angie wouldn't have thought she'd done anything that needed to be forgiven. And though realizing that didn't lessen Willa's sense of responsibility, she felt more at peace than she had for years.

Willa drew a shaky breath, unaware of the harsh-faced man who stood only a few feet behind her. "I still miss you, Ang."

The scuff of a boot in the grass startled her. As she jerked her head around, she saw Clay's denim-clad legs and her eyes shot up to his iron countenance.

Clay stared down at Willa's tear-ravaged face. He'd been prepared to rail at her, to challenge her right to be here, but the instant he'd heard her emotion-clogged voice and listened to the things she was saying to Angie—just as if Angie were sitting there with her—something inside him had started twisting.

She was turning him inside out, forcing him to feel things he wanted to ignore, deepening the conflict within him that tore open old wounds and inflicted new ones. He had softened toward Willa considerably in the three weeks she'd been here, and he hated himself for it. It wasn't right that Willa had survived the foolishness that had taken his kid sister's life. Everything good and compassionate and gentle that Willa aroused in him somehow seemed disloyal to Angie.

As he watched Willa scramble to her feet and turn fully toward him, Clay couldn't prevent his gaze from wandering downward, his mind suddenly filled with the sensuous memory of how she'd looked in that short robe the other night.

Warily Willa watched the changing emotions that crossed Clay's face. Apprehension filled her when his fingers tightened punishingly on the stems of the white lilies he held at his side. Yet when his gaze came back to meet hers, it was bleak, the shafts of pain she read there bringing a fresh sting of tears.

Neither of them said a word as Willa picked up the crumpled florist's tissue and stepped past Clay to hurry to her car.

WILLA JABBED the slender spade into the gap between the fence post and the edge of the post hole, tamping down the dirt to wedge the new post more firmly into place. At midmorning, the hot June sun was already scorching through her clothing, but Willa felt oblivious to it. She was thinking only of the call she'd made to Clay the night before.

"I've thought about your offer," she'd told him as evenly as she could, determined to hide the emotional turmoil that had plagued her in the two days since she'd seen him at the cemetery. "And I was wondering if you'd consider a compromise."

At Clay's gruff "What is it?" Willa tentatively accepted the offer he'd made to find a foreman and a couple of ranch hands for the Circle H—but on the condition that she have final approval of who was hired.

Silence followed her counterproposal, but the instant objection she'd expected never came. When Clay reminded her about the other part of his proposal—that he send over some of his men to work on the Circle H—she'd accepted.

"But until you find a foreman, I'd like to stay on and keep working. There's more than enough to go around," she added, then waited for what felt like an eternity before Clay spoke.

"Paige's condition for providing the money for expenses was that you leave the ranch," he reminded her, and Willa felt herself wilt a little at his outspoken determination to have her go.

She had pressed a shaky hand against her forehead, grateful that she'd called Clay rather than gone to see him face to face. "I've just looked over the accounts. There's enough money to cover the outstanding expenses and supplies if I'm careful. I've kept a good record, so Paige can reimburse the accounts after I'm gone. Besides, it might take you a while to find a foreman."

Clay said nothing for so long that she thought they'd been disconnected. Resentment shot through her.

"I realize you and Paige are counting the minutes until I'm out of your lives forever," she said to break the silence, unable to keep the sarcastic edge from her voice, "but Aunt Tess doesn't feel that way, and she wouldn't understand if I suddenly turned everything over to you and disappeared."

A soft curse came over the line and Willa's temper flared. "If you decide you can live with my counterproposal, you can send over a couple men to help me replace that section of fence that borders Orion. If you can spare more than two, I could use someone else to ride fence and check on the cattle in the south section along the highway." Willa took a quick breath. "Tell your men to pack their own lunches if they expect to eat. I'll be starting on the fence at seven." She hung up the phone before Clay could agree or not.

When she'd arrived at the fence line that morning just before seven with the wire and fence posts needed to do the job, two of Clay's men were waiting for her.

"I'm Frank Casey, and this here's Bill Johnson," Frank offered, and both men touched their hat brims in a show of politeness. "The boss sent us over to give you a hand."

Willa could detect nothing but respect in the manner of the two ranch hands and felt her mouth move into a reserved smile. "I appreciate your help."

The three of them had got right to work, removing several lengths of rusted, brittle wire to prepare for the new. Next they began digging up a few old rotted posts along this stretch of fence, replacing them with sturdy new ones. By that night, the new wire would be up and the most extensive of the repairs on this section would be made.

But Willa's relief at getting the job done and being spared the frustration and exhaustion of doing it alone was marred by the regret she felt. She should have been more considerate of Clay's feelings, more tolerant of his wish to have her gone, when they'd spoken on the phone the night before. Several times since she'd seen him at the cemetery, she'd relived those brief moments when she'd seen the pain on his face and the bleak look in his eyes.

Finding her at Angie's grave had obviously upset him, and in spite of how he felt about her, she hated causing him more pain. Although she'd felt as justifiably angry as when they'd talked on the phone, she should have made the extra effort to be a bit more patient, more diplomatic. In view of the fact that Clay thought her responsible for Angie's death, he was behaving with remarkable tolerance. Willa wasn't certain she'd be able to treat him as well if their situations were reversed. Some kind of apology was in order, though she wasn't quite sure how to make it without stirring everything up again.

As Willa finished with the fence post and moved down her part of the row to the next, she caught sight of Clay's silver-and-black pickup as it crested the hill on the Orion side and drove over the rough pasture toward her and the men.

Apprehensive suddenly, Willa made a project of using the slim shovel to rake loose dirt from the old post hole in preparation for the new post. Clay was probably here to speak to his men, so it was possible there would never be a private moment for her to say anything to him, much less voice an apology.

When Clay stepped out of his truck, Willa looked up from her work, but could read nothing in the hard black gaze that swung toward hers, then veered away as if he were ignoring her.

Willa worked on, listening to the easy sound of male voices as Clay joined his men, though she couldn't quite make out what was being said. The talking continued as she reached for the post-hole digger to deepen the hole.

Impatient, hoping yet dreading that Clay would come her way, Willa glanced toward him again, catching his eyes on her as he started in her direction. Hastily lifting a last bit of dirt from the post hole, Willa finished with the digger.

"I sent one of my men to check on the cattle," Clay said, the stony expression beneath his hat brim quite different from the one he'd just shown his men.

"Thanks," she murmured, her gloved hands gripping the digger handles nervously. Clay nodded, then started to turn toward his truck. Now was the time to say something to him about the night before. It might make no difference in how he felt toward her, but her conscience would be eased, and at least she could say she'd made the attempt. "Wait. There's something I need to say." Willa watched the stern, unfriendly set of Clay's face for any sign of softening when he turned back to her.

"I shouldn't have lost my temper last night," she said on an out-rush of breath. "I can understand how anxious you are to have me gone, and I'm sure I'd feel the same way if things were the other way around...." Willa could no longer meet the hard gleam in his eyes and her gaze slid from his. "Under the circumstances, you've been more than tolerant with me, and I want you to know that I'm sorry my being here is...hard on you," she got out, remembering how he'd told her that day along the highway that having her around again was hard, "damned hard," as he'd put it. "I plan to have the talk with Aunt Tess that I should have had days ago. That way, she'll have as much time as possible to get used to the idea. I'll be ready to leave as soon as you find a foreman.''

Willa glanced away, looking off into the distance, feeling awkward and more than a little sad, though she was careful not to let it show on her face. That Clay was sensitive enough to her changing emotions to see it anyway would not have occurred to her.

"I've got a man in mind who might make a good foreman for your aunt."

Willa's gaze shot back to Clay's as he went on. "I gave him a call this morning. He's the assistant foreman on a big ranch up by Sheridan. He's good with horses, knows cattle, and he's been thinking about finding a smaller operation closer to his sister and her family in Laramie. The Circle H might be just what he's looking for."

Willa tried not to show her surprise. Clay was evidently confident about the man.

"I'd appreciate a chance to talk to him myself before any decisions are made," she said firmly.

A look of impatience crossed Clay's face. "I want this over with as soon as possible, Willa," he grumbled irritably. "Don't make excuses to keep it going."

"We have an agreement," she reminded him stiffly.

"Some agreement," he growled. "After you got done with it, it wasn't much of a deal, was it?"

Willa's chin went up slightly. "But you accepted it, or your men wouldn't be over here this morning," she pointed out.

Clay stared down at her, his dark eyes holding hers with a glimmer that was startlingly cold. "I'd probably agree to just about anything that got you away from here and out of our lives for good.''

Willa felt herself go pale as she reeled inwardly from the impact of Clay's words. Her gaze was obscured by the abrupt dip of her hat brim as she looked downward. "I've got work to do," she murmured as she focused on the tight grip she had on the post-hole digger.

Clay didn't linger. Turning his back, he walked away from her and her eyes crept upward to watch him go. His stride was angry and swift. He ignored his men as he crossed to the Orion side of the fence line and climbed into his truck.

With her vision beginning to blur with tears, Willa turned and tossed down the digger, not seeing that the tip of one handle came down sharply next to a long patterned shape that wiggled between a roll of new wire and the fence post she was about to pick up. The warning rattle of the snake didn't sound until her gloved hands closed around the post.

CHAPTER SIX

WILLA GASPED and instinctively jerked away from the sharp pain in her left wrist, horrified to realize she'd been bitten by a rattlesnake. The sound of the rattle, the strike, the pain—it all happened so quickly she hadn't had time to avoid it. Willa watched, dazed with disbelief, as the snake slithered away into the rough grass and disappeared.

Revulsion brought instant nausea as she caught the musky scent the agitated rattlesnake left in its wake. Willa shucked her work gloves and let them drop to the ground, then unbuttoned her shirt cuff and wrenched it up to reveal the twin puncture wounds of the bite.

Clay had just climbed into his truck and was about to start the engine, when he saw Willa drop her gloves and yank her sleeve up. Though her back was toward him, he sensed instantly that something was wrong. Irritated that everything within him was suddenly alert, he watched a moment more.

Willa glanced anxiously in Clay's direction, relieved to see he wasn't driving away, until she remembered what he'd just said to her. *I'd probably agree to just about anything that got you away from here and out of our lives for good.*

The strong pulse of pain in the area of the bite reclaimed Willa's attention and she saw that her wrist was already beginning to swell. Though she'd hoped no venom had been injected into the bite wounds—she knew that happened sometimes, a "dry bite," it was called—the onset of swelling and sharper pain told her she hadn't been so lucky. Panicked at the thought that she was in a potentially life-threatening situation, and that she was as good as alone, Willa started swiftly toward the Circle H pickup.

Calm down, she cautioned herself as she slowed her pace. The worst thing she could do now was give in to the hysteria that threatened to claim her. Still, as foolhardy as it was, she found she was practically running to the truck, her relief at reaching it squelched when she got the passenger door open and dug into the glove compartment for the snake bite kit that should have been there, but wasn't.

"Willa?"

Willa heard Clay's shout and turned her head to see that he had just stepped out of his truck and was waiting for a response from her. Tamping down her terrible longing for his presence and his help, Willa waved him away, then leaned farther into the truck to rummage beneath the seat for the kit.

She didn't need anyone, she reminded herself. She'd got along for a long time alone. She'd survived, but until that awful moment she hadn't realized how deep and how keen the estrangement she'd suffered had gone. There was nothing but loneliness and fear deep down inside her—fear of getting too close to anyone, fear of rejection, fear of intimacy. . . .

Willa shoved those distressing thoughts aside as her fingers closed around the plastic box she'd been searching for. Trembling with haste, she pulled it from beneath the seat and worked at the stubborn catch.

"Willa, what the hell—"

Clay's voice startled her just as she got the kit open, and the contents spilled to the floor. She grabbed wildly for them, the desperation she felt making her clumsy.

"Haven't you got anything better to do?" she snapped, trying her best to conceal what she was doing from Clay. There should be plenty of time to administer the proper first aid and then drive herself to the hospital in Cascade.

"Let's see," Clay ordered as he took hold of her arm to turn her toward him. Willa winced at the fresh stab of pain, but didn't cry out.

"Damn it, Willa," he growled, then shouted for his men. Frank and Bill stopped working immediately and hurried over.

"I'll be all right," Willa told him as she tried to pull away. "I can take care of it myself."

Clay ignored her resistance and quickly inspected the puncture wounds and the swelling beneath. He released her only long enough to lift her to the truck seat. By then Frank and Bill had reached them.

"Snakebite," he told them as he forced Willa's sleeve high enough to apply a tourniquet. "One of you'd better use the CB to call someone at the house. Have them notify the hospital so they can be ready. And we'd better have a look at the size cf the snake."

"It's gone," Willa cut in.

"Have a look around, anyway," Clay directed. As his men hurried away, Clay finished tying the constricting band just above her left elbow—tight enough to impede the flow of venom through the lymph system in her arm, but not tight enough to slow the artery.

"I can do the rest," Willa insisted, and as Clay reached for the antiseptic she pulled away from him.

"Damn it, Willa, this is serious," he growled as he swiftly reclaimed her arm and spilled some antiseptic over the wounds.

"But very convenient for you and Paige, wouldn't you say?" she shot back, barely noticing the sting of the antiseptic.

"What's that supposed to mean?" he demanded, then used his teeth to rip open the cellophane that held the sterile razor as he positioned Willa's wrist to make the quarter-inch incisions through the puncture wounds that would allow the venom to drain.

"You know what I'm talking about," she told him, her voice low and trembling with more emotion than she could control. "You and Paige have been so eager to get rid of me..."

Clay's midnight eyes flashed angrily to hers for an instant before he looked down again to make the shallow cuts. "Not this way, Willa. Neither of us wants it this way and you know it." Clay reached for the suction and applied it to the fang marks.

"Oh, yeah?" she challenged, feeling nauseous and a little faint as the pain in her arm increased.

Clay raised his hand and grasped her chin to stare intently into her eyes. "Yeah," he answered, his voice rough and harsh. "And I don't ever want to hear that from you again." He didn't release her and she couldn't escape the look of anger in his eyes, which changed instantly to a look of tender concern. "You aren't feeling so good right now, are you?"

"I'm all right," she said with stiff dignity, not wanting to let Clay see that she was frightened and beginning to feel worse.

"It's going to be a rough ride out of here," he said as he released her chin to slide his calloused palm along her jaw and cheek. The soothing caress surprised her, but even more so when she realized Clay's hand was shaking.

"We don't have much choice, do we?" she asked, then saw something flare to life in Clay's eyes. He chaffed his palm gently against her cheek and slowly shook his head.

"No," he said, his voice a low rasp that moved over the surface of her emotions like rough velvet. "No choice at all, I guess."

WILLA LAY fully dressed on the hospital bed, staring at the television positioned on the wall across the room as she waited for the chaplain to stop by and give her a ride to the Circle H. It had been almost a day and a half since Clay had carried her into the emergency room and turned her over to the doctor's care. Nurses and technicians had come at her from all directions, bathing the bite area, taking blood samples, doing periodic checks of her vital signs, taking her medical history and getting an account of the bite. The antivenin had been administered quickly and successfully, but because there was the chance she'd need more, she'd been admitted to the hospital and given a private room.

Clay had stepped into the treatment area to see her before she'd been taken upstairs, but he'd stayed only long enough to learn that she was doing well and that she would need to stay in the hospital at least twenty-four hours. She hadn't seen him since.

Willa pressed the remote button that switched off the television, thoroughly weary of daytime programming. She'd needed a distraction from the unpleasant memories that had been triggered by her brief hospital stay, but television hadn't supplied it. Ever more restless, she glanced over at the wall clock, then got up, impatient to see that it was just after five. The chaplain had promised to be there by four, so Willa had already taken care of checking out.

She'd just started to make a call to his office, when the door to her room swung open. Thinking it was the chaplain, Willa quickly hung up the phone and turned around. "I was just—" Her smile of welcome faltered as Clay walked into the room, the overnight case she'd brought with her to Cascade in his hand.

"Feeling better?"

Clay stopped near the foot of the hospital bed, rotating the Stetson slightly on his fingers as his gaze swept over her. Willa struggled against the strong emotion that gripped her at the sight of him, amazed that he had this kind of effect on her. He seemed taller than ever suddenly, overwhelmingly male, and it was all Willa could do to keep her eyes from straying over his broad-shouldered, lean-hipped height.

"Feeling good enough to go home," she said a bit nervously. "As soon as Reverend Collins gets here."

"I spoke to him earlier," Clay informed her. "If you don't mind, I'll give you that ride back to the Circle H." Before Willa could respond, Clay held the small case out to her. "I thought you'd like to stop in and see Tess first, so I picked up a change of clothes for you."

Willa looked up from the case to Clay, taken aback by the personal intrusion into her life that his actions represented. If he'd truly brought her a change of clothes, that meant that he'd been in her room at the ranch and had gone through her belongings to get them. The thought gave her an odd feeling.

"That was...nice of you," she said awkwardly, then reached for the case. "I'll just be a minute."

Willa changed quickly in the room's private bath, pleased that she didn't have to wear her soiled work clothing home, but a bit pink cheeked to see that Clay had also chosen a set of her laciest underwear. The white jeans he'd selected were fine for a summer evening, and the long loose sleeves of the lime blouse would easily conceal her bandaged wrist from her aunt. He'd even thought to include a few cosmetics—just what she normally would have worn for the visit—and Willa applied them with a light hand.

"I really appreciate this, Clay," she said when she'd stepped out of the bathroom. "Aunt Tess might have worried if I hadn't stopped by again tonight."

Clay took the small bag from her. "I assumed Tess hadn't been told," he said, then gestured for her to precede him from the room.

Clay left the overnight case at the nurses' station on the floor Tess was on, then went with Willa to Tess's room. Willa was surprised Clay was going in with her, but she didn't question him. She felt unusually tired, in spite of spending most of the day resting, and although she was eager to see her aunt, she was just as eager to get the visit over with so she could go home.

"Willa!" Tess glanced past her visitor the moment Willa walked in, her instant smile widening when she caught sight of Clay. "And Clay!" she added, pleased. Willa crossed to the side of the bed opposite from where Mabel Asner stood, and leaned over to kiss her aunt's cheek.

Clay took a place at the foot of the bed, one corner of his mouth hitching up in carefully suppressed amusement when he saw the surprise on Mabel's ruddy face as she glanced from Willa to him. "Evening, Tess. Mabel."

"Are you two together?" Mabel asked, clearly bursting with curiosity.

"Willa and I are having dinner together tonight," Clay answered smoothly, and Willa felt herself reel in shock. If she hadn't sensed earlier that something between them was different, she did now.

"How are you today, Aunt Tess?" Willa asked casually to hide her confusion. The conversation settled quickly into what the doctor had said that day and who'd been by. And thanks to Mabel, Willa and Clay also got to hear the latest bit of gossip about each of Tess's visitors.

"I'm afraid Mabel missed her calling," Clay remarked as they walked to where he'd parked his car.

"She should have been a news hound for some big city newspaper. Or leastways a gossip columnist somewhere."

Willa's mouth formed a bitter line. She was unable to see much that was humorous about Mabel's penchant for gossip since she'd been a victim of it. "Then why did you tell her we were having dinner together? A piece of news like that will get all over the county in less than a half hour," she said, then added crossly, "you started something you definitely won't appreciate tomorrow."

Clay escorted her to the passenger door and opened it for her before he spoke. "You need to eat, don't you?" he asked. He closed the door before she could respond. When he'd got her case into the trunk and eased his long body onto the seat beside her, Willa was watching him mistrustfully.

"What's come over you?" she demanded to know. "Why are you doing all this?"

Clay flashed a look in her direction that skittered away as his face hardened slightly. He pushed the key into the ignition and gave it a twist. "Let's don't ask too many questions right now," he said, his voice curt and tinged with just a trace of the unfriendliness she'd come to know all too well. "Why don't we just relax and see how things go from here?"

Willa stared at him as he backed the car smoothly from the parking space, then studied his flinty profile as he drove out of the lot.

"You feel guilty about what you said yesterday," she concluded with a cynical twist of lips.

When Clay didn't have a quick answer, Willa sighed, struggling to push away all the emotions he was so carelessly arousing. She had to clarify the situation for them both.

"Look, if I'd been paying attention to what I was doing, I wouldn't have got bitten by a snake," she reasoned. "If I hadn't been bitten, you wouldn't have had an attack of conscience. I'd probably be out fixing fence right now, and you'd still be pressing me to leave Cascade."

Clay made no response to what she'd said, and Willa went tense as he turned down a familiar street and pulled into the parking lot of the Silver Spur restaurant.

"I'm not really up to this," Willa said quickly as Clay reached up to switch off the engine. Willa's green eyes had gone shadowy and the turbulence in them communicated more fear than anger. "I mean it, Clay."

Clay studied her face for a long moment before he looked away and put the car into gear. The entire ride to the Circle H passed in silence.

"Thanks for the ride—for everything," Willa said as Clay brought the car to a smooth stop in the drive. She wasted no time in levering open her door to step out. As she walked to the back of the car for her overnight case, Willa tried to conceal the weariness that was creeping over her. When Clay got out and unlocked the trunk, Willa reached for her case, but he took it for her.

"I can get that," she said as he closed the trunk, but Clay shook his head and walked with her to the back porch door. To Willa's surprise, he carried her case all the way into the kitchen and set it on the floor.

"Is there anything you need?" he asked. The sudden awkwardness between them somehow felt unnatural even though they were enemies of sorts.

"No. Nothing."

"Then I'll head on down to the barn and take care of a few chores before I go."

"I think I can handle that much," Willa told him, uncomfortable with all his help.

"You should be resting."

Anxiety flickered through her and she was suddenly frightened of mistaking any of this for genuine caring or friendship on Clay's part.

"Don't, Clay."

Her soft plea smoothed out some of the harsher angles of his face and gentled the look in his eyes. "I'll see to those chores," he insisted gruffly, then turned and walked out the back door.

Willa watched him go, then glanced around the kitchen. Any appetite she had was gone. Unusually weary, her legs leaden with fatigue and unhappiness, Willa headed for the sofa in the living room.

THE NIGHTMARE WAS the same as always—more flashback than dream—so vivid and so eerily real that it was like being wrenched from the present. Each time it managed to escape her subconscious and invade her sleep-fogged mind, Willa relived every agonizing detail of what had happened that warm spring afternoon when Angie had died.

"God, Willa, you drive like an old woman," Paige was saying as she impatiently thrust a dark skein of hair behind her shoulder. Willa had started out from the stop sign after coming to a full stop and looking both ways, but because Paige was in a hurry to get home, Willa's caution aggravated her.

Angie, who was sitting between the two cousins, elbowed Willa, and Willa momentarily turned her head and grinned at her friend, then glanced past her to a sulking Paige, who had propped an arm on the open window and was drumming her fingernails impatiently on the roof of the pickup.

Willa and Angie had taken Uncle Cal's new truck to town to pick Paige up from a friend's house, but it was Saturday, and Paige had a hot date that night with a college boy home on spring break. Paige had been a bit too full of herself all week, more bossy and conceited than usual, so naturally Willa and Angie had taken it upon themselves to have a bit of harmless fun with her. As far as they were concerned, Paige was long overdue.

Willa continued to obey the speed limit a bit more faithfully than she might have otherwise, and she and Angie shared a secret grin or two when Paige continued to squirm and complain.

Just before they reached the edge of town, Angie started to cough. "Gosh, Willa," she said after the spasm of coughing had subsided, "I could sure use something to drink." Willa had easily perceived the dry hack as a put-on and quickly took her cue.

"Me, too," she'd chimed in, then flipped on the signal to turn at the next corner.

"You can wait till you get home," Paige snapped, then crossed her arms sullenly across her chest when Willa ignored her and made the turn that would take them to a convenience store. By the time Willa pulled into the store parking lot, Paige was fuming.

"Can we get you something, Paige?" Willa had asked solicitously, seemingly oblivious to Paige's pique.

"Just hurry up," Paige said through gritted teeth, but Angie found a way to dawdle as she started counting out the change in her pocket and made a production of trying to figure if she would have enough left over for a candy bar or only a pack of gum.

By the time Willa and Angie had finally gone in to make their selections and had come back out, Paige was behind the wheel. Figuring Paige had had enough, the other two girls climbed docilely into the truck, Angie choosing the middle of the long bench seat and Willa taking the place by the door.

Provoked and in a hurry, Paige had roared out of the parking lot, ignoring speed limit and traffic signs in an attempt to make up for lost time. It crossed Willa's mind to suggest that they all put on their seat belts, but a sudden dip in the road caused her to spill her soda down the front of her shirt and she'd forgotten about the safety precaution.

A few minutes later, on the graveled back road Paige had chosen as a short cut, the truck hit a series of washboard bumps and Paige lost control. . . .

Willa awakened to blinding pain in her head and the strong, sickening fumes of gasoline. The truck lay upside down in the ravine a few feet from her and Willa moved instinctively toward it.

At first, the pain in her shoulder and arm was too great for her to crawl. Each breath she took brought a stabbing pain to her side that dimmed her vision. Slowly, agonizingly, she managed to use her other arm to pull herself along, the effort making her dizzy and nauseous. Paige, she'd noticed, was lying on the bank just above and behind the overturned truck, but Angie was nowhere in sight.

Wave upon wave of sickening fear washed through her, compelling her to get to Angie. From somewhere it registered that the gas tank had ruptured and that fire was imminent. Sobbing, struggling, fighting back the black void that tried to claim her, Willa clawed her way to the truck, the sight she saw in the wreckage of the overturned vehicle bringing with it a cry of horror.

CLAY HEARD the odd, softly keening wail just as he was about to get into his car. Sensing something was wrong when he heard the strange sound a second time, he shut the door, then hurried toward the house. Hesitating on the porch steps, he recognized Willa's voice. Fear gripped him as he wrenched open the door, then ran toward the sounds.

Willa lay on the sofa, a knee upraised as her head moved fitfully from side to side, caught up in the nightmare that had left her drenched with perspiration. Clay froze in the doorway as she again made the wailing, whimpering sound he'd heard.

"Angie, wake up."

Clay listened intently, recognizing Angie's name from the mumbled syllables. He stared a moment, too stunned to move as he watched Willa struggle with the nightmare as if she were searching for something, reaching.

"Please, Angie, wake up."

A shudder coursed through his body and landed like a fist in his chest as he recognized the words and heard the utter desperation in Willa's voice.

CHAPTER SEVEN

THE HANDS THAT GRIPPED her upper arms and shook her awake were unlike the ones that had pulled her away from the wreckage just before the truck burst into flames, but Willa fought them as she'd fought those other hands. She had to save Angie. She couldn't let herself be pulled away before she could get Angie out.

"No. No, don't. Angie's in there," she babbled wildly, then found herself sitting up, her fingers dug like claws into Clay's shoulders.

Willa stared, eyes rounded in shock as nightmare and reality clashed.

"Angie? Did she—" The nightmare dimmed and receded, leaving in its wake a soul-deep feeling of grief and terrible loss. "Oh, God," she whispered raggedly, squeezing her eyes closed as she bowed her head, her breath coming in great gasps as the sobs rose in her chest like fire.

Clay couldn't take his eyes from her stricken face. The desolation he saw there clutched at him and drew him in as the shock of what he'd just heard pulsed through him.

He realized then what he should have realized five years before—that Willa hadn't intended for anyone to be hurt. The accident had to have been the result of a crazy adolescent stunt that had gone tragically wrong. It occurred to him suddenly that it could just as easily have been Angie who'd taken that reckless chance. The tenderness that welled up inside him as he continued to hold Willa drained the last of his hostility.

"Please, just leave me alone," she said hoarsely as she shoved him away, then shifted to the end of the sofa. Too overwrought to sit still, Willa got unsteadily to her feet and walked to the west windows of the living room to stare out despairingly at the purpling sunset of the waning day. The play of long shadows mingled eerily with the lingering effects of the nightmare and Willa wrapped her arms around herself, aware of the ache in her wrist and arm as she began to shiver.

"Are you all right?"

Willa went a little more rigid as she kept her back to him and tried to control the maelstrom of emotion that roiled inside her. The nightmare hadn't come this hard for months.

"Willa?" The deep velvety texture of Clay's voice and the undisguised concern it betrayed sent more tears flooding down her cheeks.

"I'm all right," she said briskly, then brought both hands up to brush impatiently at the wetness on her face. "You did the chores?" she asked, forcing her voice to sound steady and normal.

"Forget the chores," Clay said gruffly as he came to his feet and crossed the room. Willa stiffened as

Clay stopped inches from her. "Do you have nightmares about Angie often?"

Willa bit her lip to stifle the sob that welled up in answer. The silence that stretched out was as thick and smothering as the black dreams that still hovered somewhere in the dark corners of her mind. Willa couldn't bear to have Clay pry into any of them, but she couldn't seem to form the right words to tell him so.

"Go away," she got out at last, then began to tremble as Clay's big hands came up and settled consolingly on her shoulders. She made a move to step away, but his fingers tightened, then began a soothing massage that radiated a warmth through her body that worked at the cold quivering knot deep inside. He stepped even closer as she began to shake, the heated impact of his nearness making her want to lean back and meld with his strength.

"Please. Just go away," she whispered hoarsely, her breathing fast and erratic as she tried to keep from turning and throwing her arms around him to grab for every bit of comfort his actions hinted at.

Clay felt the emotional tug of war within Willa only because the war of emotions within himself had been so acute. Compassion filled his heart.

"Not just yet, Willa," he said quietly, then turned her toward him and took her into his arms.

Willa clung to Clay helplessly, unable to resist the comfort she'd had so little of after the trauma of Angie's death and the terrible estrangement that had followed. No one had seemed to give much thought to the shock and desolation she'd felt at her friend's sudden death and the horrible manner in which she'd died. Even Aunt Tess had seemed distant and uncaring then.

"It's all right, Willa. It's all over," Clay soothed as he held her trembling body and let her cry. She felt as fragile as a small child in his arms and Clay couldn't help the protectiveness he felt toward her as he gathered her closer and led her to the large rocking chair beside the windows.

Willa's soft, pliant body molded easily to the solid planes of his as he pulled her down onto his lap and began to rock her like a baby. With the gentlest of hands he stroked her hair as her grip on him became frantic and the tears came hotter and harder.

It was some time later, when the room had gone completely dark, that the tears finally stopped. Willa rested weakly against Clay, her cheek on his damp shoulder as she listened to the steady rock of the chair and felt the calming rhythm of it to her soul. Clay's arms were still tight around her and Willa savored the security of his closeness, wondering at the meaning of it.

"Angie had her share of nightmares when she was little," Clay began, his deep voice a pleasant rumble against her chest. "Her favorite cure was the rocking chair." Clay continued to rock, raising his hand to stroke Willa's cheek.

At the mention of Angie's name, Willa went tense. Clay brushed his fingers over Willa's hair and softly ordered her to relax.

"She was my best friend, Clay," Willa whispered, the tremor in her voice a remnant of the emotional upheaval she'd just weathered. "I wouldn't have put her life in danger for anything in the world." Behind her words was the plea for Clay to at last believe this, to at last believe she hadn't caused the accident that had killed his sister. She couldn't tell him the truth outright because it would devastate Aunt Tess, yet she couldn't help but hope he would somehow realize it anyway.

Clay lowered his hand to rub her arm. "I know, Willa," he said huskily, and her heart gave a glad leap. She pressed against his chest to sit up, her damp eyes searching his in the dimness as his hand dropped to rest at her waist.

"You do?" she asked, the hope inside her swelling.

Clay's dark eyes were utterly serious. "You were just a kid," he said softly. "A kid who pulled a foolish stunt. I know you didn't mean for Angie to die."

Willa stared helplessly at him as disheartened tears swam into her eyes. He still didn't believe her, still didn't understand. Willa turned her face away and made a move to get up, but Clay didn't release her.

"I don't think Angie would be too pleased with the way things have been between you and I since then."

Willa couldn't look at Clay for a moment. When she did, she saw a tenderness and affection in his expression that surprised her.

"Angie would have wanted us to stay friends," he said. "I can see that now." Clay's fingers moved in slow circles on her back as he gripped her waist. "If there's a way for you and I to put the past five years behind us and start fresh, maybe we ought to try. What do you say?"

Willa was suddenly overcome with bittersweet emotion. Clay was forgiving her for something she hadn't done, yet offering her a reconciliation she'd not believed possible. It startled her to realize just how much she'd yearned all this time for things to come right between them, but it disappointed her that it all seemed to hinge on Clay's compassion for her rather than on the truth.

Fearful of somehow jeopardizing this truce, no matter how imperfect it was, Willa nodded slowly, bringing a trembling hand to Clay's jaw in a quick, shy caress. "All right," she murmured, the taste of new tears in her mouth as she smiled slightly and watched his eyes for any hint of insincerity.

"Good." Clay's face relaxed into a smile that eased Willa's uncertainty. "I think it would be a good idea to get our fresh start off on a full stomach. How does supper sound to you?"

Willa was too choked to answer for a moment as she sensed the first tendrils of renewed friendship forming. Surely this wasn't really happening.

"Let me have some time to freshen up and I'll see what's in the kitchen," she said as she slid off Clay's lap. Clay's hand caught hers at the last moment, enveloping her slim fingers in the hard warmth of his.

"Take your time. I'll see to supper," he said as he came to his feet.

Willa felt his fingers tighten, and she reflexively pulled back, panicked suddenly at the depth of the change that was happening between them. If Clay noticed the anxiety that made her withdraw and hurry upstairs, he didn't comment.

Willa lingered nervously in her bathroom, having splashed her face with cool water before she lightly reapplied a bit of makeup. She could hear Clay rummaging around in the kitchen and was reluctant now to join him. No one had ever seen her as he just had, not even Aunt Tess, and Willa felt uncomfortably exposed. She waited as long as she dared before she headed downstairs.

To her relief, Clay was standing at the short length of counter beside the stove with his back to her as she entered the kitchen.

"Still like your eggs over easy?" he asked as he heard her walk in.

"Over easy is fine," she answered cautiously, suddenly suspicious of Clay's earlier behavior. Perhaps he'd just felt sorry for her. Some men seemed to have trouble dealing with women's tears, and though it shamed Willa to acknowledge it, she'd just put on one heck of a show. Was it too farfetched to wonder if Clay's gentleness with her—and his willingness to forgive her—was motivated more by pity and male embarrassment than by genuine feelings? She had to find out.

Uneasy, and uncertain about just how she could discern something like that, Willa crossed to where Clay stood laying strips of bacon in a large iron skillet.

"Is there anything I can do?" she offered, watching his profile intently until his dark eyes swung toward hers.

"You could set the table."

Willa turned away to do so, noticing as she got out plates and silverware that a chocolate aroma was beginning to fill the kitchen, mingling deliciously with the smell of frying bacon.

"You don't mind bacon and eggs for a late supper, do you?" Clay asked as he watched her set the table while he waited for the bacon to cook.

"As long as it's someone else's cooking, I could eat just about anything that isn't a TV dinner," she replied.

One corner of Clay's mouth lifted. "I take it you don't like to cook."

"I don't get a lot of practice," she said without thinking. Alarmed at the bit of information she'd just given away, Willa glanced down and gave more attention than necessary to laying the flatware just right. Most larger ranches had a cook to prepare meals for the ranch hands. Clay would never guess that the cook on the D & R worked for Willa.

"I never did hear where it is you've been working the past few years," Clay said.

Willa was instantly alert. She didn't want anyone here poking into the life she'd made for herself in Colorado. Her life there was productive and secure. She was well thought of and there was no way she'd even flirt with the possibility of jeopardizing that. "I've worked several places," she answered noncommittally. "Mostly Kansas, Colorado...." She shrugged as she let her voice trail off.

"Paige said you've worked with horses," Clay persisted.

Willa turned away and opened the refrigerator door to get out a carton of milk. "I prefer working with horses," she told him evasively before smoothly changing the subject. "There's some orange juice concentrate in the freezer. Want me to make it up?"

Clay didn't ask her any more questions, but as they finished getting their meal together, Willa caught his speculative gaze on her several times and sensed his curiosity. She forgot all about it, however, when they sat down to bacon, eggs and toast, and the oven buzzer sounded.

"I saw the mix for this in the cupboard and thought it sounded good." Clay gingerly removed a pan of brownies from the oven, with the help of a tiny crocheted potholder meant more for decoration than practical use. He shifted the pan first one way then another to keep from getting his fingers scorched through the open crochet pattern. The brownies finally made it to the table with a thud and a muted curse.

"They look wonderful," Willa commented, doing her best to suppress a smile as Clay flung the potholder down and settled on his chair.

Clay caught the emerald sparkle in Willa's eyes and did a double take. It had been a long time since he'd seen anything in her even remotely resembling the impish, carefree adolescent she had been—the one he'd been so powerfully attracted to—and he suddenly ached to see her that way again.

Willa watched the darkening of Clay's eyes with more than a little apprehension. He was staring at her so intently that she felt as if the midnight black of his gaze would swallow her whole. Something contracted deep down inside her as a primitive element of her psyche understood the look and began to respond. Alarmed at the erratic skittering of her pulse, Willa fled the contact with Clay. She hastily lifted a fork of fried egg to her mouth and tried to chew normally, unnerved beyond belief.

"I've made arrangements to have the horses you planned to sell picked up and taken to the stock auction at the Cascade fairgrounds tomorrow," Clay said to break the uncomfortable silence between them as they finished their meal.

Willa glanced up, the flash of irritation she felt melding into a feeling of inevitability. No matter what she thought seemed to be changing between them, Clay was still determined to hurry her departure. Suddenly she didn't feel like resisting him. "Sounds good," she answered as she pushed her plate slightly away from herself and leaned back in her chair a moment. Her wrist was aching and she flexed her fingers beneath the table, hoping to ease the pain.

"You don't think I was out of line making those arrangements?" he asked, his gaze sharpening as he studied the faint lines of strain on her face.

Willa managed a thin smile. "Do you want an argument?"

"I might."

Willa pushed back her chair and stood to clear the table. "If you make any more arrangements for the Circle H without consulting me first, you'll probably get one." She finished stacking the plates as Clay rose to help her.

"I'll get those," he said, taking the small stack from her and carrying it to the sink.

Willa got out the dish soap and started running the dishwater, but Clay nudged her aside, handing her a dish towel.

"You don't want to get that bandage wet," he pointed out, and Willa watched with some amusement as Clay awkwardly set about washing the dishes, cringing when he banged a glass against the faucet and nearly dropped one of her aunt's good plates. But in no time, the dishes were done and put away.

"You're fairly competent in the kitchen," Willa remarked as Clay finished wiping off the stove and hanging up the dishcloth.

"I've had to cook for myself once or twice," he answered as he unrolled his shirt sleeves and rebuttoned them. He nodded toward her wrist. "I'd like to have a look at that before I go."

Willa shrugged, unconcerned. "It's still a little sore, but it's fine."

Clay reached for her left hand and gently pushed her sleeve up well past the bandage. Willa was stunned by the myriad sensations Clay's touch set off as he tenderly inspected the area around the bandage. Though her wrist still ached, there was no sign of further swelling or discoloration around or above the bandage, which the doctor had cautioned her to watch for.

"Will you be all right alone tonight?" Clay asked as he tugged down her sleeve but continued to hold her hand.

Willa looked up, her senses careening at Clay's nearness as the sensual attraction she'd been fighting to suppress came charging through her system. The combined scent of after-shave and leather invaded her nostrils and Willa felt more than a little over-whelmed.

"I don't know why not," she answered, dismayed at the breathless quality in her voice. "Thanks for...everything," she added, managing to pull her hand from Clay's grasp.

The moment they touched a current of excitement passed wildly between them. As if unable to resist the frisson, Clay reached for her.

Slowly, as though the moment were frail, he pulled her against him. Willa stared at his shirt front, fright-ened at what she sensed was coming. Contact with the male heat of Clay's body sent a tingling weakness through her and her eyes drifted closed as he placed a lean, calloused finger beneath her chin and lifted her face.

"We can't," she pleaded softly as she felt Clay's lips brush hers in a feather-light caress.

"Some things are inevitable, Willa," he whispered as his mouth continued to move enticingly across hers. "You can fight them only so long."

Willa's hands slipped around Clay's middle and locked behind his back as his arms tightened on her waist like steel bands. With each caressing stroke of his mouth, something wild was being ignited inside her, something that demanded fulfillment no matter what the cost.

Suddenly terrified, Willa managed to evade his lips, and pressed her flushed cheek against his neck. "We have to stop," she whispered, shivering with pure pleasure as his tongue found her ear and began toying with the lobe. "Please, Clay."

"All right," he relented as he gradually loosened his hold. "Maybe we are rushing things." Clay's hands lingered at her waist.

Willa shook her head. "This shouldn't be happening between us at all, Clay. It can't." *Besides, there's no real trust between us. And there never can be as long as you believe Paige,* her heart added silently.

Willa pushed away and stepped back. "It's getting late." She couldn't look at him, but felt his eyes on her as he reached for his Stetson.

"You know the phone number at Orion. I expect you to use it if you need anything tonight," he said as he put on his hat and tugged the brim into place.

Willa glanced up, then away. "I'll be fine."

"I'll be over for the horses before ten tomorrow. My men are taking care of most everything else, so you might as well sleep in." Clay hesitated long enough for Willa to look up at him again. "Good night."

Willa's voice went husky with the mad swirl of emotions that suddenly engulfed her. "Good night, Clay."

WILLA WORKED SILENTLY at grooming the aging bay, the last of the four horses she'd decided should go to the sale in town. She'd been at this for the past two hours, trimming manes, cutting burrs from tails, and now she was carefully hosing down the big animal before she gave it a final brushing, hoping the extra care she took with grooming would ensure a better price for each animal at the auction.

All four horses—two sorrels, a buckskin and the bay—were past their prime and, Willa judged, at just about the age when they would begin to cost the ranch in vet bills. Even taking into account that they hadn't been receiving the kind of workouts they needed to keep them in condition, none of the horses would have been her choice for working cattle. She'd taken time to try out each mount in the weeks she'd been there and had concluded that although the bay and sorrel geldings were gentle and well mannered enough for children, neither quite had the stamina or savvy to work cattle. The other sorrel had particularly bad habits that made her hard to handle and the buckskin mare's penchant for being easily spooked had already landed Willa in the dust more than once. The men she eventually hired would need sturdy, much more reliable mounts than these to work the almost wild cattle on the Circle H.

Willa had just finished grooming the bay and tying it with the others, when Clay pulled in with a four-horse goose-neck stock trailer behind his pickup. She gathered up the grooming brushes, combs and clothes as he drove the pickup in a wide circle in the barnyard so the truck was headed back toward the drive before he switched off the engine.

Tamping down the sudden shyness she felt as the events of the night before flashed through her mind, Willa tossed everything into the wooden box just inside the tack room and walked to the front of the barn.

"You're looking a little pale," Clay remarked as he approached, his dark eyes going over her, taking particular note of the damp muddy spatters on her jeans.

"I thought the doctor told you to take it easy for the next few days."

"He did," she returned. Then, determined to rebuff his concern, she gestured toward the horses tethered along the stable aisle. "The horses are ready if you are." At Clay's nod, Willa turned and walked into the barn to untie the bay and one of the sorrels, while Clay opened the back gate of the trailer.

Both horses loaded easily, as did the second sorrel, but the moment Willa led the skittish buckskin to the trailer, the animal drew back on the lead rope and shied nervously.

"Let me get this one, Willa," Clay said as he took a step toward her.

"No, she's fine." Willa moved to block Clay, taking hold of the lead rope with both hands as she did so. Speaking softly to calm the wary animal, Willa led her forward again. The mare shied slightly a second time, but allowed Willa to guide her.

All went well until the mare's hooves hit the metal floor of the trailer. Suddenly the big animal threw her head, then reared back, half dragging Willa with her. The swift jerk on the lead rope sent shafts of pain through Willa's arm as she fought to cling to the rope and regain her balance. Clay was at her side instantly, cursing through gritted teeth as he grabbed the rope and looped it around the mare's nose to choke her down as she bolted sideways and pulled him halfway across the wide drive. Unable to help, Willa got out of the way to give Clay room to maneuver.

Once the mare realized that fighting Clay caused the noose around her nose to tighten and close off her supply of air, she slowly calmed and submitted to Clay's control. In moments Clay had her loaded. While he secured the animals and closed the tailgate, Willa leaned against the side of the trailer, waiting for the throbbing pain in her injured wrist to ease.

"Damn it, Willa." Clay's face was stony with anger as he came around the back of the trailer.

Willa straightened self-consciously and stopped cradling her arm, automatically wanting to conceal her discomfort from Clay.

"Where does your kind of stubbornness come from, anyway?" he ranted.

"Probably from the same place yours does," she shot back as she headed for the house. "I'll meet you at the fairgrounds with the papers just as soon as I get cleaned up and get my clothes changed."

"I'll wait."

Willa hesitated at the words, then stopped and turned back toward Clay. "I intend to go to that auction," she told him coldly, not about to turn the papers over to him and sit at home. Besides, the bids were higher if someone rode each horse around the ring while the bidding was going on. She had to try to get the best possible price for the horses, since the cost of replacing them was going to be hard given her aunt's depleted resources.

"No one said you couldn't," Clay said, his stony expression unchanging. "There any reason why you can't ride to town with me?"

Willa stifled her surprise. "I can think of a few reasons," she said quietly.

"Like what?"

"You know what." Willa's voice had gone softer. "And I should stop over and have this bandage seen to at some point." Her breath caught at the way Clay's dark eyes suddenly dropped to her arm, then veered to made a slow sweep of her body. The heat that flashed over her skin when his gaze lingered too long had nothing to do with standing in the warm morning sunshine. Willa was vividly reminded of what it had felt like to be in his arms with his lips playing sensually with hers.

"I've got nothing but time today, Willa," he said, his deep voice low and faintly rough as his eyes came up to meet hers. Willa couldn't move for a moment as their gazes clung.

"You're sure?"

"More sure than I've been about anything for a long time," he answered gravely, and Willa felt a wild clash of dread and excitement.

"I won't be long," she said as she turned and walked quickly toward the house.

Scarcely ten minutes later, she emerged from the house in new jeans and a long-sleeved gold plaid shirt that intensified the green in her eyes and highlighted the sunny glints in the sandy brown hair that fell past her shoulders from beneath her Stetson. Avoiding Clay's eyes as he leaned against the truck bed on the passenger side of the pickup and watched her, Willa tossed her purse through the open window of the cab and was about to head to the Circle H pickup for the saddles she'd loaded in the back earlier, when Clay's voice stopped her.

"Already got the saddles," he said as he straightened and levered open the passenger door for her. Willa hesitated, then brushed past him to climb in, feeling an odd spurt of relief when he closed the door and moved away from her to walk around the front of the truck to the driver's side. That relief evaporated the moment he slid behind the wheel and reached for the key in the ignition.

"You're strung up tight as a fiddle, Willa. Relax," he advised as he gave the key a twist and the big engine rumbled to life. "Let's just let things happen naturally between us."

Surprised at his candor, Willa glanced sideways and released a pent-up breath of nervousness and exasperation. "I can't believe this is what you really want, Clay." Willa watched his profile carefully and decided to speak her mind. "I don't want your friendship because you were swayed by a few tears last night."

"That's good, honey," he said, turning to fix his dark eyes on her face, "because I'm not sure that what's going to happen between you and me has a whole lot to do with ordinary friendship."

Willa was speechless for a moment. "Maybe I don't want anything more than friendship," she said stiffly as she forced herself to maintain eye contact with him and conceal the truth.

Clay watched her steadily. "Am I reading the signals wrong, green eyes?"

Caught off guard by the old pet name, Willa couldn't answer. The denial lodged in her throat.

"I didn't think so," he said softly, then turned his head to check the mirrors before he put the truck into gear.

CHAPTER EIGHT

EVERYTHING'S HAPPENING TOO QUICKLY, Willa thought as she looked down from her seat in the stands and watched Clay ride the jittery buckskin into the sale ring as the auctioneer opened the bidding.

The attraction that had hovered between them since their reconciliation the night before was beginning to escalate, overwhelming her emotions and her good sense. She knew this renewed relationship was still too fragile for her to allow it to get confused with something as intense and distracting as physical desire—it was too soon for that.

Yet Willa couldn't take her eyes from the man in the ring. Her attention was riveted to his every move; she was unable to focus clearly on anything else. Clay rode the fractious buckskin with the skill of a man who'd been a good rider from early childhood, a man so thoroughly in control that the horse instinctively obeyed him. Few animals would argue with a rider Clay's size, and yet he didn't manhandle the buckskin.

Willa's eyes dropped to the large work-calloused hands that held the reins and she was instantly reminded of what they'd felt like the night before, when he'd held her and soothed away her tears. Dismayed at the strange fluttering in the pit of her stomach, Willa lifted her gaze, only to find it straying once more to his wide shoulders, his spare middle and his hard-muscled thighs.

Embarrassment brought her eyes determinedly upward as Clay rode the buckskin around the ring one more time before he dismounted and pulled the saddle to give the bidders a better look at the mare.

To distract herself, she glanced into the stands of wooden bleachers that surrounded the ring. Willa recognized the majority of bidders and spectators to be locals, then frowned when she spotted a handful who were not—and who might be bidding for a meat packer. That meant there was a possibility that the Circle H horses could end up as dog food. Willa reached up and adjusted her hat brim uncomfortably as she turned her attention back toward the ring. When the bidding stopped, Clay released the buckskin to a ringman to be led from the ring and set aside in a pen for the buyer.

One by one, Clay rode each of the other three horses into the ring. Though all four sold for less than she'd hoped, Willa felt a bit better that each one had gone to a different bidder—all locals.

"I thought we agreed I'd do all the work," Clay reminded her later when she joined him at the holding pens to help carry the saddles back to the trailer.

"It doesn't look like you left any," she remarked as he hefted one of the last two saddles to his shoulder and let the other dangle from his fingers at his side. Willa gathered up the bridles he'd draped over the fence and followed him to the trailer.

"Didn't you see anything you'd like to bid on?" he asked as he stowed the saddles in the trailer and turned to reach for the bridles she was holding.

"Nothing special," she said with a shrug. "I think I'd rather shop around a little and buy something privately." There was too much room for error in buying a horse at an auction and Willa wasn't about to gamble with her aunt's dwindling resources.

"I've got a couple of four-year-olds I might consider selling," Clay told her as he finished with the tack and stepped down to close the trailer. "Nothing too fancy, but they're sound and they've been worked some. I can show them to you later on today if you're up to it."

"Sounds good," Willa said, forcing a smile to her lips. It was hot standing in the sun and the dust. She wasn't used to feeling tired in the middle of the day and the aspirin she'd taken that morning to blunt the dull pain in her wrist had worn off a long time ago.

"I hope you made arrangements for the bookkeeper to mail you the check for the sale of your horses," Clay said pointedly as he surveyed the increasing pallor of Willa's cheeks.

Willa stiffened, automatically trying to stand a little straighter and not look as wilted as she felt. "Of course I did. That's the way it's done here, isn't it?" Without waiting for him to answer, she started around the trailer to the passenger side of the truck and got in, releasing a tired sigh as she tugged off her hat and leaned her head back.

She listened to the reassuring sound of Clay checking the trailer, then reluctantly lifted her head and replaced her hat when she heard him make his way around to the driver's side.

"Are you ready to get that dressing changed?" he asked as he opened the door and climbed in, his dark eyes flicking down to her bandaged wrist, which rested on her thigh.

"I think I'd rather have some lunch first," she answered, then added, "and since you refused to let me pay you the going rate for trailering and showing the horses, it'll be my treat."

"Your treat, huh?" Clay repeated with a grin as he slid the key into the ignition and started the truck. "How about that little steak house over on the highway?"

WILLA STOOD next to Clay in the elevator, relieved that they were finished at the hospital and would at last be going home. After having her dressing seen to and changed, they had stopped to visit Aunt Tess. One look at the deep lines of worry and concern on her aunt's face told Willa Tess had found out about the snakebite, and Willa had spent the entire visit trying to allay Tess's fears.

"Thanks for helping me with Aunt Tess," Willa murmured, then turned her head to look up at Clay as the elevator slowed to a stop and the doors swished open. "She listens to you."

"It's not that she doesn't listen to you, Willa," Clay said as he placed his hand at the back of her waist and escorted her forward. "She was worried. She's laid up and couldn't be there to help you. Plus she probably figures she was the one who put you in harm's way in the first place.''

"I can't stand the thought of her worrying," Willa said on a quaver of emotion. "She shouldn't be upset in any way."

Clay's hand slid around her waist and brought her against his side as they walked down the corridor toward the exit that led to the parking lot. Willa's arm instinctively found its way around Clay's lean middle in response.

"Tess is getting stronger every day. Besides, she's going to have to learn to deal with upsets without letting them affect her health."

"But this is too soon for her," Willa insisted, her mind filled with the memory of her aunt's collapse and her part in causing it, not to mention that Tess was still grieving for Cal.

"It's been almost four weeks, Willa," he reminded her, his arm tightening on her waist reassuringly. "She's going to be released from the hospital within the next two or three days."

"But you saw how tired she looked—and the way her hands were shaking...." Willa's voice caught on the words as her throat knotted with emotion.

"I saw," Clay agreed as they passed through the automatic doors to the parking lot and started toward the far end, where he'd left the truck and trailer. "She looked just the way you do now—tired, worked up... and about to cry."

Startled at the observation, Willa pursed her lips as she struggled to bring her emotions under control. She still felt deeply embarrassed about her crying jag the night before, and she wasn't about to treat Clay to another one.

The ride out of town passed in companionable silence. Neither spoke until they approached the turn-off to Orion.

"You still up to looking at those horses?"

"Might as well," she answered as she shifted into a slightly more erect position. The ride from town had made her drowsy and she felt impatient with herself for her lack of stamina.

"We can always do this tomorrow," he reminded her, but Willa shook her head.

"Unless it's more convenient for you to wait until tomorrow, I'd just as soon take care of this now."

Clay signaled, then turned into the graveled drive that stretched more than a mile to the Orion ranch house. Once they passed the house and took the right fork to the barns and the network of corrals beyond, Clay angled the truck and trailer to the side of the lane and switched off the engine.

In only a few minutes one of Clay's men had brought up the two horses and put them into a corral. After Willa had looked over both sorrels, Clay had them saddled and taken to a small pasture where a half-dozen cows and their calves waited.

Standing next to Clay, Willa rested her forearms on a chest-high rail of board fencing, cushioning her injured wrist on top of her other one as she looked through the rails. She watched thoughtfully as two of Clay's men worked the bunch, gathering, roping, then separating out a calf or two to show each horse's abilities.

"I thought you said they were nothing fancy," Willa said, never taking her eyes from the horses, clearly satisfied with both animals.

"I meant that they don't have the flash and the polish of the kind of horses you're used to."

Willa felt a tremor of alarm go through her at his words. She turned her head and glanced at Clay, catching the glimmer of interest in his dark eyes. "What makes you think that?" she asked as casually as she could manage.

"Tess said you worked for a big horse breeder in Colorado." The speculation in Clay's eyes deepened and Willa felt herself close up inside.

"Not so big," she said dismissively, and looked back toward the horses. "What kind of price are you looking to get?"

Clay didn't answer right away. Willa felt him study her profile for a few moments before he seemed to accept her evasive response. He named a price that made her frown.

"That's way too low, Clay. I can't let you just give them to me."

"I won't be 'giving' them to you. I'll be 'giving' them to the Hardings."

Willa chafed at the not-so-subtle reminder that Clay was only doing business through her, not with her.

"I've already agreed to let you do more than Aunt Tess would be comfortable with. I can't let you do this, too." Willa quickly named a price she felt was fairer.

Clay released an impatient sigh, then reached up to readjust his hat before he tugged it down to a determined angle over his eyes. "This is no time to be stubborn, Willa."

"I'm not being stubborn," she countered as she dropped her arms from the fence and turned to face him. "I'm offering you a fair price."

"I'm not asking for one."

"Why not?" she demanded.

Clay's expression was a mixture of irritation and discomfort. "Things turned out to be a lot worse at the Circle H than I thought they were. If I had known how much worse, I would have found a way to get around Tess's pride and done something about it a long time ago."

"You can't help someone who won't let you," Willa reminded him.

"No kidding," he muttered as he stared down at her meaningfully. Willa had to restrain a smile.

"What about the horses?" he pressed, his no-nonsense tone of voice softened by the sparkle of affection in his dark eyes.

Taken aback by the warm look, Willa glanced away, an odd kind of pain in her chest as the deep feelings she had for him came bursting up. He'd been generous enough already, sending men to work for her who were still on his payroll—men he needed to work on Orion—not to mention what he'd done to help her today, plus his agreement to help her find someone to work the Circle H full-time. She couldn't let him do all that, then allow him to sell good horses to her at half their market value.

Willa took a deep breath and shook her head, her eyes coming back to meet Clay's. "I can't pay you any less than my offer. If you won't take it, then I guess we won't be doing business today."

Clay didn't reply. His expression hardened and the soft light went out of his eyes as he glanced over her head toward where his men waited with the horses.

Willa watched the mild flash of anger come over Clay and was suddenly conscious of how precarious their renewed friendship was. The reconciliation that was barely twenty-four hours old was still far too easily imperiled and Willa felt a spurt of panic as she acknowledged how quickly a wrong word or misinterpreted action might divide them.

And in her mind it followed that if Clay were ever in the position of doubting her again, his lack of trust could end their friendship—permanently, this time.

"Miss Ross will be buying both horses, Ed," he called out. "Go ahead and load them in the trailer and take them to the Circle H."

"If you don't mind, I'd like to ride over with your men," Willa told him, the pleasure of finding two very satisfactory horses dampened. "I'll send your check back with them later."

Clay's gaze swung back to hers, but the hardness still lingered in his expression. "I was hoping you'd stay to supper."

Willa shook her head, suddenly determined to flee the ill-fated attraction she felt for him. "It's been a long day, Clay. I'd just like to go home."

"Then I'll take you in the car. Give me a minute," he said as he turned away and met his men at the pasture gate.

Relieved to be going home even if it was Clay who was taking her there, Willa started walking toward the house, where his car was parked, stopping by the truck to retrieve her purse. After a quick trip into the house for the paperwork on the horses, Clay joined her and they started for the Circle H.

"The boys'll be taking care of the chores tonight when they bring the horses over," Clay said when they reached the Circle H ranch house and he switched off the engine.

Willa tossed him an impatient look as she levered her door open. "You're doing too much, Clay," she said, stepping out when he did, her gaze meeting his over the roof of the car.

"We had an agreement, didn't we?"

Willa closed her door with a snap, reminded not only of the agreement, but of the motivation behind it: to force her to leave Cascade as soon as possible.

The faint signs of strain and tiredness on her face deepened fractionally as she nodded. "I'll get your check."

Clay followed her into the house, handing her the papers for the horses as she seated herself at the desk in the den to write out the check. She had just finished signing her name, when the telephone shrilled. She reached for the receiver.

"Circle H."

The room went quiet for only a moment. "Deke? How're things going?" she asked as she smiled, the call obviously welcome.

Clay watched the weariness disappear from Willa's face. She was smiling, even chuckling, at something this caller was saying. The warm affection in her voice was something he hadn't heard in years.

"Is the boss-lady back from St. Louis?" she asked making a veiled reference to her partner, Ivy, as she rolled the pen between her thumb and forefinger and listened. "She did? Good. I was hoping she'd go out to have a look at that one." Another pause. "I don't know yet. She'll be out of the hospital soon, but I haven't hired anyone."

The room went still enough for Clay to faintly hear the deep masculine voice coming across the line.

"You miss me, huh?" Willa asked as she leaned back in the swivel chair for a few moments. "No, don't send anyone up. It would complicate things here. I'll find someone locally." Willa glanced toward Clay. "Aunt Tess's neighbor has a lead on a foreman, and once he's hired, someone will turn up."

Willa's eyes slid from Clay's as she gave her attention to something else Deke was asking. "It's a long story, Deke," she said, the weariness creeping back into her expression as Deke made a remark. "Yeah," she answered, smiling wryly, "one of those. Anything else?" Willa listened for a moment, then ended the conversation and leaned over to hang up the phone. Clay's eyes were fixed on her with telling intensity.

"This Deke sounds a little eager for you to get back to Colorado."

The harsh edge in Clay's voice threw her for a moment.

"He's the foreman of the ranch where I work," she answered truthfully, then looked down and folded the check along the perforations.

"Is that all he is to you?"

Willa tore the check out of the ledger-sized pad, surprised at Clay's directness. "He's also a very good friend," she added as she looked up and passed him the check.

Clay took the slip of paper but barely glanced at it. "Which ranch is it you work on down there?"

Willa closed the check pad and stood to lock it in one of the metal cabinets behind the desk. She didn't answer until her back was toward him. "Just a small one. You've probably never heard of it." She was attempting to sound casual, but she was a jumble of nerves. Clay wasn't about to let her evade the question and they both knew it.

"Try me."

"I'd rather not," she said firmly as she closed the cabinet before she turned to pick up the papers and skim them before she consigned them to a file.

"Why not?"

Willa exhaled a pent-up breath, then jammed the papers into the file and shoved the drawer closed. Other than telling an outright lie, the only alternative to evasion was to tell Clay to mind his own business. And telling him that would be tantamount to waving a red flag in front of a bull.

"You're supposed to take the hint and back off," she said candidly as she turned and met the mistrust in his eyes. Stung by the look, Willa's gaze ricocheted away. "Your men should be here anytime now," she said as she headed around the desk. "I need to go out and—"

Clay caught her arm gently as she stepped past him.

"You haven't even told Tess, have you?" he concluded gruffly, his disapproval evident. "What little she knows, she's had to guess. Isn't that right?" Willa made a slight move to test the firmness of his grip. Clay lowered his voice. "Why, Willa? Why don't you trust either of us enough to answer such a simple question?"

"Why don't you trust me enough to leave it alone?" she shot back, resenting the guilt Clay made her feel.

"I thought things had changed between us."

"Not everything," she burst out, then instantly regretted the words. She tried to pull away, but Clay caught her other arm and turned her fully toward him.

"Care to explain that?"

"No, I don't," she told him coolly, forcing herself to look up into his stern countenance. "Now if you don't mind..."

"I *do* mind," Clay growled as his thumbs began to rub in calming circles on her arms. Willa's gaze fled his. She was panicked by the sensuality that radiated over her at the small gentle movements. "But it doesn't look like it'll do me any good," he added as he allowed her to pull away and take a step back. Willa felt chilled by the abrupt release. Warily her gaze came back to meet the frustration in Clay's.

It distressed her that she couldn't seem to reveal to him something as small as the details of her life in Colorado. Besides, if Paige found out about the D & R through something Clay might say, Willa was certain her cousin would find a way to use the information against her. And Willa couldn't bring herself to take the risk until she felt more secure about the reconciliation with Clay. There was also her partner to consider.

"How soon can you get that man from Sheridan down here for an interview?" she asked briskly. "You said his sister lives in Laramie. Is it possible to get him here within the next few days?"

"I can ask," Clay replied, his grim expression hardening as he accepted the swift change of subject. "I'll give him a call tonight."

Willa nodded her satisfaction. "Good. Please do that. Let me know how soon I can see him. If he seems a good choice at all, I'll hire him."

"Just like that?" Clay's voice was harsh.

"Why not?" she challenged, meeting the hard look in his eyes without flinching. "I promised I wouldn't make excuses to keep things going."

One corner of Clay's mouth hitched up in an unamused line. "No one said you had to hire the first man who comes along, either."

"I'll hire the best person available for the job," she told him curtly, "whether it's the man from Sheridan or someone else."

Clay studied the obstinate set of her features for a few moments before his expression softened. "I don't want to fight, Willa."

The quiet words cooled the anger she felt. "Neither do I," she admitted on a wavering breath.

"And I'm not exactly sure I want you to hurry back to Colorado."

Willa was stunned at the impact those few words had on her emotions and she felt herself scrambling to negate the instant meaning her heart assigned them. Clay moved forward into the short space between them, hesitating fractionally as his hands came up to rest on her waist.

"And I wasn't prying into your life down there in order to make trouble. It's just that there are a lot of things I don't know about you that I want to."

Slowly, as if giving her those scant moments to adjust, Clay lowered his head and touched his lips to hers. The tiny explosion of desire that burst deep inside her at the tender force of his mouth spread through every part of her until her entire being ached with longing. And when Clay suddenly crushed her to him, Willa's arms came up and locked around his neck. The fierceness of their feelings left them both bruised and breathless when Clay finally dragged his lips from hers.

"I've wanted to do that all day," he rasped as he appeared to struggle for self-control. Willa's unwilling sound of agreement brought his mouth back to hers with a pleasured groan. Neither of them heard the slam of the porch door or the rapid clatter of heels across the kitchen, quickly muffled by the carpet in the hall.

Paige's belatedly called "Anybody home?" caught them both by surprise as she burst through the open door to the den.

Startled, Willa drew back and broke off the kiss, but Clay didn't release her.

Near the doorway, Paige stood frozen almost in midstep at the sight of them in each other's arms. Alarm and uncertainty showed plainly on her lovely features before she seemed to recover herself.

"Well, well." Paige's voice was a bit more shrill than normal as her turbulent gaze flicked from one to the other. "It looks as if the black sheep has managed to work her way back into the fold, after all."

CHAPTER NINE

WITH OBVIOUS RELUCTANCE Clay loosened his hold and allowed Willa to take a half step away, his eyes searching hers as Paige's implication hit home.

"Willa and I have resolved our differences, if that's what you mean," he said as he turned to Paige, his unsmiling expression effectively communicating his displeasure with her remark.

Quickly taking her cue, Paige was contrite. "I suppose my comment was a bit uncalled for," she admitted with a brittle smile. Willa was surprised Paige didn't choke on the words. "It's just such a shock to see the two of you...together like that. After all..." Paige let the words drift off, knowing full well she didn't have to say more to remind either one of them of the reason for their differences.

The sound of a pickup truck and horse trailer rolling past the house to the barn out back was a welcome intrusion. Clay's men had arrived.

"I've got some horses to get settled in," Willa said, grateful for the excuse to escape the chaotic mixture of fear and suppressed rage that seemed to emanate in invisible waves from her cousin. Though Willa intended to leave Clay and Paige alone together, she was pleased when Clay followed her outside and fell into step beside her.

"I thought you might want some time alone with Paige," Willa said, suddenly needing to press Clay into a declaration of some sort.

"Why is that?"

Willa shrugged. "She's been gone a few days..." She didn't finish the sentence.

"So you think I might want to smooth things over and make up for lost time?" he said, the gruffness in his voice a mild rebuke. "I don't think you've been paying attention to what's been going on between you and me, Willa."

Clay caught her arm and gently swung her around to face him. Willa glanced self-consciously at the Orion ranch hands who were opening the trailer and about to unload the horses, but the angle of the parked vehicle prevented the couple from being seen. Clay's gaze followed the direction of hers before he backed her against the thick trunk of one of the oak trees in the backyard and bent his head to kiss her soundly.

"Now that we've straightened that out," he growled when he finally released her and left her limp against the rough bark at her back, "I think we'd better get down to the barn and see to those horses."

Willa opened passion-glazed eyes to the self-assured, supremely male look Clay was giving her, her emotions still reeling. The corners of her mouth curved up softly as she reached for the hand he held out to her, her cousin forgotten as she allowed him to tug her away from the tree trunk and slip his arm around her waist for the walk to the barn.

"HAVE YOU FORGOTTEN our little talk, or do you just no longer care about Mother's health?"

Now that Clay had gone home, Paige didn't hesitate to launch her attack. Once she'd surmised that whatever was going on between Willa and Clay hadn't exposed her yet, she was more determined than ever to ensure Willa's silence.

Willa looked up from prying off her boots and setting them in their usual place on the back porch, annoyed that she'd barely got in the door before Paige had started her harangue. "Can't this wait until tomorrow?" she asked, stepping past her cousin with the intention of heading upstairs to her room for the night.

Paige turned to follow her. "No, it can't," she said firmly, catching up with Willa in the hall. "Just how far have things gone between you and Clay?" she demanded, putting out a professionally manicured hand to grab Willa's arm and stop her.

Willa gasped at the pain as Paige clutched at her and unintentionally caught her injured wrist. Paige hesitated for a moment, surprised to feel the squared padding beneath Willa's sleeve, then quickly released her.

"What's the matter with you? Are you hurt?" Paige asked, the belligerence in her voice subdued somewhat by the obvious flash of pain on Willa's face.

Willa's lips formed a thin line. "Nothing for you to trouble yourself about," she said, then took the opportunity to turn and start up the stairway as the pain slowly subsided.

"What do you mean by that?" Paige's steps echoed Willa's all the way to the top.

"Don't you have other things besides my health to worry about?" Willa asked, unable to resist needling her cousin. As she'd expected, Paige had easily forgotten her small show of concern.

"I asked you how far things had gone between you and Clay," Paige repeated as she followed Willa into her room. "And while you're at it, how did you manage to get on his good side in the first place? What did you tell him?" Paige's violet eyes were a bit wild now.

Willa looked away and exhaled a tired breath as she tugged her shirttail from the waist of her jeans and walked toward her bathroom. Paige followed her right to the door and used her hand to prevent Willa from closing it all the way.

"I haven't told Clay any of your secrets," Willa answered wearily as she finished unbuttoning her blouse, then leaned over the tub to turn on the faucets.

Paige's voice sounded a little less anxious after that. "Then what about you and Clay?" she persisted over the sound of running water. "What's going on between the two of you?"

Willa didn't answer for a moment. She'd wondered about that, too. "Just a little mutual attraction," she called back, knowing her answer sounded annoyingly vague.

"Then you won't mind breaking it off with him," Paige said, her imperious tone of voice telling Willa plainly that she fully expected her to do just that.

Willa felt herself slump a bit at the order, saddened that she and her own flesh-and-blood relative were so deeply at odds. "Sorry," she called out, knowing full well she was tossing down the gauntlet to the one person in her life more than capable of taking it up.

THE NEXT TWO DAYS were predictably difficult as Willa tried to adjust to both Paige's presence in the house and the preparations for her aunt's release from the hospital.

Aunt Tess's earlier plans to stay with Mabel Asner in town had changed and she would be returning to the Circle H directly. Willa guessed Tess had wearied of her overbearing friend's frequent visits to the hospital and had developed second thoughts about staying with her. The fact that Paige was planning to be home for at least the next several days had probably given Tess a polite excuse to turn down Mabel's hospitality.

Not one to be easily thwarted, Mabel accompanied Tess home, anyway, her determination to see her settled in putting a damper on the cheerful event for Willa.

"Willa ought to be able to take care of the heavy housework and cooking," Mabel was saying to Tess as Willa carried a couple of the plants her aunt had received in the hospital into the living room, where the two women were sitting with Paige. Paige cast Willa a catty look and Mabel babbled on as if Willa weren't there. "She's supposed to be hiring men to work outside. No reason for her to leave all the inside work to Paige."

Willa gritted her teeth at Mabel's critical, ill-informed comment as she set the plants down carefully on an end table.

"Willa's doing so much for me now, Mabel," Tess spoke up, firmly correcting the woman. "I don't know how I could ask her for another thing."

Willa returned the fond smile Tess sent her way, then started back out to her car for another armload of her aunt's things. To her relief, Mabel was just getting up to leave as she came back in.

"You'll have to stop all this running in and out with those things for a while. Your aunt needs a nap," Mabel told her, the stern, disapproving look on the woman's puffy face making her look more shrewish than ever as she gave pointed attention to the chambray work shirt and faded jeans Willa had worn to the hospital. Paige had dressed in a smart linen suit, but Willa hadn't bothered to change from the clothes she'd worn earlier that morning to check on the cattle. Since she knew she'd be the one taking care of Tess's belongings, Willa had seen no point in dressing up.

"Stop nagging the girl, Mabel." This time Tess was clearly irritated. "What little noise she makes would never disturb me."

"Thank you for your concern, Mrs. Asner," Willa said, straining to be pleasant and hurry the woman along at the same time. "We'll take good care of Aunt Tess. She'll do just fine."

Mabel nodded, but her look of disapproval didn't alter until she glanced over at Paige. "Come along with me a moment, would you, dear? I'd like to talk to you a bit before I leave," she said, her intent for privacy clear as she bustled past Willa to the front door.

I'll just bet, Willa thought unkindly as Paige rose gracefully to follow the short, thick-waisted matron to her car.

"Lord in heaven that woman's a busybody!" Tess exclaimed the moment the door closed and Mabel stepped out of earshot. "I don't know how I could have ever entertained the idea of staying with her in town. I would have gone crazy for sure."

Willa burst out laughing at Tess's vehemence.

"And I'm sorry she was so rude to you. I'll have a talk with her about that later." Tess braced a thin hand on the arm of the sofa and got carefully to her feet. Willa automatically reached over to assist her, but Tess waved her away. "Now don't you fuss, young lady." Tess's gray eyes came up to meet Willa's, though she had to tip her head back a bit to compensate for her smaller stature. "Just give me a hug."

Willa stepped close and hugged her aunt, the taste of sentimental tears in her mouth. "Welcome home, Aunt Tess," she murmured, pressing a light kiss on Tess's pale cheek.

"Welcome home to you," Tess responded, then drew back to take Willa's face in her hands. "I want you to know how happy I am to have you home again—how proud I am of you."

Willa's gaze fled Tess's, then came back when the older woman gave her a tiny shake. "You've grown up to be just as lovely and capable a girl as I always thought you would."

Willa was too choked to speak, grateful when her aunt gave her another hug and she didn't have to.

"And now I'm afraid I do need that nap," Tess admitted as she released Willa and turned to head for her bedroom at the back of the house, leaving Willa in a backwash of emotion.

Not wanting to face Paige when she came in, Willa started toward the kitchen, but instead hurried into the den as the telephone began to ring.

"Did you get Tess settled in?" Clay's voice came over the line, his brisk tone making her stiffen a bit. At her quick answer, he went on, "I just wanted to let you know that Phil Spencer is here from Sheridan and he'll be available anytime after three for an interview and a look around the Circle H."

Willa sensed then that Clay's all-business manner over the phone was because Phil Spencer was there with him. "You can send him over anytime," she responded, hinting she wanted to conduct her part of the interview without Clay present. Clay had been able to arrange for Phil to come down for an interview quickly and Willa was hopeful that the man would be suitable so she could hire him and have him start managing the Circle H within the month. But, as per her agreement with Clay, she had final approval of the man, and if he didn't seem right for the job, she would simply not offer it to him.

Willa hung up the phone just as Paige came in, and she frowned at the unpleasant reminder that the interview and tour she'd planned for that afternoon might not be as private as she'd hoped.

PHIL SPENCER WAS a short, sturdily built man of forty whose likable personality enhanced his experience and qualifications. He impressed Willa as a good choice for a foreman. By the time she'd finished giving him a tour of the ranch—partly on horseback, mostly in the truck—she'd decided to hire him. Since she'd already read his letters of reference and discussed his resumé with him, she had only to talk salary and tell him the job was his if he wanted it. They were just getting settled in the den, when Paige came in.

"We haven't been introduced yet," Paige said, turning her best practiced smile on Phil, who seemed taken aback by both Paige's attention and her beauty.

"Phil, this is my cousin, Paige Harding," Willa said. "Paige, Phil Spencer." With the introductions out of the way, Willa had every intention of getting rid of Paige. "Phil and I will be finished in here in just a few more minutes," she prompted, hoping Paige would take the hint and leave.

Paige took the hint all right, but instead of leaving, she perversely went over and seated herself behind the desk, her officious manner as she took up Phil's resumé and letters of reference making Willa cringe.

Willa tried again. "Phil and I still have some things to talk over, Paige. I think we'd both be more comfortable with a little privacy."

Paige glanced up and fixed Willa with an icy stare. "I'd like to interview Phil myself, if you don't mind," she said, then scanned the papers before her as if she knew what she was doing.

"Go ahead and have a seat, Phil," Willa invited as she gestured to one of the wing chairs in front of the desk, resigned to Paige's interference as she seated herself opposite him in the other chair. If Phil took the job, he'd likely be exposed to a lot of meddling from Paige and it was just as well to let him experience it firsthand before any agreements were reached.

"On the basis of this resumé and these recommendations, I'd say you're just the man I'm looking for," Paige remarked as she finally looked up. "How soon could you start?"

Willa shifted in her chair, irritated that Paige was usurping her authority. "Phil and I still have a few more things to discuss before either of us makes a final decision," Willa said, feeling embarrassed for herself and for Phil, who looked faintly uneasy.

"Discuss whatever it is you think you have to, Willa." Paige got to her feet and walked around the front of the desk to shake Phil's hand. "But as far as I'm concerned, Mr. Spencer is our new foreman." Phil got up in a gesture of politeness to Paige, but Willa could tell he felt uncomfortable. "I look forward to having someone competent around to take care of things for Mother and me."

WILLA RODE the sorrel gelding to the top of the rise and reined him to a walk, giving him a chance to cool down and catch his breath. Feeling guilty for the hard, early evening ride, she reached down to pat the horse's damp neck, murmuring an apology as she scanned the network of corrals and ranch buildings of Orion in the distance.

She'd needed a hard ride after her latest no-win confrontation with Paige. She'd needed to dispel not only her ever increasing wariness of her cousin, but also the intense feeling of anger and frustration Paige provoked. That she'd also needed to see Clay again was something she didn't let herself dwell on.

Earlier, Paige had come to the den determined to go over the books—supposedly to familiarize herself with what was going on. In her usual frantic manner, she had dragged everything from the cabinet there, haphazardly strewing ledgers and papers about. She'd then demanded that Willa not only explain it all to her, but also account for every cent she'd spent so far—an accounting Paige had challenged and criticized at every turn. Easily recognizing Paige's sudden interest for the harassment it was, Willa had finally given up trying to appease her and had placed everything back in the cabinet before leaving the house.

Willa guided the sorrel toward the final gate from the pasture, leaning down to unlatch it before she rode through. Careful to secure the gate behind her, she urged the horse toward the lane that led to the back of the house.

"It's been a long time since I've seen you ride in like that," Clay remarked as he watched her dismount at the edge of the lawn and walk toward the patio. Willa glanced back the way she'd come, reminded that from where Clay sat in the lengthening shadows, he could have seen her the moment she'd ridden over the rise.

"It has been a while, yes," she answered softly.

Willa searched Clay's face as he sat on a cedar lounger with his feet up, his long, denim-clad legs stretched out and crossed casually at the ankles, his dark hair damp from a recent shower. With a lazy expression on his face and a cold beer in his hand, he was the picture of relaxation. Willa couldn't help but smile.

"You look like one of those beer commercial cowboys who kick back at the end of a hard day and do some recreational drinking."

"And you're a sight for sore eyes," he said huskily before he let his gaze roam leisurely downward. "Tell me, whatever happened to that little dress you wore to Angie's birthday party that time?"

Taken aback by the question, Willa flushed, knowing exactly which dress he was talking about. She shrugged a shoulder vaguely. "Aunt Tess probably threw it out. It disappeared from my closet shortly after the party."

Clay chuckled. "You were a mischief back then, Willa," he said, as if he were fond of the recollection. "Care for a cold one?" he offered as he tilted the bottle toward her. "I think I might even have some wine cooler."

Willa shook her head, a bit too unsure of Clay in his present mood. "Not now, thanks."

"Then come on over and sit down."

Willa nudged a padded cedar chair closer to Clay's lounger with the toe of her boot and sat down, tugging off her hat and leaning back, suddenly feeling relaxed. This is what it would be like, she mused, if she and Clay could be here together for the rest of their lives; the end of a workday could be this peaceful, this companionable.

"What's it been, a week?" Clay asked, breaking into her thoughts.

"A week for what?"

"Since we saw each other last," he clarified, reminding her that she'd not seen him since before her aunt had come home from the hospital. It had been two days since she'd met with and hired Phil Spencer, but she'd barely talked to Clay since then, what with the extra work she'd taken on trying to get the quarters at the bunkhouse ready for the new foreman.

Willa shook her head. "It's only been about four days."

Clay took a swig of his beer, his eyes on her all the while. "Have you been avoiding me?"

"I've been a little busy," she said, then added defensively, "I did call to tell you about hiring Phil Spencer."

"But you haven't returned any of my calls since then."

Willa's face showed her surprise. "Which calls were those?"

"I don't suppose Paige told you I stopped by yesterday, either," he said, his mouth twisting at the corners. "She said you were out checking cattle."

The anger and frustration she'd managed to forget about for a while came rushing back. "It must have slipped her mind, what with Tess home and all," Willa said as offhandedly as she could manage, doing her best to conceal her true feelings. Besides, criticizing her cousin to Clay would only make her look petty.

"I'd hate to have to get along on the kind of memory Paige seems to have," he commented. He took another sip of his beer before he spoke again. "You and Paige are still having serious problems getting along in the same house, aren't you?''

Willa's gaze streaked from his knowing expression. Surprised at the emotion that welled up at his perception, she looked down and toyed with the black leather band of her hat as she debated the wisdom of confiding in him.

"It won't be for much longer. Either she'll go back to New York or I'll be heading back to Colorado."

"I thought we talked about that," he reminded her, his voice going lower. "I thought you understood that I didn't want you to rush off."

Willa glanced up at the words, unable to help either the deep thrill of hope she felt or the sense of caution.

"I've got a couple of more weeks before Phil Spencer takes over," she pointed out. "That's not exactly rushing off."

Clay studied her a moment. "But when the two weeks are up, you'll be gone." It was a statement.

"I have a job to get back to," she said quietly, for the first time seeing her responsibility as an owner of the D & R as a burden.

"There are other jobs, Willa. You could find another one a lot closer to Cascade." The sternness in Clay's voice both surprised and delighted her. "If you're any good with horses at all, you could get on just about anywhere."

"I'm happy doing what I do now," she said carefully, unable to quite bring herself to tell Clay about her ranch. If he pressed her for more, she'd tell him, but until then, she'd obey for a little longer the caution she felt.

"You don't think you could be happy doing the same job for someone else?" he challenged.

"I suppose it's possible." Willa felt relieved when the frown lines on Clay's face eased and he fell silent. Letting out a deep sigh, she started to relax, until she caught the disturbing glimmer in Clay's dark eyes.

"Two weeks isn't a lot of time."

The slow smile that slanted his mouth moved through her like an electric charge as he set his beer on the table nearby, then swung his feet over the side of the lounger to bring himself face to face with her.

Willa looked deep into his half-lidded gaze and felt her blood turn thick at the message she read there. "Time?" she asked, her voice breathless with tension as she responded to the look and issued a modest sensual dare. "For what?"

"For you and I to explore the feelings between us." Willa's breath caught as Clay reached out and enveloped her hand in the hard warmth of his before he stood and pulled her to her feet. "Come on inside with me, Willa."

She froze for a moment, unable to follow Clay inside to what she instinctively understood would bring them closer to sexual intimacy, yet not quite strong enough to flee the tumultuous mixture of fulfillment and complication such intimacy would bring into her life.

She tried to think of all the reasons she had for not going in with him, for not allowing anything deeper to happen between them, but the old feeling of betrayal

simply wasn't as strong anymore. Gone, too, was her
fear that some incident could again cast doubt on her
word and destroy his trust. A sense of security she'd
not thought she'd feel again sprang to life at the realization.

"Willa?" Clay's voice was coaxing as he gave her
hand a gentle squeeze. "I knew a precocious little girl
once who wasn't afraid of anything."

Willa's pulse quickened at the affection behind his
words. "I think there's a lot more at stake here than
that precocious child had the good sense to consider," she added.

One side of Clay's mouth slipped up a notch in approval. "I'm glad she's grown up enough now to realize it."

Willa's resistance melted dangerously as she
searched Clay's tender expression. The love she'd always felt for him suddenly swelled her heart to the
bursting point and she could no more have turned
away from him and gone home than she could have
stopped her own breathing. A feeling of inevitability
stole sweetly over her and she walked with him to the
sliding glass doors that led to from the patio into the
house.

"I'd better call down to Frank and have him see to
your horse," he said once they were inside, and she
waited as he stepped into the kitchen and made the
call. It only took a moment, but to Willa it seemed
much longer.

"All taken care of," he told her when he'd finished. "I'll have someone trailer your horse to the

Circle H tomorrow. You think you'd be interested in some supper?''

The relief she should have felt at his suggestion didn't materialize. Instead she was on edge, unaware of the restless look she gave him as she tossed her hat to a chair and tried to calm herself.

"Are you?" she asked, not wanting to admit that supper was the last thing on her mind.

"Not particularly," he replied as he started her way, then angled past her toward the modest bar nearby.

Willa was stunned by the sharp disappointment she felt because he had avoided touching her.

"Can I get you that wine cooler now?" he asked solicitously as he opened the liquor cabinet, then glanced back at her. "Unless you'd rather have a mixed drink." From the slight smile that pulled at his lips Willa knew he'd seen the quick flush that had come into her cheeks and that he'd correctly interpreted it.

"How about scotch?" she replied quietly, opting for something strong.

Clay's brows arched. "Don't tell me you're in need of a little false courage?" he chided as he selected a bottle and a stout glass.

Willa slid her hands into her jeans pockets to still their tremors and turned away to wander toward the huge stone fireplace that dominated the wall between the living room and the formal dining room on the other side. "Something like that."

Clay poured the drinks and passed Willa her scotch. Before she could taste the golden liquid, Clay held his glass up in a toasting gesture. "To us, Willa," he pronounced softly as their glasses touched.

Willa couldn't pull her eyes away from the smoky sensuality in Clay's dark gaze as she sipped her drink and watched him over the rim of her glass.

The jittery feeling of tension that had pulled her nerves too taut began to ease as the heat of the strong malt began to soothe away her nervousness.

"Better?" he asked after she'd had a second sip and lowered her drink to rest on the palm of her other hand.

"Much," she replied with a smile. Clay reached out and traced her jaw lightly, his gentle touch sending a flash of warmth through her.

"You aren't in any hurry to get home tonight, are you?" he asked, his dark eyes delving so deeply into hers that she had the startling sensation he could see into her very soul.

"No," she said, the word barely making a sound as it left her lips.

"That's good."

Willa's breath caught as Clay gently took her glass and set it next to his own on the mantel.

"'Cause you know something, Willa?" he asked as he took hold of her fingers and pulled her closer. "If you're only going to give me a couple of weeks to change your mind about moving north, I think I'd like to put this time to better use." His midnight-dark eyes kindled with the fire of intent as he placed her hands on his chest, then reached down to grip her waist.

Slowly he lowered his head and brushed her lips lightly with his own, his breath mingling with hers as he deliberately flirted with her mouth. "You know how much I care for you, don't you?" he rasped, his lips maintaining their feather-light stroked as Willa's hands ventured upward. "I can't let you just run off," he whispered, his lips pressing a bit harder, clinging a bit more provocatively as Willa strained to get closer.

With each brush of his mouth, his breath became more ragged, its uneven cadence heightening Willa's excitement, until she was driven nearly wild with wanting.

Unable to bear another moment of his teasing, Willa speared her fingers into the thick hair above his collar, pulling him down as she rose on tiptoe and fused her lips to his. His response was instantaneous as he ground his body against hers, deepening the kiss until Willa lost track of everything but the primitive need she had for this man and the absolute compulsion she felt to give herself to him totally.

Clay's mouth moved off hers and glided to her ear. He took his time there before he pressed a series of light lingering kisses on the delicate spot just beneath it that robbed her body of strength. Before she realized what he was doing, he leaned down and hooked his arm behind her knees to lift her gently against his chest.

Faintly startled, Willa opened desire-weighted lashed to the burning lights that shone in his dark eyes. Understanding flickered between them and Willa made no sound of protest when Clay started for the hall that led to the master bedroom.

When he stopped at the edge of the bed, he lowered her to her feet, his mouth reclaiming hers for a fiery kiss that shocked and inflamed them both. When his lips finally released hers Willa could barely do more than cling to him.

With a slowness that served only to escalate the deep longing between them, Clay began at the open neckline of Willa's blouse, unfastening a button, then leaning down to kiss the bit of flushed skin he exposed before bringing his mouth up to graze leisurely over the silken skin of her neck. Steadily he hand moved downward, until Willa was forced to grip his shoulders tighter to keep her balance, so overwhelmed was she by the rippling tides of sensation that quaked through her.

''Willa?'' Clay's voice was rough with emotion as he parted the facings of her blouse to gently caress her lace-clad breasts. Willa heard the unasked question and felt everything within her strain to answer as she opened her eyes and looked up at him.

This was the man she would love for the rest of her life. The feelings she'd had for him years ago had survived the very worst and had somehow been resurrected into something much more mature, something much deeper than fleeting infatuation. The love she felt for him was as vital to her as her own heartbeat, and if she couldn't do something to express it now—to in some way acknowledge it—she wasn't certain she'd be able to live with herself.

Still, there was more than a little fear inside her, fear that robbed her of words and made her drop her eyes from the passionate turbulence in his.

Unable to say what she felt or to verbalize her consent, she instead trailed her fingers over the muscle and sinewed lines of his wide shoulders and down his shirt front. The pearled snaps of his western shirt gave easily to her slow, deliberate little tugs, which exposed his hair-rough chest and lean middle, until she was able to pull his shirt from his waistband and slide it off. Her eyes crept up to his. She was thrillingly aware that his fingers were moving a bit more urgently on her and that his breathing was erratic.

Clay's eyes were black with passion and desire as he pushed her blouse back and drew her sleeves down her arms to fall to the floor. Willa felt the slight tremor of his fingers when they returned to the front of her bra and gently worked the catch to free her breasts. Her eyes drifted closed in ecstacy as the sweet abrasion of his calloused fingertips was followed shortly by the warmth of his mouth.

"I want you, Willa," he breathed against her, his voice gruff as she ran her hands over the sculpted flesh of his shoulders and back, reveling in the solid male feel of him.

Willa didn't realize Clay had guided her backward until her legs touched the side of the mattress. He lowered her to the bed, then followed her down, his lips reclaiming hers as he lay beside her and slid his hard thigh possessively over hers.

'I want you, too,'' she managed to whisper, barely remembering to substitute the word *want* for *love* when Clay's lips slid off hers to nibble their way down her neck to her breast. He had just begun to toy with one rosy crest, when the telephone beside the bed jangled.

Without hesitation, Clay reached over and flicked off the bell as he continued to lavish her with attention. Nearly oblivious to the slight interruption, Willa couldn't touch him enough, her hands combing through the lushness of his hair and tracing the grooved line of his spine as he teased her nearer the unknown.

Nothing in the world mattered to her except this man and the deep compelling need she had for him. The chasm of emptiness deep within her was begging to be filled, and the more acutely she felt the need, the closer she sensed satisfaction was.

Clay had just lowered his hand to the snap of her jeans, when a loud hammering began at the other end of the house. Neither of them responded at first, so thick was the sensual haze that surrounded them. Only when the pounding began a second time did Clay show any interest in dealing with it. With a soft curse, he levered himself away from her and got up to grab his shirt, his dark eyes snapping with annoyance as he shrugged it on and hastily fastened it.

Willa slid to the edge of the bed and reached for her discarded blouse before she sat up and covered herself, her cheeks tinged with shy color.

"I won't be long," Clay promised as he leaned down, catching her chin and lifting her face for a swift hard kiss. "Wait for me?"

Willa nodded and watched him stride out as the urgent pounding began again. It was when she heard the low murmur of male voices that an uneasiness began to penetrate the sensual euphoria she was in. Sensing something was wrong, she quickly got dressed.

She had just stepped out into the hall, when she heard Clay coming through the house, the sound of his long, swift strides sending a tremor of foreboding through her.

He slowed when he saw her, the grim set of his face softening at her worried expression. Willa felt her heart begin to thud with alarm as he crossed the distance between them and gently gripped her arms as if to steady her.

"It's Aunt Tess, isn't it?" she asked, the terror she felt sending a shaky weakness through her as she clutched his muscular forearms.

Clay's grip tightened and Willa's heart plummeted with dread. "Yes, honey," he said. "It's Tess."

CHAPTER TEN

"IT'S NOT AS BAD as you think, Willa," Clay assured her. "Tess had a little spell tonight, but—" he gave her a slight shake when he saw the tears spring to her eyes "—she's all right now. Frank said Paige just called to tell us that Doc Elliot was out to see Tess a while ago and that he says she's doing fine."

"I've got to get home," Willa said, unable to keep the anxious edge from her voice.

Clay nodded. "I'll take you."

The ride from Orion to the Circle H seemed unbearably long. Clay had no more than brought the pickup to a halt beside the house than Willa flung the door open to scramble out and hurry inside. Clay caught up with her just as she reached the back porch.

"Slow down," he ordered gruffly as he braced a hand on the porch door to keep her from opening it.

Willa gave the door a futile tug before she turned toward Clay, her eyes flashing with fear and anger. "Just what do you think you're doing?" she demanded.

"If you could get a good look at yourself, you'd know."

Clay's words penetrated her anxiety and Willa made a visible effort to relax as he dropped his hand from the door and gathered her stiff frame into his arms. "You let yourself get upset too easily where Tess is concerned."

Willa bristled at the observation and pushed back slightly to give him a look of defiance. "I love my aunt. How could I not care about her?"

Clay shook his head. "Caring about her is one thing—getting yourself this stirred up is another. I told you Doc Elliot said she was all right. Besides, how much love and care are you going to show her if you charge in there after the fact and get her all excited again?"

Willa's eyes dropped to his chest and the rigidity went out of her as she accepted his reasoning. "You're right," she admitted softly, then shook her head. "But I just can't... lose her now." Willa released an impatient breath. "I know that sounds selfish."

Clay lifted his hand from her waist and used the back of his index finger to brush away the tear that had tracked down her cheek at the admission.

"Tess's going to live for a lot of years yet. Besides, worrying about it is only going to make those years miserable ones for you." Clay bent his head and touched his lips tenderly to hers, coaxing back a bit of the sensual closeness they'd shared earlier. "That's better," he pronounced as he drew away from the brief kiss and studied the more serene expression on her face. "I think you're ready to go in now."

He released her, then followed her into the house, his hand settling on the back of her waist in subtle support when Paige turned toward them from where she'd been standing at the kitchen counter.

"How could you just ride off and not let anyone know where you were going or when you'd be back?" Paige demanded in an angry tone, careful to keep her voice low. "Mother was certain you'd been thrown or that you'd been bitten by another snake."

Willa was instantly alarmed. Suddenly she regretted having ridden off without a word after her argument with Paige.

"Was that what upset her?" Willa asked, already knowing the answer.

"What do you think?" Paige tossed her dark mane of hair challengingly. "You're going to be the death of her yet."

"That's enough." Clay's voice was hard.

Paige was startled, but barely missed a beat as she daringly redirected her tirade toward Clay. "I can't believe you're defending her."

"And I can't believe you'd hold Willa responsible for this. You're way out of line, Paige."

Paige's cheeks reddened. "I'm not out of line. You just wait. She'll show her true colors one of these days. We'll see then how easily you and Mother find some way to excuse what she does."

Willa shivered at the dark glimmers of promise in Paige's eyes as she said the words, doing her best to quell the panic she felt when Paige's gaze shifted from Clay to her. She read plainly the fear-induced warning in Paige's eyes, and was shaken as she sensed more clearly than ever Paige's absolute determination to thwart her relationship with Clay.

"I think I'd like to see Tess now," Willa murmured as she stepped past Paige and escaped into the hallway. Not finding Tess in the living room, Willa hurried on down the hall to her aunt's bedroom.

Tess was sitting up on her bed, her head angled back to rest on the thick feather pillows between her and the headboard, her eyes closed, the family Bible open on her lap.

Unable to tell whether her aunt was awake or napping, Willa hesitated in the doorway, relieved to see the calm, even rise and fall of her aunt's chest.

Reluctant to disturb Tess's rest, Willa was about to back quietly away and leave when Tess spoke.

"Willa?" Tess's soft gray eyes opened and she turned her head toward her niece, a small tired smile on her face as she raised her hand to motion Willa closer. "Land sakes, child, what a look you're giving me." The tired smile broadened a bit. "But, then, I guess you're about as a big a worrier as I am."

Willa stopped at the edge of the bed, taking the hand Tess held toward her.

"How are you feeling, Aunt Tess?"

"A lot better now. Just a little tired," she said, then added, "sit with me awhile?"

"Of course." Willa sat down on the edge of the mattress, then began gently, "I'm sorry I just rode off earlier. I should have let you know where I was going."

Tess's brows drew together slightly as Willa went on, "I didn't mean to worry you."

"Worry me?" Tess asked, genuinely puzzled. "What makes you think I was worried?"

Willa's face showed her confusion. "I understood you'd got so concerned after I rode off and didn't come back that you started feeling ill again."

"Who told you that?"

Hesitant to name Paige, Willa managed to avoid answering. "That wasn't what upset you?"

Tess gave a short chuckle. "If I worried every time you got on a horse and rode off, they'd have to lock me up in a straitjacket. Sakes, girl, you spend most of your waking hours away from the house or on a horse. Why would I get upset this particular time?"

Willa searched her aunt's chiding expression, uncertain what to say. Paige had obviously engineered something here, but what? And Tess had suffered a spell of some sort this evening. If it hadn't been brought on by something Willa had done, how had it come about? The thought that her aunt had become ill for no reason was far more distressing to Willa than the thought that her illness might have been provoked by some worry or upset she'd caused.

A look of comprehension crossed Tess's face and she released a long, tired sigh and closed her eyes a moment. She murmured something soft that Willa didn't quite catch. "What was that?" Willa asked, and Tess opened her eyes and looked at her.

"Paige and I got into a little argument earlier and I was fool enough to let it bother me." Tess gave her hand a squeeze. "I hate it when Paige and I disagree." Her voice went soft as she added with gentle pride, "She's the best thing Cal and I ever accomplished together, you know."

Tess's words brought a pang to Willa, but she managed not to show it as her aunt continued.

"And you know how emotional I let myself get. Doc Elliot warned me about becoming so worked up, but I just haven't got the hang of controlling myself yet. It was no one's fault but mine and I don't want you to give it another thought, you hear?"

"All right," Willa said, able to relax as her sense of guilt eased.

"Now that we've settled that," Tess said as an impish twinkle came into her eyes, "maybe we ought to talk about just where it was you took off to so late."

Willa couldn't suppress a smile at the lively curiosity on Tess's face. "I rode over to Orion."

Tess's brows went up as she nodded. "You've been over there visiting Clay all this time?" she pressed.

Willa's cheeks colored. "Yes."

"Good. Are the two of you on as good terms these days as I think you are?"

"So far," Willa hedged.

Tess gave a decidedly unladylike snort. "Don't you dodge me on this one, Willa," she warned good-naturedly. "I can tell just by looking at you that you and Clay weren't talking ranching all that time."

The color in Willa's face deepened. "You're right about that."

Tess grinned, her earlier tiredness fading. "Are you in love with him?"

Willa didn't hesitate. "Yes."

Tess patted her hand, the gleeful look in her eyes making her seem years younger. "And does he love you?"

Willa's smile wavered a bit. "I hope," she said softly, her slight shrug communicating her uncertainty.

Tess leaned toward her and gave her a hug. "He feels a lot for you, honey, that's certain. And there's no question the two of you are suited to each other." She drew back and gave Willa a searching look. "I don't think I need to tell you how much I'd like to see the two of you together. I think the world would finally come right for you both."

If only it would, Willa thought. But no matter what happened between them now, Willa still needed Clay to see the truth about Angie's death. Although she'd been able to somehow set all that aside earlier, she knew now without a doubt that leaving the past so unresolved was potentially dangerous to their future relationship. The issue of trust was far too important to them both to allow it to be swept aside by physical desire.

"I hope you're right," she whispered.

Tess gave her another hug, then leaned back against the pillows. "Now that that's all settled, I think I might rest a little longer and read before I get ready for bed."

"Is there anything I can do for you or get for you?"

"Not a thing I can think of," Tess said with a firm shake of her head. "You just run along now and don't fret."

"All right, Aunt Tess." Willa stood up and started toward the door. "Good night."

"Good night, Willa."

Willa stepped out into the hall and eased the door partway closed, glancing toward her aunt one last time before she made her way back to the kitchen. To her relief, Clay was alone, his hip braced against the kitchen counter as he sipped a cup of coffee.

"How is she?"

"She seems fine...a little tired," Willa answered as she crossed the room and helped herself to a cup of fresh brew from the coffee maker on the counter next to where Clay was standing. "Where's Paige?"

"She took off in her car a few minutes ago."

Willa heard the smile in Clay's voice and turned toward him. "I take it she wasn't too pleased about something."

"Some*one* would be more like it," he said as he set his coffee cup aside and reached over to pull her into the circle of his arms.

"Ooops, watch the coffee," Willa cautioned as some of her coffee tippled over the side of the cup and dotted the front of Clay's shirt.

"It'd take a lot more than a little coffee to douse the fire I've got burning," he said huskily.

"Is that so?" Willa's gaze fell from his as she sipped her hot drink and tried to ignore the excitement that raced along her nerves as he pulled her against his hard thighs. If she and Clay had made love earlier, she would not have regretted it, but now that common sense had reasserted itself, she felt more cautious than ever. It didn't matter that she and Clay were becoming involved and that he had forgiven her for Angie's death; he still believed she was responsible for it.

Yet as much as she wanted to tell him everything, to make him finally see the truth, her aunt's possible reaction to it and her own sense of pride still made telling him outright impossible. Especially now that her aunt seemed unable to cope with upset of any kind, she realized grimly.

"Why don't you set that coffee out of the way, darlin'," he drawled, and waited a moment for her to place her cup on the counter behind him. Without giving her a chance to protest, he bent his head and seized her lips with a hunger that made confetti of her thoughts. When he finally broke off the kiss, they were both trembling.

"I don't suppose there's much chance of us taking up where we left off earlier, is there?" Clay asked, a wry, self-mocking twist to his mouth as he said the words.

Willa couldn't help but giggle at the look in spite of the frustrated longing that gripped her, too. "No," she answered, then sobered a bit.

"I'm still rushing this too much, aren't I?" he said, the gruffness in his voice making her feel warm and wonderfully safe with him. "I can see it in your eyes."

Willa's gaze dropped to his chest and she smoothed her fingers over his taut cotton shirt front. "I think there might be safer ways to explore our feelings for each other."

Clay took a deep breath and exhaled it slowly. "Safer maybe, but I can't shake the feeling that you're slipping through my fingers. It makes me impatient to do something about it, to make you mine." He lowered his head and sought her lips again, his breath coming in agitated gusts over her skin when he ended the kiss and struggled for control. Willa was no more in control than he as she leaned her weight against him, her body slow to recover from its love-induced languor.

"I think it would be a good idea if I headed on home," Clay said as he eased her away from him. "No telling what kind of spell your aunt would have if she came out to the kitchen a few minutes from now."

Willa walked with him to the porch door, disappointed in the light swift kiss he gave her before he stepped out into the night.

THE WEEK SPED BY QUICKLY as Willa worked to prepare the bunkhouse not only for Phil Spencer, but for the two ranch hands Clay had found for her. The future of the Circle H looked far brighter now than when she'd first returned, and Willa was more than pleased with the way things were going.

Clay stopped over nearly every day and they went out together almost every night, which never failed to distress her cousin. As a result, Paige had become withdrawn, the deep circles beneath her eyes a vivid indication of sleeplessness. Though Willa felt some amount of sympathy for Paige, she was far too busy and much too happy to allow her cousin's apprehension to daunt her.

The almost constant state of euphoria she was in because of her deepening relationship with Clay gave her a lightness of heart that had been alien to her these past five years. Though she would never quite achieve the untroubled high spirits of her adolescence, inside she felt almost as carefree.

Yet as the days rapidly advanced toward Phil Spencer's arrival, the sense of optimism and anticipation Willa awoke to each morning began to give way to the niggling reminder that Phil would soon be taking over the Circle H and that Clay and her aunt expected her to reach a decision about staying on. Neither of them knew about her part-ownership of the ranch in Colorado, and the longer Willa put off telling them about it, the harder she was finding it to do so.

It came to Willa several times that she should tell Clay about her partnership, but something had always held her back. Besides, the subject hadn't come up again, and in the past five years, Willa had developed a habit of not offering too much information about herself.

As far as Aunt Tess was concerned, Willa wasn't certain how she'd take the news, so she found herself putting it off again and again, reluctant to cause her aunt any hurt feelings until she was certain of her plans.

As it turned out, however, whatever sense of guilt Willa had felt about keeping so closemouthed about the D & R was swept suddenly away the day before Phil Spencer was to arrive.

Willa finished briskly rubbing down the sorrel once she'd unsaddled him, then turned him into his stall with his usual measure of grain and fresh water. A feeling of satisfaction settled over her as she walked through the barn toward the shade-dappled sunlight of midafternoon. Thanks to the loan of Clay's men,

most of the repairs around the ranch had been made.
And now that the bunkhouse was ready for the new
hired men, Willa felt for once as if everything were
caught up. From past experience on a working ranch,
Willa knew such an achievement was rare and fleeting, but she allowed herself to enjoy how ever many
moments of peace those accomplishments granted her.

A smile touched her lips as she walked toward the
house and saw Clay's pickup parked beside her car.
Though she hadn't expected him to stop over so early
since they were planning to go out for dinner that
night, she was glad to see him anytime. As often as
they were together, Willa couldn't help craving more,
and her relaxed stride quickened as she came up the
walk to the back porch door and stepped into the
kitchen to head for the living room.

Surprised to find no one there, Willa was just about
to call out, when she heard voices coming from the
den. Though she couldn't make out what was being
said, she could tell from the bitter tone of Paige's voice
that something was amiss.

A sense of foreboding wrapped coldly around her
heart as she approached the open door, deliberately
letting the sound of her booted feet on the carpeted
floorboards announce her arrival.

"Good. You're finally here." Paige's odd greeting
directed attention to Willa as she hesitated in the
doorway. Aunt Tess turned her head and glanced toward Willa from where she sat in one of the wing
chairs. A shadow of worry came into Willa's eyes as
she saw clearly the strain on her aunt's face, which
gave it a grayish tinge.

She walked farther into the room as Clay sat down on the edge of the desk, his long legs stretched out in front of him. Willa didn't need to see his stern expression to know that something was very wrong, or the almost fearful look of nervous agitation on her cousin's face that warned her Paige was up to something.

"Well, now that you're finally here, I don't see any reason to delay this." Paige's announcement ran like sandpaper along Willa's nerves as Paige left her mother's side and walked behind the desk. Willa's brow furrowed slightly as Paige took the check ledger for the ranch account from the cabinet. Willa didn't realize the significance of Paige's action until she flipped through the pages to a space well beyond the spot where the checks were currently being written out.

Paige cleared her throat nervously, then took a quick breath before she glanced first toward Willa, then toward her mother. Since Clay's back was toward Paige, he didn't see the look, and so couldn't have guessed at its meaning. Willa saw it clearly and understood instantly what was coming.

"As we all know, Willa's been keeping the books and has had control of the Circle H bank accounts since she's been here."

Willa's frown deepened in irritation, but Paige hurried on. "I've been trying for days to get her to explain things for me, but she's always got some excuse or other, so I decided to have a look for myself. It was when I started going through the check ledger that I started to get suspicious."

All too aware of what her cousin was up to, Willa murmured a soft "Don't, Paige," as a sick feeling hit her stomach.

"Don't what?" came Paige's belligerent question, and Willa knew then there was no stopping her.

Willa's gaze flicked aside those few inches toward Clay, but his face revealed nothing. There was no look of softness in his stony expression, and Willa suddenly found herself unable to look him directly in the eye, fearful of what she might see.

"As you can see, Clay—" Paige came around the desk and passed him the ledger "—there are three checks written out for several hundred dollars toward the back—checks we probably wouldn't have found out about right away," she hastened to add. Paige looked up and glared triumphantly at Willa as Clay flipped through the pages. "And each one is made out to Willa."

The soft sound of dismay that came from Tess penetrated Willa's shock and she glanced worriedly toward her aunt. Tess's eyes were riveted on her daughter in disbelief, but Paige hurried on.

"I couldn't believe it myself," Paige said, pressing her advantage, "until I saw the bank statement Willa got today from the personal account she'd opened for herself in town."

"Oh, Paige, no. You didn't go through Willa's mail!" Tess's exclamation went ignored as Paige grabbed for the envelope addressed to Willa and withdrew the statement. By this time Clay had tossed the ledger onto the desk and come to his feet.

Paige thrust three deposit slips into his hand. "As you can see, Clay, the figures on the deposit slips match the amounts written out of the Circle H accounts to Willa. Everything is in her handwriting, both the checks she made out to herself and endorsed, and the deposit slips." Paige took a breath that was only slightly irregular, as she feigned disappointment. "As much as I hate to think Willa would do such a thing, it looks as if she's been helping herself to Mother's money. And since she knew she wouldn't be staying on much longer, she was clever enough to write out the checks to herself from the back of the ledger so we wouldn't find out for a while. It's possible she even thought Phil Spencer wouldn't question it when he did find them, since she's family and has been in charge of everything.

Paige's voice grew stronger, condemning. "But the fact is, Willa's taken money that doesn't belong to her. Add to that the fact that none of us knows for sure where she'll be going when she leaves here, and I think she thought she'd be able to get away with it."

Willa was so stunned by Paige's accusation and the obvious trouble she'd gone to to concoct such an outlandish scheme that she was speechless. Her mind raced to figure out just how Paige had managed to arrange everything to make her look like a thief. Then she realized the scheme would have been simple enough for a child to pull off. Paige could have easily got hold of Willa's checkbook, easily forged her signature on the ranch checks, then used Willa's deposit slips to deposit the money into Willa's account at a branch bank. After all that, it would have been easier still to watch the mail for Willa's bank statement and arrange a confrontation. That Paige had grown desperate enough to do such a thing shocked her.

"I think you need to say something, Willa," Clay said.

Willa glanced over at him, snared a moment by the utter seriousness in his dark eyes, the deadly quiet about him. Did he believe she was capable of stealing from her aunt? Willa's attention jerked toward Tess at the soft moan of anguish she let out.

"Yes, Willa," Paige encouraged, seeing her mother's reaction and Willa's obvious concern over it. "What do you have to say for yourself? How could you do this to Mother? How could you violate her trust and steal from her?" She turned to Tess. "We should think about pressing charges, Mother."

Willa started to shake her head in vehement denial, when Tess's watery gray eyes came up to meet hers. The pleading look of misery on her aunt's face stopped Willa from the outraged protestation of innocence she'd been about to make. As Tess's face began to crumple, it came home to Willa in an instant just how much more traumatic it would be for her aunt if she insisted that Paige had engineered all this, rather than accept the blame herself. *"She's the best thing Cal and I ever accomplished together,"* Willa recalled her aunt's words.

"Willa?" Clay's stern voice prompted her to answer, but the words were lodged in her throat. Tess's life was more precious to her than her own reputation, and she was terrified that this trumped-up confrontation was too much for her aunt.

Why hadn't she gone back to Colorado days ago? Why had she let everything go on? Clearly Paige felt forced to do this in order to keep the truth about the accident from coming out. If Willa hadn't been so greedy and foolish about Clay and gone home when she should have, Paige wouldn't have done this. Now the door would be shut to Willa forever.

Tess was looking pale enough to faint and Paige rushed to her side to kneel by her chair.

Clay's voice brought Willa's attention back to him. "You aren't a thief, Willa, and you're no liar, either."

Willa's lips parted in surprise at the utter certainty in his dark eyes, then came together again as she glanced worriedly toward her aunt.

Which would be worse for Tess to endure? Willa asked herself frantically. Finding out that her much adored daughter was a calculating liar, or that her black sheep niece was also a thief? In those horrible moments, Willa had to decide. This could be her moment to challenge Paige, to refute everything and clear herself once and for all.

Willa started to speak, to defend herself with the truth—even to the extent of telling them all about the accident—but Tess bowed her head in shame and clenched a small shaky fist to her pale lips, effectively squelching any thought Willa might have had of telling the truth. Suddenly overwhelmed with fear for her aunt, she managed only with the utmost self-control not to run to Tess to try to hug away her distress.

Tears stung Willa's eyes as she made the only decision she felt she could make. Her voice was a choked rasp as she said, "I'm sorry, Aunt Tess. I—I'll stop in town and see that the money is transferred from my account back into yours."

Tess seemed to wilt even more at that, but Paige's arms came around her, muffling her mother's soft cry against her shoulder. Willa didn't chance a look at Clay. The fury she sensed emanating from him was enough. Unable to control the tears of despair and impotence she felt, Willa turned and hurried from the room, taking the stairs to her room two at a time.

She paced the room as if trying to escape the utter desolation that had settled over her. Then, unable to bear another moment, she dragged her suitcases from the closet and swiftly gathered her belongings. It would be impossible to live here now. From past experience she knew the condemnation she would suffer and knew that this time she would not be able to bear it in silence.

She could have Paige's outrageous claims proven wrong, she reminded herself wildly, but to do so would devastate her aunt. With shaking hands, she managed to cram everything into the cases, painfully aware that leaving the Circle H would mean leaving the two people she loved most in the world.

CHAPTER ELEVEN

WILLA PICKED OVER the breakfast of steak, eggs and blueberry muffins the cook had set in front of her ten minutes before, but she had no more appetite for this meal than she'd had for the others Ruth Miller had prepared this past week. As always, her thoughts were miles away as worry and anguish continued to knot her insides. Finally, for Ruth's sake and because she planned to put in another hard day, Willa managed to clear her plate, foregoing a second cup of coffee as she pushed away from the table.

"You're up a little early, aren't you?" Ivy called from the doorway, then made her way across the large square ranch kitchen to pour her own coffee.

"No earlier than usual," Willa replied as she started to rise from her chair. Deke and the other ranch hands would be in for breakfast soon, and Willa was reluctant for her presence to again subdue their normally boisterous good humor at mealtime.

As much as she'd tried to hide her depression, everyone at the ranch seemed to sense it from the day she'd got back from Wyoming. She was uncomfortable with the careful way everyone behaved around her now and she didn't much like to acknowledge that they all acted as if they were walking on eggshells when she was nearby. Everyone was going out of his way to be kind, but attempts to draw her back into the mainstream of the D & R were beginning to wear sorely on her nerves.

"Are you gonna to be workin' that black colt right away, or can you wait around long enough for me to eat so we can go over some business?"

Ivy sipped her coffee and waited for her partner to respond, seeing, not for the first time, the restlessness in Willa as she reluctantly nodded.

"Anything in particular?" Willa asked as casually as possible, though she was more than a little wary of Ivy's tone. Until now, Willa had managed to evade any real explanation to her friend about what had happened at the Circle H that had made her leave so suddenly. But knowing Ivy as well as she did, she could see by the determined glint in the woman's hazel eyes that she'd finally run out of patience and aimed to have some answers.

"Yes, as a matter of fact, there is," Ivy answered as her look became more determined, and Willa felt a kind of relief brush through her. Ivy was not only her partner, but her closest friend. Perhaps unburdening herself to Ivy would help lift her heartsick feelings and give her a more objective outlook. Willa was failing miserably to get a firm hold on those things alone, so maybe it was time to hear what Ivy had to say about it all.

"Then I guess I'll grab another cup of coffee and go on into the den."

Willa settled into the comfortably worn overstuffed chair opposite the short sofa in the sitting area of the den. From the sounds coming from the kitchen on the other side of the wall, Deke and their three hired hands were just coming in, and Willa closed her eyes wearily.

She remembered reading someplace that depression was often anger turned inward. As she rolled the thought over in her mind, she admitted to herself that at least in her case it must be true.

How had she allowed Paige to do it to her again? She should have been more wary, more careful of Paige. Instead she'd either tried to avoid too much open conflict with her cousin or simply ignored her.

Also, she should have swallowed a little more pride and had it out with Clay about who'd been driving when Angie was killed, while Tess was still in the hospital. Because he, too, had been concerned about Tess's health; it wouldn't have been too hard to convince him to help her keep the truth from her aunt— provided he had believed her at last. Then again, he might not have been able to mask a changed attitude toward Paige, and Willa was certain a sudden shift in his hostility would have distressed her aunt whether she knew the reason or not.

Willa let out a tired sigh. Trying to protect Tess was a never ending worry. Clay had been right. Her anxiety over endangering her aunt's frail health was making her miserable. It had kept her silent when she should have stood up for herself; it had made her sacrifice her reputation and her happiness.

A strong image of Clay came into her mind and a sharp pang went through her heart. Because she'd wanted to spare her aunt the horrible shock of knowing her only child's true nature, she'd also sacrificed her future with Clay.

"You aren't a thief, Willa, *and you're no liar, either.*" She went over Clay's words in her mind as she had again and again since she'd left the Circle H. Had there been a spark of sudden comprehension in his dark eyes, or had it only been a figment of her own anguished hope? Could he have at last come to the realization that she'd not lied about the accident? Willa couldn't trust herself to decide for sure. With a heart that sank deeper in her chest, Willa reminded herself for the thousandth time that he might only have been encouraging her to tell the truth about the theft from the Circle H accounts.

Willa heard the scrape of chairs in the kitchen and the sound of the men heading out to work. She didn't bother to open her eyes when she heard Ivy come into the den and close the door firmly behind her.

"Okay, Willa," Ivy said sternly as she seated herself on the sofa and took a quick sip of her coffee, "time's up."

Willa opened her eyes and smiled weakly.

"Let's hear it."

Ivy's demand brooked no argument and Willa didn't even try as she slowly began to relate what had happened. Ivy interrupted her right away and prompted her to start much farther back than she'd intended—especially the part about Willa and Clay reconciling and what had been happening between them since. Then, as was Ivy's habit, she continued to interrupt Willa at frequent intervals to dig for more details.

When Willa was finally allowed to get to the finish, Ivy swore colorfully for a moment, then grew quiet, her brow wrinkling in thought.

"Paige sure managed to home in on your weak spot," she finally commented, then issued a gentle challenge. "Do you think you can stand never seein' Tess again and havin' everybody you know back there—especially Clay Cantrell—thinkin' the worst of you?"

Willa shook her head sadly. "No. And it's tearing me apart, I'm afraid."

Ivy leaned forward and patted Willa's hand encouragingly. "I think your Aunt Tess's got a lot more sand in her than you give her credit for. If it were me, I think I'd be more upset and hurt because I'd lost the company of my favorite niece than I would be to find out the truth."

"'Only' niece," Willa corrected quietly.

"All right then, *only* niece. But I don't care how many nieces she's got, don't you think that losing you again hasn't upset her and jeopardized her health?"

"I knew she would be upset either way, Ivy," Willa explained tiredly. "I just thought leaving and letting Paige win would be less an upset. You don't know how much she dotes on Paige."

"Sounds to me like Tess dotes on you just as much," Ivy persisted.

Willa shook her head. "I can't take the chance."

"Heck, you took a big chance, anyway, by tearin' off like that," Ivy pointed out irritably. "I'd be downright shamed if my niece thought I was that fragile." Ivy's voice softened in regret at her characteristic outburst as she let out a deep breath and leaned back on the sofa. "But I understand, Willa."

The room grew silent until Ivy spoke again. "What about that Clay Cantrell? You think he fell for Paige's story this time, too?"

"I hope he didn't."

"Anyone who knows you, Willa, knows you couldn't have stolen from your aunt," Ivy declared emphatically. "And if Clay Cantrell couldn't see through Paige this time, he's sure not worth much."

Willa lowered her face to rub her forehead. "I thought for a moment he could see what Paige was trying to do—I even thought he might have finally realized that Paige had lied about the accident, too. But when I took the blame about the missing money, he was so angry." Willa's voice faded to a whisper. "Even if he'd doubted Paige's claims and that phony evidence, I'm certain he believed her when I said that." Willa dropped her hand and raised tear-glazed eyes to her friend as her mouth moved into a crooked, self-mocking smile. "I've made my own bed, haven't I?"

"I reckon so," Ivy agreed, "but ol' Paige was standin' right there handin' you the sheets."

Willa had to chuckle at Ivy's humorous way of putting it. "Well, have you got any enlightening words of advice that I probably won't take?" she invited, trying to lighten her own dismal mood as well as give her friend the subtle assurance that she'd eventually pull through all this—despite the fact that she herself secretly doubted it.

"You know I'm just brimmin' with advice," Ivy said with a wry grin, then sobered. "Have you thought about givin' Paige a call or goin' back up there and tellin' her you'll give her just so much time to fess up and straighten everything out before you talk to Clay and your aunt and do it yourself?''

Willa's brow furrowed and she shook her head. "It would never work, Ivy. Paige would never tell the truth about the money or the accident—especially the accident. She already admitted to me that she couldn't have gone through what I did after Angie was killed. She felt desperate enough to do this to me, to keep everyone from finding out the truth because she couldn't face being an outcast." Willa suddenly felt sad for her insecure cousin, in spite of everything. "Paige has always had to have everyone's attention. She always had to be the belle of the ball."

Ivy snorted. "Don't tell me you feel sorry for her!"

"Just a little," Willa had to admit.

Ivy threw up her hands in exasperation and thrust herself back against the sofa. "You're so danged softhearted it's spread up to your head, girl. No wonder you can't think straight."

"Gee, thanks. You know how much I like compliments," Willa kidded, trying again for a little humor.

Ivy stared at her hard for a moment, then released a frustrated breath. "I'm sorry, Willa. I thought things would get straightened out for you. Before I read your uncle's obituary and got you thinkin' about goin' up to Wyoming, I was beginnin' to feel like you'd finally got over everything back there. If I'd known you were gonna to end up like this I'm not sure I ever would have mentioned it."

"Don't be sorry, Ivy. You did what any good friend would have done. It wasn't your fault I let everything get so far out of hand." Willa sat up straight in her chair and got to her feet, leaning toward the coffee table to pick up her empty cup. "And what's done is done," she said, forcing a sureness to the words, which she didn't really feel. "Hearts mend after a while, but work just keeps piling up," she added, effectively changing the subject. "And if that black colt doesn't pitch me in the corner of the corral again today, maybe I can get to some of it."

"You just watch yourself out there, Willa. This'll be only his second time with a rider, and he's purely full of vinegar. We didn't name him Jack-in-the-Box because he's so easygoin', you know," Ivy reminded her, then added, "and give some thought about headin' up to Denver with me for the show the end of the week. If you're bound and determined to leave things the way they are back in Wyoming, I think you need to go someplace and do somethin' different, have some excitement. I don't like the way you been workin' since you got back. A little fun'll lift your spirits some."

Willa glanced back at her friend and smiled, glad for the suggestion. "Sounds good to me," she said, then carried her cup to the kitchen on her way out to the barn.

"ALL RIGHT, HARDCASE, let's try it again," Willa murmured with a grim smile of determination as she picked herself up from the hard-packed dirt and reached again for the reins and a hank of Jack-in-the-Box's black mane. The colt had been almost as fractious this morning as the day before, and Willa mounted cautiously, trying to ignore the pain that shot through her hip as she swung her leg over and slid her boot securely into the stirrup.

"It's about time you learned which one of us is more stubborn," she crooned softly as her grip tightened on the reins and she prepared for the bunching of muscles that would signal another fit of bucking.

Instead the colt moved easily forward, seeming to accept her weight as he pranced around the outer edge of the steel-railed corral. Willa was not fooled. As was the colt's habit, just when she thought he was cooperating he seemed to enjoy leaping into the air, coming down with his front legs stiff and his hindquarters high for the jarring buck that had unseated her three times, two days in a row.

Though Willa didn't favor the method of encouraging a horse to buck and riding it to an exhausted standstill, she was starting to give it mild consideration as the aches and bruises on her body began to flare into muscle-cramping stiffness. It had been a while since she'd had so much trouble with a young horse, and she was trying to decide if it was because of some error she was making in his training or simply because the colt was a handful.

The next half hour went smoothly. Willa was pleased the colt was already beginning to take signals from the reins and the guiding pressure of her legs. She murmured words of praise and reassurance in a calm steady voice and gave the horse an occasional pat, finally feeling satisfied with his progress by the time she rode him through the corral gate and dismounted to lead him to the barn to unsaddle him.

But the moment she started for the barn and the colt wasn't claiming her close concentration, the melancholy she'd managed to escape for a couple of hours settled over her once more. She might never see Clay again, or her aunt, and the very thought dragged her heart down as she was reminded again of how much she'd felt compelled to give up to in order to protect Tess's frail health. Willa rubbed the sore spot on her hip as she tried to walk out the stiffness, grateful at least that the new aches were physical this time.

"You're damned good with a horse, Willa."

Willa jerked her head up at the words, startled as Clay Cantrell stepped out of the shadows just inside the barn.

She froze in her tracks, her heart twisting with love and uncertainty at the sight of him. Tall and lean, his dark eyes and part of his face shaded by the brim of his black Stetson, Clay was an imposing male presence. His white shirt emphasized the width of his shoulders and the depth of his tan, his lean hips and long legs were encased in new denim. Willa couldn't help the raw pain that pulsed in her heart as her yearning for him grew acute. It seemed like forever since she'd been held against that hard, strong body, and the compulsion to run to him and throw herself into his arms was overwhelming.

But Willa didn't move, couldn't speak, as she tried to read his stern expression, terrified to see rejection and hatred, but unable to keep from looking.

"It's too bad you aren't as good with people."

Willa's heart lurched sickly at his harsh tone, plummeting lower, if that was possible. "H-how did you find me?" she asked in a near whisper, doing her best to recover from the fresh emotional blow that had dashed her hopes once and for all.

"Your license plates were from Elbert County, and I've been over at least half of it asking for you." Clay's face still revealed nothing but sternness.

"Did Paige and Aunt Tess decide to press charges?" she managed to get out, rallying at the stirring of anger she felt. If Paige intended to go that far, she was in for a fight.

"No charges," he answered gruffly.

Relieved, Willa gathered the colt's reins tighter. "Then why are you here?"

"I'm after my own pound of flesh."

Willa paled at that, oblivious to the black colt who nudged against her arm impatiently.

"But you'd better get that colt put up first." Clay stepped aside and Willa numbly led the horse past him, stopping just inside the barn to lift the stirrup and begin loosening the cinch. Clay stood behind her and she could feel his dark eyes on every move she made as she tried desperately to keep her hands from shaking.

That Clay was very, very angry was no secret, but what he was doing in Colorado was. In those tense moments that she quickly stripped the colt of the saddle and turned him into the nearest stall, Willa tried to guess what he'd meant about being here after his own pound of flesh.

Finished, Willa squared her slim shoulders against whatever he would say and turned toward him.

The instant she was facing him, she found herself caught in a steely embrace as his lips came down on hers with nerve-shattering force. Willa couldn't help that her arms were suddenly around his neck. She welcomed the near punishing pressure as if she were starving. His lips gentled, but he continued to plunder her mouth as if he couldn't get enough, and Willa was helpless to keep from allowing it, giving herself over totally to his demanding kiss.

For the next moments, their world diminished until there was only the two of them. Everything else flew from Willa's mind and her head spun as joy rocketed through her. He was here; this was real and right. He was hers and this kiss was the seal, the brand that seared them both.

Clay tore his lips from hers and held her even tighter as he pressed his lean jaw against her hair and mumbled raggedly, "How could you do it, Willa?"

Unable to reconcile his words with the powerful emotions that had just swept through them both, Willa went still, her heart barely slowing from its wild cadence as it began to thud in dismay.

"How could you just run away and not give me a chance?" Clay released her then just enough to grip her upper arms and keep her just inches away as he stared down at her bleakly. "Did you think I'd be fool enough to believe that damned crock of bull Paige cooked up?"

Willa couldn't speak as sadness welled up inside her. The hurt was vivid in the deep emerald of her eyes as she recalled the other time he'd believed Paige's story over hers.

Clay cursed softly and his grip tightened. "I wasn't out of my mind with shock and rage over a senseless death this time. If I hadn't been so crazy with grief over Angie I would have seen through Paige's lies five years ago." Clay's voice lowered to a choked gruffness. "I probably knew it on some level all along, but when I saw how Paige was setting you up about the theft—could see her in action—suddenly it all became clear."

Clay crushed her to him, pressing desperate kisses into her light hair. "My God, what we've made you go through, sweetheart. There aren't words enough to tell you how sorry I am."

Willa could hear the tears in his voice, and felt a flood of her own cascade down her face and dampen the front of his shirt as she pressed her cheek against his chest.

Over and over Clay repeated, "I'm so sorry, baby, so sorry."

Clay was shaking as badly as she was when he drew just enough away to lift her chin with the side of his finger. The lips he pressed to hers were infinitely tender.

"I should have believed you back then, Willa. I should have and I didn't." His face was full of regret. "I can't give you back those years and I can't take away all the pain you must have felt, but I'm hoping one day you'll be able to forgive me."

Willa had a hard time finding her voice, but when she did there was no hesitation over the words. "I already forgive you."

Clay kissed her again, then hugged her tightly, and Willa reveled in the love and security she felt in his arms.

"What about that pound of flesh you said you came for?" she asked as she remembered what he had said, totally unafraid now of what he might have meant.

Willa heard the catch in Clay's chest as he gave her a squeeze. "I wanted that because you didn't try to get everything about the accident straightened out with me when you first came back to Cascade, and because you let Paige get away with her lies a second time. The truth is, though, it's you who deserves to get your pound of flesh—from both me and Paige." Clay pulled back and looked down into her eyes. "I thought I'd go crazy when you just walked out and disappeared. I was afraid I'd never find you again." His lips twisted wryly. "Then that red-haired partner of yours gave me a good going-over up at the house."

Willa laughed at the picture of Ivy giving Clay a hard time, mildly surprised that he had managed to get past her. "What made her let you see me?" she asked curiously.

Clay's face was utterly serious. "I told her I was in love with you and that I intend to take you home to Orion to be my wife."

Willa searched his eyes intently. "Because you want to make things up to me?" she asked, her lips trembling a bit at the disheartening thought.

"Hell, no," he burst out before his voice once again gentled. "I want to marry you because that sixteen-year-old child I tried so hard not to fall for grew up to be the woman I'm going to love the rest of my life. You had me by the heart from the moment I saw you at Cal Harding's funeral—much as I tried to fight it," he admitted with a self-mocking twist of lips. "I'd already decided I was going to declare myself and ask you to marry me before you could leave Cascade again, but then Paige gummed up the works with that damned stunt." Clay's brow grew dark with anger at the mention of Paige.

"What's happened to Paige?" Willa asked, still a bit awed by everything he was saying. "Is Aunt Tess all right?"

"Tess's fine. Worried about you, but fine. She'd already guessed about the accident sometime ago, but kept hoping she was wrong because she couldn't quite face the idea that Paige could have lied about it. She went through a rough patch for a day or so after you left, but she's dealing with it well enough to get by. I don't suppose, though, that she'll start feeling better until she sees you again and knows for sure you're all right."

Willa was relieved at that news. "And Paige? What about her?"

Clay's face went a little rigid. "After you left the den, I told her flat out I knew she was lying and that I knew she'd lied when Angie died. She finally broke down and admitted everything. Afterward, Tess made it clear that she still loved Paige and that the door was always open, but that until Paige made things up with you, their relationship was going to be strained. Tess more or less insisted that Paige see a psychiatrist, and I hear Paige left for New York on Thursday.''

Willa was quiet a moment as she tried to absorb it all. ''How do you feel about that?'' she asked gently.

''How do I feel?'' Clay thought for a moment, then released a deep breath, weariness flashing over his face. ''I'm not sure I can forgive Paige for either Angie's death or the lies about you—but I think I'm in need of so much forgiveness myself that I don't have a leg to stand on.''

Willa saw clearly the uncertainty in Clay's eyes as he said the words, the silent plea for reassurance that made him seem oddly vulnerable. Her heart ached at the look.

''I love you, Clay,'' she said with simple earnestness. ''I said I've forgiven you and I mean it. I'm sick of letting the past hurt us.''

''Then . . . do you think there's a chance you'll ever agree to come back to Cascade and marry me?''

Willa searched Clay's face for an indication that his proposal of marriage was in any way a kind of penance, but instead saw the love and longing in his eyes that mirrored her own.

Clay appeared a bit nervous at her hesitance. ''You could keep your partnership in the D & R, if you want. I'm not opposed, although I'm going to miss you like hell every time you think you need to come south to check on business.''

A soft smile touched her lips. ''Thank you for not expecting me to sell out. This ranch and my partnership with Ivy was all I had for a long time.'' Willa's hand went to his cheek. She loved him more than she ever thought possible.

"Well? Are you going to say yes and put me out of my misery?" he prompted gruffly. "Or are you going to send me back past that red-haired lady wrangler and let her make good on her threat to pepper my hide with buckshot?"

Willa laughed, not at all certain whether her quick-tempered friend was above such a deed or not. Clay's lips came down lightly on hers, capturing the laughter and enticing more of the sweet, carefree sound of it as he ran a tickling finger lightly up her side.

Between the giggles and the kisses, Willa at last managed to get out a breathless yes before Clay's mouth fused hotly to hers, securing forever the bond between them that nothing would ever break again.

She'd usurped his inheritance—
then stolen his heart!

DIAMOND VALLEY

Margaret Way

CHAPTER ONE

BRETT STOOD on the upper balcony of the homestead and watched the Beech Baron soar over the edge of the escarpment and begin its descent into Diamond Valley.

Jay would be at the controls. Morton and Elaine would be hunched up in tense discussion behind him.

John Carradine had two sons, but only one of them could replace him. John Benjamin Carradine was a brilliant and extraordinary man; he had built up a great pastoral empire. Now he lay dying, and his sons were returning to divide up the spoils.

And I'm one of them, Brett thought with a shuddering, dry sob. She had gradually stopped crying, knowing the family were coming and she would have to be strong.

Whatever she did she was a Carradine possession. It had begun when she was a small child and in time John Carradine had assumed complete authority over her life. Carradine money had sent her to boarding school, then on to university. She had a degree now, but as yet, no job. She was barely twenty and still dependent upon the man many people believed to be her father.

'There's something about her that reminds me of J.B.!' one of the Carradine cousins had whispered to another, and the ten-year-old Brett had reported it to her mother as very strange. How could *she* remind anyone of Mr Carradine? Mr Carradine was the god in their lives.

That was the first time she had ever become aware of the terrible aura that surrounded her and her mother. And yet her mother was so beautiful: dark hair, luminous grey eyes, fine patrician features. Her young widowed mother had been appointed housekeeper to the great station after the boys' ailing mother had died.

It had bitterly offended the very best people, which of course included all the Carradine cousins. The only recommendation Brett's mother had had was the fact that her late husband had been a Carradine employee. Her physical beauty had given rise to a lifetime of speculation and gossip.

The stories were legion. Brett had heard them all and had been hurt by every one of them. Only J.B. was beyond common gossip. Beyond considering marrying Brett's mother. If she had been his mistress, and not even the most charitable soul had considered that she hadn't been, the underlying message was appallingly clear: even in the grip of obsession Carradine men only married women of their own social standing. Beauty appealed to them greatly, but there was never any danger that their hearts would dominate their heads.

Yet Brett had been treated extremely well—perhaps because, like her mother, she possessed that disturbing beauty. If John Carradine rarely showed love or affection to his two sons, he had showered it on Brett. Such perversity was cruel, and much as Brett had wished it otherwise, his tender indulgence had greatly diminished her chances of ever being liked or accepted by his sons.

Morton had veered between being overbearingly haughty or a cruel tease. Jay, that strange mixture, had protected her without ever showing the slightest interest. Jay was handsome, arrogant, high-mettled. He was forever at odds with his father, but his particular creed didn't allow him to direct anger or resentment at a mere girl; he was too much the quintessential male.

As a small girl Brett had idolised him with a woman's fervour; as an adolescent she had retreated behind a deep veil of reserve. Unlike her tragic mother Brett did not wear her heart on her sleeve. There was a hard knot of pain deep inside her that would never become untied. For all J.B.'s indulgence the humiliations of her childhood had made her fiercely protective of her own status and identity. Self-respect was all-important to her. If the conditions of her mother's life had made her subordinate to a rich and powerful man, Brett thought she would rather die than pay the same price. Yet hadn't her mother been trapped? Trapped by love and a small child. From the age of ten Brett had decided her life would be different, and such was the force within her small breast that she had made people, even her mother, start calling her 'Brett'. She had been christened Marisa Elizabeth Sargent. Her father, the man who *had* married her mother, had been called Brett. So Brett she was and Brett she stayed. No one had ever asked her about her extraordinary decision.

Now she stood on the balcony, slender arms clenched around her tense body. The Baron made a perfect touch-down and began to taxi along the all-weather strip to the great silver hangar that was out of Brett's sight. A chain of electrical storms had delayed their arrival and the western sky was still banked up with great curling clouds of purple-black laced with silver. She had flown through electrical storms two or three times with Jay and she had never forgotten the experience.

Nothing seemed to beat him, even the elements. Diamond Valley had once belonged to the Chase family and it was still said John Carradine had taken it off them unfairly. The boys' mother had been a Chase. The story was that she had surrendered an impossible life when Morton was about twelve and Jay two years younger, not long before the time Brett had been born. Morton favoured his mother's side of the family when the Chase family worshipped the alien, Jay. Jay was meticulously fashioned in his father's image, right down to the dark, stormy good looks and dazzlingly blue eyes. It was quite, quite extraordinary that they had never agreed. Sometimes Brett thought it was because J.B. feared his own son. Morton he could dominate; Jay he never could. Jay's rebellion, according to his father, had started when he was one day old. Jay too had idolised the mother he had lost, and his father's indifference to her had tempered all his perceptions. Between the two men a strange love-hate existed.

Yet Jay was the only one to love the station with a passion, though these days Diamond Valley was only a small part of the Carradine Corporation. The two brothers headed the top companies that made up the corporation, but John Carradine possessed majority stock in each company, ceding only nominal power to his sons. An empire that had begun with horses and cattle now encompassed aviation, real estate and mining.

Jay had walked out on his father a dozen times, but each time that proud and ruthless despot had effected a reconciliation. No one ever knew for sure if emotion played a part in it or if J.B. knew his son was far too valuable to the Corporation to lose. There were rival companies desperate for men of Jay's outstanding calibre. Jay always further outraged his father by pointing out that he was only looking after his mother's money. There was too much truth in it for even J.B. to explode. It was an open secret that John Carradine had seized on what was left of his wife's personal fortune, even if his brilliant strategies had made it grow beyond anyone's imaginings.

Lightning struck in a vivid flash and Brett turned away with a wince of pain and grief. Of all of them she had been the only one John Carradine had turned to. She had been offered a minor academic position with the History Department but been forced to reject it so that she could return to Diamond Valley. For better or worse she was caught by her love for the man who had been her own and her mother's protector. Instinct told her he was not her father, and both he and her mother had sworn to her, her mother in anguish, J.B. with great sadness, that all the gossip was totally unfounded.

'There's nothing in this world I'd love more than to be able to claim you for my daughter,' he had told her. 'You are the daughter of the only woman I have ever loved and in that way you are my daughter too. This I swear.'

For the past two months, Brett had watched the man she called J.B. die by inches. With almost his last strength he had attempted to engineer a fatal accident, but though he had worked it out boldly, chance worked against him. After that he lacked the strength to drive or ride and was confined to his bed with a nurse in full-time attendance.

It was a terrible way for anyone to die, and all the more pitiable in such a vigorous man. From a big, rangy man well over six feet he had wasted away with a cancer, accepting much less medication than he needed so he could be alert to talk to Brett. Often at two or three in the morning when the trauma seemed the worst, as Nurse Reed put it, Brett was always on call, but whatever was required of her seemed little enough. John Carradine was a legendary figure in her life, the only father figure she had really known, and his need for her presence was ferocious.

Her presence or her mother's? He often called her Marian. With such a depth of feeling in his heart Brett could never accept why he had chosen to throw such a dark shadow over all their lives. Her mother had not only been beautiful, but gentle and refined. She had never been good enough to become the second Mrs Carradine. Such rejection, for whatever reason, had affected Brett profoundly. No matter how much a woman could come to love a man, she could never trust him.

It would take about ten minutes for them to get up to the house. Brett turned away from her blind contemplation of a magnificent sky and walked into her bedroom. It was as beautiful and softly formal as if it belonged to a true daughter of a historic homestead. Her canopied bed was a Georgian four-poster, the fall-front secretaire was French and the lovely still life over the white marble fireplace was eighteenth-century Dutch. She was recognised but never accepted.

Brett turned and looked at her reflection. In contrast to her magnolia pale skin her hair looked very dark, almost black. Her eyes were grey; large with a strange luminous quality. She never knew if she was beautiful or not. She wasn't pretty. There was a certain aloofness about her features, yet her looks made an impact. As much a part of her as a destructive mystique had been part of her mother. She wasn't tall, in fact she was petite and slender enough to float away. Her outward demeanour was one of cool, swan-like composure. Inside did not necessarily coincide. All her life she had been kindly treated by a rich and powerful man. Inside her burned a wish for freedom.

Alice Reed, the nurse, was just coming out of the master suite when Brett moved down the long gallery.

'He's asleep,' she whispered, giving Brett a smile full of warmth and comfort. 'I heard a plane. Is that the family?'

'Yes.' Brett hoped that her nervous tension wasn't showing. 'They should be here any minute. Toby was standing by to drive them up. Mr Morton Carradine is bringing his wife.'

'I see.' Nurse Reed, a pleasant, competent-looking woman in her mid-forties, only nodded. She had met Elaine Carradine only once and given the option would choose not to have to meet her again.

'We'll take it as serenely as we can,' murmured Brett. 'Mrs Carradine may not have been happy that I chose you, but I'm sure she's been made aware that you've been wonderful with Mr Carradine and great support to me.'

'Don't worry, dear,' Alice Reed put out her hand and patted the girl's delicate right shoulder. 'I'll just keep out of the way. Dinner with Mrs Mac in the kitchen. I'm used to difficult people. My only concern is my patient. *And* you. You've borne the brunt of it, you know. All those broken nights are beginning to tell. There are shadows under those big eyes.'

Brett reached the landing of the great divided staircase just as the family moved into the entrance hall. Morton, a handsome, slightly fleshy blond giant, was frowning, and though the equally blonde Elaine looked up, she didn't bother to acknowledge Brett's presence. Toby was staggering under the weight of four very expensive pieces of luggage, and there was no sign of Jay.

'What is it this time, Brett?' Morton demanded. 'Another false alarm?'

'Your father is dying, Morton,' Brett answered quietly.

'Tell us again at the next summons,' added Elaine in her sharp, brittle fashion. 'Travelling makes me so irritable.' She looked down in disgust at the impeccable freshness of her yellow linen pant-suit. Elaine had been a society girl turned top fashion model before her marriage. If anything her image was even more brilliant.

'Where's Jay?' Brett's luminous grey eyes went beyond them.

'What's it to you, darling?' snapped Morton. 'There's always been an odd little bond between you and my brother.'

'God, Morton!' Elaine gave her husband a furious stare. 'The things that occur to you, occur to nobody else! Jay doesn't take the slightest notice of Brett.'

'No?' laughed Morton. 'He's taking a look around, lake eyes,' he said coolly. 'You look like you might shatter at a touch. Nerves, perhaps?'

Brett ignored him and walked swiftly towards the door, and as she did so Morton caught her around her small waist, trapping her in a bear's hold. 'Don't play the princess with me, sweetheart. Hard to know how you developed *that* little touch!'

Behind the hostility was a barely concealed lust. 'Let me go, Morton,' she said tautly, her body communicating her dislike of him.

'About time you had a man to handle you,' he said jeeringly. 'Or do you secretly fear them?'

Elaine, eyes blazing, decided to take a hand, but before she had time to snap anything off, Jay walked from the fading twilight into the brilliant light.

'Brett?' His startlingly blue gaze whipped from his brother to her, his expression so taut Morton instantly dropped his arm.

'Take it easy, brother,' Morton cautioned in half-mocking, half-wary tones.

'I'm afraid young Brett here rather fancies herself as a seductress,' Elaine offered abruptly.

'Or good old Mort couldn't bring himself to allow her to go past,' returned Jay in a quiet, deadly voice. 'We're here because J.B. is dying. It's Brett who's sat with him day after day all these long months. I don't want anyone upsetting her in any way. Is that understood?'

'We don't want Jay to be cross with us, do we, darling?' Morton moved towards his wife and took hold of her arm. 'We'll go upstairs and get out of the way.'

'How is he, Brett?' asked Jay when they were standing alone in the silent hall.

'Going fast.'

'My God, is it possible?'

'It's very hard to accept.' Brett, overtired and overwrought, felt unable to go on. There was stark pain in Jay's eyes, a rare show of emotion on his dominant dark face. It affected her deeply, and Jay had to take hold of her shoulders so he could get a better look at her face.

'You're closer to him than anyone else.'

She shook her head, aware of the turbulence in him. 'He *loves* you, Jay,' she exclaimed with pained emphasis. 'He can't tell you, that's all. It's trapped inside him, unable to come out.'

'I don't require a special explanation,' he said cuttingly. 'Anyway, it doesn't matter now. Can we go to him? That's if he wants to see us at all.'

'Please don't be bitter, Jay,' she begged.

'Don't plead with *me,* Marisa.'

'Sometimes I think you hate *me!*' Brett sighed.

'Why would I feel anything so extreme?' His hands tightened with bruising strength on the fine bones of her shoulders. 'You're as much a victim as the rest of us.'

'I know my head aches.'

'Aren't you sleeping?' His brilliant, narrowed gaze moved over her still, pale face and dark cloud of hair. Her eyes were like great shadowed pools of light.

'He likes to talk at night,' she explained with difficulty. 'The pain must be at its worst then.'

'And what does he call you—*Marian?*'

'Don't torture yourself, Jay. Torture me.'

'*Does* he?'

'Yes.' She bowed her dark head.

'He must have loved her.'

'God knows. What's clear is he wouldn't admit that either.'

'Carradines don't take their housekeeper to wife!'

Brett turned her head up at his cruelty, but there was only cynicism and pity in his eyes. 'You can't escape your own bitterness,' he told her.

'Some must be inevitable,' she admitted. 'It can't destroy my feelings for him, Jay. Your father has been the power figure in my life. He's been very good to me.'

'Considering all the talk I should think he would have to be.'

'He's *not* my father, Jay.'

'I *know* he's not!' His dark vibrant voice had the crack of a whiplash. 'Whatever else you are, you're not my little half-sister.'

'Why are you so sure?' she whispered.

'Because I've examined and tested every feeling I've ever had for you. I've had plenty of time.'

'And there's no deep affection?'

'No. Nothing so simple,' he said bitingly. 'There's no blood tie. Just an unresolved ambivalence.'

His downbent gaze never wavered. It was almost as though he wanted to break her, and Brett, tired and grief-stricken, lost control. It was shocking the power he had to hurt her. Shocking that he knew.

A little sob escaped her that she quickly smothered, ivory hand to her mouth. 'I see through you, Jay!'

'Yes, you do!'

Tiny little charges of electricity seemed to be exploding in her brain. 'You're cruel! You're planning some cruelty right now.'

'Not planning, little one,' he corrected. 'I'm going to pull it off.'

'And I'm certain it has something to do with me!'

'Isn't your real name Marisa?' He grasped hold of her delicate shoulders. 'Why don't you use it? Can't you *bear* to use it?'

She took a shuddering, deep breath. 'No.'

'Because you're certain about nothing. Can't you use your instincts?'

'And what are they supposed to tell me?' Brett raised her hands to her ears. 'That I can never look at you? That I have to look someplace else?'

There, she had said it, as he wanted her to say it. He had shocked it out of her. 'Why don't you leave me alone, Jay?' she cried defensively.

'And allow your conflicts to become a permanent part of you?' he held her still. 'You used the name Brett as a means of coping with all the anxieties ugly gossip aroused. In a sense you felt abandoned by everyone. Your mother, your real father who was tragically killed, you mother's lover, who just happened to be *my* father. You were an angry-anxious child, and you still are underneath the many veils of reserve you've developed. You still don't know who you are and you're still suffering from your fantasies. My father claims to love you, and God knows you'll rate a considerable mention in his will, but he could have set your tormented little soul at rest with a simple blood test. But no. As he came increasingly to care for you the more he allowed this thing to go on. He wouldn't legalise his relationship with your mother, and for all his strong feeling for you he's allowed you to continue frightened and insecure.'

'He *told* me he wasn't my father,' Brett sobbed.

'He could have done much more than that,' Jay pointed out harshly. 'How could anyone sort out their feelings about the man? How could anyone accept the many terrible things he has done? You don't really think he would have allowed you to take up your university post, do you? After all the care and attention that was lavished on you? More, in fact, than I'm sure he would have given his own daughter. Especially if she'd been a blue-eyed blonde. He didn't hold them in very high esteem. He didn't hold any woman in very high esteem, Marisa—your mother, my mother, you. All of you loved him and he played too large a part in your lives. Parental love he never gave. When *we* were kids, Brett, we were aching for love. Mort used to cry himself to sleep—I remember that vividly. I had my own stresses, but I was shaped another way. When you were a little girl, you wanted to love me in whatever role figured in your dreams. My father saw that, so he had to provide us with an insurmountable barrier; an anxiety so strong it was intended to warp our whole relationship. My father couldn't love me, and he couldn't bear *you* to love me. He did everything in his power to increase guilt feelings in both of us. There are rules about loving your half-brother. He knew *I* would never accept his cruel machinations. My father is like some ancient king, Marisa—he can't bear for his own son to have everything after he's gone. I know for a fact he was planning to marry you off to Lee Kennedy. He regarded Kennedy as a vassal he could govern. Both of you would remain dependent on him.'

Brett was beginning to feel dizzy. 'I don't believe you,' she whispered. She was afraid she was going to faint.

'Hasn't Kennedy flown in here at least a dozen times since you've been back?'

'To see your father.'

'Of course. And to see you. You've been so taken up with trying to find out who you are that you can't even see yourself. Your features have the purity of a little saint's, but your aura is all sexual. Men want you, Marisa. It's something very basic, even primitive which is why you're going to keep out of Mort's way.'

'How *dare* you!' Brett's smoky eyes were now smouldering with a small flame.

'You know, given just the slightest encouragement he would snap,' drawled Jay.

'Then you tell him to keep away from me!' Brett's angry cry spiralled around the empty hall. 'He's brought his wife with him, in case you've forgotten.'

'And he certainly chose poorly,' Jay gritted in a voice impossible to overhear. 'It's only women like you a man has to fear.'

'Like my *mother?*' The grief swelled up. 'You've never forgiven her, have you? She had so many names. You'll never forgive me—never, never.'

Brett put her white hands to her temples, and the sight of her seemed to incite Jay to madness. He scooped her up almost violently so that she inhaled the male scent of him. 'The evil is going to die with him!' Jay exploded furiously as her head fell back against his arm. '*I'm* here, Marisa, if you can't save yourself.'

SOME TIME after midnight Brett sat up in bed in a panic. Someone was knocking on her door, and as she stumbled across the darkened room she heard Nurse Reed's voice.

'Brett dear, you'd better come. *Brett!*'

Brett had never seen Alice Reed crying, but she was crying now, her capable face weary and ravaged. Brett only turned to snatch up her satin robe, pulling it on over her long flimsy nightgown. She had lived with this moment for months, but it now came as a terrible shock.

They were all assembled around the bedside with John Carradine's personal physician in attendance. It was one of the most terrible sights Brett had ever seen and one she knew would be burned into her brain. By far her worst experience had been the afternoon they brought her mother in after her horse had bolted and thrown her. She had begun to cry first, then scream, and someone had taken hold of her and hidden her away in his arms. But not before she had glimpsed her mother's crumpled body, her white still face, the angle of her neck. The someone had been Jay.

Now as she stood frozen on the threshold in perhaps the clearest indication of her lack of true identity Jay held out his hand again. His face was a graven mask and it told her the end was very near.

'Did you really have to call her, Nurse?' Elaine demanded bitterly, and for once Morton sent her a glance, heavy with anger and contempt that shut her up.

'Brett's the daughter he never had!' he hissed in a voice that wavered, then cut out.

Brett went forward, the breeze through the open french doors lifting the hem of her long robe and fanning it behind her. Love had so many faces, she thought. Everything Jay had said was true, but still she wanted to kiss J.B.'s cheek, stroke the silvered hair from his fine brow. Whatever he was, whatever he had done, he had served as the only father she had ever really known.

As she moved closer to the bed, something stirred within the dying man and he suddenly opened his eyes.

'Marian!'

The shock was so great, the expression on his face so intimate, so radiant, she almost slumped to the floor. Much as John Carradine had called her by her mother's name, it was a kind of forgetfulness having its origin in the pain of loss. Now he truly saw *her*.

'Marian, my love!'

Brett didn't think she could move, trapped by that terrible, avid glance, but Jay plucked her up and almost lifted her to the bed.

'I'm here,' she whispered, the tears pouring down her cheeks. 'I'm here, John.' She supposed she would never know why she had called him by a name she had never used before.

'Please, Marian, don't cry.' He stretched out a hand to her and she caught it and pressed it against her cheek. It felt like paper, not flesh.

'I love you.' The words simply flowed.

'I didn't think I'd see you this side of the grave!' J.B. made a sound that was almost a harsh chuckle. He stroked Brett's shining dark head, then frowned fiercely, stared up at his younger son.

'Still planning to take her for yourself?' There was a peculiar, jarring shift to a crafty lucidity.

'Too bad you'll miss it, Father,' Jay returned impassively, his blue eyes glazing like gems.

'Take your pick of anyone else,' his father warned him. 'Marisa is not for you, and you know why.'

'You've lost control, Father,' Jay admonished him in a quiet, deadly voice of imminent authority. 'Can't you just die in peace with us all?'

'I'm sorry, no!' Something midway between a snarl and a smile bared the old man's teeth. 'I'll admit I always had a problem with you, Jay. You always had a notion to usurp me—unlike your older brother. One way or the other I've done it all wrong.'

'It's not too late, now,' said Jay in an urgent voice. 'I'll beg if you want me to.'

J.B. shook his head. 'You will, but never for yourself. I've only met another man as hard as myself, and that's you.'

'And I've got a lot of years ahead of me,' Jay said in a soft, tingling voice. 'Tell her, Father. You love her, don't you?'

'I never loved anyone else.' The old man let out a rattling sigh. 'Not a one of my family ever did understand. Your mother, she settled to keep Diamond Valley. *Her* father sold her to me. 'Course, they didn't call it by that name. Very important family, your people, the landed gentry. A glamorous name, but they took the money. Your mother turned you against me, Jay.'

'You just like to think that,' Jay shook his raven-sheened head. 'My mother is the only good memory of my childhood. I couldn't do anything for her then, but I've been doing it ever since.'

'I know about your attempts to gain control, Jay.'

'Then you'll know how I've succeeded.'

'Please!' Brett rose urgently from her knees, coming between father and son. 'Please, Jay.' She put out a hand to him, aware of the tension in his superbly lean body.

Suddenly Elaine began to cry; great, wailing sobs. No one thought for one moment it was grief. J.B. had never approved of her and she referred to him only as 'that bloody old tyrant'. The sobs were ones of pure frustration and rage. No matter what, J.B. would never turn to his elder son. Not to Morton. His heir.

Yet he did, trying to speak, but his outburst, his last contest with his younger son had made him too weak.

'Dad!' Instead of a towering big man Morton fell like a stricken adolescent to his knees. All his life he had waited for one word of love and acceptance from his father, but John Carradine was demonstrating that he intended to die as he had lived. These were his final moments and still he chose to reject his two sons. Brett, then and now, was the focus of his attention.

Her slender body was trembling violently. She was profoundly grief-stricken, the more because all attempts at reconciliation had been destroyed by what had gone before.

In his own way, John Benjamin Carradine had sacrificed every one of them, yet with a heart full of compassion Brett bent over him and kissed his brow.

Death was so terrible, so painful, she had tried to block it from her awareness, but it was here now in the Valley.

A few minutes later, it slipped in through the closed door. Not even an empire-builder could keep a permanent hold on life.

CHAPTER TWO

THEY CAME FROM everywhere for the funeral: politi-
cians, pastoralists, business tycoons, family. The rich
and powerful and a sprinkling of humble Carradine
employees who somehow had managed to cadge a ride
to the Outback stronghold.

The homestead was full of people, hard-drinking,
hard-talking, most genuinely saddened and shocked,
others openly speculative about the contents of J.B.'s
will. It was common knowledge that John Carradine
had adopted a strange attitude towards his two sons;
all the more strange because John Jnr was held to be
a 'chip off the old block'. It was even whispered that
Jay Carradine through his better blood would sur-
pass his father's grand achievements, and maybe even
Morton would shape up, freed of his father's harsh
control.

Amid all this speculation the old stories were given
another airing, so Brett found she had to be very brave
to get through the day. Many of the women had
judged her mother cruelly, none of them having succeeded in diverting J.B.'s attention, so they were prepared to believe the worst of Brett now. Whatever her
parentage, and opinion was divided, it was generally
agreed that she had done her darnedest to engage John

Carradine's affections and so gain a place amongst the will's beneficiaries.

Strangely, the most powerful female member of the Chase clan, the boys' grandmother, Lillian Chase, supported her. Life was full of ambiguity and paradox, and though from most people's point of thinking Brett's mother had pulled the Carradine marriage apart (which simply was not true) the elderly Mrs Chase had stretched her tolerance to look kindly and even favourably on Brett as an individual.

'Nothing has been easy for you, child. Absolutely nothing,' Mrs Chase told her in a free moment they were together. 'You've given back all you got one hundred-fold. No one else could have coped with my son-in-law half as well as you did. Show a brave face to the world.'

Diamond Valley buried its own dead, but the Carradine patriarch had made it clear that he wished to be cremated and his ashes released over the shifting rose-red sands of the desert he had loved so well. There were great stories about J.B., and this was another one of them.

Towards sunset, when the western sky put on one of its legendary displays, Jay took the Beech Baron up and his brother went with him. No one else was invited and no one else wanted to go. Morton at that moment was content to allow Jay to assume his natural authority. The duel for supremacy would take place later, but it was impossible for anyone to think Morton would win. John Benjamin Carradine had thrown a shadow over the entire Valley, but his younger son was and always had been a free spirit.

'I've never enjoyed anything more than watching Jay stand up to his father,' Lillian Chase was heard to reminisce. 'It was the classic story of a shameless autocrat being defied by his own image.' At thirty-two, still a bachelor, devastatingly handsome with a nationally known name, John (Jay) Carradine was the kind of matrimonial prize girls only dreamed about. Highly visible at any time, his air of tightly leashed grief as he walked about and talked to the important people and the great families who had arrived for the funeral threw many a woman into a passionate turmoil. They had come to pay their respects to the father, not fall madly in love with the wilder of his sons. Jay's open clashes with his father made people value him all the more. For one thing, people feared in the late J.B. a ruthlessness which was entirely unaffected. To have stood up to him, boy and young man, must have taken guts of a high order. It was equally well known that the first born, Morton, had been very nearly destroyed by but somehow managed to survive his father's brutal dictatorship. By the same token he was currently held to be under the thumb of his grasping wife and her family, giving rise to the theory that Morton Carradine couldn't function without a high level of control.

Only Jay Carradine was reckoned to be a big enough man to step into his father's shoes, and it was high time Jay Carradine took himself a wife. This more than anything was the reason all the landed families that had them brought along a marriageable daughter, praying those brilliant blue eyes would fall on their offspring with favour. Quite a few of these smooth, gilded girls had older sisters, married now, who had enjoyed varying success at securing Jay's attention, but not a one of them believed they didn't have more to offer.

It was a strange funeral; almost a grand social occasion, with so many people from so many spheres of interest present. Anecdotes about the old days and the way J.B. had accumulated his vast fortune abounded, some sharp, some humorous, some sad, some charming. A Chase uncle, a much liked and very distinguished man, was a natural at telling stories, and he more than anyone evoked a vivid picture of John Benjamin Carradine as a young man. As he was a Chase some of the stories were delivered with an exquisitely malicious pleasure. Nothing had ever been so bitter for the Chase family as losing the jewel of their holdings, Diamond Valley. It was the Chase family who had blazoned the pioneering trail westward. The Chase family who had built the magnificent homestead which John Carradine had bought lock, stock and barrel, because as Mrs Lillian Chase once put it in private, 'he never had the taste to do it himself'. What he did have the taste for was money and power and the young and beautiful widow of one of his outstation managers.

No one who had ever sighted Marian Sargent, however briefly, had ever forgotten her haunting beauty, and once again they were confronted by that same disturbing quality in her daughter. It wasn't simply a matter of a cloud of dark hair, white skin and eyes like crystal; there was a kind of thrall behind the delicate grace. Many dark-haired women do not wear unrelieved black well, but against the sombre severity of her mourning dress Brett's magnolia skin had a stunning purity.

It was early evening before the will was read behind locked doors in the cedar-panelled trophy room with its lavish collection of silver cups and plate and gleaming blue ribbons. The portrait over the high mantel was not of J.B. as it was in the magnificent library. It was of Charles Thornton Chase, the boys' great-great-grandfather and founder of Diamond Valley. Jay often said that particular room had the real feel of the house and looking up at the portrait of his ancestor gave him great pleasure. Not that Jay bore much physical resemblance to the Chase side of the family, where blond hair, sky-blue eyes was the order of the day, but for all that he was clearly the family favourite. His grandmother doted on him and his uncles held him up as a model to their own sons.

Now around twenty people sat about the spacious room while Edward Cavendish of Cavendish, Manning, Ward read out the long and detailed will. Bequests were made to various institutions, charities, certain younger members of the Chase family, the boys' cousins who had accepted Carradine domination, staff who had given long and loyal service, but the bulk of his personal fortune, as well as controlling interests in all his companies, instead of being divided between his two sons was split three ways.

'My God, he can't *do* this!' Elaine all but exploded in the electric silence.

'Doesn't it say everything?' Morton exclaimed bitterly. 'He made her ambitious. He made her clever. He would say things like "you've got a good business head on your shoulders''. All these months she's had a lot of time.'

'Except they never talked about his will.'

'Do you know? Were you there?' Morton flushed at the severity of his brother's tone. 'I can't accept this, Jay. I don't see how you can either. To hell with all the fool stories! Brett's no Carradine.'

'Mr Morton, please!' begged Edward Cavendish in a distressed voice. 'You may be interested to hear that Miss Sargent has been in your father's will from as far back as the seventies when her mother died.'

'Not to the same extent, I'll wager!' Morton burst out violently.

'Perhaps not.' The lawyer looked uncertain and hooked his glasses back up his nose.

'Would you be quiet, Morton,' ordered Lillian Chase, in a frosted voice, 'and let us hear what else is in this surprise packet of a will.'

Brett got up and started to walk to the door, but Jay called crisply, 'Brett!'

She turned, the new heiress to a great fortune, looking not triumphant but surpassingly sensitive and proud. 'Yes, Mr Carradine?'

'*Sit down.*'

'Please, child.' Mrs Chase, looking suddenly old and frail, took a sip of water.

'If *you* would like me to stay, Mrs Chase.' Brett returned to her leather armchair.

It would hit her soon.

There was silence in the big, mellow room while the solicitor's rather ponderous, plummy voice continued to read from the legal document, but Brett remembered none of it. From a pawn to power. Many women had tried to marry John Carradine to secure what she had been given. The will could not be contested. No one had been in sounder mind than J.B. He had meant to give her the balance of power and drive an even deeper wedge between his two sons.

She left the trophy room in uproar. One by one private planes and charter flights had gone off, but the family were still in the house and several guests who intended leaving first thing in the morning. A scene had to be avoided at all costs. Morton and Elaine had turned on her like jackals, and only the cold fury of Jay's temper had silenced them without preventing their devouring her with their looks. She dared not defend herself. Not then. Later perhaps Jay's wrath would fall on her. She had heard Jay and his father vent a terrible anger on each other. How could she hope to survive that? She wasn't made of the same stuff, and she didn't want to be. She was Woman, compassionate, caring, supportive, enduring. From childhood she had been witness to and victim of terrible male anger and aggression. If Jay turned on her... if Jay turned on her...

Brett fled.

Mrs Chase sent for her about an hour before the appointed time for dinner, and Brett, looking pale and composed, went along to the master suite. J.B. had never used the main bedroom after his wife had died, preferring another of the twenty bedrooms. From the earliest days Diamond Valley homestead had played host to countless guests, as many as forty at a time, and hundreds on gala occasions, camping out, so there never had been any difficulty finding something to suit.

The master suite was palatial, almost overpowering in its Victorian grandeur, and Brett could understand why J.B. had chosen cosier rooms in the opposite wing.

Mrs Chase was resting quietly on the dramatic-looking bed, and she beckoned Brett in.

'You're coming down to dinner, aren't you, Brett?' Grand lady though she was, Mrs Chase was entirely without the pretentiousness and arrogance that marked Elaine and her friends, for example.

'I thought not,' Brett responded quietly. 'I'm not family, am I? I'm not known to your guests.'

'I will see to it that you are.' Mrs Chase gestured to an armchair with a fragile, bejewelled hand. 'Remember what I said to you earlier. You must show a brave face.'

'I was trying.' Brett resisted the cushion at her back.

'I know, and I was proud of you.'

'Thank you. That means a lot to me.'

'You're shocked, aren't you? Stunned by what's happened?' said the old lady.

'I never expected anything beyond a mention. A little money...'

'Ah, yes, but he loved you.'

'Why did he love me?' Brett looked into the old lady's eyes as though she was afraid of what she might hear.

'I suppose,' Lillian Chase reasoned quietly, 'because you greatly resemble your mother.'

'I would think you would find that unforgivable.'

'My dear, how could I hold you responsible for anything? You were, as Jay often says, the innocent victim. Anyway, my daughter and the boys' father were never happy together. Oh yes, Sarah loved him, or thought she did, and my husband believed it would work out, but there is no substitute for passionate, obsessive love. The marriage was basically a business contract worked out between two men. Sarah was so dazzled she thought it was all she wanted. *She* wasn't all he wanted. She was sweet, good, generous, loyal. You would have liked her and she would have been good to you. She didn't have the power to haunt or take over a man's mind. It was everyone's tragedy that your mother did.'

'It's been said, too often, that he was my father.' Brett dared not look at the old lady's face.

'Nonsense!' Mrs Chase almost hissed. 'He tried to make you believe it even as he told you so tenderly that it simply wasn't true. From what I know of your father, Brett, what I've made it my business to find out is there was no question of a relationship while he was alive. From all accounts your parents were a happy and devoted young couple who rarely saw anyone as exalted as J.B. Their paths didn't really cross until your father was killed. Believe it, Brett. It's true.'

'Yet he made me equal to his sons?'

'Forgive me, my dear, if I say a lot of it was spite— spite directed towards *my* family and a desire not to have Jay outshine his achievements. J.B. was a very complicated man, a tortured man in some respects. Morton, his first-born, was a tremendous disappointment to him. He so obviously looks like us. Jay was fashioned in his physical image, but Jay has a strong protective streak towards women, and he championed his mother. You were perfect to lavish his affections on—a helpless and dependent little girl. Later on you genuinely commanded his respect. Quite frankly, Brett, I think you deserve it. The only thing of great concern to me is, how are you going to use your power?'

DINNER WAS a sombre meal. No one was hungry. It was appearances only. The only thing that really went down well was the wine from a superlative cellar and later the port, when the gentlemen retired to the trophy room for some hard talking. Nothing changed on Diamond Valley. It was the ultimate sexist society, Brett thought. Man was king and women were chattels under the old feudal system.

Mrs Chase led the ladies into the Music Room, a room she had redecorated and which she particularly liked. It was much smaller and far less formidable than the main Drawing Room and contained a collection of musical instruments and exquisite Chinese Export wall panels. At J.B.'s insistence Brett had taken all manner of extras at boarding school, one of which was piano lessons, and, innately musical, she had taken to them extremely well. How often she had played for J.B. in this very room, but it was no time for music now.

Brett excused herself on the pretext of a headache, and although Mrs Chase had instructed her to come down to dinner she accepted Brett's excuse without demur. Elaine was in a particularly malignant mood and there was no guarantee she would continue to control it. Brett was not a Carradine. She wasn't married to a Carradine and there was no way she was even fit to sit on the board of any Carradine company, let alone become a major share holder. Her sensational figuring in the will was in the minds of everyone, including the hitherto benevolent Mrs Chase, but there was no telling what anyone would say after she was gone.

'Why did you do this to me, J.B.?' Brett asked as she picked up the small silver-framed photograph of him that she always set on her bedside table wherever she was. He had been a brilliant man, nobody denied that, marvellously effective in so many areas, but he had been a failure as a father: rigid, inflexible, ruthless. Jay and Morton had completely missed out on the joy of life in their historic home, and Brett was painfully sensitive to the fact that J.B. had used her to hurt his own sons. It was shocking, but it was true. Her inclusion in the will and to such a phenomenal extent was a deliberate piece of barbarity. Spite, Mrs Chase had called it. In any event, an outrage.

Not normally given to taking medication of any kind, Brett swallowed a couple of painkillers and prepared for bed. There was no question that she could remain at the house, although she was part owner of Diamond Valley. None of the household staff was antagonistic towards her, in fact she had long been treated as the legitimate daughter of the house, but even that could change. J.B. seemed to have hit on the exact formula for ruining her life. When she got back to the city she would take legal advice. There was a price to pay for overnight riches, and it was too high. She had never felt so alone in her life.

She had been in bed an hour or more when the chanting started; a curious high moaning melancholy sound that swept across the valley. It was the station aboriginals, of course, marking the departure of 'The

Big Man' from their lives. It was incredibly eerie and it upset Brett so much she put the pillows to her ears. Tears poured down her face and everything inside her cried out for comfort. She had always been so alone, so terribly, terribly alone. Helplessly she drifted over to the window, looking out towards the tree-screen gullies that were the aboriginals' secret world. Strange to say for such an authoritarian man J.B. had shown a surprisingly egalitarian approach to the tribal leaders—just another of his perversities.

The cool night air was wonderfully sweet-scented with all the punjilla in flower and the moon so brilliant Brett could see the lagoons towards the south-east glinting like sheets of silver. Even the distant sandhills were sharply outlined against the soft purple sky.

Old Wongin, who was a mystic, was the highest ranking at such gatherings. Once he had been a dreaded Kadaitcha Man, the tribal executioner who dealt in strong magic, and even now it really seemed as if he had been given exceptional powers. In his own way he had the same power as the white man to whom he had been so intensely loyal. To the ordinary aborigine Wongin's every word, every wish was law. He was obeyed without question and at once.

One by one the lights went out all over the homestead and a few french doors, even shutters, tightly closed. The chanting would go on until dawn, by which time John Carradine's spirit would have been taken up into the sky. But the sound was very strange and upsetting, rising and falling as it did, stopping suddenly, only to begin again, so even the nerves in one's body began to twitch.

Smoke from their fires twisted up in a cloud, but Brett, who usually loved aboriginal corroborees and ceremony, felt distraught enough to run crying through the house. Such chanting was designed to protect John Carradine from harm on his long journey, but Brett thought there was a limit to what she could take. She had seen through these last months. *She.* No one else had been prepared to watch J.B. dying.

Underneath the ritual chanting the small drums gave tongue. Brett found herself tossing and turning with the ever-changing tempo. It was impossible to sleep— *impossible,* yet she tried to keep a firm hold on her deep agitation. The wailing was heartrending, carrying its stark message across the valley. A legendary figure would walk the earth no more. Through their ancient ritual was he being helped to the Sky World.

Brett lay for a while longer in an ever-tightening misery, then she sprang out of bed, fingers of moonlight picking out her slender figure in a nightgown so fine it appeared as insubstantial as a cobweb. One thing was clear: she wouldn't get a moment's sleep without help. She had no idea how much Scotch or brandy she had to drink to relax her nerves, but she would pour herself a large measure and find out. Just about everyone else at dinner had drunk enough to drown their grief.

She was outside in the long corridor, still dimly lit by wall brackets as there were guests in the house. She didn't need any lighting beyond the moon to find her way through the house. She knew and loved every inch of it. Did no one realise what Diamond Valley meant to her? It was in her blood; the great homestead and the million acres of a landscape so powerful it had struck awe into the early explorers. The lonely grandeur. It had entered into Brett's soul.

It seemed to her as she moved silently towards the trophy room that J.B.'s spirit still hovered in the house, and she even threw a swift look over her shoulder, feeling a sharp thrill of superstitious fear. That chanting was enough to fan anyone's blood to white heat!

The room was in darkness, but so radiant was the moonlight she didn't look to turn on the light. The vast collection of silver cups took on an eerie luminescence, and she swallowed dryly and moved barefooted across the velvety Kashan rug to the low sideboard on the top of which stood a number of crystal decanters, glasses, and the finest spirits money could buy.

Brett was no connoisseur. Anything would do to gain some temporary peace. For a girl who had just been given everything, she was trembling like a leaf in a storm, fearful of trespassing on someone else's wood.

Man had always been a hunting animal.

The Carradines, every last one of them, were excellent huntsmen.

Brett reached out her hands towards a square decanter, and as she did so a tall shadow passed before the tall, mullioned windows. It almost stopped her heart.

She spun around in a mindless, atavistic dread, hands fluttering to her heart, an agonised little cry stifled in her tightened throat.

The tall figure was coming towards her, blocking out her vision of the full moon. His feet did not seem to touch the ground, yet she knew the set of his head, the wide shoulders and lean-hipped, dangerous body.

'Jay?' She tried to speak, but her vocal cords weren't working properly.

To a mind floating out of control he continued not to walk but to glide, and so great was Brett's trepidation she thought she would faint.

His hands were on her, on her shoulders, and oddly she felt that firm, moderate pressure might force her to her knees.

'I would have thought you'd be scared of coming down here, Brett?' he challenged her in a perfectly controlled, mocking voice. He was looking straight down at her, turning her slightly so the moon fell on her lovely, upturned face and filmy-clad body.

'What is there to scare me?' Even her voice jumped.

'Me.' He laughed deep in his throat. 'I've been drinking fairly heavily.'

'I think I've come down to do the same thing,' she quavered. 'I've had a terrible time trying to sleep—the chanting is so unnerving!'

'We wouldn't want J.B. to get lost, would we, on his way to the Great Sky Country?'

'*Don't,* Jay!' She was shocked by the dreadful irony of his tone.

'Starting in already to give orders?'

It was more like the flick of a whip than a rap on the knuckles. 'I've been waiting for *your* wrath to fall on me,' she said quietly, and dropped her head.

'It hasn't fallen on you at all. Yet. So what are you going to have, my little . . . friend?' Jay turned away.

'Anything.' His mockery blasted her. 'I've got wheels within wheels going around in my head.'

'I'll bet.' His caustic humour should have shrivelled her up.

'If you'll just give it to me, Jay, I'll go back upstairs.'

'The hell you will!' He put the glass into her hand. 'You float in here dressed in moonbeams, now you have to stay. Seeing you're part of it all. Part of me, *my* life.'

She seemed to sway before him. 'I don't want the money, Jay. I don't want anything. I'll see a solicitor as soon as I get back.'

'My dear girl!' He gave a jeering little laugh. 'You want a solicitor? Use your own. There are quite a few on the Carradine payroll.'

Brett could smell the whisky in her glass and it seemed to brace her. 'I had no idea what J.B. intended.'

'Really?' He took a quick step around, all power and lithe grace. 'I thought you had a tremendous insight into my father's devious, manipulating mind?'

Her white flesh flushed and she turned away, but Jay caught her as deftly as a big cat with its prey.

'Strange!' he mused quietly. 'I can see your skin change even in the moonlight. It's like a pearl, incandescent. Come over here and sit down. We'll parody a friendly talk.'

She couldn't allow herself to be so weak, so foolish. 'It's a funny time for it,' she protested.

'You never let me talk to you earlier today. Of all the people present you were the only one to keep out of my way.'

'I had nothing to say.'

'I kept track of you all the same. I never thought there was such a thing as a woman looking alluring in a mourning dress, but that's the kind of woman you are.'

He took her wrist and drew her nervy, apprehensive body towards the cushion-piled banquette under the tall bay windows. 'We'll drink a toast,' he told her almost cheerfully. 'It's not every day a little changeling inherits a great house.'

The pain was so great Brett couldn't even see straight. She was no butterfly to be pinned to a specimen board. She tried to wrench her hand out of his grip, but he jerked her to him so violently the crystal tumbler she had almost forgotten flew from her other hand. It crashed to the beautiful antique rug, where it shattered into colourless diamonds, and as she looked down in consternation Jay clipped at her, 'Don't move!'

His own glass banged down on a table and abruptly he lifted her, swinging her high in his arms. 'What do you weigh? As much as a sparrow?'

Just to be so close to him was a tumultuous shock. Something between sexual surrender and anger swept her. For years she had done little else but drink in the way he looked and moved and spoke; now she was engulfed by this shocking physical proximity. She could feel the radiant warmth of his taut powerful body, catch the aroma of the finest malt whisky on his clean breath.

He didn't put her down as she thought, but continued to hold her. 'Now this is something that hasn't happened in a long time,' he murmured, with humour. 'The last time I recall having you in my arms was five or six years ago when I had to remove you from an ill-intentioned horse. I don't think I've ever moved so fast in my life!'

'I *do* remember being hauled off. *And* blasted.' She was afraid to be in the dark with him. Afraid to let her head rest against his shoulder. 'Aren't you going to turn the lights on?'

'Why?' He started to move with her. 'The moon-light is quite extraordinary. It's truly like being trapped in a dream. Here, try my Scotch. I'll pour myself another.'

Brett tucked herself back into the corner, a terrible excitement, like an agony, pouring into her veins. She understood what he meant by a dream. She had been dreaming the same dream for years, one she would never indulge in daylight.

'Sure you can't move back any further?' he mocked her.

'Give me a break, Jay!'

'You mean you aren't getting enough?'

She closed her eyes and tilted her head back against the mullioned window. Her eyes seemed to be full of shining tears. 'I guess all you Carradines have a cruel streak?'

'You've been safe from me, so far.'

'Don't drink any more, Jay,' she said weakly. 'I know how you're hurting.'

'You know all about hurt at that,' he agreed sombrely. 'You don't run away from it.'

'No.'

A silence fell between them, then abruptly Jay turned to face her, curled up as she was amid the silk-fringed velvet cushions. 'I tried to hate him, and it wouldn't work.'

'Hating is not the way.'

'So show me another!'

Brett saw the sudden flash of his eyes, the hard sensuality of his expression, and an answering passion spurted into her blood.

'You've got no rights over me!' She dug one narrow, naked foot into the plush seat trying to push herself back even further.

'Who the hell are *you?*' His brilliant eyes narrowed over her and he reached for her as she had always known he would.

'Jay!' She gave one despairing little cry, a tight-throated, fearful sound, but he drew her up along his body, his hands clasping her head as his mouth came down over hers in a voluptuous wash of hunger.

She was drenched in it, drowning under an invincible excitement.

The first time, she thought. And it could only happen once.

He was still dressed in what he had worn at dinner, minus his jacket and black tie, and she could feel the dark mat of hair on his sleekly muscled chest gently graze her soft skin. His heart was pumping strongly against her breast, dredging up that memory of her childhood when he had lifted her clear of danger.

I cannot get free of him now.

Jay pulled her further along his body, then half turned her so that she was lying between him and the padded back of the banquette, her slender legs stretched out.

'You can't get away,' came his dark, vibrant voice.

'I *could* give you a fierce shove.'

'What, *you,* little Marisa?'

'I *can't,* Jay,' she sighed.

'No? You can't just walk away from your fate.'

'*What* fate? You're crazy!' Her will was being defeated by the urgencies of her body.

'Look at me,' said Jay deeply.

'You've had too much to drink. You've admitted it.'

'I'd need a lot more not to know what I'm doing.'

'What you're doing is taking your pain out on me.'

'And you're not giving me a little help?' He ran a finger from the tender hollow at the base of her throat to the cleft between her half exposed breasts.

Her skin seemed to burn, not with heat but with radiance. She thought it might even be lit.

'We should pick up the shattered glass,' she said weakly.

'I'd rather make love to you.'

'I must be way down the line.'

'Not you, Marisa. You're a real winner. One would only have to look at you to know you were destined for the big time.' His blue narrowed eyes glittered at her.

'I'll *give* it away!' she cried emotionally.

'You're damn right you will. It's mine anyway. *You're* mine.'

'You're just like J.B., when you think about it,' Brett said weakly.

'Aren't you sorry you comprehended too late?' He lifted her up and away from the cushioned bench.

'Jay, what are you *doing?*' Her voice was high with alarm.

'Trapping you, little bird.'

'Wait,' she begged. 'Oh, *please* wait!'

'I might have been able to do that once. Not now.'

Moonlight spilled through the great stained glass window that began at the landing and soared up into the next storey. Jay carried her safely up the stairs and along the darkened passageway that led to the turret room he had occupied since he had been a boy.

No light remained burning in the wide room, but he didn't seem to need one. Enclosed by windows on four sides, the room overflowed with silvery light, the barley twist posters rising sharply from the pale coverings on the huge bed.

'So it's come to this!' Brett gave a mutinous cry.

'Yes, and you get in there as fast as you can!' He threw her so that her slender body bounced gently on the firm springs and she sat up rapidly, glancing this way and that for some weapon to put her hand to.

'That's enough!' He closed on her, pushing her back against the pillows. 'You made your choice long ago.'

She continued to try for escape. 'I would *never* choose you—I promise you that!'

'Very fiery, but I don't believe you. Why don't you admit it, you little hypocrite?'

'How you Carradines relish your male power. Don't think you're going to use *me!*'

He came at her so suddenly she almost screamed.

'Leave it, Brett. Don't say any more. I like my illusions.'

'And what will you call yourself instead of a rapist?'

A bitter smile crossed his face. 'I'm not going to rape you, little one. I'm only going to keep you here all night.'

'And how else am I going to entertain you?' she hissed furiously.

'God, whatever you like.'

'You're crazy, Jay,' she said a little helplessly, checked by the stark weariness of his tone. 'It would be fatal to keep me here.'

'I'm going to do it all the same.' He unbuttoned his shirt completely and pulled it out. 'I want comfort too, Brett. Can't you believe it? You *lavished* it on my father.'

'That's not the same.'

'What's our relationship, then?' He bore her backwards.

'Jay...oh, please, Jay.' She was a half-second away from revealing her soul.

'Out of a hundred women why did I have to choose you?' he grated.

'You want what I've now got. That's the awful joke.'

'I surely do.'

'And what you want you think you have the right to take?'

'Don't be horrible, Brett.' His glittering gaze consumed her. 'I've caught you countless times following me with your eyes. Eyes are the windows of the soul, are they not? What do you suppose they told me?'

'That I'm just waiting my chance to destroy you. I really *hate* you, damn you!' She half lifted her body from the bed to hiss at him, half exalted, half fainting with the emotions that blazed in her. If she let him kiss her, explore her body, she would never truly be her own self again. She would twist in ecstasy, agony, beat her hands against his chest.

'Stop that, Brett. You'll only hurt yourself.' He quickly checked her, catching her hands and holding them above her head.

All she could think of was a hollow triumph. 'Don't you remember the old stories?' she cried starkly. 'If they don't stop you, *nothing* will!'

'Tell me.' Jay's voice dripped to a menacing whisper.

'You and I.' Brett turned her head violently along the counterpane. 'We are children of the king!'

His eyes flashed like diamonds and he turned her face forcibly. 'Let's settle that right now, shall we? All the old stories were lies. I've done everything in my power to help you distinguish fact from black magic. You know what my father was—the master manipulator. He gave you the truth, but he did everything in his power to prevent you from accepting it. I'm going to make love to you, Marisa, and *you're* going to decide what I am to you.'

'And what if it destroys us?' she whispered.

'But it will *not*.' He looked directly into her wide, distraught eyes and she looked swiftly away.

'I hate you, Jay!' It was a cry of love and rage and pain.

'Marisa,' he whispered against her mouth.

The agony turned to flowering. Limbs like tendrils seeking and gaining a hold on his head, his shoulders, his long legs. His body was the most exquisite weight, so wondrously real, his man-scent mingling with her own.

Had she a heart of glass it would have exploded. Her anger had only been a prelude to passion, a feeble defence that faded into transparency. Jay was draining her mouth of the sweetness he seemed to crave, and a powerful exultation snapped the invisible chains that held her and caused them to break away.

There were a lot of years in her involuntary, headlong response. A sexual urgency that roared through her body. Her small pointed tongue darted around his sculptured mouth, taking a step nearer to learning his fabulous male body. She had never been so profoundly aware of what it meant to be a woman, the most desired of all creatures.

When his masterful hand claimed her breast she went utterly still, heart pounding, every nerve stretched so taut it quivered like a plucked string on an instrument exquisitely fine-tuned. Her nipples were like tight buds, so abnormally sensitive an intense thrill, like a jolt of electricity, shot through to her womb as he twisted them first through the tantalising veil of fine lace and a moment later with moonlight illuminating their delicate, naked contours.

'You're so beautiful,' he marvelled. 'Satin-skinned.'

Brett couldn't stop him—didn't want to. It was a powerful yet real disorientation. She was going back on her dreams—the times he had come to her at night. Yet her innocence had never allowed her this ecstasy. A phantom hand and a phantom mouth had never aroused such frantic, concentrated excitement. Sensation was inexhaustible as his male drive increased.

'We're doomed, Jay!' Her voice palpitated like a wild bird's.

'Well then, we're doomed.' He sounded utterly uncaring.

'You can't afford this.'

'You want it too.' Only for a second did he lift away from her body.

'But there's a price to be paid for everything.'

'Sure there is,' he drawled. 'I've been paying all my life.'

'So when does the learning start?' She twisted her head so that her mouth was against the lean column of his throat.

'I've learned, Marisa.' He knotted his hand through her silky cloud of hair. 'You're the one who was tricked. I hold you in my arms and you flutter and gasp. I can feel the high throb of your heart, see the blood move in your blue veins. I could have made love to you when you were fifteen years old. You were ready then—a miraculous female creature just emerged from the chrysalis. Yet here you are at twenty, still a virgin.'

'You don't *know!*' she protested.

'I know. If you don't call *that* self-denial you can walk out of here right now.'

'Can I?' She rolled swiftly, lifting herself up.

'It's not so simple. I locked the door.'

'Then I don't have a choice.' She looked back at his handsome, mocking face, the insolent arrogance of his male grace.

'A choice. Let's see.' His arm snaked out, encircling her narrow waist and drawing her back to lie beside him. 'What about control of your voting rights? Mort will be sure to want to sell Diamond Valley. There are other areas, more lucrative areas we could invest our millions in. We don't need a desert stronghold any more, and it has too many powerful reminders of J.B. You can promise me to thwart him and dear Elaine on that.'

'And I leave here unharmed?' Brett stared up at the plaster mouldings on the high ceiling.

'What harm?' Jay turned his dark head to her. 'My hand on your breast? Your mouth against mine?'

'So *you* assume control. What do *I* get?'

'What do you want?' He swung about so he was resting on his elbow.

'Are we dealing, Jay?'

'We are.' He moved his hand along her cheekbone, the whorls of her ear, the pure line of her jaw.

'I never thought to see the day,' she sighed.

'Really?' His voice sounded almost normal, clipped and controlled. 'I've been expecting it for ever.'

'Now you sound as bitter as I am. How often, I wonder, did my mother lie with your father and wish with all her heart that he would honour her as well as lust after her body. Many, many nights, I'll wager.'

'My God, this isn't your roundabout way of telling me you're thinking of marriage?' grated Jay.

She ignored the black humour. 'Yes, marriage,' she said in a harsh little voice. 'Why not?' It had never remotely occurred to her before. 'Marriage in memory of my terribly wronged mother.'

'My dearest Marisa, you could have taught her a few lessons.'

'What do you say to marriage, *John* Carradine?' There was a strange, rapt look in her great luminous eyes.

'God damn it if you mightn't be a chip off the old block!' he exclaimed.

'This is no laughing matter.'

'Little one, you sound as hard as nails.'

'I was taught by masters,' she said drily.

He laughed again. 'It's not as though I'm terribly interested in anyone else.'

'Are you very sure of that? Kerri Whitman thinks she's stepped back into the picture.'

'Kerri is a very attractive girl, no more,' he shrugged.

'Oh? Didn't she follow you to the island for a week?'

'It was ten days at least.'

'Let me up.' She drew her nails along his strong, imprisoning arm.

'Not until I bring our discussion to a close. Tell me in detail what you want.'

'I don't want *anything*,' she said flatly. 'I told you that.'

'You're a rich young woman now. *Very* rich. You've had no experience whatever of business or control. You're just an innocent little babe in the woods. I know you're a clever girl, but your world has been strictly limited. When you weren't at boarding school or university you were here. You know nothing of the real world. Even Elaine could eat you up.'

'Not for long.'

'Long enough!' he silenced her drily. 'You're beautiful, and there's no way I can deny that I want you. I'm even fond of you in my fashion. I trust you're fond of me?'

'Not at all. In general terms I would say I find you both intimidating and dangerous.'

'And when have I ever hurt you?' he asked bluntly. 'Why, you ungrateful little wretch, I'd say I saved your precious skin at least one hundred times.'

'You were kind the same way you'd be kind to a stray kitten,' shrugged Brett.

'This is all very telling, but I thought we were talking business?—God Almighty, if they don't stop those drums I think I'll go down to the creek myself!' He sounded violent, twisting up to look out over the moon-drenched river flats.

'They're hammering inside my head.' She pressed back against the pillows.

'I'll shut the windows.'

'No. They still go on, and *I* have to go.'

'We'll go riding at dawn. It's the best time and it will blow all the nightmares away.'

'I *can't* stay here, Jay,' she protested.

'It must be a hundred feet to the ground at least. Anyway, I'm going to sleep.'

'So what am I *doing* here?' She sat up, pleadingly, her hands going out to him.

'Providing emotional support.'

'You're the hardest, most self-contained man I know,' Brett sighed.

'To a certain extent, I am, but I'm tied to you, in a strange way. Also, I love power. Marry me and I swear I won't ravish you as I desperately want to. Marry me and let me act for you in all things.'

'For how long?'

'You're too damned smart for it to take a long time. Say until you're twenty-one.'

'How do I know you won't take all the money from me?'

'We'll have Cavendish draw up a contract. He's the soul of discretion. I won't take your money, Brett. I'll at least double it. But I cannot have my hands tied. You'll marry me and you'll bear my son. Is that settled?'

'I want time.' She heard the deep panic in her own voice. 'I can't give myself to a man I don't love.'

Jay gave an ironical laugh. 'Princess, I thought you were dying for love of me.'

'I'll marry you and bear your child...children. I want the right to say when. Is that enough?'

'Enough for now. You're going to be a great wheeler-dealer.'

He lay down again, and though she rolled away from him across the wide bed he lifted her back. 'I want to hold you. It wouldn't be a deal otherwise. I know who you are. You're the sweetest little girl who used to stare up at me with great silvery, starry eyes. Nowadays, of course, those same eyes nearly blow me across a room.'

'I can't sleep like this,' she protested.

'Sure you can. You're going to be doing it for the rest of your life.'

Brett relaxed in amazement, her eyelids so heavy, it was a great effort not to close them with a sigh. Because Jay was who he was she was nearly accepting this incredible situation.

'Of course, we don't have to wait for a wedding if you don't want to?' He lifted her face and stared into her eyes.

'My wedding night will be my first time,' she told him. 'And probably not even then. I can't see myself loving you by then.'

'Ah, the lies you women tell!' Jay lifted her more comfortably back into his arms. 'Did I ever tell you, Brett, I loved my father?'

'I know, Jay.'

He nodded and relaxed his taut body. 'I suppose it's not unexpected for a little witch to know everything.'

CHAPTER THREE

A SOFT LIGHT fell into the room, piccaninny light when the pearlised sky was sheened with lemon. The pre-dawn breeze that fluttered around the bed was sweet and cool, causing little shivers to run along Brett's exposed skin. She made a movement of drowsy protest, then her eyes flew open as consciousness rushed into her brain.

She sat up in agitation, her heart leaping so violently she lifted a hand to her throat as though to keep it there. 'Dear God!' she whispered throbbingly. It was fantasy to be in bed with Jay; the fabric of her tell-tale dreams. She trembled in tingling shock and crossed her arms over her instantly yearning breasts. Her blood whipped into life and for an agonising instant she fought not to wake him with her lips against the clean chiselled curve of his mouth. He was as handsome as handsome, with a terrible power. His skin was very finely textured, with the colour of bronze. Hair, long thick eyelashes, brows, emphatically black. Darkness like that surely demanded dark eyes? One could scarcely absorb the shock of burning blue.

Such looks had made her, betrayed her. She had sold herself to him.

The ritual of mourning had ceased at the creek. An immense silence reigned in the short lull before the valley resounded with the heart-stopping songs of millions of birds. Brett felt as pent-up at dawn as she had ever felt the night before. What was the bargain? Jay would take her, control the fortune his father had left her, in exchange for a bitter victory. Marriage.

Her face crumpled and Brett twisted abruptly to get up. Heartache and confusion was all she had ever had from the Carradines. She thought she would get away, but an arm snaked out and drew her back with compelling force. She thrashed a little, but Jay rolled so that she was lying back against the pillows and he was leaning over her.

'Did I hear you cursing just a moment ago?

'Did I wake you?'

'You could have done it better. With a kiss.'

'No kisses.' She stared up at him with her great luminous eyes.

'Then I'll take one.'

'Jay...' Her mouth trembled.

'Need I point out that I keep to my bargains? Incidentally, more than flesh and blood can stand.'

'I have to get out of here,' she muttered.

He bent his head. 'Who would have believed such a beautiful young enchantress could be so cold?'

With his mouth against hers the very air seemed to melt.

'Jay.' She put her hands against his shoulders, pushing with ineffectual strength.

'You're damned right,' he rolled away from her abruptly, 'if you're going to get out of here at all, you'd better go now.' He swung up and moved to the door, opening it and looking down into the long corridor. 'Can't see a soul.'

Brett slipped her robe over her nightgown and lifted her hair over the neckline. 'Would you care if you did?'

'We could use ropes,' he mocked her. 'I could lower you down to the next floor.'

'*Are* we going riding?' she asked him.

'I have to clear my head.' His blue eyes were skimming her delicate face and body. 'If anyone asked me I could tell them you're just as beautiful first thing in the morning.'

'Whereas you have to shave.'

Jay ran a hand over his lean cheek. 'Hell's going to break loose when we announce our plans. You know that, don't you?'

'I'm used to a lot of fireworks.'

'Is there any possibility that you're going to want to get out of it?' His blue eyes seemed to burn into her like a brand.

'No.' She tilted her head to look at him. 'It's very important to me to get what my mother missed out on. You'll be a great man, Jay. Different from J.B.—more heart.'

'Anyway, we're quite fond of one another, aren't we?'

She saw the irony in his cool expression. 'My mother always told me I should be grateful to you, Jay.'

'What?' There was a searching frown on his face.

'Morton wasn't exactly nice to me, nor were any of your cousins. I could always see the contempt in their so civilised faces. I can remember once your knocking Morton down because he was teasing me.'

'You were just a little girl.'

'I remember.' She went past him to the door. 'You might have been a friend, but for what was between us. Pity moved you, Jay, and the same protective streak you had for your mother. What we have is a business arrangement that will allow us to guard all our interests.'

'Remember I want to sleep with you as well,' he pointed out drily. 'There are some things I can't do by myself.'

Brett saw no one on her way back to her room, and fifteen minutes later she was down at the stables where Jay had already saddled up the horses.

'We'll go east,' he said. 'Towards the rising sun.' There was a certain grimness to his expression as though he knew the next months would be very difficult to get through.

Brett sat her excited chestnut, admiring as she always did Jay's bearing in the saddle. He sat up tall, even after a hard day, never a slouch. There was a fascinating grace to his hard male body, something as superbly fit and disciplined as a top athlete and dancer combined.

The sun was beginning its ascent into splendour, flaming on the horizon and now the birds were out in their hundreds; the great formations of budgerigars flashing vivid green as they put on their incredible displays over the flowering flats. This was one of the great sights of the Outback, the tens of thousands of beautiful little birds winging and wheeling against a dazzling blue sky. There had been just sufficient early spring rain for the vast flood plains to be softened by a miraculous carpet of wildflowers cropped by the horses as they galloped towards the ruined sandstone

castles that marked the beginning of the hill country.
To the aborigines of the desert every strange natural
feature told the legend of a spirit ancestor, but many
of the stories were secret knowledge.

This early morning ride was balm to Brett's grieving spirit as it offered comfort to Jay too. They shared
a deep abiding passion for this ancient environment
from its extremes of aridity to a wonderland of wildflowers. Even the desert rivers had many moods,
flooding to run fifty miles wide, then subsiding into
chains of tranquil shallow pools. In the history of the
station, stockmen had been drowned in flash floods
and the homestead isolated by a great inland sea. Diamond Valley was a world apart, as bizarre and spectacular as the cratered surface of some new planet.

They were riding parallel to the line of billabongs
when the wind wafted a soft woman-keening aloft.

'For God's sake, what's wrong now?' Jay reined the
black mare to a halt, turning his head and listening
intently. 'I don't like that at all.'

'Still for J.B., maybe?' Brett too felt a tightening of
her nerves. The aborigines had all kinds of curious
undulating cries and chants, but something sounded
different from the ritual mourning chants of last night.
The sound that now ran their blood cold was more like
the departure of a tribal kinsman.

They rode down through the flowering bauhinias
and bright acacias to a stand of small ghost gums
standing white against the silver-green flash of lake.
Here, a handful of women were gathered around a
prone figure. One was at the figure's head, on guard,
and all of them turned to gaze at Jay and Brett as they

dismounted and began to walk soundlessly across the thick grass tussocks to the shaded clearing.

'Oh, *no!*' exclaimed Brett.

'Wongin,' Jay agreed grimly. 'Stay there.'

While Brett remained at a respectful distance, Jay went to the head woman, who fell to her knees and began stroking the old man's head. 'He go now,' she muttered, sweeping Jay with her black liquid eyes. 'Wongin blood brother to King Carradine. You know all about that.'

Jay dropped to his knees, laying his own hand on the old aborigine's head as the women started up their low keening again. Like the night before, it was a form of respectful homage and an important stage in the transition of Wongin's spirit from this ancient watercourse to the Great Sky Country.

Jay remained for a few moments with bent head, even now after a lifetime with these people marvelling at their mystical powers. Wongin had chosen to die; there was no doubt about that. His surrendering up of earthly life had been symbolic of the deep bond between tribesman and white master. 'King' Carradine had gone to his hallowed place, and Wongin, who had given him life-long allegiance, had conducted his journey into the spirit world before electing to join him. It was as simple and extraordinary as that.

Brett sat down sharply in dire distress, and one of the women, a young lubra, came to her and plucking some wild herb that grew in the vicinity crushed the silvery-grey leaves between her brown fingers and held them under Brett's nose.

'There,' she whispered. 'There.'

The scent was sudden, delicious, neither flowery nor citrus but incredibly aromatic. Brett inhaled it and gripped the emerald tussocks on either side of her. The plant's powerful fragrance cleared her head and something else beside. Within moments she felt better as though she had swallowed a tranquillising drug.

There was genuine concern and friendship in the young lubra's eyes, and Brett smiled at her and accepted a hand to get up. All aborigines had a profound kinship with nature and there were many, many wonderful herbalists and botanists among them. Jay's maternal grandfather, bitten by a desert death-adder, was commonly held to have been saved by some potion the station medicine man quickly brewed up. The white man had done everything to no avail; the brown man had survived desert living for more than forty thousand years.

The family were at breakfast when they returned to the homestead. Jay told them Wongin had passed over at dawn and, used to the ways of the aborigines, they sadly accepted this extraordinary occurrence. All except the city-bred Elaine.

As Mrs Chase's prayerful little cry was dying on her lips, Elaine burst out bluntly, 'I don't know how you can accept this superstition. The old guy was already three-quarters dead.'

'He wasn't at all!' Morton very nearly bellowed.

'Don't get your back up!' Elaine said in some amazement. 'May I please have more coffee?'

Morton got up to ring for more, placing a hand on Brett's shoulder as he passed. 'Already sitting at the family table?'

'Dear, dear Morton,' said Mrs Chase with a pained expression, 'I think you'll have to accept finally that Brett *is* family.'

'You realise we intend to contest the will?' Elaine drew in a hard breath.

'Who is *we?*' Jay raised his shocking blue eyes.

'Why, all of us, aren't we?' Elaine looked from old Mrs Chase at the head of the table back to Jay's dark, dominant face. 'We could make a very strong case.'

'Along what lines?'

Jay was reacting so oddly Elaine looked in some consternation at her husband. 'We all saw what she was doing to him—manipulating his mind.'

Jay gave a blistering laugh. 'No one, but *no one,* Elaine, will accept that image of J.B.'

'We can get something on her,' claimed Elaine.

'Would it help this conversation if I left?' Brett composedly folded her napkin and stood up.

'My dear, please have your breakfast,' Mrs Chase implored.

'Sit down, Brett,' Jay's voice cracked out. 'No one is going to hurt you. I hadn't planned to make any announcements now, but it might save Morton and Elaine a whole lot of time.' He switched his position so he was facing his grandmother, staring into her eyes and taking her hand. 'Grandma,' he said gravely, 'immediately the time's right—say six months from now—Brett and I are going to be married. It's what we both want, but you know ever since I was a little kid I've wanted, *needed,* your blessing.'

Morton cursed profoundly and Elaine jerked back so violently her chair scraped across the parqueted floor.

Mrs Chase said nothing, as though Jay was only in the middle of his story. As indeed he was.

Brett left her chair and went to stand beside Jay, and he reached up his arm unexpectedly and looped it around her narrow waist.

'Brett and Jay,' murmured Mrs Chase, almost to herself.

'You're shocked, aren't you, Grandma?' Morton shouted.

'I hear you, Morton.'

'Hell, no wonder J.B. was afraid of Jay! I didn't realise he could outmanoeuvre the old master himself!'

'This won't happen, you hear me?' Elaine cried. 'All the endless talk about you two—it could be true!'

'I have made it my business, Elaine, to establish that all the whispers were malicious lies,' the old lady said sharply, with a return to severity. 'I'll hear no more of it.'

'You know what they're doing, though, don't you, Grandma?' Morton implored. 'They're trying to cut me out.'

'Of what, my boy?' Mrs Chase, though she didn't relinquish the younger brother's hand, looked sympathetically at the other.

'No one would have to tell *you*,' Morton's drawling voice grew impassioned. 'Just as J.B. took Diamond Valley off Granddad, Jay wants to take everything off me. He wants to wield total power. All those fights with the old man! They're two of a kind.'

'How about talking a bit of sense?' Jay advised his brother shortly. 'What joy do you have in taking control? You don't even want Diamond Valley.'

'Who says?' Morton's throat was dry.

'You ought to teach your in-laws to keep their mouths shut.'

'Aaah!' Mrs Chase gave an agonised little moan. 'We must *never* let Diamond Valley go. The pain that it caused me when your grandfather had to sell out was just bearable when I knew it would come back to you boys.'

'With Brett here, in the middle.' Elaine gave the younger girl a terrible glare. 'You know he wouldn't even look at you but for the way things turned out. Why, he's been seeing Kerri Whitman right up until a week ago. They had a private suite on the island. You saw her only yesterday. As far as *she's* concerned, Jay loves her. After all, she's from one of the old families, not an insignificant little no one!'

'Insignificant little no one?' A contemptuous smile crossed Jay's mouth. 'Brett could take her place anywhere, Elaine, and you know it. Not only is she beautiful, she's highly intelligent and accomplished. I consider these things far greater assets than coming from an old family such as the Whitmans. I don't intend to discuss *my* business, but I've never told Kerri I loved her, neither did we share a suite on the island. I didn't decide to marry Brett overnight—I've had it planned for a long, long time.'

'He could at that!' Morton turned his blond head to stare at his brother. 'There's no telling with Jay. He knew J.B. wouldn't leave Brett unprovided for. He might have even known just how well. The two of them could have planned it together.'

'There were no plans, Morton.' Brett looked at him with light-filled eyes. 'Never in my wildest dreams did I imagine Jay would want to marry me.'

'So how did you fall in love?' shrieked Elaine. 'Or doesn't *love* have anything to do with it?'

'*You* certainly don't,' Jay returned with icy arrogance. 'You overstep your place in this family, Elaine. You're my brother's wife. You're free to make a comment when your opinion is sought, otherwise keep out of it.'

'Are you going to let him speak to me like that, Morton?' Elaine asked awkwardly, an unbecoming flush on her high cheekbones.

'God, what do you want me to do? Let him break my neck?'

'I'd like to speak to you, Brett, when you're ready to talk to me,' Mrs Chase said. 'I know my grandson well enough to realise he permits nothing to get in his way. I'm not saying that he mightn't want you very badly, but you must show me what *you* want.'

Their talk didn't take place until late afternoon when Morton and Elaine took the jeep out on a long inspection of the property. Elaine was visibly subdued and Morton appeared to be in a state of shock.

'Sit down, Brett,' Mrs Chase said gently. 'You know I've always been fond of you so there's no need to be nervous. You're very young—twenty. You have no one—no woman relative outside of me so I want you to think of me as your honorary grandmother.'

'Were I ever so blessed.' Brett moved gracefully to sit opposite the old lady. 'What is it you would like to know?'

'Only one thing really,' Mrs Chase sighed. 'Do you love my grandson?'

A wave of emotion flowed over both women. The older disguised it through long habit, the younger reacted as if in pain. 'Do birds fly?'

'Would you like to tell me exactly, my dear?' For the first time Mrs Chase smiled.

'I can't remember when I didn't love him,' Brett confessed. 'I idolised him as a child, then as I grew up it went deeper—so deep I thought it was hidden.'

'And you've known Jay wanted to marry you for some time?'

I can't lie to her, Brett thought. To Morton, Elaine, anyone, but not to Mrs Chase. 'Jay asked me to marry him last night. I don't really know his reasons. Jay's no open book. He's a man who makes plans, so I expect my inheritance has a great deal to do with it. I think *he* thinks of it as Chase money. He's always had a thing about your side of the family that intensified with the years. He's always been determined to get his mother's money back. Even to this day his parents' failed marriage is an open wound. I don't think Jay holds marriage very sacred.'

'There's no question he's been very wary of coming into it,' Mrs Chase looked deeply reflective. 'I'm intensely anxious about this, Brett. I don't want you to get hurt—you've been hurt enough. It's my view that Jay has a deep attachment to you. You've shared so much. You've lived in the same house—'

'Neither of which has influenced Morton.'

'Morton isn't immune to you either. You're a very beautiful girl, Brett. You don't need me to tell you that.'

'Beauty may gain attention, but it doesn't turn a lover into a husband,' said Brett quietly.

'It's worth stressing that J.B. didn't marry your mother for *Jay*. Whatever the clashes between them they were father and son, very much alike in lots of ways. Much as J.B. provoked the conflict, he couldn't begin to cope with the idea of setting your mother up as mistress of Diamond Valley and stepmother to the boys. Jay, and Morton to a much lesser extent, was markedly affected by the whole tragedy. He was at the wrong stage of his emotional development to lose his mother the way he did. She had acquired a knight and Jay considered he had lost the battle. It says a great deal for his affection for you that he has always looked after you, no matter how high-handed it might have appeared at the time. Both of my grandsons have had to cope with a lifetime of frustrations, but now that's all over. It's inevitable that Jay will gain power and control. The differences between the two boys are great. I can't really see that Jay needs your voting power at all. Everyone within the corporation will look to him as the next chairman. He has always been more powerful, more aggressive, more dominant than Morton. He's perfected a very authoritarian manner, and compared with J.B. he's positively loved. J.B. liked people to fear him, but Jay likes to dominate through achievement. The one thing he cannot do is subdue you. What it seems to me is, you and Jay have arrived at some kind of resolution of the unhappy past.'

'I don't think he loves me,' Brett said poignantly.

'Then how can you go into this marriage, dear child?'

'Maybe I'm neurotic?' Brett suggested wryly.

'Not *you*, though we all have hang-ups, my dear. I suppose at your deepest level of thought you wish to avenge your mother?'

'I can't deny it,' said Brett. 'Maybe it's the ultimate symbolic gesture. At the same time I know I can make Jay happy if he'll only let me. My heart is exclusively his. I gave it up as a child. I suppose a psychiatrist would call it obsessive love—but Jay is such a romantic man. He's so vivid and vital, incapable of a mean action. J.B. had brilliant intellectual capacities, but he did a lot of terrible things. Jay, I know, makes a clear distinction between driving a hard bargain and being utterly pitiless. There's nothing in this world I want more than to be beside him. He doesn't just use the land to make money; he cherishes it like I do. For all J.B.'s dealings in stock and land, and how consummately shrewd they were, his personal fortune came before everything. He wasn't a great philanthropist like your own family. Chase money built hospitals and schools and endowed research institutes.'

'Well,' Mrs Chase sighed, 'if J.B. gave very little away he certainly died an exceedingly rich man. Diamond Valley in the old days was a very happy place. Of course so much changed after the Second World War. Very few of us, even the very rich, could afford to maintain the old Edwardian splendour. My own dear father employed fourteen gardeners. Needless to say he had a passion for gardening and hothouses and shade houses but my husband's family owned thousands of acres at one time, with a chain of stations running from the Gulf of Carpentaria to the markets in Adelaide. They built many magnificent houses, as you know, the centres of great pastoral communities, but two wars robbed them of the sons they desperately needed, and my own dear husband, though an exceptionally good man, lacked his fore-bears' legendary fire and genius. He was no match for J.B. He simply rode in one day as handsome as a dispossessed archangel and struck up a bargain. The bargain included my daughter. J.B. as a self-made man always had a hunger for position. I saw love in my daughter's eyes. I saw ambition in J.B.'s. I would not like to see history repeat itself.'

Whatever the truth, Brett thought, I have to face it. No matter how brutal that truth might be. It was impossible not to see the parallel.

Brett was dressing for dinner when Elaine came to her room, thin face tense, blue eyes glittering.

'Don't you think it's time you and I had a little talk?' she gritted.

Brett was suddenly very angry. For years she had endured Elaine's appalling arrogance; now she had withstood enough.

'How dare you come into my room like this!' she cried, seizing up a precious silver-backed brush as though she intended to fling it. 'There's no way I could go to yours and just force my way in. I'm not the helpless child I was, and this is now as much my house as yours—more, and I'd like you to leave.'

'I'll leave when I get some answers,' Elaine returned unpleasantly, and flounced into one of the moiré-upholstered armchairs. 'Don't play the heiress with me. Whatever good fortune has happened to you, you're still the housekeeper's daughter!'

'And what the devil are you, the scion of some noble family? Your grandfather made his money tinning sausages. Snobbery is not the democratic way,' retorted Brett.

'Most of us take it to our bosoms.'

'What do you mean, *most*? All you society layabouts?'

Elaine sprang up, eyes blazing, and slapped Brett across the cheek. 'You're a very rude girl—ill-bred. It's quite impossible for you to marry into this family.'

Brett saw her chance. She deplored physical violence but ended up choosing it. She bent swiftly and jerked the small silk Qum rug from beneath Elaine's booted feet. It seemed to her almost a blow below the belt, but she wasn't going to have the likes of Elaine slapping her face.

'You bitch!' screamed Elaine as she went down.

'Don't expect me to apologise.' Brett regarded the older girl contemptuously. 'If all the civility you can muster is slapping my face you can't expect I won't return the insult. What I do is no business of yours, nor of Morton's, unless it infringes on business. I know you've come here to tell me all about Kerri Whitman's affair with Jay. I know she's a friend of yours and I reject all your lies.'

'No lies!' Elaine, flushed with rage, struggled to her feet. 'You'll pay for that!' Incredibly her lip trembled. 'Don't think you can hide behind Jay.'

'I never have, so why would I start now? I've always had to take on opponents much bigger than myself.'

'You do realise, of course, that Jay is using you? You're supposed to be a clever girl, so try to be rational. On your own admission you never in your wildest dreams—wasn't it?—aspired to becoming Jay's wife, yet immediately J.B. dies and leaves you equal beneficiary with his own sons, Jay proceeds to propose. We all know Jay. I can hardly afford to be too friendly. He's seeking absolute control—you know that, don't you? He's seized on your windfall to get it. Your combined clout will rob my husband of his rightful place as chairman of the Carradine Corporation.'

'I know nothing about high intrigue.' Brett turned away and dropped the silver brush on the dressing table. 'I do know Jay is J.B.'s logical successor. Morton, even if he is the elder, had no such ambitions until you succeeded in getting your claws into him. I realise your father and brothers are behind you. No doubt they regard it now as *their* money, or at the very least your children's inheritance. Isn't that the dynastic *modus operandi?* Empires have to be protected.'

'I see you have some grip on the situation,' Elaine said acidly. 'This must seem like the impossible dream for you, but go ahead with it and believe me, it will turn into a nightmare. He's got a showdown with Kerri to face. You don't spend a week with a man for nothing. I had a long conversation with her only yesterday, and Jay led her to believe he would marry her quite soon. Oh, Jay denied it with his customary arrogance, but I suspect you have your doubts. Only a fool wouldn't wonder why his proposal came out of the blue. Jay can think a whole strategy out in seconds. Don't worry, we all admire him, but he's not his father's son for nothing. Morton has nothing of J.B. Jay has too much.'

'Which makes him irresistible to me,' Brett feigned cynicism. 'As I'd like to point out, I cared a great deal for J.B. He was a hard man, a very hard man, but he offered me security and protection. I'm not glad he saw fit to raise me to the status of his own sons, but I am pleased in a sense to give it all back. I'm much too ignorant of big business to expect to take over some of the reins myself—not yet. But I've a good brain and I intend to learn. I promise you I won't remain too long in the dark. Jay isn't the only one good at decision making and making real use of unexpected opportunities. I chose Jay as much as he chose me. Our motives don't concern you, but if you're in any doubt that he's not attracted to me, you and Kerri Whitman can put that out of your minds. Jay knows exactly the kind of wife he wants. *Me.*'

'And while you're ticking off your attributes,' Elaine told her viciously, 'put balance of power at the top of your list. Jay's played the field in the past. He's a handsome, virile man and women chase him wherever he goes. He doesn't love you, so he won't be faithful. Thought of that? You'll be stuck here on Diamond Valley—always supposing you're fool enough to want to keep this great white elephant, and Jay will be jetting around. You're much too young at twenty to know it all. There's a dark side to Jay, and you're going to find out!'

CHAPTER FOUR

SOMEHOW BRETT CONTRIVED to get through the following months. Diamond Valley was much too isolated to be a home base for either Jay or Morton, so they continued to live in Adelaide—Morton and Elaine in the Lodge, that was part of the original Chase estate; Jay in one of the three pieds-à-terre he retained in the Southern capitals.

Brett remained on Diamond Valley, where she worked much too hard to be lonely. With a great deal of money put at her disposal she began refurbishing the house, consulting often with Jay's grandmother, not only as a mark of respect but for the old lady's excellent advice. They shared a classic eye and both wished to preserve the spirit of the great homestead. It was more a question of using what was to hand; an abundance of antique furniture and art works of all kinds, plus the treasures Brett unearthed; possessions overlooked for many long years. Walls were treated, curtains changed, sofas and armchairs re-covered, some of the guest rooms entirely re-done.

The only room Brett left severely alone was the old master bedroom suite with its sweeping views of the valley. It was as though she could hardly believe she and Jay might eventually sleep there. As it stood it was overpoweringly splendid, a relic of the Victorian era, but she knew how she could turn it into a luxurious, light and welcoming haven.

It remained unchanged, as did her curious relationship with Jay.

In the early months he had taken her on a long tour of the Carradine holdings. He treated her more as a trainee executive than a fiancée, though the formal announcement of their engagement was being withheld until a more appropriate time. The ring Jay had given her, a magnificent sapphire flanked by diamonds, dangled from a fine gold chain she wore around her neck. It was part of a matching set comprising necklace, pendant earrings, bracelet and ring that had been acquired at a Sotheby's auction some eighty years before. Brett knew the whole story. It had once belonged to an important English lady, and often as Brett fingered it she tried to visualise the woman who had first owned it. She must have had a fine and delicate hand. The band was small, but it fitted her fine-boned hand perfectly. Jay had not consulted her on the choice of ring. He had selected it himself from a considerable collection of family jewellery.

'The rest you'll get the day we're married,' he told her. 'You mightn't know it, but your eyes pick up colours like the dawn sky. I've seen them smoky blue, and lilac—even a tender green. You'll make a beautiful bride.'

Not a happy one. How *could* it be, when she wasn't much loved?

Mrs Chase approved the choice. 'I'm so glad Jay found it,' she said. 'The ring, of course, was much too small for me, but I did wear the necklace and earrings on a few occasions, mostly grand ones. My daughter never wore any of it to the best of my knowledge. We were considered beauties in our day, but we never had your heady quality, Brett. It makes for storms in life. That's why I worry.'

As Mrs Chase had predicted, there was no power struggle within the Corporation. Any coups had been pre-empted by the stunning news that Jay Carradine was to marry his father's little-known ward. For all Jay's formidable business genius, deep jealousies existed. Morton, since he had married into the Amery clan with its wide business interests, was being pushed along in his ambitions which were not normally excessive. He knew he could not compete with his younger brother at any level, and for much of his life this fact hadn't bothered him. In fact the two brothers, given the same harsh conditions, had been very close. The Amerys had changed all that. It was said Elaine Carradine had more aspirations in her little finger than her husband had in his whole six-foot-plus body. Unfortunately, when it was put to the vote, Carradine board members voted in a predictable way. None of them owed blind obedience to Amery interests and the Carradine Corporation was seen to be still a one-man show. John Carradine in his lifetime as head of his own organisation had exercised near-absolute control. Factions existed, but they had been held under restraint. Board members saw clearly that John Carradine Junior was the only man for the job. Furthermore, his soon-to-be bride was an important board member.

In this vein, Brett turned her attention to the study of economic corporations. She had always been an excellent student and now her major aim was to learn as much as she could about large-scale operations. She read widely from a pile of books an economics lecturer at her old university sent her, also all the literature she could find on the Carradine Corporation. She was unaware that she had made a very good impression on Carradine board members, many of whom thought as traditional chauvinists that she would be very easily controlled and manipulated. It seemed she had a brain, to be expected in a twenty-year-old man but an unexpected plus in a pretty girl when it wasn't really imperative.

Brett worked hard, on all things. Jay came and went. His attitude towards her could not even remotely have been termed 'loverlike'. Neither was it warmly affectionate as to family. It was strictly businesslike. She was a welcome addition to the Carradine Corporation and she was shaping up well. She received lots of impassive praise and active encouragement. She did not receive any more of the lovemaking that had awakened her body to sexual ecstasy. In all important respects they had made a business deal.

This didn't help her when the mail arrived, along with certain items forwarded by the interior design firm working with her on the refurbishing. A brief note from Jay informing her that he would be bringing guests for the long weekend—seven in all—two personal letters for herself—girl friends from her university days—a stack of mail for Jack Moran, the station manager, and a padded post bag that had to be business because it bore her name and address on a white sticker.

She opened it first to get it over with, never expecting the sheaf of glossy photographs that spilled out. They were all of the same two people, Jay and Kerri Whitman. Pretty monotonous, really. Jay and Morton were both crack polo players. One of the photos showed Jay leaning down from his polo pony receiving a congratulatory kiss from an excited and radiant Kerri. She appeared to be gripping him tight around the neck, no doubt in an excess of emotion. Others showed them enjoying leisure moments, on a yacht. Kerri was wearing a minuscule bikini that couldn't find a flaw in her long, lithe body. They were smiling into one another's eyes at a dinner table. Kerri was wearing a low-cut strapless dress and a wonderful-looking necklace, and her lips looked full and glossy. Dates were stamped on the backs of the photographs. The photographs purported to be recent. Brett put them away and didn't look at them again.

Jay and his party flew in on the following Friday afternoon. Brett wasn't surprised to see Kerri Whitman among their number, but she was surprised by the warmth and friendliness of Kerri's greeting.

'How lovely to see you, Brett!' Hazel eyes sparkled. 'Jay's been telling me all about your efforts at interior decoration. I can't wait to see them.' The words were certainly ambiguous. The smile seemed straightforward.

'Brett!' Jay compelled her to him, turning up her chin and staring into her eyes. Then he lowered his handsome dark head and lightly brushed her mouth.

The public image.

'I've missed you.' As soon as his lips left hers Brett gave him a slow, enchanting smile. It hinted of many things—all of them illusions.

Jay narrowed his eyes. 'Let me introduce David Cooper,' he took hold of the arm of an attractive, grinning young man. 'I think you know everyone else. Dave is just back from a working tour overseas. He's a lawyer by profession. I'm trying to convince him to join our team.'

'Not *trying,* Jay,' David Cooper smiled, and then to Brett, 'this is one hell of a man you've got here, Brett—I may call you that?'

'Please.' Brett liked him at once. He had thick, glossy brown hair and humorous brown eyes. No hooded arrogance to David's open regard, and Brett found it thoroughly pleasing.

A moment later she was greeting Jay's other guests. People who had once virtually ignored her now sought her company. It had to be money.

'You'll be friends with me, won't you?' Kerri begged. 'I swear on my honour I'll try to cure myself of Jay.'

Brett smiled serenely. 'I'm so pleased there are no hard feelings, Kerri.'

The cruellest kind of training now stood her in good stead. She was a success with everyone at dinner. Jay wanted no shadowy figure at his side; he wanted a woman with a mind of her own and the ability to express it. It was fortunate she was highly intelligent and had been given the opportunity to receive an excellent education. The conversation ranged over a wide sphere of interests, and though Kerri Whitman did her level best to engineer a few bright-eyed put-downs, it was very obvious who was the more intelligent, the more informed of the two.

Afterwards David asked her to stroll with him in the garden. He had scarcely taken his eyes off her at dinner, but whether because of her looks or conversation Brett didn't know.

'How poised you are for such a young woman,' he complimented her warmly. 'Why, I could give you eight or nine years, and I feel like a schoolboy by comparison.'

'I think you're being very kind to me, David.'

He lightly took her elbow and guided her down the wide, shallow flight of steps. 'I'd heard of you, naturally, but I didn't *see* you the way you are.'

Brett could well imagine. 'I insist you tell me what you heard?' she countered lightly.

Darkness covered David's faint flush. 'Why, that you were as beautiful as night. You were John Carradine's ward. Young—no more.'

'Suitable?'

'I think Jay is very much to be congratulated,' David responded gallantly. 'I think you're the perfect match for him.'

'May I ask why?' Brett lifted her lovely face. She was wearing her dark cloud of hair in a loose roll to complement the almost Grecian line of her white dinner dress, and it emphasised the purity of her features. Her voice matched her looks.

David was enchanted. 'For one,' he said ardently, 'Jay deserves the best. Enormous success has come to him very early and it's not easy being the man at the top. He holds the reins of power. From what I've seen, power can be dehumanising. You're a caring, com-

passionate young woman. I've been listening to you at
dinner, and I like your views, the tolerance of your
attitudes. Obviously you have a good brain and you
intend to use it to the full. Speaking as a male, I think
women have been held back too long. You'll be good
for Jay, good for the Corporation. I think women
bring a saner approach to business. You'll act as a fine
balance. The whole character of the Carradine Corporation was moulded and established by Jay's father. It's generally accepted that he was an autocrat
solely responsible for company decision and policy.
Jay's a man who looks for solutions when Corporation interests conflict with the interests of particular
individuals, or even the ecology.'

'I know what you mean.' Brett nodded her head.
'Jay convinced the board to take a stand with the
conservationists. There'll be no more clearing of the
rainforest on Carradine holdings. That wouldn't have
happened in J.B.'s day. Jay cares deeply about the
land—that's the Chase heritage. It often seems strange
to me that Morton, who resembles so strongly the
Chase side of the family, should have little feel for his
home and this extraordinary environment. He con-
siders the homestead a white elephant. It certainly
costs a great deal to maintain.'

'It's absolutely splendid!' David burst out raptur-
ously, turning to look back at the brilliantly lit mansion. 'The first time I've been here, as you know. It's
quite, quite breathtaking to come on in what could be
a great wild-life sanctuary. It's positively unique.'

'Well—unique to this part of the world,' agreed
Brett. 'The old squatocracy was the equivalent of the
British aristocracy. Many a second son made a great

fortune here, so he built the kind of house he was used to. The homestead has the same importance as the Home Country's castle. It was possible for certain men, the great cattle kings like Kidson and Tyson, to build up vast estates the size of England and more. Diamond Valley homestead is an excellent example of the golden years. It's still in the hands of the same family and it still retains its original glory.'

'Another thing I was wanting to compliment you on,' David told her. 'Twenty years hardly seems enough for you to have learned so much. The refurbishing—isn't that what you call it?—is positively brilliant. I can tell you the whole place has knocked me absolutely flat!'

'I would never have done so well but for Mrs Chase.'

'Ah yes, a marvellous lady! Full of vigour.'

'She spent a very long time here. To me it's still filled with her presence. It was she who lavished so much loving care on the home gardens,' Brett told him.

'Extraordinary!' David was still reaching for superlatives. 'By far the most striking aspect of it is the enormous size of the plants. One would have thought it would be very difficult indeed to grow anything in a desert environment, but all this is absolutely beautiful!' He waved a hand over the richness and extent of the gardens. 'One wonders how so much wealth fell into the hands of the one family.'

'*Two* families,' Brett corrected gently. 'Chase and Carradine, and it didn't just *fall*. There was a lot of agony mixed up with the exultation. You would only have to visit the station cemetery. Before the days of the Flying Doctor Service the Outback was no place to be if anything went wrong.'

'I can imagine,' David retorted. They were walking along a softly lit corridor of cypresses and he turned quickly, to peer down at her. 'For all its magnificence, Brett, you don't find it a lonely prison?'

Her silver eyes seemed to flash. *'Never!'* she said fervently. 'Diamond Valley is no prison to me. It's my protection.'

'A strange word, surely?' David found himself countering. 'Why would a beautiful, clever girl like yourself wish to hide?'

'Did I say *hide?'* She gave him an enigmatic smile.

'Damn it, I'm sorry. The fact of the matter, Brett, is you're the sort of girl one gets awfully emotional about. I've only just met you and I'm under your spell. Are you quite sure you're mortal?'

'If you pinch me I'll pretend it doesn't hurt.'

'Why have you been here all these months?' David's brown eyes darkened.

'You mean I shouldn't sit back and let certain things happen?' Brett asked him almost bluntly.

'Jay doesn't give a damn about Kerri Whitman,' David immediately betrayed his knowledge of the situation. 'I only meant I would have thought Jay would want you by his side. I know I couldn't bear to leave you out of my sight were you my fiancée.'

'And how would the refurbishing have been done?' Brett moved on, the top of her head reaching David's shoulder. 'No, David, it suits us both to get things done. We have the rest of our lives.'

'And Jay is getting a jewel.'

When they came in some fifteen minutes later, David was looking both exhilarated and excited. Brett had promised to take him out riding first thing in the morning, and such is the mass of contradictions human beings are, as much as he admired and respected Jay and indeed was thrilled at the prospect of joining the Carradine Corporation, he was allowing himself the outrageous hope that Brett might see him as a second choice. Love at first sight wasn't particularly uncommon, though circumstances made people hold their feelings in a suspended state. Brett was Carradine's fiancée; a powerful deterrent, yet already David was allowing himself to be impelled towards danger.

Kerri, sitting on the sofa, seized on David's giveaway expression. She lifted her head to Jay and said something that brought a hawklike watchfulness to his lean, handsome face. Brett in her white gown was the picture of patrician elegance. She was smiling, a real smile that reached her dazzling eyes, but no more. There was a visible aura of rapport between them, but when Kerri swung about to gauge Jay's expression all she received was a clear view of his arrogant profile.

THE SOFT RAP on her door brought Brett to attention. She had been sitting at her dressing table brushing out her hair preparatory to going to bed. Her head was a kaleidoscope of thoughts and for one ghastly moment she thought it might be Kerri. Kerri, who appeared to be so friendly, was a powerful enemy— Brett knew that, as she was meant to know. Kerri was playing secret games. The Whitmans, winners for so long, wouldn't sit still and lose everything now. If there was a way to break up this extraordinary engagement they would call all their formidable resources into play. The photographs were only the start.

Brett was clasping her hairbrush so tightly her knuckles showed white. She was determined to be proud and brave—she had no other choice—but her heart was thumping uncomfortably. A session with Kerri Whitman was the last thing she wanted. Nevertheless she swallowed hard and went to the door, the hem of her long aqua peignoir just brushing the floor. She was glad now that she could afford such glamorous nightwear. It shouldn't, but it did make her feel more sure of herself.

Instead of Kerri, Jay was standing outside the door, one hand resting against the jamb in an attitude of mild impatience.

'My dear Marisa!' He gave her a sweeping bow.

'Yes, Jay?'

His blue eyes were amused, searching. 'You're obviously deeply surprised to find your fiancé outside your bedroom door.'

'Actually, yes,' she returned coolly. 'I thought we shook hands an hour ago.'

'My dear, I'm sure I kissed your cheek.'

'And believe me, I'm very grateful.'

'May I come in?' he asked airily, one black eyebrow lifting at the acerbity of their exchange.

'Oh, do.' Brett turned away from his unsettling regard. 'It will give us a chance to talk over the last months.'

'I must say I adore that nightgown and robe. It's simply gorgeous. You're not expecting a visitor, surely?'

'One can't be certain of anything in this house.'
Brett slid into an armchair and indicated the one opposite her with her hand.

'You did very well tonight.' Jay didn't sit but allowed his gaze to move around the room. 'I knew you were boning up, of course, but I had no idea how intensively. You're a very bright girl.'

'I'm delirious with your praise!' she said drily.

He swung his head back and something in his eyes silenced her. 'Don't complicate things, will you?'

'It would be a bonus if you'd tell me what you mean.'

'Have you any idea how much Dave wants to come and work for us?'

'David?' She frowned. 'What has David to do with this?'

'David is a man like any other. He can be seduced by a pair of sparkling eyes. You know how the song goes.'

Brett gritted her small white teeth and pushed up out of her chair. 'If this is an exhibition of jealousy, Jay, it's extremely unsuccessful.'

'It's Dave I'm concerned about,' he remarked drily. 'It would be a mistake to give him the lightest encouragement. He's a man I don't care to lose.'

'You don't need to drop *your* admirers, of course?' Colour swam into her cheeks. 'Engagements shouldn't take all the fun out of life.'

Jay didn't answer that at all. He even acted as though she hadn't spoken. 'Don't think I'm blaming you, Brett,' he drawled pleasantly. 'I know you can't help this fascination thing—it came with you at birth. Put simply, I don't want to risk losing Dave. For his sake, if not mine, nip his infatuation in the bud. You know perfectly well nothing can come of it. All that *will* happen is a ruined career.'

'I don't believe this,' she said slowly. 'I thought you'd be only too pleased to see me getting on with your friends, the people you bring here.'

'I don't want you to seduce them,' Jay said brutally. 'You're gifted that way.'

'Just who have I seduced in all these years?' she asked tightly, unaware that anger was heightening her beauty. 'How can you accuse me of such a thing?'

'Forget the dramatics, Brett,' he advised in a clipped voice. 'I've already said I know it's not really your fault. I just want to get this thing straight. Dave is attracted to you—'

'I don't—'

He held up his hand. 'Agreed?'

'I'm too confused to tell,' she sighed.

His laugh made her nape tingle. 'Do you think no one noticed you when you came in from your walk?'

'Oh, God, Jay!' She put up her hands and pushed her fingers through her dark cloud of hair. 'This is crazy! The reason I went with David was to please *you*. I like him, certainly, but I never considered even the mildest flirtation for one minute. I'm not looking for affairs; I'm not even looking for love. I've learned enough to know that it's in very short supply.'

'So it is!' Jay shrugged his wide shoulders, the very picture of arrogant self-sufficiency. 'You needn't look like that either. I *know* you, Brett. You're no different now from that heartbroken little girl. You conceal the intensity of your feelings under that swan-like disdain.'

'You're devastating when you're kind!'

He levelled his brilliant blue eyes at her, as intimidating in their fashion as a loaded gun. 'Dave is fast losing his habitual good sense. No artifices are necessary with you, but that was a bravura performance tonight—the princess locked away in the enchanted wilds. Dave's reaction was immediate and passionate—I should know. You told him you'd take him out riding in the morning?'

'And what if I did?' Brett's dark hair framed her face, that haunting face now filled with emotion.

'I'll come with you, that's all.' The smile on his handsome mouth left no trace in his eyes. 'You *are* my fiancée. You can't expect me to take too kindly to Dave's involvement—or anyone else's, for that matter. I've never read a signal wrongly in my life. Dave thinks because I've kept you here he's freer in some way, but he couldn't be more wrong!' He looked at her long and mockingly, more handsome than the devil.

'I could change my mind,' she challenged him, her nerves stretching as they always did at the sight of his lean, lithe elegance.

'Not you, Brett.' His brilliant gaze returned hers. 'We're two of a kind. Both of us know how to survive hostile environments. Both of us *should* be emotionally burnt out. I want no other woman but you. You suit me very well.'

She moved closer so that he was inches from her, searching his eyes as if to penetrate the layers of concealment that masked his heart.

Ice turned to fire, anger to abrupt passion.

Jay took her nerveless wrist and drew her hard against his strong, sleek body. 'What are you, Brett, my Nemesis? Goddess of retribution?'

'Kiss me,' she said strangely—not a pleading but an affirmation of her power.

'I'll let nothing destroy me. Not even you.'

'Kiss me, Jay.' The stillness of her expression did not alter, but her eyes grew enormous, shimmering like ice crystals.

'You'd like to bring me down, wouldn't you? Revenge a childhood filled with little humiliations.'

'You've always been in my deepest fantasies,' she said quietly.

'Did you think I didn't know what was happening to you?' He lifted a hand and grasped her by the hair. 'You talk of rape. There was never a question of rape between you and me. In the end it would have been impossible for you not to give yourself to me. I'm looking into your eyes, Brett.'

'They have secrets, just like yours. Is it possible you're a little frightened of me?' She was speaking softly, slowly, as though she sought to put him in a trance.

'So frightened I've stayed away.' He began to twine her silken hair around his hand. 'Dave couldn't take his eyes off you at dinner. You'd only have to snap your fingers and the poor devil would throw up a brilliant career. Your beauty doesn't end at admiration. It's black magic. Not a shadow show, the real thing.'

'So why don't you kiss me?' she whispered.

His reaction was sizzling. His grip so powerful it almost cut off her breath. She was bent backwards over his arm while the heat that was in him scorched her mouth and her body. Passion rose in a great wave.

She should have screamed for the bitterness.

'Jay,' she whimpered against his violent kiss, 'you're cracking my bones!'

His hands travelled over her. She knew from their strength and authority what could lie ahead of her. There was a whole world of sensuality hidden behind her marriage vows.

The aqua peignoir fanned to the floor. It was as though he had to get nearer to her than the glistening film of satin. She was faintly conscious that she was moaning, turning her head as he drew his mouth along her throat.

He was her everything. *Everything*. Yet words of endearment were lodged in her throat. Love. Obsession. Maybe obsession was the better word for it.

He lifted her and turned with awful slowness towards the bed. His jaw was clenched and there was a primitive flare to his finely cut nostrils. The image of a conqueror leaped into her mind. His eyes were brilliant, the only living things in a golden, taut mask.

She came down on the cloud bed with a sense of falling through space. The lace strap of her nightgown had fallen off her shoulder and her small, high breasts were almost exposed to his view—dazzling white skin, wonderful rosy peaks.

She turned her head to look up at him, but he was still staring down at her with the same hard and consummate mastery. What was she anyway but a possession to be subjugated?

Unless she could foil him.

She slid across to the other side of the bed and stood back against the wall. A small bronze figure of a dancer was always on her bedside table, and she seized it up and held it like a threat.

'It would be terrible to harm you, Jay,' she warned.

Incredibly he smiled. 'Are you aware what you look like? I don't want to rob you of any confidence, but I could smother you in a second.'

'Is that what you *want* to do?'

'What I want to do is put my brand on your flesh. You tend to revert to the wild.'

'Dominion over a woman's body isn't dominion over her heart.'

'I know that, Brett,' he returned sombrely, and turned away from her as though weary of the conquest.

She came away from her place of retreat beside the waterfall of silk curtain and moved towards the bedside table. How was it possible to feel wounded yet desperate for more? What was she, a masochist? Why was there excitement in wishing Jay would subdue her? She wanted him, that was why. She wanted him so much she was exhausted with the force of it. Desire was like tongues of fire licking at her flesh. Jay represented all she had ever really wanted in life. Jay was her past and her future, but where was love?

In the end he took the exquisite little figurine from her, placing it gently on the bedside table. He moved, as she well knew, as swiftly as the wind. She stood before him, incapable of movement, and all at once he turned into the Jay of her childhood: champion of weeping little girls.

'Come here,' he said quietly, his high-mettled face, so stormy at times, filled with a rare empathy.

What then?

In the next second he lifted her and put her down across his knees. 'Honest to God, Brett, sometimes you wring my heart! You've taken so much. We *both* have, yet we can't abandon the old grievances. Sometimes I think we even fight to hold on to them.'

'Why did you kiss me so savagely?' Despite herself she took comfort from his strong body, leaning back so that her dark head was against his shoulder.

'I can't help kissing you savagely,' he returned crisply. 'Where *you're* concerned I am a savage. Fighting me is like slamming a knife into my heart.'

She rose up swiftly, staring into his eyes. '*What* did you say?'

'So you can start carving it up?'

'I want truth between us, Jay.'

'Then supposing *you* start?' There was a faint bite to his voice as though there was no room for lies.

Brett's eyes glowed in her face. Her cheekbones were shadowed with soft colour. 'I've always wanted to be honest with you, Jay, but I never have.'

'I don't think you especially like how you feel.'

'Feel about you?'

'I don't mind if we talk all night. I think I have to kiss you hard to tranquillise you.'

She sighed deeply and leaned back against him. 'You shouldn't try to torment me with Kerri Whitman.'

'Don't be dumb,' he said shortly. 'It doesn't suit you.'

'Really?' Her temper matched his in less than a second. 'If you promise not to be embarrassed I'd like to show you something.'

'I think you'd better put your robe on, then.' His eyes burned over her shoulders and breasts, the graceful line of thigh and slender legs.

'Fine.' She moved off his knee and picked her peignoir up.

'In the meantime I should take a running jump into a cold shower,' said Jay drily.

'You stay there. You won't need a shower when this is over.'

'Marisa, I'm shocked!'

'I mean it.' She was angered by his mockery.

'All right, I'll just sit here and admire the femininity of your room. How come you haven't started on the master suite yet?'

Brett shook her head. 'I'm going to stipulate on this famous contract that we're to enjoy separate rooms.'

'What makes you think I would ever agree to that?' he asked lazily.

Brett took the large yellow envelope out of her bureau and pushed the drawer back. 'Not to mention accommodation for lovers.'

'Any lovers *you* might decide to take will be quickly buried. God, I damn near threw poor old Dave out of the house.'

She stopped before him and passed him the padded envelope.

He sat forward, his expression sharp. 'What is this, Marisa?'

'Guilty already?'

He glanced up at her with narrowed eyes. 'There's nothing you like more than a bit of mystery. I guess in another time I would have had to rescue you from burning.'

'Nobody ever stops to put a label on a man. Some people might call *you* a devil.'

'A devil by any other name.' Jay drew the photographs out slowly, not a trace of response in his face. 'Don't they have one of us in bed?'

'Did you want one of you in bed?'

'I get more out of just looking at you. This isn't a crime, is it, Marisa? Not a real crime. I see a man and a woman. Incidentally, one of these is years ago.'

'There are dates on the back.'

He leaned back and threw the photographs into the fireplace. 'That's my response to these. They're just a bunch of you-know-what, intended to hurt you. I'm so glad they failed.'

'Well—I guess there are more. I'll probably get the one of the two of you in bed yet.'

'So what?' His blue eyes flared. 'Sleeping around is common these days. I would have made love to lots of girls—you know that. *You* were a child. Maybe I didn't love 'em, but that was all right in their book. All of them I still count among my friends. Most of them are happily married, for that matter.'

Brett nodded, aware that what he was saying was perfectly true. Women had chased Jay for years. *That* was magic, if you like. 'And what about Kerri?'

'Kerri can eat her heart out.'

'Elaine said you got around to talking marriage,' she said.

'And what do *you* think?'

'As a matter of fact I think I'd be very surprised.'

'Well then, Marisa,' Jay returned coolly, 'you know me better than you think.'

CHAPTER FIVE

BRETT ROSE next morning with every intention of doing what Jay told her. Perhaps David had been a little more attentive than necessary, but she was still surprised by Jay's reaction. She had merely been pleasant to a personable young man, but if it was going to jeopardise David's position in any way she would have to be very careful and controlled in her manner. Kerri Whitman would just love to stir up a little trouble!

She stood in the middle of her bedroom and surveyed her slender figure. Her cotton shirt and jodhpurs looked neat and businesslike, her riding boots had a commendable shine to them. She was a small girl, but no one could deny she was a fine rider. Her deep love of horses went back as far as she could remember; in fact during her lonely childhood horses had been the source of her greatest pleasure. On a great station like Diamond Valley it would have been unthinkable for her not to ride, and even her mother's tragic accident, terrible though it had been for her, could not change her affinity with these miraculous creatures. J.B. had been fascinated by her trick of singing to a favourite mount, and Brett had always told him it was a song of joy. Riding released all her tensions, and the trails on Diamond Valley were limitless.

'You look beautiful this morning, Brett,' murmured David as soon as he saw her.

'David, you mustn't flatter me too much,' she responded lightly, thinking perhaps Jay hadn't been exaggerating after all.

'Not flattery, Brett, the simple truth.' His brown eyes warmed. 'This is a first for me, you know. I've never been out on an early morning ride in my life.'

'But you *can* ride?'

Last night he had told her he could. Perhaps he had been joking.

'Put it this way, I can stay on providing I have a tame beast.'

'Ah well,' Brett couldn't help smiling at him, 'we have horses that understand every kind of rider. I talk to the lot of them.'

'Do you really?'

'Not only that, they talk back to me. Some of them won't shut up.'

'You really do look super in that gear,' David told her. 'I could literally worship at your booted feet.'

'By the way,' she turned her dark head, 'Jay is coming along with us.'

He went a little pink. 'I was afraid he might.'

'*David!*' She opened her large eyes.

'Is it too terrible to want you to myself?'

'You understand I'm engaged,' warned Brett.

'Jay has to be the luckiest guy in the world.' He held the door open for her as they walked through to the morning room. The intention was to have a quick cup of tea and delay breakfast until after their ride. Early mornings were superb. The air was so pure, and the vast plains and the desert fringe responded sublimely

as the direction of the light varied. The intensity of
colour was remarkable—the dramatic ochres, orange, yellow, chocolate brown, the glowing blood red
of the sand dunes, the great purple chasms; it was this
that gave Diamond Valley its unique character. Brett
was looking forward to initiating another, sympa-
thetic human being into all this peace and beauty.

Kerri Whitman and Jocelyn Nolan, wife of one of
the Corporation's top executives, were already seated
at the large circular table enjoying a really lavish
breakfast. Both of them were pencil-slim, but one of
the great rewards of staying at the homestead was to
eat everything that was put on. Very few guests ever
stuck to their normal programmes, and Brett had long
since found she had to go sparingly on the delectable
breakfast bakery that issued from Mrs Martin's
kitchen. The brioches and croissants in particular
simply melted in the mouth.

'Oh, there you are!' Kerri called gaily. 'Come on
and sit down. Why not sit beside me, David? I'm sure
you're just dying to make inroads on all this delicious
food. I'll have to starve for a week, but it's worth it!'

David and Brett smiled and said their good mornings, and Brett explained that they only had time for
a cup of tea.

'And perhaps one of those golden little rolls.' David
too seemed distracted by the sumptuous morning
spread.

'Have you seen Jay?' asked Brett, walking to the
large bay window and looking out. 'He's coming riding with us.'

'*Was* coming riding, dear,' Kerri amended. 'The
manager was up here a while ago and carried him

off—something about the sale of some Droughtmasters. He told me to tell you to go on. He'll probably be with Moran for some time.'

David brightened as if he had been touched by the sun. 'That's it then,' he downed his cup of tea. 'Is this not a beautiful day?'

'Sure is, Dave,' Kerri agreed laconically. 'Be good.'

There was always a man at the stables, and it was he who saddled up a quiet gelding for David.

'Gosh, you're not going to ride *that!*' he exclaimed as Brett accepted a leg-up on to her beautiful, dancing mare.

Brett's silver eyes were glowing. 'Say hello to Rain Dancer.' The mare lifted, then shook her finely chiselled head, her big bold eyes showing her generous and animated temperament.

David, who didn't understand the display of excitability, saw it as a threat to the petite Brett.

'Hi there, Rain Dancer,' he called a shade apprehensively. 'Sure she isn't a bit too big for you?'

'Miss Brett can ride anythin',' the aboriginal hand grinned. 'It's you that's got to watch yourself, mister!'

While Rain Dancer was raring to go, the gelding's instinct was to walk back into the stables. Brett leaned over and gave it the slightest tap on the flank and it responded immediately.

They moved off.

It was possibly the most enjoyable morning Brett had experienced for months. David was quite content to sit his horse while she gave Rain Dancer periodic bursts of galloping. It was too much to expect either of them to keep to David's sedate pace, but for the most part they rode along companionably, side by side.

It was coming on to the Wet in the tropical North of the continent and they had been experiencing short downpours like mini-storms in the early mornings and around sunset. As a consequence the limitless flats were covered with mile upon mile of mulla-mullas, waving like the pussytails the desert dwellers called them, pink parakeelya, poppies, lilies, desert nightshades, annual saltbush and bluebush, the firebush cassia and the blinding mantle of white and gold paper daisies.

'It beats me how they call this a desert!' Brett exclaimed. 'The flowers go on for ever!'

'You're seeing the land in its time of glory. When rain falls, even a passing shower, the living desert springs to life. The seeds of these wildflowers are wonderful creations—they only need a drop of water to germinate. Later, in summer when the big heat is on, all these endless miles of wildflowers will fade and die. That's if the North doesn't flood from cyclones or heavy monsoonal rain. Then the Channel Country goes under. We've been cut off on plenty of occasions. All this, for instance, would be under water. People call it the Dead Heart, and it can be, but after rain or flood it's Nature's most incredible garden.'

David shielded his eyes from the dazzling glare of the paper daisies. 'At first glance from the plane, I thought how could anyone live out here, no matter how grand the homestead. It's so vast and lonely. That's the first impression. The isolation, I felt, would be too much for me. It's almost like living on your own planet. But this ... *grandeur* lifts my heart.'

Brett was delighted with his sincere appreciation. 'Have you seen the Centre, Ayers Rock, the Olgas? Uluru and Katajuta, the aboriginals call them.'

'Actually, though I've been all round the world and in every major city of my own country, this is my first visit to our great Outback, and it's affecting me profoundly,' David told her. 'Without realising it I have the most extraordinary place on earth at my own back door.'

'I suppose that would have to apply to the oldest continent on earth. By the same token we have enormous wilderness areas, great natural landscapes in a world where the wilderness has all but disappeared. I'm so glad you're finding all this special, David. I'm quite passionate about Diamond Valley.'

Brett's voice was low, vibrant, thrilling, and David looked at her with an almost poignant longing. It seemed to him he had never met such a girl in his life. Even the way she rode, free like the wind, excited him. She looked as delicate as a white camellia, yet she abandoned herself to the great outdoors. It was wildly unsettling.

A fine herd of shorthorns was luxuriating in the rich pastures, and Brett allowed David to inspect them before taking him down to the serpentine creek. The pebbles on the shore shone white and the whole area was a glowing canvas of rose-pink and green. Even the graceful gums were reflected in the mirror-still dark green water.

'This is fantastic!' David breathed. 'Wouldn't it be just perfect for a swim?'

'We really should go back,' Brett smiled at him. 'I can smell rain on the breeze.'

'You can?' He looked up at the peacock sky in astonishment. He had missed the mauve clouds on the horizon.

The rain came down before they gained shelter, but neither seemed to care. It was, in fact, wonderfully refreshing, and Rain Dancer, true to her name, began to react to a good soak, going into an extravagant routine not unlike the haute école of the famous Lippizaners of the Spanish Riding School.

David was entranced. He had never had such an experience in all his city-bred life. The rain was wonderful. The horses were wonderful. The whole Valley was fantastic, but most of all, the girl.

They were laughing helplessly when they arrived back at the stables. The attendant had disappeared for a moment and David quickly dismounted and went to Brett.

'Here, let me help you. Honestly, you're soaked to the skin!' He had seen plenty of girls in the rain. Very few of them actually glowed like a flower.

Brett put her hands to her glistening head, then removed her feet from the stirrups, unaware that David was looking up at her as though she was the goddess of the hunt. 'Needless to say, it's all over. The showers are short and sweet.' She needed no help to dismount herself, but David obviously thought she did.

She slid down, and with her back against the mare David suddenly gripped her shoulders. He was on the point of kissing her; she knew it. She liked him so much she was shaken to discover he had developed such feeling for her so early and so unwisely.

'David—' she began.

His sun-browned face, his glossy head was poised over hers. Her expression was one of a supplicant.

'So *there* you are!' a familiar voice called ringingly.

David dropped his hands at once and Brett froze. Neither of them had heard footsteps in the courtyard, yet here were Jay and Kerri, dressed for riding.

'You obviously didn't wait for us,' Kerri accused them with mock grievance. 'Jay, do you really think you should allow your fiancée to go riding with attractive young men?'

Jay's brilliant blue eyes moved abruptly from David to Brett. His face wore an expression Brett knew well; a glittery arrogance that didn't bode well for David. For either of them, for that matter.

Brett didn't wait for his answer; she rushed to her own defence. 'You were the one who told us not to wait, Kerri,' she said decisively.

'Not *me,* darling.' Kerri laughed good-naturedly. 'I was only fooling, you know. Jay knows he has nothing to be jealous about.'

David jerked up his head. 'Is this some kind of joke? Brett asked you where Jay was and you said he'd gone off with the station manager.'

'So I did!' Kerri responded wide-eyed. 'Hey, don't let's make an issue of this. If you didn't want to wait, you didn't want to wait.'

'You told us to go, Kerri,' David replied sternly.

'Shouldn't you two get out of those wet clothes?' Jay intervened. 'Whatever you *thought* Kerri said, I did intend for us all to go out together. No matter. Breakfast is waiting.'

'What about that Kerri?' muttered David as they walked back to the house. 'She turned the tables on us, and it had to be deliberate.'

'I'm used to troublemakers,' Brett said briskly. 'I take them in my stride.'

'Jay looked kinda intimidating.'

'It comes easily to him.' Brett flicked a smoky look into his face, then looked away. 'You want to join the Corporation, don't you, David?'

'Obviously—that's why I'm here.'

'Perhaps it might be better—'

'If I didn't appear to enjoy your company so much?'

'I have enemies, David,' Brett warned him.

'I think you'd better include Kerri Whitman among those people,' David went on. 'I suppose you can't expect her to be fond of you. There was a time when Jay was going to marry her, wasn't there?'

'That rumour was put about,' she agreed.

'A lot of people heard it. I'm only back from overseas and I heard it. Wait a little minute, Brett.' He caught her arm. 'Normally I hate gossip, but I think it's obvious that I really like you. Be on your guard.'

'Can't you at least warn me from whom?'

'Has it ever occurred to you that Morton is very jealous of his brother?'

'Not right now, David. We have to change.' Brett walked on. 'I grew up here, you know. I know Jay *and* Morton as if they were my own family. Morton was never jealous of his brother until he married and his wife and her family convinced him he ought to be. Morton isn't as sure of himself as he appears to be. He and Jay had the same upbringing, and believe me, they're very close. If and when it really comes to it, blood will tell. Morton may be manoeuvred into any number of little skirmishes, but no one on this earth is going to make him raise his hand against his brother. Morton *loves* Jay. He doesn't hate him. But he could be persuaded to hate *me*.'

Some of their guests were still seated over breakfast when Brett and David eventually made their way back to the morning room. Brett, who believed in taking the bit between her teeth, looked across at Jocelyn Nolan. Mrs Nolan was keeping her husband company while he enjoyed a late, leisurely breakfast.

'We missed Jay,' Brett told her conversationally. 'Didn't Kerri tell us to go ahead?'

'Why, I believe she said to stay.'

'Oh, surely not,' intervened David, trying not to sound contemptuous.

'Well, I thought so,' Jocelyn Nolan replied apologetically. 'Excuse me, won't you? I have to get my sunglasses. I've never experienced such quality of light!'

'I've a feeling dear Kerri has something on Mrs Nolan,' David said later. 'She didn't want to lie, but she had to.'

If Kerri was feeling at all malevolent she managed to hide it well. For an outsider it would have been easy to believe she was taking this engagement very well. Her manner with Jay was that of a lifetime good friend spiced with the inevitable man-woman banter. She was provocative, certainly, but it was an integral part of her nature. Towards Brett she was friendly, albeit in a gently patronising way—something that might be expected of an experienced sophisticate in her dealings with a girl barely out of the classroom. Occasionally Kerri was downright indulgent, giving the impression that Brett needed all the support she could get.

It was a tour de force of acting.

For the remainder of the weekend, Brett never found herself alone again with David. She regretted the faint constraint this caused, but she realised it had to be. Jay had lost no time admonishing her.

'That's where it ends, Marisa,' he told her. 'Dave's a damned fool allowing himself a romantic daydream. We wouldn't want it to go sour, would we?'

'Showing the *real* you?' Brett found herself taunting him. She had intended to tell him about Kerri's piece of mischief, but Jay could be shockingly arrogant when he chose. Let it seem she had been attracted to David. It sweetened her mood. Jay's highhandedness went beyond his rights. She shuddered to think what he would be like after marriage.

Less than half an hour after their brief clash he had announced to the whole party their wedding date: December the twentieth. He held her to him; he had to. Brett's leg muscles abruptly gave out.

Brett went down to the airstrip to see them all off. Although she had lived with the idea of her approaching marriage these past months, she couldn't believe Jay had set the actual date. Hadn't he ever heard of asking the bride? Not that she was a bride—more a business partner. Even business partners had to be consulted.

David shook her hand, a kind of driven urgency beneath the courteous, pleasant sentences. 'If you ever need someone to come to... someone to help you, or just listen, please think of me,' he murmured quickly as Jay turned away to check under the Beech Baron.

Was that David's way of saying he thought she was being used?

Kerri smiled at her with curving lips and blank eyes. 'If I can't be a bridesmaid, at least throw the bouquet at me!'

She had to get to the altar first. All these people, and probably not one of them believed Jay loved her.

'A kiss before I go,' Jay called to her, and Brett could see the mockery blazing out of his eyes.

She moved gracefully towards him, a small, slender girl in an amethyst silk top and matching pants, a double belt resting on her narrow hips. She expected the usual display of allegiance, but some devil had got into Jay. He lifted her clear off the ground so their mouths were on a level, then he kissed her with a sensuality no one was likely to forget.

Brett was reduced to breathless mumbling. 'You brute!'

His brilliant eyes sparkled, shockingly brilliant eyes. 'If there's anyone winning prizes around here, honey, it's me!'

'What in the world are you talking about?'

'I'm beginning to think Dave's a real old rogue. What was he whispering to you so heroically?'

'His phone number,' hissed Brett.

'I wouldn't be at all surprised.' Jay lowered her gently to the ground. 'See you, little one, take care. I couldn't operate if I didn't know you were safe here.'

Brett groaned. Jay was such an unnerving mixture!

'You might decide to start on our bedroom,' he added with a cool smile. 'Spare no expense. It's going to be our private sanctuary.'

He was about to go, and Brett caught his arm and lifted herself on tiptoe. 'Break just one of the rules and our deal's off,' she whispered in his ear.

'Darling!' He kissed her once again. Hard.

They were all staring out of the plane. Kerri's head was in view. Brett waved and moved away to the Land Rover.

A few minutes later the twin engines roared into life. The aircraft moved down the runway gathering speed for the take-off. It lifted and soared into a cobalt sky. Soon it was a mere speck. Only then did Brett turn away. Her life wasn't hers any more. Perhaps it had never been hers. She couldn't remember a time when it hadn't been Jay's.

THE PHOTOGRAPHS kept up as Brett knew they would. It was a standard underhand practice. She considered sending them on to Jay, but she had already had his response. The fireplace seemed a good choice, but she was still at the stage when she was questioning the morality of her own decisions. Marriage with Jay presented terrible dilemmas—for *her*. Men seemed to have little trouble differentiating between wives and lovers. On the basis of these photographs, recent because Kerri had taken the trouble to have her hair re-styled in a distinctive short cut, Jay was her constant companion at functions. Either that or she had managed to have herself photographed right beside him. Brett supposed that mightn't be all that difficult for someone like Kerri Whitman; she had always received a good deal of society coverage. Jay, of course, expected her to defer to his male superiority. Diamond Valley had never been the place to fight women's rights. Man was king. Jay, for all his strong protective streak, wasn't all that different from the knights of the Middle Ages. He expected to be obeyed without question. He expected to be trusted implicitly no matter how devastating his actions purported to be.

Brett had seen him with Kerri. For that matter, over the years she had seen him with a lot of beautiful girls. There was once a girl called Sally he had liked very much. Brett had liked her too. Whenever she came to Diamond Valley, which was often, she had always brought the much younger Brett a nice surprise. Sally had been exceptional. Kerri Whitman and her friends had treated her as an oddity in the Carradine set-up. People like Kerri and Elaine had seen that the stories abounded.

In the end, Brett didn't destroy the photographs at all; she kept them as she had the ones Jay had so carelessly thrown away. If nothing else they established beyond question that both parties were extremely photogenic. Brett decided at going on twenty-one—of course December the twentieth was her birthday—it was about time she stopped allowing people to manipulate her. It was all very well for Jay to tuck her neatly out of sight while he lived a full, dynamic life, but she had to follow her own path to true adult identity. Much as she loved Jay—and the thought of losing him drove her to despair—nothing really good could come of a marriage without love. She knew arranged marriages happened and many appeared to work very well, but such a marriage was potentially traumatic for her. Behind her hard-won reserve she was a deeply sensitive and emotional woman. Jay, if no one else, had the power to destroy her. She had given him her promise and she had a conscience about promises, but now she required guarantees.

The following week when Carradine Air Freight flew into the property with all sorts of things she had ordered Brett took advantage of a free trip down to Adelaide, the beautiful capital of South Australia. She advised no one of her visit, including Jay. With shoulder-length, naturally deep-waving hair she didn't need a hairdresser all that frequently. Often she simply trimmed her hair herself or had one of the house-girls help her amid waves of giggles. Now she decided on a style. She had seen it in a magazine. The model was her type, large-eyed, small-boned, with a curling cloud of hair. The model's hair had been graduated in length to release the natural curl and Brett thought the same style would suit her very well.

She intended to buy lots of clothes as well. The woman in Jay's life would have to realise she had a lifetime of fierce competition ahead of her. Jay radiated a vivid sexuality, and such a quality had attendant dangers. Brett was stuck with the same quality herself and failed to recognise it. She had never *used* her beauty at any time. Her mother had been a very beautiful woman and she had suffered for it. Brett identified beauty and suffering in her own mind.

To other women, like Kerri Whitman, beauty was a symbol of power. Kerri's good looks had given her endless gratification. It had begun with, 'What a beautiful baby!' and it had never stopped. Brett, for a variety of reasons, not the least of them growing up in a male-dominated environment, unconnected with family, had an altogether different conception of her femininity.

She had never been the centre of anyone's universe. With her advanced intelligence she had realised even at an early age that her mother had placed a *man* before her child. That man had been J.B. Her inheritance was his way of making reparation. She would gladly have swopped it for the kind of childhood and adolescence many of her student friends had enjoyed.

Was it possible that in marrying Jay she would only be perpetuating her mother's life? She realised now she wanted more. Much more.

IT WAS an exquisite figure indeed who emerged from Celine's Boutique. As a student and at home on Diamond Valley Brett had never had much more than a small collection of clothes. In the past hours she had had her hair styled, bought an entire range of Estee Lauder beauty products, several of the French perfumes that most appealed to her, and a high fashion wardrobe for every conceivable occasion. Accessories were included too. So unfamiliar was she with such lavish self-indulgence, she thought she must surely have outfitted herself for life. She didn't realise then how much appearance counted in Jay's world. The women in rich men's lives were expected to look superb. It was taken for granted. Even a woman whose preoccupation wasn't clothes was made to realise her appearance reflected on her husband. If she was to be seen at Jay's side, a role Kerri Whitman appeared to be usurping, she would have to look very fashionable indeed.

Celine and others had only been too happy to oblige. Celine, a Frenchwoman, who travelled back and forth from Australia to Europe, was renowned for her magnificent range of clothes, and the artist in her responded keenly to hanging favourite garments on such a beautiful clothes horse. Although petite, Brett was perfectly proportioned, with the model-girl requirements of long neck, small breasts, narrow waist and hips and long graceful limbs.

By the time Celine had finished with her, Brett felt ready for anything, even the functions Kerri Whitman and her circle were likely to attend. She was a rich girl now—not '*that* woman's daughter'. There was no need to wait for Jay to give her jewellery either; she could buy it herself. She had lived all her life under a system of male domination. As much as J.B. had favoured her, he had never set her free.

Brett had always loved pearls, so now she bought a long lustrous string and matching earrings. She was wearing a stylish silk two-piece in white patterned with swirls of blue, rose and lavender. The pearls were the perfect complement, glowing softly against her beautiful skin. No one hurried away to check on her credit. Whatever her past, she was a woman of consequence now. How money did talk! These days it positively opened doors, but tragedy and unhappiness were intrinsic to the human species. Brett had begun life with nothing, but from what she had seen she had been no worse off in terms of conflicts than the very rich.

Still, it was wonderful to be financially independent, even if in the middle of it she had to pinch herself to make sure she wasn't dreaming. No man was her master. Or so she told herself.

CHAPTER SIX

THE HEAD OFFICES of the Carradine Corporation occupied several of the top floors in the city's most prestigious executive building. Brett had never been inside until this very year; J.B. had not wanted her there. Now his death gave her instant access.

'Good afternoon, Miss Sargent,' a smart young woman said to her immediately she stepped out of the lift. The young woman was carrying a number of files she had been instructed to take down to the legal office.

Brett smiled pleasantly and walked to the reception desk. All the offices were spacious, spotless, quietly opulent. They presented the traditional look, symbolic of the Carradine way of living, rather than the bold and blunt modern format. The staff were very well trained and a smart appearance was considered a prerequisite rather than a valuable asset.

The receptionist, a beautifully groomed blonde impeccably attired, gave Brett a dazzling smile and reached for the phone. 'I'll tell Mr Carradine you're here.'

'Please—I'm looking to surprise him.'

The blonde blinked her long eyelashes. Brett interpreted that as meaning she wasn't sure that was at all wise.

It was really like a giant beehive. Every little section had its own leader, but instead of a queen bee, there was Jay. He occupied the throne room, so lately the province of his father. It was Jay who made all the important final decisions, but in general his top executives were left in charge of their own domains. Brett had put a great deal of time and concentration into studying the various phases of the business, but its scope was increasing all the time. As soon as she had learned that Morton and Elaine wanted to sell Diamond Valley off Brett had begun thinking of ways to make the homestead pay. There was no question that it cost a fortune to maintain, and there was a problem for either of the brothers to find the time to even get there. Morton considered that the many millions such a pastoral jewel would bring could be put to better use: expanding Carradine Aviation, for example. They could buy more helicopters, aeroplanes. They now operated one of the largest fleet of jets in Australia with a twenty-four-hour, seven-day-a-week service. It had occurred to Brett that the homestead would make a very grand private hotel for the swarms of overseas visitors, particularly from Japan and America who had heard of the powerful scenery the Australian Outback offered and wished to explore it. With Carradine Aviation already operating in the area charter flights could be made to all the vast desert monuments, which were truly wonderful, as well as the splendours of Katherine Gorge and that paradise of the wild, Arnhem Land. Brett had had long enough to gauge the reaction of overseas visitors to the station. They revelled in the splendid comfort of the homestead. They were amazed at the starkly sublime beauty of the Centre and the incredible lushness of the North.

It was a thought, and so far she had kept it to herself.

Jay's secretary ran her territory like a general. Unlike the receptionists she was neither young nor beautiful. She was a rather severe-looking woman in her late forties and she enjoyed executive status.

'Ah, good afternoon, Miss Sargent.' A discreet but extremely thorough head-to-toe examination. 'How well you look! This *is* a surprise.'

'Mr Carradine in?' Brett returned the practised smile.

'Why, yes.' The secretary gave her another packed look. 'He's extremely busy, but I'll tell him you're here.'

'Please—don't bother.' Brett realised she *had* altered. She would never have spoken like that once. Surely it had a dash of Jay's cool arrogance?

Jay was sitting behind his desk, head down. He looked intensely handsome, intensely formidable in his dark business clothes.

'Leave it there, thank you, Avril, and get my brother on the phone.'

'Is it too far to walk down the corridor?' asked Brett.

His head flew up in startled recognition. His blue eyes seared her to the spot.

'If looks could kill!'

'As in devour?' He stood up. 'I was wondering how long it would take you to fly the coop. I figured on just about now. You look exquisite.'

'I do?' She gave him a little cool smile that actually concealed a tremendous, chronic longing.

'Exquisite is an understatement.' He held her shoulders and allowed his gaze to roam all over her. 'I think you've been here before. You know too much to have learned it in one lifetime. I didn't think it possible to paint a lily, but the effect is dazzling. Where did you get those pearls? I don't recall having seen them.'

'I bought them with my own money.'

'It used to be a husband's privilege to buy his wife's jewellery,' he pointed out drily.

'I couldn't wait,' shrugged Brett.

'No one ever said you *had* to wait. Tell me where you bought them.'

'Oh, a jeweller. A very good one.' She threw back her shining head. With the full weight of her hair layered it framed her face in a dark cloud of waves and curls. It was normally parted on the side, but the stylist had changed it to the centre, accentuating the perfect symmetry of her features. In one stroke he had created the ideal look for her. Her beauty was essentially classical, and the manner in which she now wore her hair embellished that look.

Jay seemed amused by her insouciance. 'Am I allowed to kiss that glossy mouth?'

'Since when did you *ask?*' she said drily.

'Since when did you start looking like a millionairess? You aren't little Brett any longer. I guess you've passed your final test.' He bent his dark head, his mouth just touching hers.

It was extraordinary. She wanted to move away, knowing he was tormenting her, for whatever reason, but her yearning was too much. Her sweet breath came into his mouth as a fevered little sigh and abruptly, masterfully, he folded her into his arms.

They stayed like that together, mouths locked. There was a starburst behind Brett's eyes. Her body agonised to be closer to his. He was kissing her so deeply she could hardly stand.

'Jay!' She might have cried to him, 'Help me!'

'I want you so much I can't take this any more.' His fingers circled her breast, then he pushed back abruptly.

'Where are you staying?' he asked.

She named the hotel, breathing deeply to overcome her raging blood.

'Does Gran know you're here?'

'No one. I thought it was about time I did my own thing.'

'I want you to go to her.'

'She may not want me.'

'You can't believe that,' he challenged her, almost curtly. 'I don't want you in some hotel by yourself. There's no need. I'll put through a call to Gran now.'

A moment later he was speaking to his grand-mother, then he passed Brett the phone. The warmth and pleasure in Mrs Chase's voice brought comfort into Brett's guarded heart. Making the transition to *family* would be easy with such a generous, gracious lady, but Brett knew she might never be accepted by other members of a tightly knit clan.

'I'll arrange for your things to be sent over from the hotel.' Jay turned back to his desk with his quick, lithe tread. 'I wouldn't bother mentioning to Gran that you checked into a hotel. She'd be hurt.'

'I think she might understand,' Brett murmured, low-voiced. 'I'm bound to see Morton and Elaine.'

'I expect so, if you pass the lodge every day. Morton's all right, Brett. His feelings are mixed about you. He always wanted to like you, but he couldn't. The way J.B. brought us all up was enough to tie anyone in knots. For a long time Morton couldn't deal with J.B.'s rejection. All those rages and the cruel teasing were a result of jealousy, a terrible state of rivalry J.B. created. Now that he's gone, we can all settle down. In a very short time you're going to be my wife.'

'Aren't you going to add "when we straighten out the details"?' queried Brett.

'*What* details?' he asked softly, a brittle smile on his mouth.

'We don't love one another, Jay, I know that, but I would need your promise to be faithful. I'd never allow you to touch me if you weren't.'

'Do you want to bet?' His voice dropped dangerously, an insolent smile in his eyes.

'It won't come to that.' She bit her full bottom lip. 'Marriage without fidelity would lose all its value.'

'There's a genuine mystery here,' Jay said shortly. 'Who the hell am I going to be unfaithful with? Is it Kerri? *Again?*'

'Well, more photographs did arrive.'

'Which *you* think have some significance?'

'Don't go all glittery with me, Jay. I learned to cope years ago. What I'm really saying is, whatever your relationship with Kerri Whitman in the past, it would have to stop.'

'You offensive little brat!' he growled.

'Not at all—I'm just your fiancée. If I ever get your ring on my finger, that is.'

'So where is it now?'

'I pawned it around noon.' Brett couldn't hold the sharpness in. He took a few steps towards her and she made a convulsive little movement of retreat. 'It's in my bag.'

'What happened? Couldn't you bear it between your breasts?'

'Jay, the gold chain wouldn't go with the pearls.'

He put out his right hand and lifted the lustrous strand.

'Surely you're not going to rip them off?'

'I'm funny about a lot of things.'

'Jay!' she protested.

His brilliant glance slanted unpleasantly over her. 'You think you know me, little one? You're just learning. *I know we don't love one another,*' he brutally mimicked her words. 'What *is* love, do you know? All those feelings you can't control. *I* can't control. I'd have to suggest to you that it's the longest lasting lust on record. Maybe it even happens every hundred years. Get *my* ring out of your bag.'

Colour burned along her high, delicate cheekbones. 'Do you expect me to obey that tone of voice?'

'I certainly do. You're a beautiful, articulate, intelligent girl, Marisa, but I'm much stronger than you are. I'll just take hold of you—'

'I'll get it. I'll get it to avoid an unpleasant scene.' She walked to his huge mahogany desk and picked up her soft leather handbag. 'I suppose if I'd been someone else you'd have given me a party.'

His eyes narrowed to slits and the lean line of his jaw tightened. 'What is it you're looking for, to go over my knee? We held off as a mark of respect to J.B., or have you conveniently forgotten?'

'I'm sorry.' She felt herself go a little white. Jay when he was angry was all glittery male energy. She took the ring out of her bag but couldn't hold it, her hands were trembling so much. It slipped through her fingers and rolled on the carpet.

'We'll have dinner tonight,' he said curtly. 'Just you and me. You can have the biggest party you like a week before the wedding.' He bent and picked up the ring. 'You're *not* going to get out of it. Clearly you're getting cold feet. I promise to stay stone cold sober. I promise not to touch you unless you want it. I will *not* promise to be faithful. I consider it a serious slur on my character. Someone starts a rumour and it spreads. You'll hear plenty of rumours when you're married to me. You're a major problem in yourself. I can see you haven't got a clue what I'm saying,' he added. 'Don't you ever look in the mirror? What do you think you're seeing, little Snow White? You're an enchantress, Brett. Men are going to fall for you in droves.'

'If you want to break my fingers, you're doing a good job,' she cried emotionally.

'I want to wrap your hair around your throat and strangle you, if you want to know.' His blue eyes were flashing warning signals.

'You're horrible, horrible! You push the ring on my finger.'

'For God's sake, stop it!' He pulled her into his arms, dragging her head back. 'Stop it, do you hear?'

She shut her eyes as though she couldn't bear to look at him, and his mouth came down and covered hers.

Anger raised their passion to a new key. Brett thought she was surely fainting. Her graceful body seemed to go slack against his, but he wouldn't release her so easily. He kissed her into a half dazed submission, then with appalling suddenness lifted his head.

'You deserved that. You know you did.' Sexual hostility glittered in his brilliant eyes.

Brett's whole body was trembling from the force of his passion. She could barely open her eyes, her small panting breaths betraying her extreme agitation. 'I'm sorry I came here,' she whispered.

'You ought to be sorry for a lot!' grated Jay.

'*Tell* me,' she gasped. 'For the past twenty years? For my *mother*? For J.B. because he cared for me? Probably you're only thinking of marrying me to get your hands on the money!'

'It certainly couldn't be love,' he laughed harshly, his face darkly relentless.

She wanted to hit him. She *hated* him. She hated him so much she was barely able to keep from sobbing her heart out.

Jay muffled an oath and grasped her creamy nape. 'I have a feeling, Brett, that we're getting angry for the same reason. I don't know what it looks like to you, but you're in my blood. You know my history. I know yours. We're hopelessly entwined.'

Memories took wing and her face crumpled in pain.

'Don't you cry,' he said softly. 'Don't you *dare* cry.'

She let her head fall forward against his shoulder and abruptly his hand lost its tension and fell to caressing the long line of her neck. Jay's other arm caught her into him, the fire transmuted to an odd tenderness.

'Do you really think I want your money?' he asked sardonically.

Brett shook her head.

'I can't hear you, Marisa.'

'No, Jay.'

'I think I'm doing a pretty fair job of increasing your fortune.'

'I had so much to tell you,' she sighed.

He lifted her head and tilted up her chin. Her eyes were enormous, shimmering with tears. 'It breaks my heart just to look at you,' he said quietly.

'Is something wrong with my face?' She blinked her lashes quickly, thinking her delicate make-up might be ruined.

'God, what a question!' His mouth twisted wryly. 'You've lost all your lipstick, but I don't think it matters—men kiss their fiancées all the time. The ring is on. Keep it on. We've waited long enough.'

THE BOARD called an important, unscheduled meeting for the following week. Brett attended, but her part was restricted to listening to what Jay and various members said. Inside information had been leaked to a senior Carradine executive that a rival air-freight company, generally believed to be thriving, was having significant internal problems and was ripe for a take-over. The current Managing Director, known to everyone at the table, outside Brett, was said to be failing to maximise profit, a cardinal sin. As well, management were having increasing problems with their personnel. The company, the Board was told, was riddled with conflicts and though it was highly unlikely it would collapse in the short term, in the long term it was risking bankruptcy. The time for Carradine to act was now. Westgate could not rival Carradine, but the board agreed that a take-over would greatly increase Carradine power. One thing was important, however: until Carradine made its raid there was to be absolute secrecy as to the Board's intentions. A leak to the business world, to the press, would be fatal. Industrial spying was a constant threat to modern business. The Carradine informant was a key man in the Westgate hierarchy. As a trade, he expected to be given a similar position within the Carradine Corporation.

It seemed to Brett he wasn't much of a man to be trusted, but it seemed he had worked long and hard for his own organisation, but when he couldn't change the present decision-making, he justified his actions by saying he was ultimately concerned with the survival of a business he had helped build up.

It was on this issue the Board argued. Finally it was agreed that the Westgate executive had been motivated solely by his anger and impotence at seeing in his own words, 'a good company go fast down the drain'. As a rationale it was generally understood. No money was involved. The aim was to save Westgate. A take-over by Carradine represented in terms of profit, efficiency and control the best option available.

Voting was unanimous.

Brett was returning to Jay's office when she saw Elaine walking down the corridor. Elaine, with her attenuated figure, was looking very high fashion in a torso-hugging jacket and narrow skirt in elegant black and white. She wore a hat with a little spotted veil, and whatever their marked differences Brett decided she had never known a time when Elaine didn't look stunning.

Elaine, for her part, had decided she had better not ignore Brett's presence any more. She flashed the younger girl a bright, false smile.

'Meeting broken up, has it?'

'Just this minute. You look terrific, Elaine, as usual.'

'It's absolutely no use looking anything else,' Elaine agreed carelessly. 'Someone has obviously taken *you* in hand,' she added.

'I didn't have a great deal of money in the old days.'

'Well, you have now, dear,' Elaine drawled acidly. 'I see you're wearing your ring.'

'Jay wants me to.'

'Ummm—' Elaine couldn't seem to tear her eyes away from the magnificence of the ring, the huge central sapphire set with baguette diamonds. 'How does it feel to have snared one of the biggest matrimonial prizes in the country? A guy, incidentally, who belonged to somebody else?'

Brett threw up her head sharply, her luminous eyes trained on Elaine's face. 'It's good to be loyal to one's friends, but on the subject of Kerri Whitman you really ought to sort out the facts,' she said calmly. 'Kerri had high hopes, I know. I'm sorry if she's suffering, but even without me I doubt very much whether Jay would have gone on and married her.'

'He *told* her he would,' Elaine laughed cynically. 'I think he would have, dear, but for the nightmare of J.B.'s will. Whether you marry Jay or not, I would *worry* about Kerri, if I were you. I'm quite sure she'll be around to add to your troubles. Of course your particular case mightn't find its way into the divorce courts, but sophisticated people know how to arrange their affairs.'

'Then you ought to go shopping for a new photographer!'

It was a shot in the dark, but the effect on Elaine was spectacular. Her face went slack with shock, then as Brett continued to stare at her challengingly she adopted a façade of aggression.

'What the devil is *that* supposed to mean?'

'Shouldn't you have said, "Photographer?" and then looked blank? You didn't look blank, Elaine. You looked stunned. I might have known. Who else could it be? You and Kerri are such pals.'

'You know, I'm sorry for you,' Elaine gasped. 'You're raving! I know nothing whatever about photographs.'

'Even if they've got your fingerprints all over them?'

'I don't see how—' Elaine broke off abruptly.

'Did you use gloves, you and Kerri? If you thought *I* was going to be upset, you must be crazy. Jay put this ring on my finger because he wants to marry me. If I were you and Kerri I wouldn't worry about why he wants to marry me. *Why* he wants me to be the mother of his son. Speculation will get neither of you any-where.'

'I've come here to have lunch with Morton,' Elaine complained bitterly. 'I shall tell him what you've said.'

'I bet you won't.' Brett went on taking stabs in the dark. 'He's coming out of the board room door now. He's smiling at Jay. It's obvious enough he loves his brother, no matter how hard you've tried to change that. Tell him in front of me if you like. Tell him what I've accused you and Kerri Whitman of and I'll stick around to study his face. I think Morton understands you very well. You're the sort of woman who enjoys starting little fires. Here he comes now...'

Underneath her chic veil, Elaine's face went pale. 'I always said you're an awful little bitch,' she mumbled. 'Out to get everything you can.'

'Smile, Elaine,' Brett returned coolly. 'We're all going to be one happy family.'

Morton's tall, heavy figure loomed up before them.

'What do you say if we all go out together for lunch?' He looked from one woman to the other. It was clear he was in a good mood.

'Why, that would be lovely, darling,' cooed Elaine, 'but Brett's just told me she has an appointment.'

'Can't you break it?' Morton didn't want his mood ruined.

'It's really something I can't get out of, Morton,' Brett murmured in a disappointed tone. 'Perhaps we could all get together for dinner one evening?' Some time in the far distant future.

'We haven't taken Gran out lately.' Morton seemed infused with good spirits. 'I think we should. They tell me that new place, Colonnades, is very good. Old Berkeley's in town. We should make up a party.'

'That will be great!' Elaine's fair, faintly feral face convulsed with agonised pleasure. She moved forward a few steps and clasped her husband's arm. 'We should go, darling, if we want them to hold our table.'

Morton laughed again. 'And when have they ever failed to do that? See you later, Brett.' His blue eyes took on their familiar hot glow. 'As someone said in the boardroom just now, you look a dream.'

Something was missing from the dream.

AT SIX O'CLOCK that evening Brett received a phone call from Jay's office requesting her to meet him there as he was unable to get to the house to pick her up. They had made plans to go to the theatre, a new play, and afterwards to go on to supper, but a late appointment had delayed him. Brett did not question it; both brothers worked late many nights.

She thought her quick dressing was a shade too sketchy. She would have liked a little more time, but when she showed herself off to Mrs Chase, that gracious lady smiled with pleasure.

'Beautiful, Brett—just beautiful! I'm so glad lace has come back into fashion. That black goes superbly with white skin.'

Brett didn't hesitate. She bent down and kissed Mrs Chase's fine, dry cheek. 'You're a good girl, Brett,' the old lady patted her hand soothingly. 'You always were and you always will be. I'm happy about this marriage. You have so many fine qualities Jay can only love and respect you.'

All the way into the city, and the Chase chauffeur drove her in, Brett considered how she could secure these twin prizes, love and respect. Jay was a hunter, yet protecting his womenfolk was one of his most powerful instincts. It was easy to recall the many times Jay had put himself at risk saving her from possible injury. As a child on the station she had tried desperately to be self-reliant. Her mother had not been able to spare her a great deal of time, and because Brett so terribly needed her mother she had been driven to an exaggerated independence. Moving so freely about a great station had often put her in physical danger. Jay had always been there. To a great extent, and she saw that now, he had played a near-parental role. Jay had watched over her through every stage. It *had* to be caring. Or had it been pity for a little girl largely deprived of a normal childhood? One thing was understood: their lives, as he had said, were hopelessly entwined. Surely that was central to an enduring relationship. Perhaps, as she so desperately wanted to, she should tell him what he meant to her, what he had meant to her over all these long years. It shouldn't be difficult, yet the circumstances of her life had made her fear showing her heart. Self-denial was long instilled. She was overly cautious about everything.

There was a hush over the top floor. Everyone had gone home. Brett walked quietly down the corridor and into Jay's suite. His door was ajar, but as she went to go forward to give it a little rap she was startled by the sound of low, angry voices.

She fell back against Jay's secretary's desk. She needed to. The voices she had heard belonged to Jay and a woman he apparently couldn't get out of his life:

Kerri Whitman. She waited a minute and the voices stopped. Perhaps she had made a little involuntary sound. She wanted to run away, but she knew she had to face it. Incidents like these broke engagements. What she had been attempting to do was live a lie. She had more pride than that.

Brett drew herself up and reached for the door-knob, throwing the heavy door wide open.

What she saw seared itself into her brain. Kerri Whitman, in a dishevelled state, was trapped in Jay's arms. Another thing came to her: Jay had just lifted his head from kissing her. His face was darkened with passion and Brett felt all her flimsy hopes fly out the window. 'I think I've got the message now,' she said quietly. 'It's obvious you two can't keep apart.'

She didn't want to scream, to rave and rant: she just wanted to disappear in a puff of smoke. Like her dreams. She was pulling off the great sapphire ring, but neither was it her way to throw it. She put it down gently on one of the bookshelves that lined the wall.

'I think you might ask what the hell is going on?' Jay exploded violently, giving the incredible impression that he and not she was the one deeply wronged. He almost threw Kerri from him and she burst into near hysterical laughter.

'I warned you, didn't I, you stupid girl? You never quite got it before.'

Brett didn't need a warning now. She turned and fled down the corridor.

Jay came after her, but the lift was waiting and she closed the door in his face. Trust Jay to look like an avenging archangel! He was showing his true nature. The rules of man didn't apply to him.

He almost caught her as she hurried across the foyer. What on earth did he think he was going to say? He ought to be able to have his cake and eat it too? Men were incredible creatures. Hadn't J.B. treated her mother the same way?

There was a taxi stand on the other side of the street, and so anxious was Brett to get to it she looked swiftly both ways but not back again. A small blue sedan raced around the corner on the lights, coming directly for her, and as the taxi driver shouted in horror, he saw a man swoop from the pavement and lift the girl backwards and almost clear off the ground. The man threw himself back, but as he pivoted the sedan struck him glancingly before stopping amid a squeal of brakes.

The two of them fell to the ground.

The taxi driver waited no more. He leapt out of his car and raced to their assistance. The driver of the blue sedan, swearing profusely, pulled over into a NO STANDING zone.

'Boy, that was close!' The tall, lean man needed no assistance, but the taxi driver helped him lift the girl to her feet. 'I thought you were a goner, young lady,' he insisted. 'Probably the bloke in the car was going too fast.'

'I'm sorry... so sorry.' Brett was terribly shaken.

'*Sorry?*' The single word seemed to flame from Jay and the taxi driver raised his eyebrows.

'I think you should check nothing's broken. You okay, mister?'

'Nothing much wrong with me,' the tall man said briskly. 'Thanks for coming to our assistance.'

'Sure was a near thing. When you feel up to it, little lady, you ought to thank this nice gentleman. I reckon you'd be lying in an ambulance by now. Just look what you've done to your stockings—and oh, your *elbow!*'

'I'll take care of her,' said the tall man.

The taxi-driver decided they knew one another after all. Couldn't be lovers; their behaviour was too odd. The girl had come out of that office building. Come to think of it, he knew the guy—Carradine, that was it. Not only was he rich, he was brave.

The driver of the blue sedan needed calming and reassuring, and Brett, to prevent further interest, as a small crowd had quickly gathered, went with Jay back inside the building.

'Let's have a look,' he clipped when they were inside the lift.

'I can attend to it, Jay. It's nothing.' In fact she had badly grazed her elbow.

'You might have been killed!'

'I wasn't. You always seem to be close by.'

'Just an old habit.' He was white beneath his dark bronze tan. 'If you're wondering, I'm quite sure Kerri Whitman has gone.'

'I guess she got a kick out of seeing me nearly go under a car,' shrugged Brett. 'If she came out the front door she couldn't have missed it.'

'I'd say she went down to the parking lot.'

'The car hit you. Are you hurt?'

'Don't sound so hopeful!' he said bitterly.

'I would never want you hurt, Jay. You've been good enough to me in your fashion, after all.'

The lift stopped at the top floor and he guided her along the corridor. 'I was just about to come for you. What the devil were you doing here?'

'Ask your secretary.' Brett felt so shaken she was sick.

'You bet I will! Avril had no instructions from me to ring you.'

'Maybe not Avril. I understood it was someone from your office.'

'Man or woman?' Jay stopped and looked down at her frowningly.

'A woman. Aren't they all?' Brett slowly lifted her head. What she was going to say failed. There was such a look of anger and concern in Jay's eyes, her bitterness left her.

'Hold me,' she whispered. The very ground seemed to tremble beneath her.

Immediately his arms came around her. 'Stay here,' he murmured. 'Stay here where you belong.'

His jacket coat brushed against her tender skin and she gave a little shiver of pain.

'We'd better clean that up, I guess.'

'I've scarcely felt it.'

'You've skinned it raw. I think I'll get Kendall to take a look at it.'

'It's nothing, Jay.' She twisted her arm so she could take a closer look at her elbow. 'I've had worse falls.'

'You've never jumped in front of a cab before.'

Jay sat her down in his office while he went for the first-aid kit. Brett was feeling so shaky she left all her thoughts alone. Time for that later. She relived the moment when Jay had hauled her away from that car. She knew that he had risked injury. That dimension of their troubled relationship had not left them; when she was in trouble he went to her aid.

'I know *you* must be badly bruised,' she pointed out wretchedly when he had joined her.

'My dear Marisa, I'm tough,' he assured her.

'I suppose you are.'

'This might hurt a bit,' he warned.

Brett drew in her breath. He swabbed the whole area, gently patted it dry, then brushed it with an antibiotic powder. 'I'll just put some gauze around it, then I'll take you back to my apartment. We can have something to eat there.'

'I want to go home, Jay,' she said quietly.

'Isn't *home* with me?'

'The house we're trying to build has too many cracks in it. They seem to get wider every day.'

'Ever heard of sabotage?' He finished tying a neat dressing.

She put a trembling hand over her face. 'Not now, Jay. I feel a little sick.'

'Then you'll come with me. For better or worse, Marisa, I'm the man in your life.'

For the rest of the evening he was kind and solicitous. While Brett tidied herself up and removed her ruined stockings he went to the phone and ordered dinner for two from a restaurant he frequented. It was not the restaurant's usual practice to cater for the home, but anything for Mr Carradine.

While they waited Brett rested quietly on the richly-hued glove leather banquette. Jay's apartment was bold and masculine—powerful, like his personality. The walls were all dark, gleaming timber. The tufted leather on the banquettes around the room matched the upholstery on the antique dining chairs. The table was very modern with a top of some sparkling stone. The art works too were very modern and compelling, for Jay was a man with strong and wide-ranging aesthetic tastes and opinions. Diamond Valley was traditional; this was avant-garde.

Forty minutes later, the food arrived—avocado with seafood, lobster Newburg and a fragrant, delicious iced dessert made with tropical fruits.

Jay seated her at the table and poured the wine. It simply wasn't real. The two of them ignored the events of the past hours; Jay knew instinctively it wasn't the time to face them. Brett shut them out. Jay had an immediate and extortionate effect on her emotions. She loved him so much that though she might bleed inside she was ready to forgive him. This fact alone proved conclusively that women were more forgiving than men.

He took her home towards midnight when they were sure Mrs Chase would have gone to bed. Both of them recognised an unwritten rule that the boys' grandmother should not be disturbed or upset. Lillian Chase had suffered a number of tragedies in her life; she was entitled to a little peace at nearing eighty.

The Lodge was still ablaze as they swept past. Morton and Elaine entertained frequently, for big parties at the Main House when Mrs Chase gave her permission, but for small affairs at the splendidly renovated and refurbished Lodge. Brett glanced briefly at the driveway beneath the canopy of great shade trees and immediately felt sick to the pit of her stomach. Kerri Whitman's white Porsche stood out against the dark purple shadows.

Jay with his characteristic alertness noticed it as soon as they drove through the great wrought iron gates.

'Would you be completely rocked if we tackled this thing now?' He pulled the Jaguar over and turned to face her.

'Surely you don't want to go in now?'

His blue eyes glittered. '*I'm* going, Marisa, even if you're not. No woman makes a fool out of me!'

She could feel her whole being recoil. 'None of them are on my side, Jay. Kerri is Elaine's friend. Nothing would please Elaine more than to see our engagement break up. Morton is of the same mind.'

'I don't think you understand exactly how Morton feels. Morton is a little mixed up about you, certainly, but I can assure you he'd much rather see me with you than anyone like Kerri Whitman. Kerri is Elaine's friend, not Morton's. Morton is my *brother*. Do you know what that means? The blood bond is *real*. Kerri is a good-looking woman with lots of sex appeal, but she thinks nothing of cheap acts. I know why. Morton knows too. I just have to prove it to you.'

'All right, Jay,' Brett barely whispered.

Morton came to the door, his welcoming smile stopping short when he saw his brother's face and Brett's bandaged arm. 'Hey, what's gone wrong?' He held back the door and ushered them in. 'Elaine,' he called over his shoulder, 'Jay and Brett are here. This must be the night for upset—Kerri arrived a couple of hours ago. Elaine's been feeding her Scotch and sympathy.'

'Jay!' Elaine rushed out into the hallway, her voice more high-pitched than normal. She looked down dismayed at Brett's arm. 'Come in. Come in!'

'You've got Kerri out the back,' Jay broke in brutally. 'Trot her out.'

'What the heck's going on?' Morton rumpled his blond head.

'Let's make it short and sweet,' responded Jay, his handsome face with the strength and glitter of polished steel. 'Kerri is trying to wreck our engagement and she's getting some help.'

'What the hell!' Morton groaned.

'You know what else, old spunk?' Jay advanced on his brother. 'Your sweet wife is up to her ears in suspicion.'

Morton waved to the sofas in the living room. 'Can't we all sit down? I mean, I'm a stranger in my own home. I never know what's going on.'

Elaine looked white and a little bit tipsy. 'I don't know what you mean, Jay. Kerri came here tonight to talk to me.'

'Are you going to get her or shall I fetch her out?' Jay's white teeth snapped together.

Kerri herself appeared at the open doorway. 'Don't bother, I'm here. Is this going to be a *wonderful* get-together!'

'More like a confession!' Jay threw up his dark head, anger and arrogance in his expression. 'You're starting to wobble, Kerri. Don't you think you'd better sit down?'

'Certainly, if it's going to make you explain.' Kerri advanced into the room and sat down carefully beside her friend. 'Has dear little Brett hurt herself?' Her hazel eyes glinted with thinly veiled contempt.

Jay turned sharply, looking even more dangerous. 'I don't think you're grasping the magnitude of your mistakes. I can only point out that my influence is far-reaching. I don't as a rule make war on women, but then I've never found myself so angry before.'

'Isn't that natural?' drawled Kerri. 'Your fiancée has found you out.'

'My fiancée has been sent a lot of photographs,' Jay announced curtly. 'I advised her to throw them on the fire, as they didn't interest me. They've been upsetting her. So now I take action.'

Elaine gasped and put her hand to her heart. Jay's look of stormy vitality was never more in evidence. 'Can't you just let it be, Jay? What good would it do?'

'We could make sure who took them. We know why. Further, tonight Brett received a phone call telling her to meet me at my office instead of waiting for me up at the house as arranged. Anyone could see it as a set-up, but she went. Kerri made sure she was there before her. She staged an angry scene and obviously she saw it as a final performance, because she made herself as dishevelled as she could in the shortest possible time. She even shoved her hands through her hair and tore open her blouse—the one she's wearing now. It was intended to stop Brett in her tracks, and it did. She took off her ring and tried to put as much distance between us as she could. She was almost knocked over by a car.'

'Brett was?' Morton jerked his head around sharply.

'Fortunately I caught up with her and managed to pull her away.'

Kerri laughed.

'It's no joke!'

Elaine shut her eyes.

'What's the most startling thing here,' Kerri drawled, 'is the wild distortion of Jay's story. I could scarcely deny that I presented a—what was it?—dishevelled image, but then I've always been drawn to a violent lover. It's a case of now he wants me, now he don't.'

'I won't settle for anything less than the truth,' Jay said bluntly, ignoring her flippancy.

'Your truth isn't mine, darling.'

'I'll try to remember that when your brother comes to renew his contract.'

For the first time a chill seemed to ripple through Kerri's ultra-slim body. 'What has Graham to do with this?' It was more of an aggrievement than a question.

Jay gave a twisted smile. 'Who started out with the cheap weapons?'

'You were my lover, were you not?'

'I usually don't talk, but you don't seem to have any such inhibitions. We indulged our sexual urges from time to time. As far as I can recall it was pleasant, but so long ago it's all blurred.'

'Jay!' It was Brett who spoke. 'Please—no more.'

'Can't take it, dear?' Kerri sneered at her.

'I don't like to see you humiliated.' It was said so quietly, so sincerely, the effect was shattering.

Kerri, a strong, determined young woman, burst into wild sobbing and Elaine put her arms around her protectively.

'Are you satisfied now?'

'Why don't you tell us *your* part in it?' Jay retaliated. 'All those crocodile tears don't help. I've learned that a woman thinks she can get away with murder if she sheds a few tears. Always in *my* mind is protecting Brett. She's not a sharp-tongued snob, like you two.'

'Hang on, Jay,' Morton interrupted. 'I can understand you're angry—'

'You don't know *how* angry. Brett could have been killed tonight!'

'It's all terribly unfortunate,' Morton said helplessly. 'What the hell *did* you do, Elaine?'

'Hold on. Did I say I did anything?'

'I've had my answer.' Brett stood up. 'See this on my arm? I did that. I blame no one. I accept that Kerri once knew Jay very well, but *she* must accept that that is now over. I'm prepared to try and forget it all.'

Elaine shook her blonde head stubbornly. 'I have no connection with all this. I'm merely being a good friend.'

'You might have remembered you're attacking family before you started,' Jay told her uncompromisingly. 'I'd like a guarantee from you, Morton, that you'll keep your wife in order. She's getting too far over the mark these days. I wouldn't like to have to drop a word in Gerald's ear. If anyone knows his daughter, he does.'

'Leave it to me, Jay.' Morton stood up angrily. 'I told you there'd be trouble if you tried to marry Brett.'

'Not *try*,' Jay stormed in. 'I'm *marrying* Brett.'

'There's a little time left!' yelled Kerri.

Morton no longer bothered to conceal his disgust.

'Get Kerri's things together, Elaine,' he said in a commanding tone of voice. 'I'm taking her home.'

Brett went with Jay out into the night. She didn't know how much more of it she could have taken.

CHAPTER SEVEN

THE FOLLOWING DAY Brett received a visit from
Elaine. Mrs Chase was not at home. She had a morning appointment with her doctor, a routine check, and
afterwards she planned to have lunch with two of her
dearest friends.

'I saw the Rolls go by,' Elaine offered, when Brett
went to answer the door chimes. 'May I speak to you?'

'No arguments, Elaine. I couldn't stand it.'.

'No arguments,' Elaine agreed wryly. 'Morton and
I have been at it for hours. I didn't realise he could get
so angry! If he would give himself half a chance, he'd
be quite a guy.'

'A strange thing to say of your husband?' Brett led
the way to the garden room with its plumply upholstered wicker chairs and dazzling array of indoor
plants.

'Morton has always walked in someone's shadow—
J.B.'s, that terrible man, his brother, Jay. Maybe he
can never measure up to Jay in terms of brilliance, but
he's bright enough.'

'He'd even do better if you'd allow him to be his
own man.'

For a moment Elaine couldn't find her own voice. 'For a cool little thing you don't pull your punches!' she snapped.

'I care about Morton—at least I would if he'd let me. I know how Morton suffered.'

'I guess it wasn't your fault at that.' Elaine slumped into a chair.

'Coffee?'

'And lots of it. I have a hangover. Don't I look it close up?'

'I've never known you look anything else but good.' Brett turned her shining dark head. 'Ah, there you are, Mrs Harris. Do you think we might have coffee?'

'Certainly,' the housekeeper said. 'Good morning, Mrs Carradine.'

Elaine nodded pleasantly and waited for the housekeeper to move off. 'I haven't been very nice to you, have I, Brett?'

'Obviously you felt you didn't like me.' Brett stopped to cup the flower of a magnificent pink amaryllis, then sat down opposite her visitor.

Elaine shrugged. 'That wasn't it. J.B. did so much damage. I've even come around to thinking he was cruellest to you even when he made such a fuss over you. There were all those stories when you were a child; he could have stopped them. It was a crime really, and you got caught in the middle.'

'It's too late now,' Brett said wryly. 'Everyone has a theory why J.B. did as he did. Only the poor have to obey the rules. Men as rich as J.B. did as they liked. It's a way of life.'

'Well—I don't dislike you, Brett.' Elaine's voice was very dry and brittle. 'I admire you, as a matter of fact. And I was very upset to hear what happened last night.'

'You mean with Kerri?'

Elaine hesitated. 'I know this won't go any further, but Kerri rather forced me to go along with her. We go back a long way. Kerri's great as long as you don't cross her—in that respect she's like her old man. She urged me to help her with the photographs—a fellow called Joe Campigli took them. Jay can trace anything when he tries. Kerri was counting on your not showing them to him. I'm not pleased with what I did. Morton is shocked.'

'You got caught?' There was a note of humour in Brett's voice.

'Shocked that I tried to upset his brother.'

There was a rustling sound as Mrs Harris returned and Brett stood up and took the tray. 'Thank you. That looks lovely.'

Elaine sat back in her chair. 'Do you think you could get me some aspirin, Mrs Harris? My head is pounding!'

'I'm sorry—I'll get some right away.'

Brett looked at Elaine's strained face. 'You don't have to explain any more. Relax.'

'I can't relax until I get it over. Anyway, Morton is frantic for you to know I had no idea what Kerri was up to last night. He kept me awake for hours after he came home. He used to like Kerri—or I thought he liked her—but he's gone off her now. He thinks she has no sense of pride.'

'Pride is difficult when one's in love. I don't think it strange she loves Jay. I expect if I marry him I'll have a problem all my life.'

'*If?* Don't you mean *when?*'

Mrs Harris loomed up again with the aspirin and Elaine swallowed them down. 'Shall I pour?' she asked.

'Thank you.' Brett accepted a little cake, but Elaine waved temptation away.

Mrs Harris went off, pleased to see such harmony. She had worked for the Chase family for thirty years and was as well acquainted with family matters as any one of them.

'The point *is*,' Elaine picked up the conversation, 'I want no more of this. I expect Kerri will give me a bad time. She might even divulge one or two things I'd rather be kept quiet. Your life is in *your* hands, Brett. I expect a lot has happened to you for such a young woman—all that money, Jay... There couldn't be a woman alive who wouldn't go mad for Jay. To be frank, I made a play for him myself. We both know he's had quite a few affairs, but *you* were always different. Some people might think he's taking over where his father left off, but I think he loves you.'

'Why *me?*'

Elaine unexpectedly laughed, then winced as it hurt her head. 'I've never met anyone without vanity before. You're beautiful. Surely you know that?'

'If that's all Jay wanted he could have made up his mind long ago,' sighed Brett.

'Then doesn't that answer your question? Hell, even I know he's always been there for you. Obviously he's been waiting for you to grow up. Of course, it's much better now you're rich!'

Brett sat there for a long time after Elaine had gone. There was no gentle way to say it. Her inheritance had certainly brought Jay to the point.

THE NEXT TIME Brett entered the Carradine building she met David. She watched the colour flood his sun-browned face. 'I think of you and what happens!'

She smiled and held out her hand. 'How are you, David? Jay told me you're the latest whizz kid in the legal department.'

'It's great. I'm settling in well.' His brown eyes, in-telligent and warm, were transparent in their pleas-ure. 'How are *you?*' He broke off as a harassed businessman bumped into him without apology and hurried off. 'Going up to see Jay?'

'I was.'

'I think you'll find he's completely tied up. There's been some sort of disaster. Nothing I'm sure Jay can't fix.'

'Why, what happened?' Brett allowed him to ma-noeuvre her into a quieter, safer place.

'None of us have the details yet. I know Jay was looking like thunder and telling Morton to get in on the double. Probably something poor old Mort's done.'

'Maybe I should go up?'

'Maybe you shouldn't,' David warned. 'At least, not for a half hour or so. I'm shooting out for a bite of lunch. I've been working on something long and tedious and I haven't had the chance yet. Why don't you join me for a cup of coffee? That way you'll miss the worst of the storm.'

Brett stood there, undecided. Finally she reasoned she would only be in the way if she went up to Jay. 'All right, that'll be nice.'

It was long past the recognised lunch break, so they had no wait. David ordered a crumbly butter-rich crab quiche and a salad, while Brett kept him company with coffee and a small slice of a spectacular gateau that tasted like chocolate velvet.

'I think I'll have to have some of that,' David remarked. 'You look beautiful, Brett, as always. Are you happy?'

Brett raised her delicate black eyebrows. 'Wait a second. Don't I look happy?'

'Being happy is a difficult matter. There seem to be shadows in those luminous eyes.'

'Maybe my eyeshadow is all wrong.' She kept the quizzical smile on her face. 'I'm happy, David. How could I not be? I'll be a married woman in a few weeks.'

'You don't think you ought to wait?'

'David, stop that! Jay is your boss!'

'And I want to say he's great, but you're so young!'

'Twenty-one on December the twentieth. I just missed out on being a Christmas baby.' I just missed out on a lot.

'I was wondering when I'd see you again,' David's brown eyes very nearly smouldered. 'I know I have no right to say that.'

'It's a little foolish, David,' Brett pointed out gently. 'It could be self-destructive.'

David's smooth skin reddened. 'To think I had to meet you now! Why not a year ago?'

Something in his expression moved Brett's tender heart and she stretched out her hand.

'David, it wouldn't have made the slightest difference. Jay's in my blood, in my bones.'

'God damn him,' muttered David, shaking his head.

'David, if you feel like that why ever did you accept a position within the Corporation? Where is your loyalty to Jay? I think loyalty is terribly important.'

'Of course it is,' he agreed seriously, putting down his fork. 'In our professional lives I'm loyal to Jay all right. I'd probably have to be certified crazy if I weren't. In fact Jay would find out immediately and sack me. I wouldn't care to cross him. I respect him as a person, as a boss. If anything, I'm like the rest of them—I grovel at his feet. The only thing I don't like about Jay is, he's got *you.*'

Brett was shocked. 'David,' she said finally, 'you make me nervous.'

'You know another funny thing?'

'Really, I don't think I want to know.' Brett felt like her coffee cup would fall from her fingers.

'I fell in love with you on sight.'

'It's a good thing that's so unreliable.' Agitation was flushing Brett's magnolia skin with wild colour. 'You don't know me, David. We're almost strangers.'

'That's just it—we're not. You don't feel strange with me. I don't feel strange with you.'

'David,' she said helplessly, 'I'm terribly embarrassed. I do like you, but I love *Jay*, remember?'

'I don't think Jay's right for you.'

'Surely *I* should decide.'

'Please don't be angry, Brett,' he begged her. 'I know I'm out of line, but I can't seem to help myself. You want a friend. You *need* a friend. I know you're without family. Sometimes there's a look in your eyes and I think, why, she's just a little kid. Getting married is an awfully big decision.'

'You would like to make it for me?' Brett gave a strange little laugh like a bell in her throat. 'David, I think we'll have to forget this conversation. You might want to work for the Corporation, but it could become impossible.'

'Oh, Brett, you'd never give me away,' he exclaimed ardently. 'You shouldn't be pressured into this thing.'

'And how do you know I *am?*'

David's eyes fell to his neglected lunch plate. 'People talk.'

'And *people* think I'm being pressured, do they?'

'Please, Brett,' he caught her fingers. 'All I think about is you. Whether Jay can make you happy. Women are crazy about him—lots of women. I've seen them throw themselves at him with my own eyes. It's understandable, I guess: he's as handsome as the devil and he's filthy rich. The thing is, women like that aren't going to care whether he gets married or not. They won't think of you. Especially not you. All they'll think of is what they can get out of him. One of the girls in the office brought her sister up just so she could get a look at him. I mean, I ask you! Probably it would be like being married to a movie star. Some goddamn sex symbol.'

'The only thing you've omitted,' Brett pointed out quietly, 'is that Jay doesn't even *see* the women who chase him and when he does, he gets intensely irritated. I think you're forgetting I've known him all my life. I've seen the same things you have. I've seen how Jay reacts. He's thirty-two and I can tell you he doesn't fall in love easily.'

'Can you swear he's in love with *you?*'

Brett stood up with calm dignity and gathered up her soft leather handbag. 'A real friend, David, would not say these things to me. A loyal employee of the Carradine Corporation would never allow themselves to become trapped in such a situation.'

'Brett, forgive me.' David jumped up, a muscle beside his mouth working. '*I am* your friend, believe me. I would do anything for you. *Anything.* Just ask me.'

'Why don't you, darling?' a voice asked behind them, and both Brett and David broke off in a shocked panic.

Kerri Whitman's face popped around the side of the adjoining high-backed banquette.

David swore. A thick vein stood out on his forehead. Brett felt sick with disgust.

'I suppose you've been deliberately listening!'

'Sure have.' Kerri stood up. 'Would you like me to play it back? Really, David, you ought to have your head examined. When I send this to Jay,' she turned her head to indicate some device, 'your career is over.'

'But you're not interested in David, are you? You're only interested in me. And I doubt very much if you walk round with a micro-recorder in your bag. Though all things are possible.' Brett made a swoop and in front of Kerri's outraged eyes emptied her handbag out on the table.

'How *dare* you!' Kerri who exulted in laying traps bitterly resented being a victim.

'Please—it's quite all right.' Brett rummaged through the assortment of objects on the table, exactly the sorts of things a woman usually carried in her handbag. No recording device of any kind.

'Tell me, you weren't here when we arrived. Did you go past the window and nearly fall over?' she asked Kerri.

'As a matter of fact, I did.' Kerri slumped down in the banquette. 'The two of you were so engrossed in each other you didn't even see me. I've never heard such rubbish! Just how did you think you were going to work for Carradine and doublecross Jay?' she asked David bitterly. 'You're so awfully nice, aren't you? A cut above me. Yet you're prowling around Jay's precious little half-sister.'

'You're disgusting, Kerri,' Brett said scornfully. 'It's the only thing you seem to understand.'

'If I can make trouble for you, I *will!*'

Kerri looked so white and wretched Brett passed a hand before her eyes. 'Please, David, sit down. Mercifully the restaurant is almost empty, but even then Jay will get a report back. Kerri,' she sat down beside the older woman, 'do you think I'm so insensitive I can't feel your pain? I know you're in love with Jay, but it's time you went after a little help. He's not in love with you. I doubt if he could be barely civil to you these days. What you're doing is very foolhardy and it will become a matter of grave concern for your family if you persist.'

Kerri laughed harshly. 'I no longer try to follow you, Brett. If anyone tried to take my man I'd kill her!'

'Then aren't you really saying Jay *isn't* your man? You *know* he isn't. Please try to leave your emotions aside and think this out. So you had a rapport? There have been other women in Jay's life. Remember Sally Grosvenor?'

'Yes, I do, boring creature.'

'She rated pretty high with Jay. She was very kind to me.'

'Have you ever thought that's why?' There was a kind of anguish in Kerri's hazel eyes. 'I lost Jay the moment you grew up.'

'I'm so sorry,' Brett said.

'The incredible part is I believe you are, but that changes nothing. Without you everything would be different.'

All at once Brett could see it was useless. Kerri had withdrawn beyond help. 'Please don't make trouble, Kerri,' she begged.

'If you imagine I'm going to let that snake off the hook. I'd do anything for you, Brett—*anything*,' she mimicked David with extravagant scorn.

'Isn't it a little bit like what *you're* doing?' Brett asked quietly. 'I might be a curious person, but I can only feel pity for people in love. It's the same for everybody, the brilliant and the ordinary, the rich and the poor. Sometimes I think it could be treated as a disease. No one seems to have any control over what they're doing. You're a confident, glamorous woman, yet a pathetic jealousy has taken you over. David is considered a brilliant legal brain, yet he's caught in some fantasy about me. I can barely remember a moment of my life without Jay. Keeping us together seems to be first on Jay's list of priorities. He's determined to marry me. What else can I say—to both of you? You may beat me down, but how are you going to beat Jay?'

'Well, I am going to have a damn good try,' Kerri gave a harsh laugh. 'It's all very well for you to play the real lady, but ladies usually wind up getting crushed.'

The street outside was filled with people, light and the rumbling sounds of traffic. 'I'm through,' David said bleakly. 'For years I've been working towards this kind of job, and now I've messed it up.'

'She mightn't say a thing,' Brett pointed out.

'I don't think you understand Kerri Whitman's kind of woman. She's been utterly cruel about you, yet you show her sympathy.'

'She needs it,' Brett told him soberly.

'I don't think there's any chance she won't use what she thinks she's got on us both.'

'Then I'll deny it,' Brett decided. 'Kerri seems to think I won't lift a finger to help myself, but she's quite wrong. Of course what I'm trying to do is help *you*. You'll get over this, David—this little infatuation. It's a passing thing. You're working towards a long and satisfying career.'

'I'd place *you* first.'

'Oh, David!' Brett didn't feel she could take any more. 'Can't you see you're setting yourself up for disaster?'

'And no more able to help myself than Kerri Whitman,' David agreed wryly. 'You don't need Jay's permission to have coffee with me. Kerri's a woman who's made lots of trouble. There's a good chance Jay mightn't believe her. I don't intend to drop out of the organisation until I'm fired.'

HE WAS FIRED the same day.

Brett knew it from one furious, blazing look.

'What the hell does he think he's doing around here?' Jay propelled Brett into his office, towering over her.

'I met him downstairs. We had a cup of coffee.'

'Just like that?' Jay laughed. It sounded menacing and dangerous. 'I gave him credit for more damned sense. Did he actually think he could step on my toes? I could swat him into oblivion like a mosquito.'

'It sounds like overkill.'

'Sit down, Brett,' ordered Jay. 'I'm not coming down hard for nothing. I saw all the moon-eyed looks back on Diamond Valley. Of course I'm a reasonable man; I'm even a tolerant one. I gave him a chance. You do inspire a compulsive idiocy.'

'Thank you.' Brett threw up her dark head. 'Mercifully you don't suffer from it.'

'It's disloyal, Brett,' he said harshly. 'It's disloyal and it's underhand.'

'And who says? Kerri Whitman?'

'Brett,' Jay rasped grimly, 'I'm extremely harassed today. I'll get around to that in time. Kerri did manage to get through to me, posing as her mother. She had quite a story.'

'And you believed her?' Brett asked feelingly.

'You bet your life I did!' The jagged mockery of his tone cut through to her heart. 'Kerri's a born provocateur on the one hand, but I've been doing some observing myself. Dave's so far gone he thinks nothing of pursuing a girl who's damn near at the altar. That's bad enough, but how about this? He *works* for me. I offered him a job—a good job. The chance to go as high as he likes. But it seems that's inadequate weighed against you.'

'Kerri's lying.' Brett spread her hands. They were very pretty hands: small, fine-boned, long-fingered. The sapphire was as clear and blue as some wonderful subterranean grotto, the surrounding diamonds blazed in the light.

'Look at me, Brett.' Jay sounded very severe.

She lifted her head, the colour racing under her beautiful skin. 'It was all quite innocent, I assure you.' At least she might save David's career.

'Do you imagine I can't read your eyes? I know everything about you.'

She gave a muffled little exclamation and leapt to her feet. She put out her hand and gripped his wrist. 'Please don't fire David,' she begged.

'Pleading, are you?' His eyes, as blue as her sapphire, slanted over her unpleasantly.

'How could David hurt *you?*' Brett pleaded.

'My dear Marisa, it appears he's having a damned good try. When have you ever pleaded for me? Your eyelashes are all wet.'

'Jay, I'm asking you,' she said with soft poignancy.

'And the answer is David is getting his walking papers today.' His brilliant eyes glittered under their lids. 'I can accept an unwilling attraction. I cannot accept sabotage.'

'But *I* have to accept it from Kerri.' Now Brett's silvery eyes filled right up with tears. 'I have to accept lots of things, whereas you accept nothing.'

'That's right.' He caught her delicate shoulders. 'Anyone who tries to get to you answers to me. Finally it seems someone went directly to Gunn at Westlake and informed him of our intentions.'

Brett heard what he was saying, but for a moment couldn't take it in. 'Westlake,' she repeated.

He prodded her memory bluntly. 'Don't tell me you've forgotten our recent Board meeting?'

'So what has it to do with me?'

'Maybe Dave decided he wanted you and an alternative career?'

'I'm sure nothing could be further from his mind!' Brett looked and sounded shocked. 'Why is David the only one you've thought of?'

'Surely I wouldn't think of *you.*'

'*What!*' She looked up at him in amazement and distress.

'It has been suggested to me.'

'Morton?' Her sensitive face was shadowed with pain.

'Morton, my dear, is sufficiently on your side to write that sick suggestion off. You have one hell of an aura, Brett, but no one who knows you would ever accuse you of double dealing. You're incapable of treachery. My brother and I know perfectly well you had nothing to do with it. The suggestion was very neat—too neat. Some people seem to go out of their way to set themselves up for a fall. David Cooper is one of them.'

'David didn't do it,' Brett shook her head.

'David Cooper has done enough.' Jay's hand closed under her chin. 'He's no one to cry about.'

'If you sack him I promise I—'

'*What?*' His hard fingers pinched.

'*Please* don't sack him, Jay,' she begged.

There was a cold hostility in his eyes, an arrogant set to his handsome head. He looked incredibly like J.B.

'No one—but no one—plays me for a fool. Cooper goes.'

THE LEAK LED to an intensive inquiry, but no one asked Brett any more questions.

Elaine, on the other hand, was distraught. 'You've got to help me, Brett,' she whispered over the phone. 'I just don't know how this thing will finish.'

Brett invited her up to the house so they could talk—about what, Brett didn't know. Surely Elaine couldn't have had anything to do with it? Elaine was a woman who worked untiringly in what she saw to be her husband's interests. The engagement party was scheduled for the following Saturday night. Brett found, even with help, there was a great deal to do. She hoped what Elaine had to say wouldn't take long. She still had a last fitting for her dress, which was being made by a top designer. It was a black tie occasion and Brett realised she would be very much on show. It was almost impossible to jam all the things she had to do in.

'Thanks a lot for seeing me,' Elaine burst out in a rush. 'I know how busy you must be. Incidentally, if there's anything I can do please let me know. Gran in?'

Brett nodded. 'She's resting in her room. She says she wants to be at her best on Saturday night.'

'She has always favoured you. I could turn into an angel, but it wouldn't make any difference. I know she doesn't think a great deal of me.'

'That's not true, Elaine,' Brett glanced at her quickly.

'Oh, don't worry, I can see you're embarrassed. Gran takes a very strict view of certain things, and I know I haven't come up to scratch.'

'I know you would do anything for Morton's sake.'

'Gran thinks I'm a bad influence in his life.' Elaine sat down.

'Not a *bad* influence, Elaine—scarcely that. Maybe she thinks Morton is more capable than you allow. He affects that very casual style as a cover. He's really a man of brain.'

'In the man of brawn?'

'Jay tells me repeatedly that Morton is blooming,' said Brett.

'Now J.B.'s gone?'

'J.B. *was* the major influence on Morton's life. While Jay fought him at every turn, Morton's way was to conform. A lot of people thought he would simply collapse, but in fact Jay has given him the one thing he lacked—direction. Jay's very clever with people. More importantly, he loves his brother.'

'I *know* that, Brett,' Elaine agreed, meekly for her. 'If Jay is the ideal, *my* husband is proving he's no mediocrity. Foolishly I thought Jay might shove him in the background. I *really* thought that. So did Dad. We didn't see anything between J.B. and Jay. We didn't see all the decency. J.B. never looked on Morton indulgently in his whole life. Jay pushes his brother further and further on. You could say Dad and I were J.B.'s dupes. We thought after he had gone Jay would take his place. Even Dad had to admit it showed our poor judgement, and that's quite a thing for *my* father to admit. Jay has backed his brother all along. Belatedly I realise that for the past few years I've been doing all the wrong things. Morton talks wistfully about a family. I've sought to keep up my social life and my figure. You more than anyone have made me feel a poor thing.'

'But what have *I* done, Elaine? I'm grappling with my own problems.'

'You've got something that Gran's got—a kind of high-mindedness, a disdain for anything dirty or underhand,' Elaine explained.

'I can't imagine your doing the things I've done. You came out of that business with Kerri with dignity, although she can't accept that she can't be the winner. It's Kerri I want to talk to you about now.'

'She's not on the move again, is she?' Brett asked dismally.

Elaine lit a cigarette and exhaled a great gust of smoke. At Brett's age she had been a picture of glowing prettiness, but her model-girl aspirations and later the right sort of clothes had set her on the path of smoking to alleviate her hunger pangs. Now she gestured furiously.

'I don't care what she does to me. This whole thing is getting me down—I can't sleep, I'm drinking too much and I smoke one cigarette after another.'

'Why don't you give it all away and have a baby?' Brett said suddenly. 'You're not happy, Elaine, the way you are. I don't like to see you abusing your body. All those cigarettes are really bad. I won't bore you by going on, but obviously you're now thinking of starting a family. You *couldn't* smoke if you were pregnant.'

'I wouldn't.' Abruptly Elaine put her cigarette out. 'My mother is always at me too. The thing is, Brett, when Kerri and I were friends...'

'You're not now?'

Elaine laughed. 'I guess we were never friends. I have to re-read the whole book. Kerri and I were bosom buddies, or so I thought. Actually our friendship wasn't all that bad. It was a lot of fun. We obviously did what we liked.' She swallowed and gave a pathetic, shamefaced grin. 'Once when Morton was away I had a bit of a—'

'You don't have to tell me, Elaine. Your affairs are your own.'

'You have to know what this is about,' insisted Elaine. 'It seems very remote now, a passing aberration, but Kerri reminds me of it every so often. The implied threat is that she would tell Morton. He would never understand—Morton is that extraordinary thing, an entirely faithful husband. I want you to believe this, Brett. It's most important that you do. In passing I happened to mention to Kerri that we were planning the Westlake take-over,' she added.

'Oh, my God!' Brett cried expressively, instantly seeing the rest.

'Brett.' Elaine grabbed her hand. 'I never thought for one moment Kerri would repeat it, let alone pass on the story. It just popped out as things sometimes do. I'd been telling Kerri things for years and years. It was as if she was my sister. Kerri has never done anything to hurt any one of us.'

'Until now.'

Elaine pulled out a handkerchief and dabbed her eyes vigorously. 'Oh, Brett, what am I to do? I'm terrified of Jay. Sometimes I don't know who he is. He can look so much like J.B. All that charm turns to a kind of caged ferocity.'

'It was a mistake, an indiscretion,' Brett began.

'If Gran knew she would detest me for life.'

'You meant no harm, Elaine,' Brett said in a worried voice. 'Was it Kerri who went to Westlake?'

'I don't know precisely if it was Kerri. It was Kerri who set up the meeting. She boasted about it. The incredibly foolish part was she thought it would reflect on *you*.'

'But Jay knows me,' Brett pointed out dryly. 'Anyway, I'm on the Carradine Board. Why would I work against my own interests?'

'To spite Jay.'

'My God, how extraordinary! I'm afraid Kerri Whitman has too devious a mind.'

'Be sure of it,' Elaine groaned. 'Do you think you could possibly go to Jay? I'm so madly upset. If Morton was to know! I think he'd probably divorce me.'

'Why don't you tell him everything and set the record straight?'

'I can't, Brett,' Elaine said simply. 'Would *you* like to tell Jay you'd had an affair? If you couldn't tell him now how do you think you'd tell him if you were married?'

Brett grimaced. 'But if there's the possibility that Kerri would tell Morton anyway, wouldn't it be better if he heard it from you?'

'There's a chance he won't hear it at all if you get to Jay. Jay's the great fixer.'

'He may already know.'

Elaine moaned miserably. 'If he does, he hasn't told his brother.

'Telling wouldn't be Jay's way. You might be hurt, but equally so would Morton.'

'Could you speak to Jay for me, Brett?' Elaine begged. 'I swear, I *swear* my indiscretion was entirely innocent. It never occurred to me at that time Kerri would do anything with the information.'

'I can try, Elaine,' Brett promised.

'You're a pal!'

'Whatever is happening to Elaine these days?' Mrs Chase asked afterwards. 'Didn't I see her kiss you when she left this morning? I happened to be looking through my window—the roses are glorious—and there was Elaine acting like a real woman for a change!'

What Elaine did not realise was that relations between Brett and Jay were strangely taut. Engagement parties, weddings were going on, but the atmosphere between them was electric.

Brett rang Jay's office and when she got through to him he sounded very crisp and businesslike. She had to choke back an answering briskness and asked him quite sweetly would he mind calling in to see her.

'Better still, I'll call and pick you up,' he told her.

'You don't have to bother to. . .'

'Got it?' he asked bluntly, and hung up.

He arrived about six-thirty, spent some time with his grandmother who was delighted to see him, then escorted Brett down the wide, shallow stone steps to his car.

'This *is* an honour, Marisa,' he said with something of his brother's easy drawl. 'I do like that dress—such a beautiful colour. What would you call it, jacaranda?'

'Jacaranda, lavender-blue, deep mauve, any of those.'

'Hungering for my company, are you?'

Brett's temper was rising, but she had sense enough to try and turn his hard mockery aside. 'Surely I can call the man I'm going to marry in a little over a week?'

'I'm so glad you remember,' he drawled.

'I do.'

He stopped before he pulled out the gates. 'You just listen to me, little one. There's going to be no fool contract between us. I've treated you like a piece of precious jade. All I've allowed myself is a few reverent strokes. On our wedding night, you're *mine.*'

She seemed to recoil. In reality her whole body came so shudderingly alive she had to arch back against the contoured seat.

'Whatever's in your mind, forget it. Just be grateful I've appreciated your youth and your innocence so far.' Jay pulled the gear lever into drive and the Jaguar took off with velvet smoothness. 'You'll be twenty-one, my wife, and if it's any consolation I promise I'll make you a great lover.'

'Then why do I get the impression you'd like to beat me?'

He looked at her and laughed. 'I thought you said, eat you. There's a better thought. Have I ever actually struck you?'

'Yes,' she said. 'At least, you shook me and called me a stupid little twit.'

'And when was this?' Amusement softened the hard handsomeness.

'I was inside one of the horse stalls, and you thought I'd been kicked at first.'

'I didn't know then that you and horses were on such friendly terms,' Jay said drily. 'Where do you want to go for our honeymoon?'

'Really, you're *asking* me?'

'I'd get a lot more pleasure out of being given your preferences. You're very unusual, Brett, for a fiancée.'

'Perhaps I've never felt like one?'

'You'd feel like one if you ever tried to get away.'

They stopped at a red light and Jay glanced down at his watch. 'Where would you like to go for dinner?'

'Somewhere different. Somewhere where everyone doesn't know you're the great Jay Carradine.'

'Also, they don't know *you*. You've been getting yourself in the social pages lately. You take a great photograph.'

'So do you.'

Dinner was spiced with the same kind of barbed banter. Brett kept her end up very well, but inside she cringed from approaching the subject of the Westlake leak. Also one bad experience precluded ever discussing deeply personal or sensitive matters in a restaurant again.

'So what is it you've been mulling over all through dinner?' Jay asked as they were leaving.

She could scarcely control a little sigh. 'How do you know there was anything on my mind?'

'You're nervous and you don't really want to talk about it.'

'I'm glad that's over.'

He put her into the car and came around the other side.

'Are you sure you have the right address?' Brett asked as they turned towards the city.

'I'm not taking you home yet, Marisa.' He moved out to overtake a slow-moving taxi. 'So anyway, what's bothering you?'

'I don't think I can face it without a stiff drink.'

'*That* bad?'

She nodded. 'I'll tell you when we get to the penthouse. If things get awkward, I can always jump!'

BRETT WAS deeply conscious of the quiet of the penthouse. Unlike Diamond Valley or even the Chase mansion, no magnificent chandeliers were appended from the ceilings. Jay's designer had created a miracle of modern lighting where the whole system was virtually hidden yet created myriad effects. There were lights on the pictures, and these with one or two others brought drama and mystery to the large L-shaped room. It was a study in gold and black and crimson, and Brett felt her heart begin to flutter in a strange fear and excitement.

She sank down into one of the soft, rich banquettes and fervently closed her eyes. It was safer than following Jay's every move. His body spoke to her. Every lithe movement. He was so much a part of her she couldn't exorcise him for a minute.

He must have touched a switch, because music insinuated itself seductively into the atmosphere. Brett recognised the work: Stravinsky. It wrapped its way around her senses, the throb and thrum of the strings touching chords deep within her. Music very often reduced her to tears. For years, instead of human companionship, she had only had music and her beloved horses to turn to. They had never let her down.

She shivered and her eyes flew open when Jay ran a finger down her cheek. 'Why the poignant expression?'

She turned her head to look up at him. 'I was just thinking of the things that have always given me pleasure.'

'It's only right and proper that music should be one of them. It even releases *my* demons.'

'Well, I'll allow you a few,' she sighed.

'Want that drink now?'

'I'm no drinker, Jay.'

'I know that, but you told me you needed some Dutch courage.'

'Are you going to sit down or are you going to prowl around the room?' she sighed.

'I *can't* sit beside you.' Jay's vibrant voice was low and mocking.

'Why not?' It came out as a little gasp.

'Well, I'm not all that near to you now and you're trembling. I can almost feel the flutter of your heart.'

'What I have to tell you won't make you happy.' She didn't look at him as she said this, so she didn't see the sudden glitter in his eyes.

'So long as you don't tell me you plan to ditch me at the altar?'

'No, nothing like that,' Brett shook her cloudy dark head. 'It's about Westlake . . .' she trailed off.

'I wouldn't think of discussing that now.' Jay shed his jacket and stripped off his silk tie. 'If you aren't going to have a drink, join me in a mineral water.'

Brett appeared to be oblivious to his refusal. 'You've said things in confidence, Jay, that you never intended to be repeated?'

'What I don't intend to be repeated I don't pour into irresponsible ears.'

'Won't you please come and sit down?'

'Certainly, darling. Alongside you. But be sure my behaviour will be pure and wholesome. I may be scorching inside, but I have to wait until my wedding before I gain possession of my so beautiful bride. You will allow me on our wedding night, won't you, Marisa? I think I'd better start getting some guarantees that I'll be allowed access to the marital bed.'

'Jay, this isn't any joking matter!' she protested.

He sat down so close to her, Brett slipped her feet out of her elegant evening pumps and drew her legs under her.

'Won't you crush your dress?' His sapphire eyes slid satirically over her arching, slender body.

'It's uncrushable. Or almost.' She recognised his sardonic mood and it didn't bode well for her.

'Why don't I just put you out of your misery?' he said coolly. 'I won't allow Cooper back into Carradine, but I spoke up for him with Hall, Mackenzie. Gavin's a very discreet man. I had to tell him something close to the truth, otherwise they would have questioned why I sacked him. I guess even a man can understand love, or more explicitly, infatuation. Cooper couldn't stay with us any longer; that would be continually feeding the flames.' He swept his blue eyes over her. 'Satisfied, little one? You won't think me a beast?'

'You mean you saw to it that David got a job?' She leant forward, her smoky eyes soft and melting.

He stirred somewhat impatiently, his handsome face tight. 'Why shouldn't I respond to your piteous little pleas? I can please you there if nothing else.'

'Oh Jay!' she sighed, and put her head on his shoulder. 'As far as David is concerned I'm very pleased. I know he was foolish, but the oddest things happen. He was drawn to me, and I didn't know.'

'Shouldn't you forget it now?'

She put her arms around him. 'Thank you.'

'Strange how someone else can inject a little warmth!' mused Jay.

'What do you mean?' Brett lifted her head and stared into his eyes. They were very close. She only had to move an inch and she could brush her mouth against his bronze, polished skin. He had very fine white teeth and the edges of his handsome mouth were slightly uplifted and cleanly delineated. She could almost taste its texture.

'What are you staring at?' he asked crisply.

'You.'

'You must want something else?'

'I do.' Her sigh was a tiny sound at the back of her throat. 'I don't want to bring this up all over again, but I have to. I promised Elaine.'

'*Elaine?*'

There was so much disgust, incredulity, both, in his tone, Brett tightened her hands together.

'I'll have to keep remembering I'm twenty-one in a little over a week. Twenty-one means one is all grown up. I have things to say and I'm going to say it. I'm frightened.'

'What the hell!' Jay looked at her intensely. 'Your face *is* white.'

'I don't think you know how really intimidating you can be.'

'What—to you? I can't accept that, Brett.' He sounded angry.

'Well, I fight very hard not to show it.'

'What?' It was said so sharply she might have jabbed him with a knife.

'You've had to be tough, Jay.'

'What, whips and all that?' Arrogance burned in his eyes.

'I know you've been good to me. J.B. was good to me, but I've told you, you have a very powerful aura. It's been strengthened over the years. Elaine was afraid to speak to you...'

'*Elaine* was afraid to speak to me,' he cut her off. 'Now you've got me really curious! Elaine has been handing me a line for years—it's her nature. What's she done now? Played up when Mort was out of town?'

Brett decided to speak out. 'In an unguarded moment she let slip to Kerri Whitman that the Board were thinking of taking over Westlake. She meant it in the strictest confidence, of course. She and Kerri Whitman have been friends for years, but Kerri decided to use it against you. *Me,* I suppose. She thought you would blame me and your anger would drive us apart.'

Jay sat and stared at her as though he couldn't speak.

Brett's tongue came out and explored her top lip. 'Jay?'

He stood up and walked through the sliding glass door to look out at the star-studded night. After a moment Brett decided to follow him, very small without her high-heeled evening shoes.

They stood together looking out over the dazzling lights of the city. Finally, Jay spoke. Brett had been expecting a fierce wrath, but instead his voice was cool and dry. 'It seems our dear Elaine spilled the beans for nothing. *You* happened to say to me that you didn't altogether trust our informant from Westlake, and it's not my way to trust informers either, though they do come up with highly classified information. Our informant was working both sides. By the time I'd finished with him he let it all out. I then went to Westlake and proposed a deal—a deal I expect they will take. Kerri Whitman's name was never mentioned. I've already spoken to her father as I knew I would have to. Kerri is going to have to work herself out overseas. I expect what she threatened Elaine with was nonsense. She's not such a fool as you all think. Trying to undermine Carradine would be like declaring war. WhiTec would never hand us *that* piece of paper. Kerri was lying, trying to frighten you. You should have come to me at once.'

'You mean Kerri meant it as a sick joke? That she never went to Westlake at all?'

Jay smiled unpleasantly. 'My dear, you need to toughen up yourself. I told you, Kerri wouldn't be such a fool. In hurting me she would only be hurting her father and brother, and that's something she would never do. I've another piece of information for you and Elaine,' he added. 'Kerri has already left for Hong Kong. She intends flying on to the U.K. and Europe. With any luck at all she might find herself a husband. She'll only have to mention that her family own one of the largest sheep stations in the country— the Golden Fleece and all that.'

Brett turned away quickly. 'She might have been kinder to her friend. Elaine was quite frantic!'

'Good. I hope it cures her entirely. Important business matters shouldn't come into casual conversation. Even Mort is frightened of talking in his sleep.'

Brett said nothing but returned inside. She picked up her shoes, then sat down to put them on.

'Where do you think you're going?'

Jay spoke so tautly a cold tendril of panic writhed through her. 'Aren't you taking me home? You work so hard I wouldn't want to rob you of sleep.'

'Don't ride me hard, Brett,' he warned.

'It's just everyone is so *cruel*,' she cried emotionally. 'It seems I've never known anything but cruelty all my life!'

'Strong words indeed!' He seemed to turn into a panther, so with a quake of fear, she saw him lunge and she became a victim in his arms. His eyes were blue and blazing, the golden light glanced off his high cheekbones. 'When was *I* ever cruel to you?' He tilted her head back, catching her silky hair in his hand. 'You should say a prayer, lady, that I was around.'

'No, no, not you, Jay,' she moaned.

'Are you going to deny me your mouth?' He shifted his hand and gripped her chin, his hard male sensuality unleashed and roaming free.

She could only look at him. She couldn't speak. At the centre of his eyes was a flame. Abruptly he brought her body so close up against him she felt weightless, liquid, her blood running molten. She knew she gave a little cry as his encircling arms turned to steel, then her lashes fluttered like dark wings against her cheeks as his head came down over hers.

She was taken over. Mastered. Jay's exclusive possession.

The moment his mouth covered hers her slender body expelled all strength. Her soft weight pressed against him and recognising her weakness he picked her up like a mere doll.

Night surrounded them, enchanting music that rose and fell. Brett trembled on the edge of surrendering up her heart. Desire stabbed through her like an actual agony. She, who was incapable of putting voice to her passion, was wild for this hard ravishment to go on.

'What are you wishing for—a gentler lover?' Jay's handsome face was darkened with hot blood. 'David Cooper, maybe? You're no wife for him.'

He strode into the bedroom and threw her on to the wide bed. 'I know how you think of me, Marisa—a tyrant like my father. You think I'll take all you have to offer and give nothing in return. You think I'll try to subjugate you like J.B. did your mother. You think I'm only marrying you because you've now got the money to further my ambitions. You think I'm incapable of love, only lust. If that were indeed so I could have taken you at fifteen. You were raised thinking a woman was no more than a man's property. I would have thought a higher education would have set you straight, but you're still locked up in the old nightmares. You've had plenty of time, but you still fail to realise *I am not my father!* The old king is dead. I'm *me,* and I ache for some tenderness from you. You plead for someone like Cooper, and though it's against my own judgement I make sure he gets a second chance. You even plead for Elaine who has given you hell over the years. Now I have to listen to you telling me I'm too damned tough by far. So I terrify you, do I?'

'Please, Jay, I didn't say that,' she whispered.

'Take off that dress.'

Brett put her hand up to her throat. 'Jay, I...I can't...I wanted...'

'Take it off,' he repeated curtly. 'I don't want to ravish you, my darling, I simply want to pay court to your beauty. You have a slip underneath, haven't you? I have some idea how chaste you are, Marisa. That impenetrable reserve.'

She stared at him in bewilderment, but he turned away from her and walked to a vivid, abstract painting that hung above a magnificent brassbound Korean chest. The painting swung out and now Brett could see it masked a wall safe. Jay put his hand in and extracted a long velvet-covered case. Brett had seen it before. It housed the diamond and sapphire suite she had been told she would receive on her wedding day. Obviously Jay intended to see her in them now.

'Well?' He began to walk back to her, his smile twisted and caustic. 'Tremble all you want, but you have my word I'll keep my bargain to court you like a princess. A princess is expected to reserve her body.'

Brett lifted herself shakily off the bed. She put a hand to the top of the zipper at the back of her dress and pulled it down. The slip she wore beneath was the same beautiful jacaranda blue, designed especially for the gown it matched.

'Really, if I could kiss you the way I wanted, you'd be bruised all over!' muttered Jay.

She gave a little shiver, though the air was warm.

'Come here.' He held up the necklace and it glittered blue and ice fire. 'Jewels must be seen against skin,' he told her. 'Hail, Princess Marisa. You've achieved what's never been done before—you've brought me to my knees.' He turned her with one hand on her delicate shoulder and clasped the exquisite necklace around her long, slender throat. It felt cold and rather heavy, but he made her walk to the wall of mirrors in the adjoining dressing room.

Her slip dipped very low, the lace curved away to reveal the slight upper swell of her breasts. The gossamer thin material clung to her narrow torso, her waist, and slender hips. The lace hem hid her trembling knees. She should have looked ridiculous, but she looked incredibly erotic.

'Now the ear pendants,' Jay said briskly. He sounded for all the world like a jeweller making an important sale. 'No need to push your hair back, I like it all loose and cloudy. Well, perhaps just a little.' He flicked at a side curl. 'If I had to describe you, Brett,

I'd say you were priceless. And consistent. Being consistent is very important. There!' He held her shoulders and stared at her. The top of her head came up to his shoulder. She was as white and slight as a geisha girl, but her silver glance could never have been mistaken for an invitation. She continued to look beautiful and stricken.

'I did intend giving these to you on our wedding day, but Gran tells me you've chosen blue for our engagement party. She thought it would be splendid if you wore the sapphires then. You should capture all hearts.'

'Are you done, Jay?' she asked quietly.

'I won't ask you for a grateful kiss, even though I've had to be satisfied with the occasional kiss up to date. A lesser man would be howling.' His blue eyes were startling, as blue as the sapphires she wore at her breast.

'Thank you, Jay.' She looked down and touched the glowing stones while the pendants swung against her cheeks. 'I can't believe anyone would give me such a fabulous present. It makes me feel shaken inside.'

'So I'll settle for a smile. Isn't that how a princess behaves? A word here, a smile there. Always so gracious but never letting anyone know what goes on inside.'

'Don't be like this, Jay,' she entreated. 'I can't bear it. Why am I making you so angry? I try. I think I've been trying very hard.' Her voice broke.

'Don't cry,' he warned her with a half-blind impatience.

'Oh, *leave* me!' She tried to twist away, but as she did so his hand slipped over her shoulder and seemingly without his volition sought her naked breast.

The mirrored gesture was so sensual Brett thought she would faint. Her legs actually gave way, and he caught her under her narrow rib cage and pulled her back against him.

'Dear God!' he groaned. It was no blasphemy but a raw plea for help.

She began to cry, and quietly he gathered her up, jaw tight, nostrils flaring with the intensity of his feelings. In a daze she lay on the wide bed and he came to her, kissing her mouth, her face, her throat, the peaks and valleys of her breasts. His mouth, his hands, were so strong, so sure, so sensitive, her heart began to hammer in an excess of emotion. Her blue veins were trails of fire his fingertips set, and she began to allow him intimacies that went beyond anything she had known before.

Man was the true aggressor. It was a woman's nature to submit. Jay had a power over her impossible to withstand. It overwhelmed her with its force so that she didn't even know she was half-sobbing his name.

He lifted his head abruptly, staring down at her: white skin, japanned brows and lashes, rose satin mouth, tears like glittering diamonds spilling out towards her ears. Even the nipples of her small high breasts blossomed, suffused with colour from his touch. She looked drugged with ecstasy and a kind of virginal terror combined.

Jay never doubted he could take her then. She was so very young and vulnerable after all, immensely

susceptible to him as she had always been. His palms
slid across her satin skin and her eyes suddenly opened
wide, settling dazedly on his dominant dark face, pale
beneath its patina of golden bronze.

'I never meant to make you cry,' he said quietly, and
smoothed back the gleaming hair that framed her face.
'I promised you I'd hold back and I will. God knows
I've had to learn a powerful self-discipline.'

Her eyes were huge, glittering like ice crystals. Sapphires and diamonds gave off an unholy light. For the
first time she truly realised what marriage with Jay
would mean. A new dimension. Some fantastic world
that altered space and time. Passion was a living,
breathing entity. There were no theatricals to match it.
Pleasure was so violent it had put her whole being into
a sexual trance. Only Jay had stopped her surrender,
though the planes of his face were as hard as a rock.

She tried, but found she couldn't speak normally.
Her voice was a mere whisper, her skin so translucent
the light seemed to shine through it. 'Oh, Jay, what's
going to happen when you find I'm not woman
enough for you?'

'You're *not?*' His velvet voice was deep and sardonic.

'You must know I was nearly fainting now. Going
right away.'

There was amusement in his brilliant eyes. 'Do *I*
look so prosaic and solid?'

'You look very real and strong.'

'Well, I'm real enough,' he stroked around her ear.
'I don't know about strong. I'm waiting for my blood

to subside. I made a pledge and I'm just going to have to keep it.'

'But what are you feeling about me?' Brett insisted desperately. 'There are so many secret places of the heart. I have nothing to go by. *Nothing.* I read books by the score. What do they tell me? Heroines tremble, they don't flake out.'

'It's a big world. Lots of different women in it.'

'I feel like a flame burning out of control.'

'Because, my dearest Marisa, you *are.*' There was a faint taunt buried in it. 'I shouldn't worry if you were going to be woman enough for me. Sooner or later you're bound to be too much!'

'I don't understand,' she faltered.

'Of course you don't,' he countered, rolling away and standing up. 'That's our problem.'

For goodness sake, taking it in the matter of boiling out,' Mrs Close suggested. 'I know it's your duty—'

Bran, by nature a peacemaker, put the suggestion to Daisy very sweetly. Daisy, cumulatively buxom ..... One had to threaten someone else's best point, after all.

CHAPTER EIGHT

THERE WERE TO BE two celebrations—the actual ceremony and a grand reception in Adelaide, beautiful city of churches; another scheduled for Diamond Valley the day after. The Outback was not going to be deprived of the glorious opportunity to offer its congratulations to one of its most illustrious sons. Around two hundred people were expected to make the great trek to the historic station where they would set up camp like the pioneers of old.

Air Carradine was kept busy flying in the huge loads of provisions needed for such a celebration—it was expected to go on for days—and the household staff was augmented by well trained personnel including top caterers. The florist who had the huge commission of arranging the flowers for all three occasions had already jetted in and out to get an idea of what he wanted to see in the house, but the great banks of flowers, including the beautiful Queensland orchids, were to be delivered as late as possible to the station.

It was an exciting time and everyone became a trifle unhinged. Elaine, whose habitual manner was so laid-back it resembled a study in inertia, became astonishingly active. From opposing the marriage she now acted as though it had all been her idea.

'For goodness' sake, ask her to be matron of honour,' Mrs Chase suggested. 'I know it's *your* wedding . . .'

Brett, by nature a peacemaker, put the suggestion to Elaine very sweetly, and Elaine compulsively hugged her. One had to remember Morton was best man, after all.

'Dear God, how are we going to get through it?' Mrs Chase was heard to wail, but she, perhaps more than anyone, was filled with romance and excitement. She hadn't really taken to Elaine, so her elder grandson's marriage, though feverish, was untouched by the special aura she perceived in this wonderful occasion. Though she had never put it into actual words Jay had been her great favourite from the moment her daughter had placed him in her arms. He had waved at her—yes, he had actually *waved*. *That* story had been told, but to avoid complications Lillian Chase had never played favourites. One would have had to be a dyed-in-the-wool snob not to welcome Brett as one's own. She was as beautiful as a dream, and her character had the same classic harmony as her looks. Mrs Chase was well pleased.

The engagement party, in itself one of the social events of the year, gave a clue what the wedding would be. Brett couldn't remember much of it except that her beautiful, romantic dress had to be altered that very morning. The pace had become hectic, and though she was remembering to eat she was losing weight. The final touches on the master suite at Diamond Valley were still to be taken care of, and there were still a hundred and one things left to do.

As it was winter in the Northern Hemisphere, they had decided not to forsake the sun. There was all of the South Pacific to be explored, endless blue lagoons, palm trees and white sand. If they wanted to go shopping there was always Singapore and Hong Kong. The possibilities were all there to be decided on. What Brett really wanted was to come true. They would spend their wedding night at Diamond Valley, and old ghosts would be laid to rest.

Brett had asked her three closest friends from her university days to be her bridesmaids. They were thrilled to accept, and Brett immediately relieved them of all financial worry by explaining that Mrs Chase had insisted on paying for all the dresses, headpieces, Brett's veil and accessories. She had already assumed the position of grandmother to the bride.

'I know I'm not supposed to know what's going on,' Jay told her in one of the rare moments they had together. 'But I insist on a veil.'

'*You* want a veil?' Brett tried for lightness to balance her mounting tensions.

'No little hats, big hats, bows or whatever. I want a veil—a long veil. Tons of it. I want to throw it back and stare into your beautiful face. I've discovered I'm a very traditional man.'

Mercifully Brett had planned a veil all along. She had even decided on the romantic image Jay so plainly wanted. As a summer bride she felt the emphasis was on something delicate and cool, so she finally chose a beautiful embroidered white organza over strapless silk taffeta. The scalloped edge just touched her collarbones, the sleeves were big and billowy to match the full romantic skirt and the waistline was small and tight. It was a young, very soft look, and it brought tears to Mrs Chase's eyes. The bridesmaids too were to wear embroidered organza in the same delicate shade of pink, the pink of the rosebuds planned for their bouquets and the circlet of pure silk flowers, pink and white, they were to wear on their heads. All three had thick, shining dark hair and varying shades of blue into green eyes, and the beautiful blush of pink colour suited them extremely well. Elaine had chosen something more sophisticated; a lovely gown featuring hand-made lace on Swiss voile with rose satin beneath. Brett hoped Jay would allow the elegant little pillbox hat their designer had devised. It was certain Elaine would not part with it. Almost as much time was spent deciding on Mrs Chase's outfit. She was as excited and exacting as the girls. There was something about weddings that brought out the young girl in everybody.

'Blue is always beautiful,' the designer suggested. 'Especially with blue eyes. I see a simple, very elegant flowing dress with a lace jacket. I know you have wonderful jewellery, Mrs Chase. Now the hat is important...'

So it went on until everything was perfected.

Brett could scarcely believe what had seemed like a dream from which she must surely wake was almost a reality. In a few days' time she was to marry Jay. A magnificent reception was planned. No one, however, said it was going to be a breeze. Both Jay and Brett were so pressured they scarcely found the time to communicate. Family and attendants were having all the fun. Jay couldn't even find the time for the church rehearsal, but Morton was too nervous about his role not to make it. Nothing was to go wrong. It was to be the wedding to end all weddings. The most sumptuous presents had arrived, so lavish Brett's eyes were dazzled. She had started life very differently from what it was now—and all because a rich and powerful man had desired her mother. He had never offered her the joy of marriage, yet Jay had chosen her daughter for his wife. The wheel had come full circle. Shouldn't she accept it?

The Chase mansion still retained three of its original ten acres and the reception for two hundred and fifty people was to be held in the house and the magnificent setting of the long established grounds. Brett was out in the garden watching one of the silk-lined marquees going up when she saw Elaine racing across the lawn, almost knocking into a stack of white garden chairs.

Brett knew immediately that something was wrong and her heart began to hammer in a fast-rising panic. She had never truly believed she could ever be so lucky. The gods had only briefly smiled on her before slamming her down.

Beads of nervous sweat stood out on Elaine's brow. She gestured frantically to Brett, calling her away from the scene of activity.

'What is it? What's wrong?' One look at Elaine's blanched face and a wave of nausea rose to Brett's throat.

'I've just come in,' Elaine waved a backward hand at her diamond-blue Mercedes parked along the drive.

'I just heard a newsflash. One of our helicopters is down. It crash-landed in the hills near the Hislop estate.'

Brett flinched.

'Oh, God, Brett,' the words expelled from Elaine in a violent rush, 'weren't Morton and Jay making a sweep of that area? I never pay attention, but I'm sure Morton said they were interested in buying acreage out there?'

'What did the bulletin say? Who was in it, who was hurt?'

'That's the only information they gave. A helicopter from the Carradine Corporation crash-landed in the hills. They'll have more information when it's to hand.' Elaine was almost babbling in her panic.

'It only takes a second to turn one's life upside down,' Brett said strangely. 'I'm going out there. Right now.'

'There's the car. You'll have to drive—I can't.'

'We have to stop word of this getting to the house.' Brett started to move swiftly across the lawn.

'Gran could have a heart attack,' Elaine panted.

'We don't know *who* was in that helicopter,' Brett said grimly, surprised by the control she was keeping in her voice. 'We can only pray it wasn't Morton and Jay and that no one was badly hurt.'

Despite her shock and apprehension the Chase housekeeper assured Brett she would monitor all calls.

'Shouldn't I start making a few phone calls myself, Miss Brett?' she asked.

'It's just *happened!*' Elaine cried, so white she looked like a powdered and painted doll.

'We're going up there now,' Brett explained, grasping Mrs Harris's arm reassuringly. 'Take all calls, and whether the news is good or bad don't tell Mrs Chase. You *must* wait for our return.'

'I understand, Miss Brett,' Mrs Harris promised soberly.

'I'M ILL!' Elaine muttered as Brett turned out of the driveway and on to the road. 'It's just like some terrible nightmare. You never think anything is going to happen to you, to yours, then right out of the blue, just when everything is going right...'

Brett didn't answer. Life had made her a fatalist. She had lost father and mother; the man who had made her his ward. Her life had been a series of hard knocks, but if anything happened to Jay it might as well be over.

She pressed down harder on the accelerator and the powerful V8 engine responded with a deep-throated grunt. They were out of their beautiful garden suburb in the foothills and climbing towards the blue shimmering ranges. The needle hit 120, 140, 160k's.

'Brett, we'll be arrested!'

The car was performing brilliantly, revelling in a speed comfortably within its range. Brett's foot on the accelerator never slackened. It took a tremendous effort of control not to go faster. No policeman on a motor-cycle would stop her. She would go to jail if she had to, but first she had to get to Jay. It was too much of a coincidence that a Carradine helicopter was in the Hislop area. Unlike Elaine, she always listened. Jay was planning on securing a considerable holding in that district. One didn't need psychic powers to feel Jay and Morton had been in that helicopter.

They went a long way in a short time, when terrifyingly they saw cars parked haphazardly across a field. Two were easily distinguishable as police cars, another wore the logo of a local T.V. station, but the one their eyes were fixed on was the bright yellow coronary unit.

'Don't worry about the car,' cried Elaine. 'Take it over.'

It wasn't the kind of track the Mercedes coupé was meant to ride. They went zigzagging cross-country and now they could see the helicopter rising out of a shallow depression.

'Brett!' In her agitation Elaine almost tore Brett's arm from the wheel. 'It looks okay, doesn't it? I don't see any... I don't see...'

Any bodies, Brett supplied grimly in her mind.

The uniformed policeman ran towards them, waving his arms in a warning motion.

'Stop, Brett—you're supposed to *stop!*' Elaine yelled.

'I'll stop when I get there.' For the first time in her life Brett disobeyed a lawful signal. She swept on by and jammed the car to a halt parallel to the ambulance.

'Gosh, Brett,' Elaine exclaimed in awe, 'we might be in trouble.'

'Who cares!' Brett's eyes were huge, the pupils dilated. 'If anything has happened to either of them our lives have come to a stop.'

They swung out of the car, leaving the doors open. The policeman who had signalled them down now advanced on them with a fellow officer, but Elaine cried out in a loud voice.

'I'm Mrs Carradine . . . Carradine!'

Until then Brett had taken the initiative, but now it suddenly seemed she was through. Some man in jeans and a pink shirt was trying to show Elaine a card, but she didn't even bother to read it. She raced towards the helicopter and disappeared down the slope.

'Please miss . . .' Now the policeman was coming towards Brett. He was saying something, but she couldn't seem to catch it. There was a muffled sound in her ears as though she was swimming underwater. What did it matter anyway? There was no sign of Jay and the ambulance was empty.

'Amazing . . . simply amazing . . . I just don't know . . .' The policeman looked at her, saw her pallor, and took hold of her arm.

Was this her destiny, to meet tragedy head-on?

She didn't fight the policeman's firm grip. She walked on with a kind of terrible directness.

'That's him. That's him!' the policeman was saying, then like a miracle she saw Jay; a tall, lean and powerful form against a cobalt blue sky.

'It's okay, miss. *Really* . . . okay. Seems the pilot suffered a heart attack. Fairly young bloke too. As soon as the paramedics are finished with him we'll get him straight to hospital. I wouldn't like to think what might have happened if the Carradines didn't know a lot about different kinds of aircraft. Seems one of them brought it down.' It must have struck him as somewhat wry, because he gave a gruff laugh.

'*Jay!*' Brett's eyes held relief from a great anguish.

He was suddenly upon them, reaching for Brett and folding her into his arms. He pressed her head against his chest and spoke to the policeman. 'They're about ready to shift our pilot now. He's responding quite well, thank God.'

'Right, sir.' The constable executed a little salute. 'I expect my partner has finished off our report. Seems like a miracle the chopper wasn't a write-off.'

'It *was* rather like sky-diving,' Jay shook the hand that was thrust at him. 'Thank you for coming so promptly. Your efficiency probably saved Ray's life. I'll be speaking to the Commissioner in any case.'

'Thank you, sir.'

Brett lifted her head and the policeman smiled at her. 'Too bad you had to get such a terrible fright, miss. I understand you're getting married tomorrow. If I may say so, your fiancé had the greatest incentive possible to stay alive.'

They waited in a quiet little group, Brett and Jay, Elaine and Morton, while the semi-conscious pilot was put into the back of the ambulance. The T.V. cameraman was still filming, and Elaine drew a sharp breath.

'Wouldn't you think they'd leave the poor man alone? Is he going to be all right?' She lifted her eyes to her husband.

'God, as far as I was concerned he'd dropped dead. One moment Jay and I were talking, the next we were falling from the sky. I know one thing: if it had been just me up there, we wouldn't have stood a chance. I couldn't seem to think, I couldn't seem to move. It was all happening too fast. I tell you something,' he added. 'I'm going to get really fit. While I was staggering back in my seat, Jay was blasting into action. I know—I was there.'

Jay put a hand on Brett's hair. 'Why don't you two go on? The car's here. Go home.'

'Thanks, pardner,' Morton sighed gustily. 'I don't mind if I do. Remember that time in North Queensland when we flew through an electrical storm? The goddamned plane was bucketing around like a brumby. It even rolled over in thick layers of clouds. All I could do was throw up and wait to die—didn't even care—while you had to stick there and pull it out of a dive. How come the two of us are so different? The only other man I ever knew so damned cool was J.B.'

'Do you want to go back with Mort and Elaine?' Jay bent to the quiet and pale Brett.

'I'm staying here.' She raised her arm and put it around him.

'Okay, so we'll go back to town with the T.V. boys. I promised them about two words when I caught my breath. I have to speak to Ray's wife and organise for the chopper to be brought in. It's nowhere near as badly damaged as I thought.'

IT WAS ALMOST two hours later before Jay was able to call it a day. Brett waited in his office and his secretary, unexpectedly motherly and solicitous, brought her tea and sandwiches.

'Eat them up, dear,' she advised. 'Something in the tummy counteracts shock.'

Eventually they were able to go.

Good wishes came from every side. Jay's manner could not have been more charming and carefree. He was a man with nine lives; a man on the eve of a blessed marriage. Brett nodded and smiled. It was quite, quite extraordinary. Her delicate features had assumed an ethereal quality with the intensity of her feelings. The shock of the morning was continuing to give her pain.

She wanted to feel elation, but she could not. She hadn't forgotten how fragile was the link to life; the way she had stared mesmerised at the upper section of the crashed helicopter. Remnants of that terror still held her in its steely claws.

'I'll change my clothes before we go back to the house,' Jay told her. 'We can have a few quiet moments together.' His voice was as calm as ever. 'Are you feeling all right, Brett?'

'Much better now.'

He continued to watch her with brilliant, hooded eyes.

While he changed out of his suit Brett wandered around the penthouse aimlessly picking up objects and setting them down. It had taken one startling and terrifying incident to make her realise she had been acting like a child who could not put her feelings into words. They had made passionate love, yet never once had she told him she was brimming with love for him. She had never found a way to say it. *Never*. Her childhood had marked her. She wanted so much to be free and unscarred. Love was the ultimate healer.

When Jay came back into the living room, so vivid and handsome, she went to him with a little cry.

'Tell me what's in your mind,' he begged her. 'This moment. *Say* it, Brett.'

'I love you.' The words were tight and choked.

'Say it again.'

'I love you.' This time they flowed more easily. 'Utterly, irrevocably. You are my life.'

He stared into her eyes for an endless moment, then cupping her face in his hands, he kissed her with a tenderness so exquisite she knew she would remember it for the rest of her days.

'That wasn't so terrible, was it?'

'No.' Her eyes were very soft and shining.

'Wait a minute, you're so small.' Jay swung her up and carried her back to a deep leather armchair where she curled up in his arms. Her gleaming hair fluttered against his neck and his chin.

'You could have been killed,' she said shakily.

'I wasn't!' This, very firm.

'All I could think was I'd never told you how much I loved you. I've withheld it from you all this time. It was crazy and self-destructive.'

'I'll have to admit it did give me a few bad moments.' He tilted back her head and kissed her on her forehead, her nose and her soft, tender mouth. 'In fact it might have driven me nuts. I dared not speak to you, touch you, until you were all grown up. God,' he groaned feelingly, 'all these years! I feel badly about your shock and upset this morning, but if it helped, and it obviously did, I'd be prepared to go through it again. Perhaps not to the same extent,' he smiled wryly. 'There's nothing like a nosedive to give a man wings.'

'*Don't!*' shivered Brett.

'At last I have you,' he said quietly. 'I can't remember a time when you weren't very special to me. A small girl with big, silvery eyes. All those years we could have enjoyed but for J.B. He was about as complicated a man as one could ever get. He told me once he'd make pretty damned sure *I* would never get you. All your life I think he mixed you up with your mother. But that's all over.'

'It *is*.' Brett lifted herself up and clasped her slender arms around his neck. 'Love can vanquish anything—hatred, enmity, pain. You've been my hero-figure, my champion, ever since I can remember. I never expected for you to love me, but miracles *are* possible in this world. Tomorrow we're going to be married. Tomorrow we fly back to Diamond Valley. From this moment I dedicate my life to you. I'm going to be the best wife in the world.'

'Perfect!' Jay gave her a blue, brilliant look. 'Remind me tomorrow night!'

In June, get ready for thrilling romances
and FREE BOOKS—Western-style—
with...

WESTERN *Lovers*

You can receive the first 2 Western Lovers titles FREE!

June 1995 brings Harlequin and Silhouette's
WESTERN LOVERS series, which combines larger-than-
life love stories set in the American West! And WESTERN
LOVERS brings you stories with your favorite themes...
"Ranch Rogues," "Hitched In Haste," "Ranchin' Dads,"
"Reunited Hearts" the packaging on each book
highlights the popular theme found in each WESTERN
LOVERS story!

And in June, when you buy either of the Men Made In
America titles, you will receive a WESTERN LOVERS title
absolutely FREE! Look for these fabulous combinations:

◆ Buy ALL IN THE FAMILY
   by Heather Graham Pozzessere (Men Made In
   America) and receive a FREE copy of
   BETRAYED BY LOVE by Diana Palmer
   (Western Lovers)

◆ Buy THE WAITING GAME
   by Jayne Ann Krentz (Men Made In America)
   and receive a FREE copy of
   IN A CLASS BY HIMSELF by JoAnn Ross
   (Western Lovers)

**Look for the special, extra-value shrink-wrapped
packages at your favorite retail outlet!**

HARLEQUIN® Silhouette®

WL-T

Take 4 bestselling love stories FREE

Plus get a FREE surprise gift!

THREE BESTSELLING AUTHORS

HEATHER GRAHAM POZZESSERE
THERESA MICHAELS
MERLINE LOVELACE

bring you

THREE HEROES THAT DREAMS ARE MADE OF!

The Highwayman—He knew the honorable thing was to send his captive home, but how could he let the beautiful Lady Kate return to the arms of another man?

The Warrior—Raised to protect his tribe, the fierce Apache warrior had little room in his heart until the gentle Angie showed him the power and strength of love.

The Knight—His years as a mercenary had taught him many skills, but would winning the hand of a spirited young widow prove to be his greatest challenge?

Don't miss these **UNFORGETTABLE RENEGADES!**

Available in August wherever Harlequin books are sold.

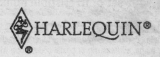

HARLEQUIN®

Fifty red-blooded, white-hot, true-blue hunks
from every State in the Union!

MEN MADE IN AMERICA! Written by some of our
most popular authors, these stories feature some of the
strongest, sexiest men, each from a different state in the
union!

Available only until June, at your favorite
retail outlet.

In June, look for:

THE WAITING GAME
by Jayne Ann Krentz (Washington)
ALL IN THE FAMILY
by Heather Graham Pozzessere (Virginia)

**This June is our last month of MEN MADE IN
AMERICA, so if you've missed any titles, act now
and complete your set of irresistible hunks!**

See below for details.

Announcing
the New Pages & Privileges™ Program
from Harlequin® and Silhouette®

Get All This FREE
With Just One Proof-of-Purchase!

- **FREE Hotel Discounts** of up to 60% off at leading hotels in the U.S., Canada and Europe

- **FREE Travel Service** with the guaranteed lowest available airfares plus 5% cash back on every ticket

- **FREE $25 Travel Voucher** to use on any ticket on any airline booked through our Travel Service

- **FREE Petite Parfumerie** collection (a $50 Retail value)

- **FREE Insider Tips Letter** full of fascinating information and hot sneak previews of upcoming books

- **FREE Mystery Gift** (if you enroll before June 15/95)

And there are more great gifts and benefits to come!
Enroll today and become Privileged!

(see insert for details)

 PROOF-OF-PURCHASE

Offer expires October 31, 1996   BR-PP2

If you are looking for more titles by

MARGARET WAY

Don't miss these fabulous stories by one of
Harlequin's most renowned authors:

Harlequin Romance®

#03295	ONE FATEFUL SUMMER	$2.99	☐
#03331	THE CARRADINE BRAND	$2.99 U.S.	☐
		$3.50 CAN.	☐

(limited quantities available on certain titles)

TOTAL AMOUNT	$
POSTAGE & HANDLING	$
($1.00 for one book, 50¢ for each additional)	
APPLICABLE TAXES*	$_____
TOTAL PAYABLE	$_____
(check or money order—please do not send cash)	

To order, complete this form and send it, along with a check or money order
for the total above, payable to Harlequin Books, to: **In the U.S.:** 3010 Walden
Avenue, P.O. Box 9047, Buffalo, NY 14269-9047; **In Canada:** P.O. Box 613,
Fort Erie, Ontario, L2A 5X3.

Name: _____

Address: _____ City: _____

State/Prov.: _____ Zip/Postal Code: _____

*New York residents remit applicable sales taxes.
 Canadian residents remit applicable GST and provincial taxes.   HMWBACK1

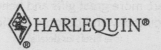